**Two brand-new stories in every volume...
twice a month!**

Duets Vol. #89

Just in time for the holidays—a delightful
Double Duets from *USA TODAY* bestselling author
Jacqueline Diamond! Christmas and Cinderella are
two of the fun themes in the aptly titled
Cindy and the Fella and *Calling All Glass Slippers*.
Ms. Diamond never fails to "make your head spin
and leave you laughing..." says *Rendezvous*.

Duets Vol. #90

The celebrations continue with
Hitched for the Holidays by well-known
writing team Jennifer Drew. This talented duo always
"gives readers a top-notch reading experience with
vibrant characters...and spicy tension," says
Romantic Times. Rounding out the volume is
popular Barbara Dunlop with the quirky
A Groom in Her Stocking. Enjoy the fun
when Santa delivers not one but *two* fiancés
to the dateless heroine!

Be sure to pick up both Duets volumes today!

Cindy and the Fella

"I love this song!" Cindy exclaimed.

She began to shimmy. "Take me in your arms."

Hugh's throat tightened, and he looped one arm around her waist and took her hand in his. Before he knew it, they were pressed together so tight that he could practically measure Cindy's bra size. For the first time he understood why the Puritans had disapproved of dancing. Those fools!

Caught in the moment, Hugh lifted her chin and touched his lips to hers. When her tongue flicked against his mouth, he claimed a deep, thorough kiss.

What was happening? Shocked, he drew back.

"Hugh, are you upset?" she asked worriedly.

"I'm sorry. It's my fault."

"No, it's not. We shouldn't have tempted fate." She caught his upper arms as if to steady him. "Look, I have to go. I'll see you tomorrow, okay?" She collected her purse and went out the door.

His midsection still suspiciously tight, Hugh glanced at his statue of a fertility goddess standing in the corner. He could have sworn she wore a Mona Lisa smile.

"This is all your fault."

For more, turn to page 9

Calling All Glass Slippers

"We can get together again tonight—"

"No," Laura said.

"What do you mean, no?"

"No dating and no more sex," she said. "I'm sorry, Jared, but I think we need to keep our distance."

He understood, even if he didn't share her apprehension. "We could do nooners," he said hopefully.

When she shook her head, her red hair gave a suggestive bounce. "It's not that simple."

"Don't tell me you're not tempted."

Pink tinged her cheeks. "Please accept my decision. I'm sure I'm doing the right thing. We both lost control last night, and, well, wonderful as it was, I don't want to repeat the experience."

Glumly Jared accepted that she meant it. But it wasn't only sex they were giving up. He wanted to spend more time together doing things— dancing, joking, talking. Yes, it was probably for the best. So why did he feel as if he'd lost something?

For more, turn to page 197

HARLEQUIN DUETS

ISBN 0-373-44155-X

Copyright in the collection:
Copyright © 2002 by Harlequin Books S.A.

The publisher acknowledges the copyright holder
of the individual works as follows:

CINDY AND THE FELLA
Copyright © 2002 by Jackie Hyman

CALLING ALL GLASS SLIPPERS
Copyright © 2002 by Jackie Hyman

Cindy and the Fella

Jacqueline Diamond

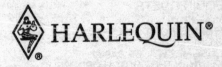

HARLEQUIN®

TORONTO • NEW YORK • LONDON
AMSTERDAM • PARIS • SYDNEY • HAMBURG
STOCKHOLM • ATHENS • TOKYO • MILAN • MADRID
PRAGUE • WARSAW • BUDAPEST • AUCKLAND

Dear Reader,

Sometimes a "minor" character comes along who refuses to fade away quietly. When absentminded English professor Hugh Bemling made his first appearance writing bad poetry in *Excuse Me? Whose Baby?* he was anything but heroic. He bobbed up again in *Heaven Scent*, writing outrageously hokey poems to a psychologist who clearly didn't return his affections. After she ran off with a rancher, Hugh seemed destined to disappear into the stacks of forgotten supporting characters.

It was not to be. This time he's front and center when Cindy McChad comes barreling into town. She's totally unlike the willowy ladies after whom Hugh pines, and she's in love with someone else. But the juxtaposition of opposites was too much for me to resist.

I hope you have fun with their story, as well. Please write me at P.O. Box 1315, Brea, CA 92822, or contact me by e-mail at Jdiamondfriends@aol.com. I'd be happy to send an autographed flier of my upcoming books. Thanks!

Warmly,

Jacqueline Diamond

Books by Jacqueline Diamond

HARLEQUIN DUETS
2—KIDNAPPED?
8—THE BRIDE WORE GYM SHOES
37—DESIGNER GENES*
44—EXCUSE ME? WHOSE BABY?
55—MORE THAN THE DOCTOR ORDERED**
65—THE DOC'S DOUBLE DELIVERY
78—HEAVEN SCENT

*The Bachelor Dads of Nowhere Junction
**The Mail Order Men of Nowhere Junction

For Virginia Mercier,
who did such a wonderful job of raising my husband.

MIDDAY AT A NOISY off-campus café was not the best time to make a romantic gesture. The Lunar Lunch Box, crowded with students and smelling of burgers and onions wasn't a setting to thrill a poet's heart, either. But Hugh Bemling was determined.

From behind a dog-eared menu, the bearded English professor peered at the loveliest lady in Clair De Lune, California: Blair Riley, a teaching assistant in Comparative Literature. In Hugh, she had inspired three odes, two sonnets, several quatrains and a late-night limerick, which he had crumpled and discarded as inappropriately lighthearted.

Until now, the exquisite T.A. had known nothing of his sentiments. Merely from watching her beautiful form move along the hallways of the English and Comparative Literature Department, Hugh had fallen in love with her.

He'd imagined himself in this state many times before, but it had never hit so hard. The memory of his former flames faded before this slender beauty, her black hair gleaming, her green eyes glowing and her crop top revealing a bare midriff of unparalleled perfection.

There was, Hugh admitted silently, a slight impediment to his plan to touch the lady's heart. That would be the handsome man sitting opposite her, holding her hands across the table.

The fellow was tall, with broad shoulders and golden

hair. De Lune University was a small world, and without half trying Hugh had learned that the newcomer went by the name of Roland Greenwald, hailed from Minnesota and was a graduate student in Medieval Studies.

Steeling his spine, Hugh reminded himself that faint heart ne'er won fair lady. And he had every intention of winning. He planned to launch his opening sally the moment he stopped hyperventilating.

Nervously he brushed a hank of prematurely gray-tinged hair off his forehead. Since the lady and her escort were taking their time paying the bill, Hugh removed his wire-rimmed glasses, breathed on them and wiped them with his shirttail. Now he was ready.

Blair arose, tossed her gorgeous mane, and smiled at Roland. The man smiled back, clearly besotted. How little he suspected that he was about to be bested in a lovers' duel!

She began walking toward Hugh, her hips swaying as masculine heads turned to watch. He sprang to his feet. From one of his overstuffed pockets, he pulled the poem he had stayed up all night revising. Clutching a small bag of rose petals in his free hand, he read aloud:

> "There once was a T.A. named Blair,
> To whom none on earth can compare."

Wait a minute! This wasn't the poem he'd labored to perfect, it was the discarded limerick. In his usual absentminded manner, Hugh must have stuck it in his pocket by mistake.

Yet he couldn't stop. The entire room was staring at him.

The owner, Stu Crockenmeyer, paused openmouthed with an order pad in one hand. Behind the grill, the chubby cook, Daffodil O'Foy, froze, her metal spatula raised like a tennis racquet.

Helpless in the grip of his own momentum, Hugh read on:

"I'd be there in a jiff
If I might take a whiff
Of the fragrant perfumes in her hair."

His heart sank as he heard a guffaw from one of the onlookers. Then Blair said, very gently, "Did you write that poem for me, Professor Bemling? How sweet!"

Roland merely gawked at him. Apparently people didn't make this kind of gesture in Minnesota.

The pair turned away and the blond man held the door, admitting a rush of warm November sunshine. Panic seized Hugh. She was getting away before he'd finished! Hurriedly he grasped his small mesh bag and shook it into the air.

A draft from the door sent velvety pink petals fluttering into the open mouth of Stu Crockenmeyer. The heavyset man spat them out in disgust. His face burning, Hugh hurriedly paid his bill and departed.

He regretted the poetic switcheroo that had foiled what would otherwise have been a glorious tribute, but it had been worth humiliating himself to make the attempt. Perhaps, if angels came with rearview mirrors, Blair might at least have seen the petals and been moved by them. Even so, now that she knew of his feelings, she should gradually lose interest in the empty-headed hunk at her side.

Hugh wished that fate had bestowed on him a husky

build and tawny hair, but even so, his heart beat as
fiercely and honestly as any man's. Someday, Blair was
going to realize it and love him in return.

A BRISK WIND, HINTING of the approaching Minnesota
winter, swirled colorful leaves across the softball field.
Although autumn wasn't the usual season for the sport,
the children of Oofdah took advantage of any spell of
good weather to hone their skills.

At home plate, the ball whizzed past a four-foot-tall
player, who waved his bat wildly. "Strike three!" cried
the umpire.

Mutters of protest wafted from the bleachers. A man
sprang to his feet. "What're you, blind?" he yelled.
"That ball nearly took my son's nose off!"

"Then he shouldn't have swung at it," someone said.

"He was protecting himself!"

On the sidelines, a tall, stocky woman held up the
score: 4-3. "Congratulations, Tigers!" she announced.

"Congratulations, my butt!" roared the outraged father as he shoved his way through the bleachers. "That
was the most boneheaded call I've ever seen! The Mam-
moths aren't out, and my son deserves another turn!"

As soon as he reached the ground, it became obvious
that the man towered over the slender umpire. One of the
coaches started toward him, then hesitated as the giant
raised a fist menacingly.

"Dad," said a small voice. "It's okay."

"It's not okay, and you shut up!"

That was when the stocky woman got annoyed. She
showed this by setting down the scorecards and straightening her large-framed glasses.

She walked calmly toward the enraged father. The
woman lacked several inches of his height and, even with

the added bulk of her sweater, she couldn't match his muscular mass. But there was something about her that made the crowd fall silent.

"You're new in Oofdah," she said.

"We've been here a few months." He frowned. "You're the second-grade teacher, right?"

"Cindy McChad." She extended one hand. "And you're Al Saxon, I believe."

Apparently realizing he was on the brink of being co-opted, Al ignored her hand and growled, "Get out of my way."

"I don't think that would be a good idea," said Cindy.

Around the field, the young players watched with fascination. In the stands, one of the parents tried to take bets on who would win the confrontation, but when he sided with Miss McChad, no one would bet against him.

The father appeared to have transferred his anger from the quivering umpire to the unflappable woman blocking his path. "For the last time, move!"

"I'm president of the Softball Boosters," said Cindy, her blue eyes placid behind the large lenses. A few pale blond hairs, blown free from her long braid, wisped around her face. "If you have any complaints, you can bring them to me."

"Don't say I didn't warn you!" Hunching his shoulders, Al barreled forward like a football player intent on making a touchdown.

As to what happened next, the observers never did agree. Some said that Miss McChad sidestepped and stuck out her foot. Others claimed she leaped away in slow motion like a mystical Chinese kung fu warrior, and the man lost his balance and tripped from his own weight.

Whatever the case might be, the man went sprawling. At that moment, a flock of geese swooped from the heav-

ens and zoomed inches above his head, honking loudly
and then bursting away in an explosion of wings. Perhaps
they'd mistaken him for Myrtle Sandfelter, who was
waiting with bread crumbs by the pond on the other side
of the park. The effect, in any event, was startling.

With a cry of alarm, the man flailed at the air. When
he peered up again, another odd thing happened: a breeze
eddied around Miss McChad, raising a swirl of leaves.
From the ground, it must have appeared almost super-
natural, the way the many-hued bits flew around and
around her.

At last the leaves settled and Al Saxon staggered to
his feet. Taking his arm, Cindy escorted him from the
field. "I'm sure you'll want to join our booster club,"
she was saying when last heard. "You'll find we all get
along splendidly."

ON THE WAY HOME, Cindy stopped at the food bank to
bag groceries for the needy. A little old man with droopy
eyebrows, working alongside her, said, "Have you heard
from Roland?"

"He's been careless about returning phone calls lately,"
she said. "You know how he gets, all caught up in his
studies. He even forgets to eat unless I remind him."

"If I were you, I wouldn't have let him go all the way
to California," the man said. "Remember that time at
the football game when he started to carry the ball in the
wrong direction? I don't know what would have happened if you hadn't run out on the field and turned him
around."

"I'm sure he'll be fine," she said. "That was ten years
ago."

"At my age, ten years doesn't seem like very long,"
said the man.

Next, Cindy stopped at the library and volunteered to shelve some books. As always on Saturdays, it was busy.

"I expect you'll be checking out our wedding books pretty soon," said the reference librarian, while scrubbing chewing gum off a computer keyboard. "Next June, isn't it?"

"We haven't set a date. I'll have to consult my fiancé," Cindy said, even though she and Roland both knew that she was the one who would make the decision.

Although he'd never gotten around to buying her a ring, he'd have been happy to get married six years ago when they graduated from the University of Minnesota. But then her father had died and her mother needed her more than Roland did.

He and Cindy had been best friends since fifth grade, when his family moved in across the street and she bested him in a snowball fight. They'd dated through high school, gone to university together in the Twin Cities and taught at Oofdah Elementary ever since.

When Roland announced that he'd won a scholarship to get his master's degree in Medieval Studies, she'd agreed to let him go, even though it meant he'd be away for two semesters in Southern California. He loved the subject, and Cindy liked to see people grow and flourish.

She got back in her car and drove between billowing maples through the town where she'd lived all her life. She passed the white clapboard Church of Oofdah, where her father had been minister for more than twenty years. Her mother still conducted the choir, which had recently cut a rock 'n' roll CD version of "A Mighty Fortress Is Our God."

Cindy nearly, out of habit, stopped at Ahmed's Swedish Deli to pick up some meatballs and nettle soup, then remembered that Roland wasn't home. Until two months

ago, he'd lived across the street in his parents' old
house—which he'd inherited—amid piles of books, papers, mail and clothing carelessly flung across the
furniture.

It was Cindy who'd sorted his bills and made sure his
laundry got done. During his absence, she was keeping
an eye on the renters. After she'd taken their dog to obe-
dience school, they'd settled in nicely.

When she pulled into her driveway, she glanced across
the street and saw smoke rising from the chimney of
Roland's house. How cozy it looked! Next winter, amazingly, Cindy herself would be living there, all snuggled
up with that big handsome man, yet close enough to in-
stall her mother's storm windows and clean out her
drains.

Snuggling with Roland. Cindy tried to imagine what it
would be like, once they went beyond the hugging and
kissing in which they'd indulged so far. As a minister's
daughter, she'd held fast to what was proper, and Roland
hadn't objected. She hoped his reticence wouldn't persist
once they were married, however, or how would they
ever get children?

Inside the one-story brick house where she'd grown
up, Cindy found the lights blazing and the welcome scent
of baked chicken wafting from the kitchen. "Hi, Mom!"
she called.

She was answered by the crash of piano keys in an
unholy chord. "Oh, my!" came her mother's sweet
voice. "You startled me."

Cindy went into the living room. Frances McChad,
who seemed far too small to have given birth to such a
large daughter, sat dreamily on the piano bench staring
at the printed music.

"How was your day?" Cindy asked.

"Exciting." On the instrument, the pink-cheeked woman launched into a dance rhythm that set her gray curls bouncing. It took Cindy several moments to recognize the melody as "Silent Night."

In her opinion, the carol didn't work well as a cha-cha. Politely she said, "How creative."

"I'm so full of ideas, I can't tell you!" With a smack, Frances dropped the cover on the keyboard and stood. She barely reached her daughter's armpit. "We'll talk at dinner. See you in half an hour."

How odd. Usually Frances couldn't wait for Cindy to get home so they could discuss the events of the day. After her husband's death, she'd clung ferociously to her daughter.

That hadn't been true for some time, though, Cindy reflected. Recently her mother had taken to drifting in with a sack of store-bought fried chicken or hamburgers after a long session with the choir. Cindy had assumed it was due to the thrilling but temporary business of cutting a CD to raise funds for the church.

Perhaps Frances was making another one. On the piano, next to "Silent Night," stood a copy of "The Little Drummer Boy" with the handwritten notation: "Try it as a tango." Oh, dear, Cindy thought.

She proceeded to the small front bedroom she'd occupied for as long as she could remember. The walls were enlivened by posters promoting the softball team and the Oofdah Elementary School Science Fair, which Cindy had organized for the past three years. The red-and-white checked curtains added a cheery picnic quality reminiscent of summer outings at the park.

On the doily-covered dresser stood a photo of Roland and Cindy as homecoming king and queen. As a sign of school spirit, they'd both worn football uniforms to the dance, much to the amusement of their classmates.

Impulsively she switched on her computer to check her e-mail. Although she tried to tell herself she was seeking messages from her little students or their parents, she knew she really hoped to hear from Roland.

What could be keeping him so busy out there in California? Probably he was too absorbed in his medieval research to return phone calls and e-mails, that was all.

When she clicked onto the Internet, she saw that, as usual, she had mail. But was it the right mail?

There was a newsletter from the Oofdah Friends of Foster Children, a notice of a PTA meeting, a Booster Club note about next week's fund-raising wienie roast, and a subject line that said, "From Roland."

Cindy's heart leaped into her throat. She hadn't wanted to admit, even to herself, how worried she'd been. Everything was right with the world, now that Roland had responded.

Eagerly she clicked open his message. It was longer than usual, she noticed.

She began to read.

"My dear friend Cindy…" Usually he addressed her as "Dear Cindy."

"Do you remember the day we got engaged?" As if she could forget! "It was our senior year in college and we'd come home to ride on a float in the Founders Day Parade."

Cindy's father, who'd organized the annual event, had needed someone to play the town's first mayor, Farmer Oofdah. She and Roland had had a friendly dispute over which of them got to play the character. In the end, they'd both donned overalls, grabbed pitchforks and spent the entire parade tossing hay on each other and laughing as the float rattled down Oofdah's main street.

"When we got back," Roland wrote, "your father asked, 'When are you two getting married?' I said, 'As soon as Cindy sets the date.'"

She smiled happily. Apparently he was thinking the same thing she was, that they'd waited long enough.

"It seemed like the most natural thing in the world to plan a future together," he went on. "You had always been my best friend, and that hasn't changed a bit."

No, it hadn't, Cindy thought with pleasure. Lots of people had commented over the years that the one constant in their lives was Cindy and Roland, never wavering in their mutual loyalty.

"I love you as much as ever," Roland wrote. "However, recently, I've come to understand that it's a brother-sister type of love. That's why neither of us was in any hurry to tie the knot."

Frowning, Cindy reread the last paragraph. What did he mean, a brother-sister type of love? Uneasily she read on.

"What made me realize this is that I've fallen in love with a woman I met here in Clair De Lune."

Cindy shook her head. Somebody else's e-mail must have crossed hers in cyberspace, dropping an errant sentence into place. Roland, in love with another woman?

Her heart squeezed. Without Roland, her whole world would be empty. He couldn't mean this. It must be a mistake.

"I'm sorry, but I have to break off our engagement." The words stared back at her pitilessly. "I was going to wait until I saw you, but I decided it would be unfair to break the news at Christmas. Cinders, you're my best buddy. I hope you'll forgive me, so we can go on being friends.

"Love, Roland."

There was no longer any question of an errant e-mail from a stranger. He'd used his pet nickname for her and he'd signed his own name.

How could he drop such a stink bomb out of the clear blue sky? How could he be so cruel?

Imprinted in her mind, his handsome face regarded her impishly. Cindy wanted to ruffle his thick blond hair and watch the sunrise as he flashed his brilliant smile.

Sure, they goofed around together, but they were far more than buddies. Years of shared experience and intimate conversations had matured their friendship into love, or at least it had for Cindy.

A tap at the bedroom door roused her. "I'm sorry," she told her mother. "I forgot about dinner."

"That's okay." Frances smiled and wiped her hands on her apron, which was printed with tiny roosters chasing tiny hens. "It's not quite ready, but I can't wait any longer to tell you the news."

Cindy didn't think she could take any more news today. "What's that?"

"I've accepted the job offer I mentioned last week, as choir director in Rochester," said her mom. "I know I promised to turn it down, but I changed my mind."

"It's an hour and a half away," Cindy replied automatically, still struggling to absorb Roland's words.

"I'm going to find an apartment near my new job. I'll sell the house as soon as you get married," Frances said.

"What—why—?"

"The pastor in Rochester called to say the local radio station is playing my CD and it's a runaway hit!" replied her mother. "He said his choir can't live without me. In fact, they want me to conduct an entire Christmas concert of updated carols. My brain's been humming all day. Don't you think 'O Little Town of Bethlehem' would sound perfect with a salsa beat?''

Cindy hated to disagree. She did want her mother to realize her potential. Still... ''What will the choir here do without you?''

''They can drive to Rochester twice a month for rehearsals,'' Frances said. ''It's perfect. To tell you the truth, I'm tired of having the responsibility for a house.''

Wasn't it only a few months ago that she'd begged her daughter to stay because otherwise she might have to give up their home? Well, no, it had been more like a half-dozen years. Yet it seemed impossible that she and Roland should both have changed so drastically.

In the space of a few minutes, Cindy's world had turned upside down. Her mother no longer needed her. And the man she adored believed himself in love with someone else.

Believed was the operative word. She refused to accept it. Alone and lonely in a strange place, Roland had been vulnerable. It was like that time on the football field when he'd gotten confused and run the wrong way.

Which was pretty much what Frances was doing, too. Of course she enjoyed the pastor's flattery, and it was only right that her talents should be recognized. That didn't mean she should abandon her home on an impulse.

''All your friends live in Oofdah,'' Cindy said. ''You belong here.''

''Everyone needs a change now and then,'' said her mother.

''I'll tell you what,'' Cindy said. ''Tell the pastor you want a probationary period. Rent a room in Rochester for a few weeks and give it a try.''

"But, dear, I've already agreed."

"Don't burn any bridges," Cindy warned. "You've got roots here."

"You have a point," Frances said. "I can hold off on moving my furniture, but I did promise to start work next week. I hope you won't mind being left alone."

"Actually I'm going to take a little trip to California," Cindy said. "I'll tell you all about it after I wash up for dinner."

"Very well, dear," said Frances, and went out with tiny pucker lines dimpling her forehead.

Cindy's thoughts whirled. She would have to take at least a month's leave, but what else could she do?

She must confront Roland in person or he might never come to his senses. Besides, it went against her nature to simply sit and do nothing.

The second-grade students at Oofdah Elementary would need a good substitute. Cindy's friend Doris, who wanted to resume teaching after full-time motherhood, would be delighted to get the work.

Above all, she reminded herself, her fiancé needed her. And she certainly needed him.

2

PARKING HER LARGE SUITCASE beside her on the porch, Cindy rang the doorbell a second time. There was still no response from within the house.

She'd e-mailed ahead to say when she was arriving, so what could have befallen her landlady? Perplexed, Cindy stared around, as if force of will could compel the woman to materialize.

Forest Lane was a quiet residential street not unlike those in Oofdah, except for a preponderance of stucco and the smaller size of the lots. However, the weather was quite different. Although November had arrived, the afternoon air lacked even a trace of chill.

The landscaping up and down the block struck her as fanciful: fat palm trees resembling giant pineapples, rose-bushes still in bloom, flower beds spilling over with pansies and primroses. Those were spring flowers, as everyone knew.

At least her landlady had a more sober turn of mind. The house, reminiscent of a witch's hideaway in a fairy tale, featured dark shingled siding, gingerbread trim and an overarching tree that blocked the sunlight. Instead of flowers, the beds harbored spindly herbs.

To her left, at the head of the driveway, rose a free-standing garage with a small apartment on top. Cindy, who'd found the place listed on the Internet, considered the rent quite reasonable. Best of all, the landlady, Mrs. Pipp, hadn't minded leasing it for only a month.

"I'm willing to be flexible," she'd said on the phone. "The only thing I loathe are boring tenants, and you don't sound like one of those."

Again, Cindy pressed the bell. No answer. Was Mrs. Pipp ill? She was considering whether to force the door when a slim man with a distracted expression strolled down the walkway from the sidewalk.

In baggy slacks and a tweed jacket with elbow patches, he looked supremely professorial. Long bangs and a squarish salt-and-pepper beard nearly obscured his high-boned, intelligent face. Lost in thought, he was halfway up the porch steps when he spotted her and halted.

"Excuse me," Cindy said. "Are you Mr. Pipp?"

"Am I who?" Frowning, he pushed up the bridge of his wire-rimmed glasses. Instinctively Cindy mirrored his action and adjusted her own frames.

He was kind of cute, she thought, although only about her height, five foot nine. Without thinking, she smoothed down the long skirt and coordinating sweater she wore beneath her open coat.

"Are you Mr. Pipp?" she repeated. "Mrs. Pipp's husband."

"There is no Mr. Pipp," he said. "Or perhaps there was, but I've never met him. Mrs. Pipp, well, we all call her Dean Pipp. She's retired now. I'm Hugh Bemling, by the way. Professor of English and Comparative Literature."

She shook hands. "I'm Cindy McChad. I teach second grade in Minnesota, and I'm renting a room from Mrs. Pipp. But she doesn't seem to be here."

"Looks like her note fell off." The fellow pointed to a slip of paper lying on the doormat.

After picking it up, Cindy read aloud: "'Ran out to the bookstore. Back whenever.' That sounds like it could take hours."

"With Dean Pipp, you never know." The man patted his bulging jacket pockets. "I brought her mail. Some of it still comes to the department by mistake. I'll just leave it inside and be on my way." Without explanation, he knelt by one of the herb beds, retrieved a spade from behind a bush and began digging.

"If you don't mind my asking, what are you doing?" Cindy said.

"Retrieving her keys." Hugh glanced up at her. When seen from above without the interference of glasses, his eyes were bright blue. "She buries them when she goes out. Otherwise, she loses them."

"I don't suppose there'd be one to my apartment, would there?" she asked.

He lifted up a plastic bag, shook off some dirt and retrieved a key ring. "One of these probably fits your door. Hold on."

Cindy waited while Hugh tossed a couple of crumpled letters onto a table inside. After locking the house, he led the way across the driveway and up a weathered staircase next to the garage.

At the top, he said, "Oh, I forgot," turned abruptly and reached for Cindy's luggage. "Let me help you."

Their hands bumped. Hugh had strong hands for someone so slim, Cindy noticed. Perhaps because she was wearing a heavy coat in mild weather, she felt unexpectedly hot.

She released the handle, even though they were right at her door. "Thank you."

"You're most welcome," said the professor. One tug on the heavy valise and he nearly fell off the landing.

Regaining his balance, he fumbled with the key and, after several tries, turned the knob.

Normally Cindy would have thanked him again and sent him on his way. However, her head felt light, most likely from the flower-scented breeze drifting past, and she let the professor escort her inside.

The room was large and sunny, furnished with a convertible couch, a desk and a chair. Behind the open door, Cindy found a kitchenette with a small dining counter, refrigerator and stove.

Regretfully she supposed that she shouldn't be alone here with a strange man, not even one as likable as Hugh. "Well, goodbye," she said.

Absorbed in a struggle to wrest her key from the ring, he didn't seem to hear. Suddenly it flew off, sailed across the room and slid under the couch.

Hugh gazed around. "Where'd it go?"

"Under there." Cindy pointed.

The professor frowned. "I don't suppose you've got a jack?"

"I can lift it," she said. "You climb under and get the key."

"Right." Dropping down, he peered beneath the sofa.

Cindy found herself wondering how it would feel to be the one lying on the floor while Hugh loomed over her, holding the edge of the couch like Atlas. He'd be adorable, flexing his muscles—surely there were muscles beneath that jacket, weren't there?

She didn't understand why she was thinking this way. She'd never fantasized about Roland's muscles, although he had plenty of them. In fact, if he'd been here, they'd have conducted a wrestling match to determine which one got to play strongman.

Returning to the present, she hefted the sofa and Hugh

reached underneath. "Got it!" He lifted the key and, at the same time, turned sharply toward her. Before she could call out a warning, he banged his head on the bottom of the couch and collapsed onto the carpet.

Wonderful. She'd barely arrived in town and already she'd coldcocked her first guest.

STARS AND STRIPES WHIZZED through Hugh's brain. He sensed that a poem was being born, rather like a galaxy, in a swirl of astral glory.

It was a short poem, because his head hurt. "A lady from the Midwest came to put me to the test," he muttered, then dropped the effort.

"Try rolling to your left," said a resonant female voice. "I can't pull you out and hold the couch at the same time."

For want of a better idea, he obeyed. The only difficulty was overcoming inertia. Once he got rolling, he rather enjoyed it.

"Stop!" said the woman. Beside him, the sofa settled into place with a soft thud. "Are you all right?"

Hugh tried sitting up. The front of his head hurt, but he was always knocking into one thing or another, so he was used to it. "I'm fine," he said.

The woman sat next to him on the floor. Through her glasses, sympathy shone from cornflower-colored eyes. "I'm sorry. I don't know what happened."

"It was my fault, not yours." Hugh was pleased to find himself able to talk easily. It meant he didn't have a concussion. It also meant he'd at least temporarily overcome his usual shyness around women.

"You should stay until you're feeling steadier," Cindy said. "I'll make you a cup of whatever's in the cupboard, and then I hope you don't mind if I unpack."

"I don't mind at all." Slowly he hoisted himself into a chair and, after a few minutes, was pleased to accept a cup of cinnamon tea. Sipping it, Hugh watched his hostess unlatch her suitcase and begin stowing her gear.

Cindy didn't appear to mind having an audience as she hung up her clothes and arranged her shoes in the closet. She was statuesque, definitely not his type, Hugh reflected. Still, that long thick blond braid brought to mind a figure from Teutonic legend. Brunhild, perhaps.

From the bottom of her suitcase, she lifted a framed photo and set it reverently on the desk. Hugh adjusted his glasses. Surely he was imagining the resemblance…

He got up for a closer inspection. "It is him," he said in surprise. "Looks like you played football with Roland."

"You know him?" She beamed. "He's my fiancé. I didn't play football, though—that's what we wore to homecoming."

Her remark rattled around until it came into focus. "The two of you are engaged?"

Cindy nodded happily. "We're getting married next summer."

Here was a perplexing development. Hugh remembered hearing somewhere that a person shouldn't interfere in other people's private business, but for heaven's sake, this was *his* private business, too. "You'd better tell Blair Riley. I think she's under the impression that he's available."

"Is that her name? Blair Riley?" Cindy came to stand beside him. Her nearness gave Hugh a pleasant buzz. Although his taste ran more to delicate princesses than to legendary queens, he appreciated femininity in all its forms. "Unfortunately Roland's under the impression that he's available, as well."

"How is that possible?" he asked.

"He has a very loving heart and he's far from home," she said.

This explanation of Roland's behavior made sense to Hugh. He'd never understood romantic relationships, aside from purely literary ones.

Since he first acknowledged the existence of girls in junior high school, he'd regarded them with some confusion. His parents, whose idea of a romantic evening was to do research together at the library, hadn't been much help.

Writing love poems helped overcome Hugh's awkwardness at expressing his feelings. Over the years, the poems had won him a number of dates and had sparked a couple of more serious involvements. Yet always the passion had faded, on both sides, within a few months.

He didn't understand what was missing. Cindy, on the other hand, radiated confidence when she talked about Roland. And if she knew how to pry loose her fiancé's attachment to Blair, Hugh would welcome her assistance.

"I think we should join forces," he said.

"Why?"

He hesitated, seeking the right way to express what he knew intuitively. "Blair and I, well, I can't say that we have an understanding *yet,* but the Fates have decreed that we should eventually come together," he said. "So I'm willing to assist you in any way I can."

When his companion didn't answer immediately, a cloud descended upon Hugh's spirits. Being around this upbeat newcomer gave him an unaccustomed sense of well-being, and he wanted to experience more of it before they went their separate ways.

HOW APPEALING THE MAN WAS, Cindy thought, with his earnest talk about the Fates bringing two people together.

She didn't have a romantic bone in her body, but she enjoyed the quality when she observed it in others.

Still, she hesitated to form a partnership, however temporary. Ganging up on Roland might seem like a betrayal of their trust in each other, a trust that she still believed in.

"It won't be necessary," she said. "All I need are directions to wherever Roland hangs out. I think it would work best if I run into him casually."

She didn't want to appear pushy. Besides, she hoped that a few minutes' conversation would reawaken the natural, unbreakable bond between them.

"They often eat at the Lunar Lunch Box." Hugh set aside his empty cup. "It's at the corner of Debussy Street and De Lune Boulevard, just a few blocks from here. I can walk you over, if you like."

The prospect of strolling beside Hugh gave Cindy a pleasantly squiggly feeling. "If it's not out of your way."

"I live two blocks the other side," he said. "It's no problem at all."

Cindy was tempted to wear her coat on the principle that it was November and people ought to respect the seasons. However, sunlight streamed through the window and, if she weren't mistaken, the temperature outside hovered in the upper seventies. Also, she didn't want to sweat around Hugh. "Ready when you are."

They were descending the steps when a small, elderly woman rushed toward them. Dressed in a gardening smock, she had a pair of binoculars slung around her neck and a camera held in front of her face. She began snapping away to Cindy's puzzlement and, judging by his expression, Hugh's annoyance.

"Dean Pipp?" Cindy saw no reason for her landlady to act like paparazzi. "Please stop that."

"I'm not Dean Pipp." The woman lowered her camera, revealing an accusatory expression. "What I want to know is, are you two married or are you living in sin?" She brandished a cell phone. "My friends want all the details."

Cindy tried to fathom this remark. "Are you from a church group?"

"Heavens, no!" The woman drew herself up to her full height, on the shy side of five feet. "I'm a gossip, and a good one, too."

"Esther Zimpelman lives across the street," Hugh said. "She's very nosy."

Indignation flared on the woman's face. "You're jealous because no one bothers about you. If I'd recognized you in time, Professor Bemling, I wouldn't have taken your picture." To Cindy, she said, "The last time I tried to share some tidbit about him, my friends threatened to cut me off. They said he's not scandalous enough."

"I'm Cindy McChad." She extended her hand, then realized the neighbor didn't have a free one. "I'm pleased to meet you, Mrs. Zimpelman, but you should do something more productive with your time. I'm sure the local hospital could use volunteers."

"The Hospital Guild kicked me out when they caught me reading the patients' medical charts." The small woman backed away. "You're very tall. I hope you're not violent."

"Only when provoked." Cindy would never lay a hand on an old lady, but she didn't want to be gossiped about, either.

"Welcome to the neighborhood. Try not to behave

yourself.'' Lugging her equipment, Mrs. Zimpelman marched across the street.

"Clair De Lune has its share of characters," Hugh observed when the woman was gone.

"Not too many like that, I hope," Cindy said.

"Not exactly." His answer was as far as he would commit himself.

They set off down Forest Lane, their strides matching. Cindy found herself swaying a bit too close to Hugh and forced herself to move farther away on the sidewalk.

At Hugh's suggestion, they detoured a few blocks north to swing through De Lune University. It would be helpful to have a guided tour of the campus, in case she wanted to visit Roland there later, Cindy decided.

Besides, it was only four o'clock, too early to find anyone in a restaurant. If she went later, she could eat dinner while she waited for Roland to show up.

The campus, she discovered, was much smaller than the public university she'd attended and had ivy-covered brick buildings organized around a grassy quadrangle. Students in summer clothing bicycled and skateboarded beneath delicate trees that Hugh called jacarandas.

He pointed out the glass-and-steel Faculty Center and waved vaguely toward a distant, unseen science center. At the back corner of the campus, they glimpsed the large, modern Student Center located behind the quadrangle.

When a narrow leaf blew down and lodged in Hugh's hair, Cindy plucked it off. His hair was soft and full, she found, and fought the urge to run her fingers through it. Although it was turning gray, he didn't appear older than in his mid-thirties.

"Do you always touch people?" he asked.

"I'm used to dealing with my second-graders," she admitted. "Do you mind?"

"No." He gave her a bemused smile.

"Hey, Professor Bemling! How ya doing?" called a couple of students cutting across the grass. Without waiting for an answer, they waved and vanished.

"Which class are they in?" Cindy said.

"I have no idea. I can't keep my students straight except by their work, and unfortunately they don't walk around with their papers pasted to their foreheads," he said.

"Second-graders sometimes paste their papers to their foreheads," she said. "I try to discourage it. By the way, where's your department?"

"Right here." Hugh indicated the building they were standing next to.

"Why didn't you say so?" Cindy longed to peek inside. "Aren't you going to invite me in?"

"There's nothing much to see." In a fit of self-consciousness, the professor thrust his hands into his pockets, then promptly pulled them out. Half a dozen papers popped out, too, and went whirling in the breeze.

When Hugh began chasing them down, Cindy joined in. She grabbed four pieces and he collected two. As she handed them back, she noticed that one contained a verse.

"You write poetry?" she asked. "May I read it?"

He nodded, wariness warring with eagerness in his eyes. As she did with her students' poetry, Cindy spoke the words out loud.

"There once was a T.A. named Blair,
To whom none on earth can compare."

"Not that one!" Hugh plucked it from her grasp. "I've written a much better one, if I can find it."

The light wind teased at her cheeks. "We should go inside," Cindy said. "Someplace where we can talk privately."

"You mean…my office?"

"Don't you let people into your office?" she asked, feeling a bit envious. Second-grade teachers didn't get offices. "If I had one, I'd show it off."

"It's cluttered," Hugh said.

"Like your pockets?"

"Worse." He gave her a self-deprecating grin. "I don't mind showing it to you, though. You're not the type who finds fault with everything." With a gait so quick it was almost a skip, he escorted her inside.

NO ONE BUT HUGH EVER WENT into his office. The janitor refused to clean it on the grounds that he should receive hazardous duty pay. Students waited outside and called "Professor Bemling!" until he responded.

Although most faculty offices were small, this one abutted an empty storage space. Over the years, the intervening wall had crumbled, and Hugh, without realizing it, had kept wedging in bookcases, so that the narrow pathway between them now ran a mazelike course that seemed to cover miles.

The shelves were crammed with volumes he'd picked up at used bookstores, or been sent by fellow professors and by publishers. Several shelves were filled with magazines, including a few copies of *Better Homes and Gardens,* to which he'd once submitted an article entitled "The Flower of Chivalry." He thought they'd returned it, but he could never find anything among the stacks of paper on his desk.

A tall file cabinet was stuffed, the top drawers with student records and the lower drawers with poems, articles and lecture notes. He kept a separate file of love poetry that dated all the way back to adolescence.

Hugh had once been fond of a girl named Melanie, whom he'd warned that to break his heart would be a felony. There'd been Sarah—no one could be fairer—and Isabelle, who tempted him to kiss and tell. It was only a poetic conceit. He never had kissed her, and felt certain he wouldn't have stooped to bragging about it if he had.

The loveliest of all, of course, was Blair. He'd put extra copies of his poems about her in the file, including the one he'd meant to read at the Lunar Lunch Box.

As he strained to open the balky file drawer, Cindy stood amid the clutter, reading the book titles on the nearest shelf. "You have such wide-ranging taste in poetry," she said. "Limericks. The works of Byron. Oh, here's *The Idylls of the King.* I love stories about King Arthur."

"I don't know how I'd have survived adolescence without them." The tales had given Hugh a belief in the triumph of principles over brute strength, and the courage to defy bullies. He had often been bruised, but he'd never been cowed.

Still, few women these days appreciated a man who liked poetry, however extraordinary his dreams might be. They preferred knuckleheads with broad chests, like Roland.

Uncomfortably Hugh remembered that Cindy was engaged to Roland. He refused to let it bother him.

"Where's the poem you wanted me to see?" she asked.

"In here." Hugh riffled through the file to the ones written for Blair. He passed odes to two old girlfriends:

Betsy ("Your namesake sewed our flag. My love for you will never lag") and Carmen ("utterly charmin'").

His throat tightened as he extracted a copy of his favorite work. For some reason, it mattered very much to him whether Cindy liked it.

She accepted the sheet carefully, as if it might break. Aloud, she read:

> "Green are your eyes, green as jade,
> Green as the trees or a grassy blade.
> I'm green with envy and blue with yearning.
> One glance from you turns me red from burning
> With passion that's yours and yours alone.
> Someday I pray you'll make me your own."

Hearing the words pronounced in Cindy's no-nonsense voice made Hugh see how silly the thing was. "The rhyme scheme is simplistic, isn't it?" he said before she could comment. "It doesn't scan very well, either."

Cindy pressed the paper to her bosom, which, he couldn't help noticing, was generous. "The emotion rings out clear and true. You feel things deeply, don't you?"

Hugh felt himself blushing. "I suppose I do."

"Any woman who would critique a love poem isn't worth bothering with," she said. "How did she respond to it?"

"She hasn't heard it," he said. "I took the wrong one by mistake. I made a fool of myself, I'm afraid, but I don't care. Love is worth it."

"She'll fall into your arms when she hears it," Cindy said. "A woman who would do less doesn't deserve you."

No one had ever spoken to Hugh this way. He almost

wished that Cindy weren't engaged to Roland so he could write a poem for her, but of course, a romance between them would never work.

Although she was fun to be around, she wasn't willowy or soft and she didn't make his knees quiver. She was more like good friend material, someone whom he could trust to read his poetry without fear of mockery.

"I'm going to take it to her right now." He folded the copy into his breast pocket. "She'll probably be at the restaurant with Roland."

"That's a good idea," Cindy said. "I was kind of worried about how Blair might feel when he breaks up with her. It'll be much better if you're there to cushion the blow."

So they were joining forces, at least for one evening. The prospect buoyed Hugh.

"Let's go, then," he said.

"You got it," said Cindy, and they went out together.

3

EXCEPT FOR A COUPLE of office buildings, downtown Clair De Lune was dominated by one- and two-story shops and cafés, mostly built of stucco or funky wood. The buildings were squeezed together compared to those in Oofdah, but Cindy liked their cheeky style.

A cutout of a full moon with a smiling face topped the shake roof of the restaurant, outside which she and Hugh stood gathering their courage. Petunias, fearless in this frost-free zone, spilled from planters beneath a row of mullioned windows.

Cindy's heart rate quickened. Now that she was on the verge of seeing Roland, her impulsive cross-country jaunt began to seem a bit presumptuous.

She thought she knew her fiancé better than the back of her hand, but did she? What if he did love someone else? Her breath caught in her throat.

"Having second thoughts?" Hugh asked. "It goes with the territory, you know."

"What territory?"

He paused while a group of students surged by them and went inside. Through the open door, Cindy heard the chatter of voices and the clink of dishes and cutlery.

In answer to her question, Hugh said, "Taking emotional risks is the most nerve-racking activity on earth, worse than white-water rafting. Or so I presume."

"You're right." The youth group at Cindy's church

camped out in northern Minnesota for one week every summer, and she and Roland had worked as counselors during college. The two of them had dared each other to try every sport they came across, including rafting.

Then, it had never occurred to her to be frightened. Not like now, when she had to fortify her will.

"You mustn't allow yourself to be frightened of failure," Hugh advised. "Our suffering is minor in light of our magnificent quest."

"I don't often fail, and when I do, I regroup and try again," Cindy said. "But this time, I can't bear to think about losing."

"It sounds like you've had more successes than I have," said Hugh. "But I never give up."

"I'm sure you've won over plenty of girls. You're so..." She caught herself before uttering the word *cute* and substituted it with *"attractive."*

"I've had a few girlfriends, but no great love affair." Hugh sounded wistful. "I don't know how to make a relationship work in the long haul."

"I've had lots of experience with the long haul." Cindy found herself on safer ground at last. "The trick is to stock the other person's favorite snack foods and make sure to alternate who gets to pick the movie."

"That doesn't sound hard," Hugh said.

The temperature was dropping rapidly, making Cindy wish she'd brought her coat. She couldn't help suspecting that, despite the ballyhoo about Southern California's warm temperatures, a frost would sneak up on them in the night.

"Let's go in," she said.

"Right."

Entering the Lunar Lunch Box was like walking through a wall of sound. The linoleum floor, wooden furniture and silvery walls, which were painted with scenes of fantastical voyages to the moon, resounded with the clamor of the diners.

Swarms of young people clustered around tables. Through their midst scurried an overworked waitress carrying a tray piled with food.

Even in this crowd, how could anyone miss Roland? He sat in profile to Cindy, his chair pushed back from the table to make room for his long legs. Those broad shoulders and that gleaming blond hair, which had grown several inches since she last saw him, dominated the restaurant.

"We wouldn't need full-size horses," he was saying to a group of rapt companions. "Professor Needham has a stable full of ponies. Since she's one of the faculty sponsors, I'm sure she'll rent them to us cheap."

"What are we going to use for lances?" asked a young man. Even through the din, Cindy found her ears attuned to the conversation at that table. For a teacher accustomed to supervising recess, it wasn't difficult.

"There's all sorts of possibilities." All Cindy could see of the woman who spoke was the back of her swingy black hair, but her throaty voice came across distinctly. "We can scout the home-improvement stores and the costume shops."

It was daunting to see Roland so confident and at ease in his new environment. And to observe how many friends he'd made whom Cindy knew nothing about.

Hugh touched her shoulder with gentle reassurance. She took courage from his quiet strength and from the fact that, in a way, they were both in this together.

A puffy middle-aged man in a white apron nearly ran into them as he scurried about the restaurant. "Excuse me," Cindy said.

"You'll have to wait for a seat." He waggled an order form in one hand. "We're full, and I'm short a server."

"No problem." When he departed and Cindy returned her attention to Roland, she saw that he had slung one arm around the back of the chair next to his. The woman's pageboy grazed the thick muscles visible below the sleeve of his T-shirt.

Seeing Roland so close to another woman was an affront to the natural order. Still, Cindy didn't take it too seriously. A few years ago, she'd dampened a New Year's Eve party for herself by getting annoyed because he'd flirted with another woman, only to watch him completely lose interest when the newcomer confessed she hated football.

Cindy strolled closer. "Hi, Roland," she said, as if they'd seen each other only the day before.

He turned with a half smile that brought out the cleft in his chin. The smile froze. "Cindy?" Roland nearly choked on her name.

"None other," she said.

Remembering his manners, he stood up. With his longer hair, he resembled a Viking, so handsome he took her breath away. "What are you doing here?"

Cindy realized she should have prepared something to say next. "I happened to be in the neighborhood" wasn't going to work.

"I thought we should talk in person," she said as calmly as she could with a whole tableful of strangers eyeing her.

Hugh moved to her side. "They're engaged," he told Roland's dark-haired companion.

She stood up, too, and glanced from Roland to Cindy. The most striking thing about her was the emerald-green eyes, brilliant beneath two perfect, straight brows. She was slender and shapely, a fact that no one could miss thanks to her midriff-baring halter top and tiny shorts. Bracelets jingled on her slim wrist as she pushed back her hair.

It was easy to understand how this beauty had dazzled Hugh, but that didn't mean he was in love. No, just a minute. She didn't mean Hugh, she meant Roland.

"Uh, Blair, this is Cindy McChad," her fiancé was saying. "Cindy, Blair Riley."

"You're engaged?" the woman asked in a husky, musical voice.

"I broke it off," he said. "Cindy, I'm sorry you've wasted your time coming all the way out here to California."

Any show of emotion would embarrass everyone, including herself. Nevertheless, Cindy couldn't hide her disappointment that her old friend was treating her so shabbily. "I don't think it's appropriate to break off a six-year engagement by e-mail, do you, Roland?"

He got that shamefaced, little-boy look she'd seen in one of her students the other day when she caught him dropping a lizard into a girl's backpack. "I guess not." Doggedly he added, "But it's over. Cindy, I don't want to hurt you or make you angry. The truth is, I've changed."

"I hope you don't think I deliberately came between you," Blair said. "I had no idea he was taken."

Cindy liked this straightforward young woman. "It's not your fault. I don't blame Roland for spreading his wings, either. But have you thought about the fact that, after he earns his master's degree, he's going back to Minnesota? You'd hate it there. For one thing, you'd freeze."

Roland's eyes took on a hooded appearance, much like

the one he'd worn when he announced out of the blue that he'd won a fellowship at De Lune University. "I'm not going back to live in Oofdah, Cindy. I want to teach college, and that means moving somewhere else. Maybe out of Minnesota entirely."

She didn't know what to say. She couldn't adjust to this turn of events so quickly.

Hugh placed a sympathetic hand beneath her elbow. After a moment in which no one spoke, he said, "Do you mind if I change the subject? I have something for Blair."

"Please do." Cindy was glad to postpone any response to Roland's painful declaration.

Pulling a sheet of paper from his pocket, Hugh faced the beautiful young woman. Tenderly he read:

"Green are your eyes, green as jade,
Green as the trees…"

Listening, Cindy wished she could be the subject of such passion. If only Roland showed more enthusiasm for her! Not simply more than he was showing now, which wouldn't take much, but more than he'd shown when, for instance, he'd asked her to the senior prom by saying, "Would you rather go to the dance or stay home and watch the game?"

Hugh would never approach a woman that way, she reflected wistfully. Why didn't Blair appreciate it? Judging by the expression on her face, his heartfelt effort failed to move her.

"That's a very nice poem, Professor Bemling," she said when he finished.

"It's for you." Hugh extended the sheet, which bore heavy fold lines.

"Thank you." The young woman tucked it into her purse. "You'll have to excuse us. Roland and I are going to the movies."

"We're late. We'd better hurry," said Roland. He had never rushed when he and Cindy went out, even if it meant walking into a movie half an hour late.

The two of them dropped some money on the table and departed. People turned to watch, and no wonder, she thought. They made a beautiful couple.

It was inconsiderate, if not downright heartless, of Roland to dismiss her so casually after all the years they'd spent together, Cindy reflected. Yet it wasn't entirely surprising.

For years, she'd tolerated his casual manner, not objecting that he changed their plans whenever something more interesting came up. She hadn't minded, because interesting things didn't come up very often in Oofdah. Unfortunately he appeared to find Blair very interesting.

Still, he'd strayed before. During their sophomore year in college, he'd split up with Cindy to date a fresh-faced cheerleader, squiring her to a couple of dances. But he'd come back, saying the girl's nonstop chatter bored him.

Misbehavior at age twenty-eight was a lot more serious than misbehavior at nineteen, but Roland's personality hadn't changed much. As he'd said in his e-mail, they were best friends, and Cindy had a big enough heart to stick around until he was ready to reconcile.

There was no point in standing here, now that Roland and Blair had gone. Hugh found them a clear table, and they sat down to eat.

After a few minutes, Cindy got tired of waiting for service, as all she did was think about Roland. Excusing herself, she collected a couple of menus from a side counter. She also poured two cups of coffee from a carafe and brought them to the table so she and Hugh had something to sip while they made their selection.

"If you want something done, do it yourself," she explained as she settled across from Hugh. Only then did she notice how dejected he looked, his chin resting on his palms and his expression solemn.

She wished she could help him. But right now, for one of the few times in her life, Cindy wasn't even sure how she was going to help herself.

HUGH DIDN'T MIND THAT HIS poem hadn't bowled Blair over. His crusade to win her, like any pursuit of a difficult but worthwhile goal, had to be conducted in stages. He counted tonight as a success because he'd made the point that his love was steadfast and he didn't give up easily.

What Cindy had experienced was a different matter. She shouldn't have to go through such a cruel rejection by a man she'd trusted.

An unaccustomed anger surged through Hugh. Only a cad would break off an engagement by e-mail, and only a fool would fail to appreciate such a devoted woman.

Now Cindy would go flying back to Minnesota, since she had no further reason to hang out in Clair De Lune. Hugh was going to miss having a fellow campaigner on the romance trail.

Seeing her study him across the table, he said, "I'm sorry Roland didn't come to his senses."

"I don't know what I'd have done without you," she said. "You gave me so much support."

"That's because I've been there plenty of times myself," Hugh said. "Who could forget that lurch of the stomach, that twist of disbelief? I've outgrown them for the most part, but the memories are as sharp as yesterday."

"By the way," Cindy said, "do you have any idea what they were talking about, that business about ponies and lances?"

"Every December, the History Department sponsors a medieval fair and Christmas boutique," Hugh said. "They're always looking for new attractions. I presume Roland and his crowd are planning a tournament." It seemed ironic, considering how little romance the man had in his soul.

"That sounds like the kind of thing Roland would enjoy," Cindy agreed. "Something brawny and physical."

"I envy him. I'd love to be in that tournament to show Blair how I feel."

"You should give it a try," she said. "If you don't mind a few bruises."

"Pain doesn't bother me, but I'd get knocked off in the first round and probably break my glasses." Given his slender physique and average height, Hugh had accepted long ago that he could be a knight in shining armor only in the metaphorical sense.

"You might not win the joust, but you'd show the truest spirit," Cindy said.

Stirred, Hugh cupped his hand over hers on the table. "Thank you. However, I try to limit the circumstances under which I make a fool of myself."

"I think sometimes physical pain is easier to bear than the emotional kind." Cindy stared toward the door through which Roland had disappeared.

Lacking any way to console her, Hugh could only sit there, holding her hand. Despite her self-confidence, she was a sensitive woman and tonight she'd been dealt a blow.

"I think we work well as a team," he said. "I wish you'd consider continuing our alliance."

Cindy's pale braid snapped back and forth as she shook her head. "Roland needs to discover for himself that this is a shallow attachment. Besides, I have no idea how to help you. The way I tend to steamroll people, I might even make things worse between you and Blair." Before he could argue, she glanced around. "If no one wants to take our order, I may go write it up myself."

"Don't get your panties in a twist. I'm here." The owner, Stu Crockenmeyer, pulled a pad from his pocket.

Stu was notorious for his grouchy temper. When not forced into service due to lack of staff, he rarely addressed patrons unless they'd broken one of his written or unwritten rules. Hugh hoped they weren't about to receive an insult, because he'd be honor-bound to defend his companion.

"I'll have the pastrami on rye," Cindy said.

"Patty melt for me," said Hugh.

Stu made a few scribbles. "No substitutions," he said belligerently.

"We didn't ask for any," Cindy pointed out.

"Yeah, but you were gonna."

"With your attitude, you're going to lose business," she said.

"Ever worked as a waitress?" he asked.

She blinked at the unexpected question. "Yes, one summer while I was in college."

"Want a job?" Stu said. "We've got an opening, and I like the way you don't put up with guff."

She considered for a moment. "Sure, why not?"

"You can start tomorrow afternoon. Four o'clock." After handing her his business card, Stu headed off.

Cindy smiled, filling the room with sunshine. "That was lucky," she said. "I can earn some money to finance my stay and keep an eye on Roland at the same time."

"You're going to stay for a while?" Hugh asked with a surge of relief.

"I wasn't planning to, but I guess I am now."

WHEN THE TWO OF THEM arrived at Dean Pipp's house on Forest Lane, the front porch light was blazing. Cindy wondered if she should ring the bell and introduce herself to her landlady.

Before she could decide, a woman in her seventies with a nest of steel-gray hair popped unbidden onto the porch. "Sorry I wasn't here earlier," she told Cindy, her shawl and gypsy-style skirt quivering in the breeze. "I'm Marie Pipp. Call me Dean, everybody else does. Hugh, thanks for leaving my mail. You can go along home now."

"Glad to be of service," he said. "Cindy, if you change your mind…"

"She won't," said the peppery landlady. "No woman ever changes her mind where you're concerned, Hugh Bemling. This is the third one of my tenants you've gone after, and the first two both got themselves married to other men. Very happily, too, I might add."

"You misunderstand," he said. "But no matter. I'll see you soon, Cindy. Have a pleasant evening." He strolled away.

What a sweet guy. She wished he lived in Oofdah so they could stay friends. It was too bad his gentle nature didn't suit her forceful personality, but she savored the prospect of seeing him again.

"He's not courting me," she told her landlady. "He's in love with someone else and wants me to help."

"He's enlisting you to woo another woman? What on earth is he thinking?" The dean made a clucking noise as she attempted to shoo Cindy into the house. "Come have a cup of tea. I grow my own mint."

The offer would have been tempting if she weren't full. "We just ate at the Lunar Lunch Box."

"Did Stu Crockenmeyer poison you with his coffee? All the more reason to flush it out with some of my tea." The dean led the way indoors without waiting for an answer, and Cindy followed, too curious to refuse.

They passed through an entryway narrowed by bookshelves on both sides. Some of the volumes were so ancient that their leather bindings flaked brown and black bits onto the wooden floor. Through a doorway to her left, Cindy glimpsed an old-fashioned parlor, also crammed with volumes. It reminded her of Hugh's office, but then, they *were* both scholars.

The dean guided her into a formal dining room papered with printed cabbage roses and dimly lit by wall sconces. Books were piled atop the antique-style sideboard and stacked on the floor. Along one wall hung portraits of Mark Twain, Edgar Allan Poe and William Shakespeare, each listing at a different angle.

At the head of the table stood a samovar atop a small blue flame. The fragrance of mint tantalized her. "I would like to try your tea, after all."

"Of course you would." The landlady poured steaming liquid into two mismatched cups, one bearing a floral design and the other depicting a shepherdess. "Now tell me about this nonsense of your helping Hugh win whatever lady he's mooning over this week."

"He asked, but I'm not going to do it," Cindy said, taking a seat. The tea, after she'd blown on it to bring the temperature down, turned out to be presweetened and delicious. "This is excellent."

"I knew you were a woman of taste the moment I heard you came from Minnesota," the dean responded.

"Why is that?" Cindy asked.

"Because they make such tasty cheeses," said her landlady.

"That's Wisconsin."

"It's in the same general region," said Dean Pipp. "People can't expect me to keep track of fifty different states all at the same time, not to mention however many foreign countries."

At close range, she had the sharp features and quick, birdlike gaze of a born eccentric. Cindy was pleased to find that the denizens of Clair De Lune could be quirky in more pleasant ways than Mrs. Zimpelman.

"You're wise not to get tangled up with Professor Bemling," the dean went on. "He's a mass of confused amorous instincts. He'll never win one of his fair ladies, if you ask me."

"He's good company," Cindy protested. "I'd like to help him, if I knew how."

The dean uttered an unladylike snort. "Help Hugh?" she repeated. "The only thing that could help that man is a magic spell."

"You wouldn't happen to know one, would you?" Cindy teased.

"Maybe there's one in here." Mrs. Pipp picked up a worn volume from the corner of the table. "I just bought this today." She handed it to Cindy.

The title was *Magical Transformations in Literature*. From what little she could read in the faint lighting, Cindy didn't see any magical cures for lovesickness. "Did you buy this for some particular reason?"

"I wrote a paper for a literary journal recently on how werewolves are depicted in TV and movies versus how they appear in folk tales," the dean said. "I got interested in the subject of people changing into something else. In literature, I mean."

"Please don't turn Hugh into a werewolf. I like him the way he is." Cindy finished her tea. "It's been lovely to meet you, but I am rather tired."

"Did you get a key?" asked Dean Pipp, taking back her book. "Good. Speaking of spells, that apartment has a knack for making people fall in love. My young women always seem to end up in the matrimonial state."

"I'm glad to hear it. I hope it works on my fiancé." Cindy had explained her reason for coming to California when she first contacted her landlady.

"So do I," said the dean. "If he's the right man, as you think."

"He is," she said. "He just has to learn not to take me for granted."

They talked for a while longer about teaching and the differences between second grade and college. Cindy was yawning by the time she let herself into her room. No wonder, she thought, realizing it was two hours later in Oofdah.

As she undressed, the idea of magical transformations danced through her brain. What image sprang to mind wasn't people turning into fantastical creatures, however, but the annual Makeover Event held each spring at the Oofdah Emporium.

It was amazing what a difference a little makeup and a change of fashion made for some of her fellow teachers. Once, Cindy had asked Roland if she should try it, but he'd insisted he liked her the way she was.

She pulled on a light-blue nightgown. No, she thought, she wasn't going to change her appearance now. It would only look as if she were trying to compete with Blair.

When she lay on the folded-out couch, the face that drifted into her mind's eye wasn't her fiancé's. Instead she saw Hugh's overgrown, graying hair, the square beard that hid his face, the shambling way he walked... Well, Blair could hardly be expected to fall in love with a man who, as Cindy's grandfather used to say, hid his light under a bushel.

Transformation. Makeover. What a great idea! Not for her, but for Hugh.

Cindy sat up in bed. She would tell him her plan tomorrow, and in no time both their problems would be solved. With her guidance, he'd win Blair, while Roland, discovering how shallowly his new flame burned, would come running back to his true love.

She lay down again, pleased at the prospect of helping Hugh, and dreamed about him all night.

4

A TERRIBLE THING HAPPENED to Hugh Bemling on Saturday morning, although at first everything seemed normal. When he awoke in his loft apartment above a bookstore, sunlight was streaming through the high slanting panes of glass. For a moment, he had the comforting sensation that all was right with the world.

But how could this be? He was no closer to winning Blair's heart than he'd been the day before.

Puzzled, he pushed aside the mosquito netting that canopied his bed and poured himself a cup of coffee from the automatic pot that sat on a steamer trunk beside his cot. The hot, strong liquid cleared the cobwebs from his brain, but did nothing to dispel the unfamiliar sense of well-being.

Hugh's mood was his first inkling that something had gone amiss. Lonely since childhood, he had come to accept a deep yearning for companionship as the norm. Instinctively he mistrusted cheerfulness, especially if it lasted longer than a few minutes.

He knew what he had to do. Writing a love poem would cure any delusions of happiness.

Hugh lowered his feet to his grass mat and walked to the carved wooden chest that doubled as a desk. Ignoring the rumpled state of his pajamas, he sat cross-legged on the floor to write.

The apartment, designed as an artist's studio, had previously belonged to a sculptor and her husband, an anthropologist who taught African Studies. The pair had returned to their beloved Africa on a grant and, along with their apartment, had transferred all their furnishings to Hugh.

He'd been delighted to get them for a modest sum, since his idea of interior decorating was limited to installing as many bookcases as possible. Although he'd saved more than enough from his salary to buy a house, Hugh had no idea what he would do with one.

Nibbling the end of his ballpoint pen, he stared down at the narrow pad left by a real-estate agent who had tried to talk him into home-shopping. It was difficult to get in the mood for love while staring at a small photo of a smiling middle-aged man, beneath which ran the motto, Bo Mallard Real Estate Is Hot To Trot!

Exactly what did it mean to be hot to trot? It sounded more like a disease than a distinction. Hugh ripped the cardboard off the bottom and turned the pad over to work on the blank side.

"Lovely Blair..."

And there his inspiration ended. He couldn't think of a single way to describe her hair that didn't strike him as ridiculous. The words that rhymed with her name all sounded stilted, too.

He treated himself to a second cup of coffee, then went back to stare at the paper. Nothing. He read some of his favorite parts of Tennyson's *The Idylls of the King,* then studied the paper again. Still blank. An entire hour went by, and yet he couldn't write a single additional word.

Hugh leaned back with a groan. Writer's block had always been his greatest fear, one never realized until now. Something had gone desperately wrong and he had no idea where to find a cure. Unless...

If he participated in next month's joust, he might regain his inspiration. The stories of King Arthur had been his refuge as a child, but perhaps rereading Tennyson's work wasn't enough. He needed hands-on experience.

After switching on his computer, Hugh clicked to the university's Web site. It featured a press release about the joust—and the thrilling announcement that Blair Riley, playing the princess, had issued an invitation for a challenger to face her champion, Roland Greenwald.

Hugh flexed his shoulders. It was going to hurt, getting knocked to the ground and possibly trampled by ponies. Although his heart urged him to dare everything, his common sense warned that he should consider a less perilous approach.

A knock at the door made him grimace. Solicitors, this early?

The knock came again. Perhaps, Hugh thought with a spurt of hope, it was the bookstore owner, who always notified him when a new volume of poetry hit the shelves. Inspiration might be literally knocking at his door.

He got up to answer it.

The grin that greeted him came from eye-level. He hadn't realized yesterday how tall Cindy was. This morning, she looked quite fetching in a warrior maiden kind of way, with her ash-blond braid curled atop her head.

"I hope I'm not disturbing you. Dean Pipp gave me your address," she said. "I have an idea to discuss."

Hugh ran his fingers through his hair in the faint hope of straightening it. "Come in." He waved toward the steamer trunk. "Coffee?"

"I already had some, thanks." Cindy stood, studying the eight-foot-tall wooden fertility goddess that dominated the far end of the loft. "That's some statue."

"So it is." Hugh was a bit embarrassed to be seen in his pajamas, but it was too late to do anything about it. "What's your idea?"

Cindy plopped onto a wicker settee. "We're going to make a new man of you, Hugh Bemling. Blair won't know what hit her."

This sounded promising. He eased himself onto the sling seat of a canvas chair. "Tell me more."

CINDY KNEW IT WASN'T POLITE to drop by a man's apartment unannounced, particularly on a Saturday morning when he might be sleeping late. She'd set out with the intention of enjoying a leisurely coffee and Danish pastry, then window-shopping until a decent hour when she would telephone.

In the bookstore downstairs, she'd browsed through several volumes about makeovers. Discouraged by the glossy photos of women with high cheekbones and men with bulging muscles, she'd put them back. The goal wasn't to turn Hugh into a movie star. All he needed to win any woman's heart was to make a few minor changes, and suddenly she couldn't wait to tell him so.

Although it had been only a little after nine, she'd climbed the stairs alongside the bookstore. Cindy didn't regret her impulsive decision, even though it meant confronting Hugh in his nightclothes. With his thick hair falling over his forehead, he wore an appealingly dreamy expression.

That didn't mean, unfortunately, that he warmed to her suggestions. Shave his beard? No, thanks. Cut his shaggy hair? Absolutely not!

"You can't deny that you need exercise," Cindy said, clinging doggedly to her final point.

"What sort of exercise?" A spark of interest lit Hugh's vivid eyes.

Cindy had been on the verge of suggesting a morning jog, but it didn't appear that mornings were Hugh's strong point. "Join a gym," she said. "Build up those muscles and increase your stamina."

As she spoke, he stiffened his spine and seemed to gain a few inches in height. "That's not a bad idea. If I were stronger, I might be able to joust." Then he added, "You'll have to join me. Otherwise I won't know what I'm doing."

Cindy was on the point of protesting, when an image of Hugh smacking a racquetball flashed into her mind. Then she saw him, hot and sweaty, lifting weights.

He was more likely to stick to an exercise program if he had a buddy, she told herself. Besides, working at the Lunar Lunch Box wasn't going to absorb nearly enough of her energy while she waited for Roland to come to his senses.

"All right," she said. "I've never belonged to a gym, although I've been involved in team sports. It should be interesting."

So, an hour later, they met at the University Health Club. Beneath Hugh's T-shirt and shorts, his pale limbs were healthy but on the thin side, Cindy thought, regarding him with the objectivity of a longtime sports booster.

She herself had stopped at a store to buy athletic clothing, since she hadn't brought any to California. It came as a jolt when the medium shorts and T-shirt didn't fit and she had to buy the large size. Did clothes run smaller in Clair De Lune than in Oofdah, or had her old ones simply stretched over the years?

They both signed up for a one-month trial membership at a discounted price. Soon they were grunting and straining on a pair of machines apparently designed by medieval torturers. Roland would love them, Cindy mused.

If he were here, the former football star would have raced through his exercises, to the pleasure of a rapidly growing knot of feminine admirers. Cindy had always taken pride in her fiancé's charisma, yet today she enjoyed struggling alongside Hugh, sharing sympathetic glances with him, free of interruptions by other women.

"How're you doing?" asked Brad, the fellow who'd sold them their memberships. "I was going to suggest you join the noon volleyball game, but our coach called in sick."

"I can coach volleyball," Cindy said. Over the years, she'd supervised almost every sport played in Oofdah.

"Really?" Hugh asked.

"That would be great," said their host. "The other players were quite disappointed. I'll see if I can catch them before they leave."

They turned out to be short one player of the twelve needed, so Cindy decided to play as well as coach. She assigned Hugh to the left rear position while she took up center back. After she explained the rules to him, the girl to her right served the ball, and the game began.

It was a new experience, shouting out calls for both teams while playing her position. Cindy was surprised how winded she got. She used to play one sport after another for hours. Somewhere along the line, she'd confined herself to the sidelines without noticing.

This was fun despite the aching lungs, she thought, as she raced forward, spiked the ball and scored a point. She just hoped Hugh was enjoying it, too.

HUGH'S FIRST REACTION on entering the gym, located a block from campus on Venus Avenue, had been to recoil from the smell and the loud echoes. He hadn't been won over by the tedious pulling, pushing and straining on the exercise machine, either.

Once he got the hang of volleyball, however, his muscles responded in fresh and pleasurable ways. There was a rhythm to the game, even when he wasn't personally handling the ball. The team seemed to share its spirit, all of them bouncing from foot to foot, encouraging each other and sharing the lift when one person leaped to make a hit.

When, halfway through, Hugh lunged forward and smacked the ball over the net, his teammates cheered. The fact that his shot was easily returned didn't matter.

Although he missed the ball several times and never repeated his moment of triumph, Hugh felt as if he were moving with a new kind of grace. Afterward, heading for the whirlpool bath, he relished the burning sensation in his arms and legs. At this rate, he might be able to tackle Roland at the tournament, after all.

Half a dozen people piled into the hot water, but most of them left after a few minutes. "They must be in better shape than we are," Cindy said, when she and Hugh were alone. "I don't know how I'm going to go carry trays around the coffee shop this afternoon."

Her braid floated on the water as she leaned back and closed her eyes. Even motionless, there was a vibrancy about the woman that caught Hugh's attention. It had been exciting, watching her play and shout directions at the same time, and knowing that she was keeping a special eye on him.

He'd never had a woman as a friend before. Among his acquaintances, the few ladies who met his romantic ideal were immediately put on a pedestal, and no one else registered on the radar screen.

Come to think of it, Hugh mused, he didn't have many
male friends, either. His only buddy was Jared Benton,
the head of the theater department, whom he'd met when
he consulted with Hugh last season on interpretations of
several classic plays in production. Jared, an outgoing
fellow who drew more than his share of female attention,
occasionally joined Hugh for lunch and teased him good-
naturedly about his poetic outlook.

Jared had never offered to help with a makeover, however. And if he had, Hugh certainly wouldn't have felt
this pleasant buzz at being alone together.

As Cindy lolled in the water, her rosy complexion and
well-rounded shape in the one-piece suit gave Hugh the
impression of innocent sensuality. He'd seen a lot of sensuality, if you counted female body parts bursting out of
skimpy clothing around campus, but none of it had struck
him as innocent.

Maybe that was why it had become so hard to write
poetry, he mused. Poetry required mystery and remote-
ness, not bare navels and thong sandals.

A woman from Oofdah, called Cindy... He couldn't go
on. There was nothing romantic about the name Cindy,
and the only rhyme he could think of was the unappeal-
ing "windy."

"A penny for your thoughts." Cindy was watching
him with interest.

"I can't write poems anymore," Hugh admitted. "At
least, I couldn't this morning."

"You're probably on poetic overload," she replied
promptly. "You've been rhapsodizing about Blair at a
heavy pace, haven't you?"

"But this has never happened before," he said. "Until
now, the words always flowed."

"What do you think has changed?" As she sat up, her

suit's low neckline revealed the round tops of her breasts. They were so lush and full Hugh could almost feel them pressing against his palms. He forced his thoughts away.

"Just that I haven't seen her much in the past day or two," he said. "Maybe it's like an artist with a model. I need the visual stimulation."

"Do you want to practice on me?" There was no trace of coyness in Cindy's tone. "I'd be happy to pose for a poem, if that would help."

"Thanks, but you're not my type," Hugh said.

A brief, uncomfortable silence fell between them. He wondered if he'd said the wrong thing. But why should she take offense at an honest reply to her question?

"I think I'll get dressed now," Cindy said. "I've got to be at work in a couple of hours and I doubt Mr. Crockenmeyer would appreciate it if I showed up in my bathing suit."

"You promised to keep me company at the gym," Hugh reminded her. "One o'clock on weekdays is a good time for me, since I've got a break from classes then. And I suppose we can pencil in Saturdays, too."

There was a moment's hesitation before she said, "Fine. I'll see you Monday." With a splash and a cascade of water, she rose from the pool, slung a towel around herself and headed for the women's locker room.

HUGH'S REMARK STUNG. When Cindy offered to stand in for Blair temporarily, she hadn't been prepared for a rejection. It wasn't as if she'd been proposing herself as a romantic object, after all.

So she wasn't his type. Well, he wasn't hers, either, but she would never say so.

Was it really impossible for a man to write poems about her? She'd never wanted such a thing before. Certainly Roland had never composed one, and Cindy wouldn't have known how to react if he had.

She tried to put the incident out of her mind. No use dwelling on something so unimportant.

That evening at the Lunar Lunch Box, she handled her duties in an efficient, impersonal fashion. Underneath, she felt an unaccustomed irritability.

When too many patrons arrived at once, and Mr. Crockenmeyer snarled at her for no good reason, she gave him a quelling stare that stopped him in his tracks. This won her a thumbs-up from Daffodil, the cook, and a sympathetic glance from the other waitress, Magda Barton.

Cindy was so preoccupied that she took little notice when Roland arrived with Blair and some other friends. She could have asked Magda to wait on them, but their table was in Cindy's station and she saw no reason to flee with her tail between her legs.

"What do you think you're doing?" Roland asked when she approached, order pad in hand. "You aren't working here, are you?"

"Tonight's special is avocado pita sandwiches with cranberry sauce and hash browns," Cindy said. "We also have quesadillas with German potato salad."

"What an international menu," murmured Blair.

"Hey, we all come here for the heartburn," said a thin fellow beside her.

"Cindy, go home," Roland said. "I don't want to sound hard-hearted, but you're just torturing yourself."

"Maybe I could get Daffodil to add lutefisk to the menu," Cindy answered.

"Yeah?" His expression warmed. "I've missed that."

"What's lutefisk?" asked Blair.

"Codfish soaked in lye." Cindy watched shivers of

distaste run around the table, except for Roland, whose nose quivered appreciatively. The small triumph, surprisingly, failed to lift her spirits. "Okay, who's having what?"

After she took their orders, she heard Blair ask Roland, "You don't really eat that lutefisk stuff, do you?"

"It's great with nettle soup," he said.

Cindy was working so hard she didn't notice when they left. The tip she found beside Roland's plate was a perfectly correct fifteen percent, down to the penny.

On Sunday, she called her mother in Rochester. Frances was philosophical about Roland's unresponsiveness.

"You always get what you want," she told her daughter. "He'll come around."

"How's the new chorus?" Cindy asked.

"Well..." Her mother's voice trailed off.

"Uncooperative?" If so, Cindy was ready to fly back and whip them into shape. "Is there a troublemaker?"

"No, no." Frances laughed. "They're fine. I'm just a bit rattled at living in a strange place. It's so much busier than Oofdah, and I hardly know anyone."

"You're lonely," Cindy said. "Oh, Mom, I was afraid of that."

"I've been wondering if I made a mistake," her mother said. "I haven't rented out the house yet. It's not too late for me to go back."

A wonderful calm settled over Cindy at the suggestion. Their home had always been her refuge, and her mother was its heart. Yet Frances needed to grow and blossom, and an opportunity like this might never come again.

With an effort, she found the right words. "Give it time, Mom. You've only been in Rochester a few days. It might grow on you."

"I don't know." Her mother sighed. "Maybe I'm too old to change my ways."

"Sixty-one isn't old," Cindy said. "You could have twenty or thirty good years left. What are you going to do for all those decades, sit around baking cookies?"

That was exactly what she wanted her mother to do, while she and Roland cuddled in their love nest across the street. If she was lucky, her life might still work out that way. But only if it was the right thing for everyone involved.

"You've got a point," Frances said. "Besides, I can't let them down now. They're counting on me for the Christmas concert."

"Absolutely," said her daughter.

ON SUNDAY AFTERNOON, Hugh graded papers, struggled in vain to write poetry and worried about that uncomfortable silence after he told Cindy she wasn't his type. She'd only been trying to help. He should have been more diplomatic.

To work off his uneasiness, he went to the gym and exercised until sweat ran down his forehead and back. Although the physical strain felt good, it didn't relieve his sense of guilt.

That evening, he considered and discarded the possibility of buying Cindy a bouquet of flowers—roses, of course—or a box of gourmet chocolates. Either one would only suggest amour, and would make them both uncomfortable again.

Hugh was frying an egg for dinner when the answer hit him. He could shave off his beard! Since Cindy had suggested it as part of a makeover, what better way to show that he valued her advice?

After eating the egg directly out of the pan, he went

to the bathroom and stared at his reflection. The man who met his gaze, with his salt-and-pepper hair and mostly gray beard, could easily pass for forty, although Hugh was only thirty-six.

Ten years ago, when the gray first began to show, he'd been grateful for the aging effect. As a child, Hugh had been obnoxiously precocious. He'd made few friends, since most kids dismissed him as a nerd. Bored with the curriculum, he'd skipped so many grades that he'd graduated from high school at fifteen and from college at eighteen. Being so much younger than his classmates had isolated him even more.

In another year, he'd racked up a master's degree, and by twenty-one was a full-fledged Ph.D. When he began teaching at a community college, he'd frequently been mistaken for a student.

The early arrival of gray hairs had been a blessing, and, when he grew a beard, he'd been delighted that it came out even grayer than his hair. Without his more mature appearance, he doubted he'd have been hired here at De Lune University, let alone given tenure and promoted to full professor.

Hugh grimaced at the fellow in the mirror. It was one thing to add ten years to his apparent age when he was twenty-five. Now, he reflected, the mop of hair and full beard not only aged him unnecessarily, they gave him the air of a hermit newly emerged from a cave. No wonder Blair didn't take him seriously.

No question about it. The whiskers had to come off.

He squirted on some shaving lotion and reached for his razor.

With all this hair at hand, he could choose from numerous variations. A full mustache and goatee. Tug, tug went the razor, and loose hairs sprinkled the sink. Not bad, not bad, Hugh thought as he examined himself from several angles. He could pass for a roué from the 1920s.

He pictured Cindy laughing at his pretensions. All right, he decided, and removed the goatee.

A full mustache transformed him into an English gentleman, ready for a night at his club. Wagers would be taken on whether the intrepid Phineas Fogg could or could not circle the globe in eighty days. Hugh debated whether he wanted to be Phineas Fogg, and decided he didn't. Off came the mustache.

Despite a hint of pallor from lack of sun, exposing the bottom half of his face made a startling difference in Hugh's appearance. He shyly examined the mature jawline and cheekbones that had developed, unseen, over the past fifteen years.

Suddenly he couldn't bear to study himself any further. That man in the mirror was an imposter. He was going to grow the darn beard back, first thing.

It wouldn't happen before tomorrow, though. At one o'clock, like it or not, Cindy was going to see the new Hugh.

5

WHEN CINDY DESCENDED from her apartment on Monday morning, she found Mrs. Zimpelman sitting in a wheelchair at the foot of the staircase. At least, she assumed it was her neighbor, although she couldn't see her face because of the camera trained directly upward.

"You're going to get a great shot of my kneecaps," said Cindy, who'd convinced herself to wear her gym shorts, although she still feared an ice storm might roll into Southern California at any moment. "Make sure you don't miss the scar. I got that when Roland accidentally whacked me with an oar at camp."

The elderly woman lowered her camera. "You can tease all you like. I'm not budging. He has to come sneaking out sometime."

"Who?"

"The man you've got stashed up there," crowed her neighbor. "You can't fool me! It's almost noon and you haven't been out all morning. Don't tell me you were up there alone!"

"I'm afraid I'm much more boring than you give me credit for," Cindy said. "I worked at the Lunch Box until midnight and I was tired." She'd slept late, then spent the rest of the morning answering e-mails from her twenty little students.

Lowering the camera, her neighbor scowled. "You owe me more than that. Honestly! Do you want to force

a poor old woman who's broken her foot to wheel herself
all over town? I need gossip and it's your job as my
neighbor to supply it.''

Cindy eyed the partial cast on the woman's foot.
''What happened?''

''It was terrible.'' Mrs. Zimpelman shook her head,
which set her binoculars to bobbing against her chest. ''I
tripped and fell off my back porch. None of the other
Snoopers are sympathetic, because I wasn't spying on
anyone at the time. Mariah said that if I can't keep up
my contributions, they might banish me. I'd have to go
to that boring Senior Center across town where all they
do is organize theater trips and sing karaoke.''

''You mean you're part of a formal group?'' Oofdah
had plenty of gossips but, as far as Cindy knew, they'd
never organized.

''Yes, and you can drop me off on your way to the
gym.'' Mrs. Zimpelman wheeled herself backward, finally allowing Cindy off the steps. ''Runcie can drive me
home. He's a ladies' man and he'll probably make a pass,
but I can take care of myself.''

''Okay.'' Cindy was halfway to her rental car before
something hit her. ''How did you know I was going to
the gym?''

''Sadie Wilkerson's grandson works there,'' said her
neighbor, rolling around to the passenger side. ''You can
help me in and fold this chair for me. Good thing you're
a big, strong girl.''

The aged car, which Cindy had leased cheap from a
no-frills company, rattled toward the campus as she followed Esther Zimpelman's directions. It was a short trip,
but, as she quickly learned, replete with local history.

''On that corner right there, Bill Sachet—he's the biggest real estate developer in town—barely stopped his car

in time before his wife Lynn jumped out, screaming that he was the biggest jerk she'd ever met,'' Esther said. ''Mariah's the one who heard them. I'll never forgive myself for missing it, a block from my house.''

''Why did his wife call him a jerk?'' Cindy didn't approve of gossip, but her curiosity was aroused.

''He was dumping her for Vanessa something-or-other—she's Vanessa Sachet, now,'' Mrs. Zimpelman said. ''Vanessa's a public relations consultant, twenty-six years Bill's junior and the biggest social climber in town. Lynn got a large financial settlement, but Bill's betrayal broke her heart.''

''How awful,'' Cindy said.

When they stopped at University Avenue, Esther said, ''The students used to stage a Mardi Gras parade along here every February, riding on floats and partying. Occasionally they got so carried away they took their clothes off. Disgusting! I'll show you photos sometime if you'd like.''

''Oh, dear,'' Cindy said. ''Do they still do that?''

''When Wilson Martin became university president six years ago, he put a stop to it,'' Esther said. ''What a fuddy duddy.''

''He sounds like a sensible man.''

''That's because you don't know him,'' her passenger retorted. ''Pull in right there.''

On a corner of the campus adjacent to the main parking lot stood an old house marked by a sign that said, University Senior Center. In smaller letters, it read, Members Only.

Cindy pulled into the circular driveway and stopped by the front porch. Some magician must have devised this house, she thought, tilting back her head to admire the three stories distinguished by balconies, a widow's walk, roof peaks and a round tower. "It's fantastic."

"In her will, Eva St. Clair left it to the university with the provision that it be used as a Senior Center," Esther said. "The town is named after her family, you know. She specified that her old friend Mariah Michaels was in charge of membership for as long as she lived. Mariah's eighty-nine now, but still going strong."

"Is she the queen of gossip?" Cindy asked.

"Far and away," her neighbor said reverently.

As Cindy was removing the wheelchair from her trunk, a husky man of around seventy marched down the stairs, his back erect and his head topped by a felt hat. "Hello, there, beautiful young lady," he said. "I'm Herbert Runciland." He extended one hand. When she reached out to shake it, he turned her palm over and kissed it.

"Behave yourself, Runcie!" sniffed Esther. "And help me up those stairs!"

As he obeyed, a businesslike African-American man came to carry up the wheelchair. He introduced himself as Hosea O'Donnell.

"Are you one of the Snoopers, too?" Cindy asked. "Don't tell me you're the King of Gossip!"

He chuckled. "Young lady, I always aspired to be an oddball in my old age, but I'm too boring. When I retired from my job as a civil engineer, I thought I'd just sit around and gather dust. Turned out these folks needed help learning how to use computers, though, so I kind of snuck into the group as a technology consultant."

"I'm afraid to ask what else you do for them," she said. "You don't use spy equipment, do you?"

"We never reveal our methods," Hosea told her. "We'll see that Esther gets a ride home. You bringing her tomorrow, too?"

Why not? Cindy had to drive to the gym, right around the corner on Venus Avenue, at one o'clock every day. "Sure, if this is a good time."

"That's kind of you," he said.

"I'm glad Esther has friends," Cindy said. "I only wish they would keep her out of trouble instead of encouraging her to get into it."

"We're harmless," Hosea said with a grin. "Mostly."

Cindy supposed he was right. Their prying might be an annoyance, but she doubted it did much harm, and clearly it kept the seniors energized.

On the short drive to the gym, her thoughts flew ahead to Hugh. Since Saturday, she'd deliberately kept busy so she wouldn't dwell on his rejection of her offer to help stimulate his muse. Yesterday, she'd attended church in the morning and baby-sat during a fellowship meeting in the early afternoon. Then she'd worked all evening.

Still, his remark haunted her. *You're not my type.* Not the type he wrote poems about. Not the type of woman who inspired him.

She didn't understand why she cared. Maybe it was because Roland, having gone temporarily insane, didn't think she was *his* type, either. Cindy didn't need to be anybody's type. She was perfectly happy as her own self, thank you very much. Yet...

Whenever he talked about Blair, Hugh's eyes filled with azure longing beneath his glasses. If Roland had ever showed even a tenth that much passion toward her, Cindy would have been thrilled, but she knew it wasn't his nature. It was Hugh's nature, though. So why couldn't he spare her enough enthusiasm to write a poem about her, even in practice?

At the gym, Cindy signed in and stowed her bag in a locker. In the exercise room, a young woman stood playing with her long blond hair while flirting with a handsome man on an exercise bike. He bore a strong resemblance to Hugh.

"Hey!" He waved. She swiveled to see if there was anyone behind her. Nope.

Then it hit her. It *was* Hugh!

Amazed, Cindy made her way between rows of exercise equipment. "You shaved it off!"

"He shaved what off?" asked the girl.

"Do you like it?" Hugh turned to display his profile to Cindy. His strong jawline and firm, full mouth surprised her.

And made her heart sink. If she hadn't been his type before, what chance did she have now that he had transformed himself into a babe magnet?

Cindy knew she had only herself to blame. The makeover was her idea. Besides, she reminded herself firmly, she wasn't available. As soon as Roland stopped acting like an idiot, they'd be back together.

"What a difference!" she said.

"He shaved something off?" The girl peered at him. "Omigosh! Professor Bemling!" Her cheeks reddening, she made a quick getaway.

"I'm going to grow it back." Hugh gave Cindy an embarrassed grin. "I feel foolish."

If he replaced the beard, he'd be his old whiskery self and only Cindy would appreciate him. But the point was to attract Blair. "There's nothing foolish about being handsome," she said. "That young lady was flirting with you. How often does that happen?"

"She was flirting?" Hugh stopped cycling. "I wondered why she kept squirming and picking at her hair."

Cindy climbed onto a nearby cycle. "Now all you've

got to do is build up those muscles, and Blair will throw herself at you.''

''I hope she throws herself slowly, so I have time to figure out what she's doing,'' Hugh said. ''I'm new at this.''

For an hour, they strained and grunted on various machines. Between bouts of hard breathing, Cindy described Mrs. Zimpelman and the Snoopers. Hugh explained about shaving off his beard, talking about his teen-age precociousness and how he'd tried for so long to appear older, until he realized it was no longer necessary.

Afterward, the two of them headed out into the absurdly bright November day. ''I need to buy a few new clothes before work,'' Cindy said.

She'd decided she might as well get an early start on next summer's wardrobe. There was no point in continuing to fight the climate, since she planned to stay here for at least a few more weeks. ''How about you?'' she asked. ''That collar's a little frayed. I couldn't tell before because of the beard.''

Hugh fingered the offending collar. ''I suppose so. Besides, this shirt is getting tight in the upper arms.''

''That's your muscles,'' she said. ''They're firming up.''

''Really?'' He flexed one. ''Ow. I think I overdid it back there.''

''Me, too.'' A pleasant ache infused her shoulders and back. What she needed was a massage, but she had no intention of suggesting it.

They rode in Cindy's car, since Hugh had walked to the gym. She parked in a lot behind the Lunch Box, and together they cruised along the sidewalk, window-shopping.

With an hour and a half to go, they had plenty of time.

Cindy usually rounded up an entire season's wardrobe in that amount of time, since she bought the same practical styles year after year.

The shops here offered more variety than she'd seen in Oofdah. For one thing, they couldn't seem to make up their minds about the season. One boutique featured wool suits and leather jackets. Another specialized in bikinis.

There were funky imports from Asia, athletic gear, formal gowns and much more—too much to choose from. Cindy was relieved when Hugh led the way into a shop called Male/Female, which had a wide selection for both sexes.

Early afternoon was apparently a slow time, and a couple of salespeople bustled toward them. Before she knew it, she and Hugh were ensconced in side-by-side dressing rooms, while their attendants brought clothing by the armload.

"You come here often?" she called over the partition.

"I've never been here," replied Hugh's slightly gruff tenor voice. "I saw Jared Benton carrying a sack with the store logo once, and everyone considers him a cool dresser."

Cindy didn't bother to ask who Jared Benton was. She'd already confirmed for herself that he had good taste in stores.

From the women's section, the saleslady brought a deep-pink skirt-and-blouse set made from a soft, flowing fabric. Although it wasn't her usual style, Cindy loved it. A gorgeous calf-length midnight-blue dress spangled with stars could be worn for everyday or dressed up with a matching beaded shawl. She added it to her selections, along with two mix-and-match skirts and short-sleeved sweaters.

When she checked her watch, she was surprised to see it was almost time for work. Quickly she went to pay.

Hugh was still trying on clothes when she left. "See you tomorrow!" she called.

"How on earth did you finish so fast?" came his reply.

"Necessity," she said. "Bye!"

It was best that she didn't see him modeling his new wardrobe, she told herself as she hurried to stash her purchases in her trunk. It was beginning to bother her, watching Hugh knock himself out to attract Blair. What a contrast to the carelessness with which Roland treated his once-and-future fiancé!

She deserved better, Cindy thought.

Better than this treatment, or better than Roland? Was it possible the two of them weren't cut out for each other, after all? She stopped outside the Lunar Lunch Box beneath a petunia-stuffed window box, while her mind struggled to answer her own question.

No answer came to her. Not wanting to be late to work, she slipped into the restaurant through a side door and put on the regulation silver apron. She barely roused herself enough to respond to Magda's welcoming hello.

Order pad in hand, Cindy headed to her station. Although it was only four o'clock, students, faculty and townies were gathering. Some evening classes started at six, she'd learned, so diners arrived early.

Half an hour later, Roland entered with some friends. They chose a table in Magda's section, sparing Cindy the awkwardness of waiting on him again. Since he sat with his back to her, she couldn't even get a good look at his face.

He might be deliberately turning a cold shoulder. Perhaps his continuing resolution was a sign that she should give up, she mused as she carried out a tray of sandwiches. Cindy believed that little clues could add up to one big cosmic sign, which in this case seemed to say, Keep Out.

She hated to throw in the towel. Yet if she didn't return soon, Oofdah's Holiday Charity Bazaar would lose her annual services as chairman and the high school basketball team might replace her as its volunteer assistant coach.

"Did you hear about Professor Bemling?" a young woman was telling her two girlfriends as Cindy delivered their plates. "He shaved off his beard and Neve says he's cute!"

Neve must be the blonde from the gym, Cindy guessed. "Who had the iced tea?"

"Me," said a redhead. Without pausing, she told her companions, "Neve must have forgotten her contact lenses. Professor Beemer, cute? Give me a break!"

"I've got his Advanced Sonnets class tonight," said the third coed. "I'll let you know."

"He's adorable," Cindy said. "Take it from me."

The three of them stared at her. "Yeah?" said the redhead at last. "No kidding?"

"It doesn't surprise me," said the first woman. "I always thought Professor Bemling had great features under all that hair. I'm almost sorry he shaved it off."

"Hugh shaved his beard?" The husky female voice came from behind Cindy. "Why did he do that?"

When Cindy turned, she found herself facing Blair. The teaching assistant's green eyes were wide with curiosity, their large size emphasizing her delicate and faintly exotic beauty.

Surely she must realize that Hugh had changed himself in the hope of winning her heart. Cindy didn't believe it was her place to make such a declaration, however, so she said, "Growing a beard was a youthful thing to do. I guess he's outgrown it."

"Isn't he kind of old to be outgrowing things?" Blair asked.

"Mid-thirties isn't so old," Cindy said.

"I thought he was, like, forty-five." The younger woman's eyebrows arched as she absorbed the information. "He's so intellectual, it's no wonder he's a late bloomer in other areas."

Was it possible Blair admired Hugh? Dismissing a twinge of dismay, Cindy reminded herself that this was a good sign for the professor's quest.

"Blair!" Roland called from across the room. "We're saving you a seat."

Try as she might, Cindy couldn't keep their eyes from meeting. At that exact moment, the café's background music track shifted into a holiday song about taking a sleigh ride together.

Instantly she was transported to last Christmas. After breakfasting with her mother, she and Roland had broken out their old sleds and gone to a nearby snowy hill. Laughing and shouting dares, they'd spent hours racing each other until their fingers and toes went numb and their coats were soaking.

On the way home, Roland had said, "I don't know what I'd do without you. I only truly feel like myself when you're around."

Now, gazing across the room, Cindy saw from his startled expression that he remembered, too. When Blair joined him at the table, he scarcely acknowledged her.

Roland really does love me. For the first time since she'd begun to consider going home, Cindy relaxed.

Her decision was made. She was going to stick around.

6

BY THE END OF THE WEEK, Hugh was thoroughly confused. Ordinarily he moved across campus in a fog of near-invisibility, greeted in passing by students and acquaintances who scarcely glanced at him. Since he'd shaved his beard and started wearing turtleneck sweaters from Male/Female, however, everything had changed.

People stopped to talk to him. Coeds consulted him about papers they'd never had any problems with before. The campus delivery service quit mixing up his mail with that of a Professor Hemming in the art department. The head librarian, who in the past had required ID every time Hugh sought to put a book on reserve, suggested he fill a vacancy on the Student-Faculty Library Committee.

The attention made him uneasy. It was as if people were seeing a different person, a stranger in Hugh's body. Campus posters about next month's Tournament of Knights no longer filled him with longing, but with apprehension. Now that participating began to seem like a real possibility, he realized he didn't want to parade around in front of a crowd like a peacock.

Still, he decided not to grow the beard back. He didn't need to hide behind it anymore.

On Friday, he met Jared Benton for lunch at Key Lune Pies. Normally Hugh bought a flattened tuna sandwich out of a vending machine at the Faculty Center, but his appetite had increased since he began exercising. Besides, he was counting on his friend for some advice.

"You're not as skinny as you used to be," Jared told him, consuming a club sandwich while Hugh devoured a veggie burger. They sat in one corner of the cottage-style restaurant beneath a Creeping Charlie plant that seemed to be trying to listen in on the conversation.

Hugh pushed aside an inquisitive green tendril and munched a fried potato. "I've joined a gym," he said.

"Good for you." The theater director returned a wave from a couple of women who'd entered the restaurant. They peered hopefully toward the table, but, seeing no free chairs, let the hostess seat them elsewhere. "You've been hiding out for too long."

On her way past them, the hostess looked with interest at Jared, but received no response. Women were always throwing themselves at him. In his early thirties, the man wasn't movie star handsome, with his slightly crooked nose and odd lavender eyes, but he projected an irresistible charisma.

"How do you handle it?" Hugh asked.

"Handle what?" His friend nodded toward a group of students who'd just spotted him and were shouting his name. "Sorry!" he called to their table. "I'm tied up."

Disappointed, they went back to their discussion.

"How do you handle the attention?" Hugh said. "Everybody noticing you."

"Do people notice me?"

Hugh decided to try a different approach. "The problem is that everyone's responding to the new me except the woman I love. I figured you might be able to advise me."

"About love?" Jared finger-combed his thick brown hair. Although nearly as long as Hugh's, it fell into smooth waves instead of awkward clumps. "I had strong feelings for a girl once, years ago, but the timing was wrong. Other than that, I haven't met anyone who motivates me to forsake all others."

"I have," Hugh said. "That's why I joined the gym."

"New clothes, too, I see. Good choice." His friend signaled to a waiter, who produced a piece of carrot cake even though Jared hadn't ordered it. "You want dessert?"

Hugh shook his head. "No, thanks. I'm not sure I should be eating a burger, either. Vegetarian or not. Poets are supposed to go into a decline when they're in love."

"Women don't get turned on by lovesick poets," Jared said. "You want my advice? Flirt with other women. Go out on dates. Make this woman of your dreams see that she's going to lose you if she doesn't get her act together."

It would never have occurred to Hugh to be unfaithful to Blair in the slightest word or deed. Once he'd fixed his devotion on her, he'd been fully prepared to pine away, as long as it didn't interfere with conducting his classes. "Are you sure about this?"

"It's reverse psychology," said the director. "People want what they can't have. Be honest. If this woman had tried to shackle you the first time you met, would you find her as exciting?"

Hugh didn't know how to answer that, because no woman had ever tried to shackle herself to him. It sounded painful, like getting knocked flat by Cindy's sofa. "I suppose not."

"One more tip," Jared said. "Solar Snips."

"Excuse me?" Hugh hoped that wasn't the name of a racehorse.

"Solar Snips," his friend repeated. "It's a unisex salon down at the corner of Solar and Jupiter. Ask for Bernie.''

"Is that a male or a female Bernie?" he asked.

"I've never been sure," Jared admitted. "Like I said, it's a unisex salon. When it comes to hair, Bernie's a wizard.''

"I'll make an appointment." Surely Hugh could trust a wizard who'd done such a good job on Jared. "Thanks.''

It was time to meet Cindy at the gym. As he said goodbye to his friend, Hugh wondered if he should take Jared's advice and ask her on a date.

How ridiculous! She'd probably refuse out of loyalty to Roland, and, if not, he doubted Blair would care in the least.

Still, the idea of reverse psychology was worth considering. If there'd ever been a master at winning female hearts, it was Jared Benton.

CINDY SPENT FRIDAY, her night off, doing laundry at Dean Pipp's house, giving her mother another pep talk by phone and mulling how to go about inviting Roland for Thanksgiving dinner. The holiday was coming up the next week.

It would be awkward to invite him in front of his friends, and she disliked the idea of dropping by his apartment, since Blair might be hanging around. On the other hand, sending an e-mail would allow him to cop out by simply failing to reply.

On Saturday, she arrived at the gym but didn't see Hugh in the exercise room. At the desk, Brad—whose desktop placard listed his last name as Wilkerson, like Esther's friend Sadie—suggested she check the pool.

There she found Hugh swimming laps among half a

dozen other people. When he saw her, he glided to the edge and hoisted himself out.

Compared to Roland, whom Cindy had observed in a swimsuit plenty of times, Hugh was on the slim side. Yet he moved with greater self-confidence than before, and his shoulders had taken on a more commanding stance.

She was changing, too, Cindy had to admit. When she'd fastened her bra this morning, she'd had to tighten it by one hook's width. Either she'd lost weight, which wasn't surprising given the absence of her mother's large-scale meals, or she'd firmed up from exercising.

"How come you decided to swim today?" she asked.

"Somebody mentioned cross-training and it sounded like a good idea," Hugh said.

She hadn't thought of him as training for anything in particular. "You mean for the tournament?"

Water dripped down his lean body as he considered her question. "I haven't made up my mind yet," he answered at last. "Anyway, I got here early so I tried the weight room, and it made me sweaty. Why don't you join me?"

"I'll get my suit." Cindy was glad she'd remembered to tuck it in her bag. "I'll be right back." About to leave, she paused to make a closer inspection. "There's something different about your hair."

"I got it cut." Hugh stood straighter, as if a weight had been removed. It was hard to tell how much had been cut in this wet state.

"It's fine," Cindy said automatically. "I'll be right back."

Her one-piece suit was by far the most conservative outfit at the pool, she discovered. One swimmer wore a thong bikini that left almost nothing to the imagination, including the exact size and shape of her posterior cheeks. For once, Cindy was grateful that her moderate nearsightedness blurred the details.

A pool attendant organized an informal game of punchball. It was every man or woman for himself and, despite the lack of scorekeeping, everyone fought fiercely to get a crack at the ball.

Once, Cindy and Hugh collided in midair, skin against skin. Despite the disconcerting contact, she knocked the ball out of his grasp and halfway across the pool.

A few minutes later, both of them jumped at the same time, trying to hit the ball. As Cindy's back smacked against his bare chest, Hugh lunged past her to make the hit. The ball flew out of the pool.

"Foul!" the attendant called.

"Who says it's a foul?" Instinctively Cindy rose to Hugh's defense even though he'd robbed her of the shot. "There aren't any rules. I say he scores two points!"

While the other players debated, Hugh wrapped his arms around Cindy from behind. "It doesn't matter," he said, "but thanks. I hope I didn't hurt you."

"I'm fine. Besides, I'm the one who ran into you." She leaned back against him. The man proved surprisingly sturdy, even though less massive than Roland. Besides, Roland wouldn't have been standing here comforting her, he'd have raced for the ball.

Since no one could agree on the rules, the game broke up. Cindy didn't mind. She was in no hurry to leave the shelter of Hugh's arms.

The worst part about having her fiancé go off to college had been the lack of anyone to hold her. Cindy hadn't realized how much she minded until now.

Hugh felt sturdier than she would have expected, and warmer. His cheek was slightly rough as it pressed against her jaw. His beard must grow quickly, she thought, and found that fact alluring.

"Everybody out of the pool," the attendant called. "For you newbies, that's the rule around here, one break per hour. We want to make sure nobody's overdoing it, or floating under the surface, either."

Slowly Hugh released her. When they got out, Cindy saw that he wore a faraway expression. "Thinking of a poem?" she asked hopefully.

He shook his head. "I'm still not feeling poetic."

Cindy's stomach twisted with disappointment, which made her angry at herself. She had no business expecting Hugh to go gooey-eyed over her, just because he'd hugged her for a moment. He'd been showing concern, not love.

When she came out of the locker room a short time later, the first thing she noticed about Hugh was his hair. Now that it was dry, its new fullness emphasized his high cheekbones and intelligent expression.

"That really is a wonderful cut," Cindy said.

"A friend of mine recommended Solar Snips," he told her, adjusting his glasses with a trace of self-consciousness. "A hairdresser named Bernie did this."

"Yoo-hoo!" Across the open foyer snailed Mrs. Zimpelman, who'd graduated from her wheelchair to a walker. "Cindy! We need to talk to you!"

She was flanked by two elderly women. One wore heavy makeup, dyed red locks and short shorts that displayed her shapely stockinged legs. The other lady, elegant in coiffed silver hair and a designer pantsuit, wrinkled her nose at the pervasive scent of chlorine.

Cindy went to meet them. "Are you all right, Mrs. Zimpelman?"

"Certainly. It's just that I didn't know if you'd be

going home after exercising, so I'm buttonholing you here," said her neighbor. "I know you're off on Fridays and I need a ride to an emergency meeting of the Snoopers tonight."

"Me, too. And we both need rides home," added the red-haired lady. "I'm Sadie Wilkerson." This, Cindy recalled, was Brad's grandmother.

After they shook hands, Esther introduced the third lady as Mariah Michaels. Aha, the doyenne, Cindy thought. When they shook hands, her grip was like iron.

"I'll be happy to bring you both," she said. "Mrs. Michaels, do you need a ride?"

"No, thank you," said the older lady. "Hosea O'Donnell is picking me up in his sports car."

"It's a two-seater," Sadie explained.

Mrs. Zimpelman gave Hugh a passing glance. "I'm sorry if this interferes with your plans, young man, but you can't have Cindy tonight."

"He could have her later." Sadie giggled.

"Well, they'd better do it at Cindy's apartment, because if they go elsewhere, I won't be able to follow, and I'll be very annoyed," Esther said. "Young man, what *are* your intentions toward my neighbor?" Before Hugh could frame a response, she uttered a little shriek. "Hugh Bemling? I didn't recognize you!"

"My goodness, he's transformed himself." Mariah Michaels whipped a pad and pen from her purse. "We must have the details."

"Excuse me?" Hugh said.

"How was it accomplished? Where was the clothing purchased and how much did it cost?" demanded the matriarch.

"I'd rather not discuss it," he said. The three elderly women glared as if he'd uttered a string of curses.

"Tell me about this emergency meeting," Cindy interjected.

"We can't," said Sadie. "It's confidential. Although I suppose since you're driving us, you could stick around and attend it yourself."

"Any reason I can't come, too?" Hugh asked.

The women regarded him with varying degrees of speculation. "Until today, I would have said absolutely not," Esther admitted. "You're on our D.B. list. Definitely Boring."

"We don't waste time on those people," added Mariah.

"But now you're kind of cute, even if you *are* close-mouthed," said Sadie.

"Besides, Mariah, if Hugh joins us, we can grill him about his transformation," said Mrs. Zimpelman.

Mrs. Michaels weighed these arguments. "I don't see why not," she said at last. "Besides, we could use an insider at the university."

Now Cindy really was curious.

Before they left, Sadie went to the reception desk and engaged in a low conversation with Brad, who then handed her a rumpled sheet of paper. "What's that?" Cindy asked when Mrs. Wilkerson returned.

"Just some notes." The woman gave her a Cheshire cat smile.

"We have spies everywhere," said Mrs. Michaels.

"I've heard about your group from Cindy, and I must say, you're living up to your reputation," Hugh told her. "I'll look forward to seeing you all tonight."

As he walked away, Sadie Wilkerson murmured, "Who'd have thought it? Hugh Bemling a stud!"

"I'd give his butt a score of eight," Esther said. To Cindy, she explained, "That's out of a possible ten."

"Your fiancé Roland has a nine," noted Mariah. "Runcie scoped him out for us."

"He gave Blair a ten," said Sadie. "But then, he's partial to girls."

As she escorted the women out of the health club, Cindy made a point of never turning her back on them.

HUGH HAD BEEN CURIOUS about the old St. Clair house, and it more than lived up to his expectations. Inside, it was beautifully maintained, with intricately carved dark wooden moldings, furnishings from the early 1900s and unexpected passageways that were reminiscent of those in a Victorian novel.

After entering unchallenged by the Snoopers, Hugh explored a bit, poking his head through several doorways as he wandered down the hallways. In a chamber that resembled a war room from a movie, he saw walls lined with maps of the town.

College yearbooks, scrapbooks and videotapes filled the shelves. Between two large file cabinets, an easel displayed a posterboard flow chart. On it, the names of Clair De Lune's notables were connected with a spiderweb of multicolored lines, apparently indicating relationships.

Although he would have liked to investigate further, he didn't want to get thrown out. Hugh followed the sound of voices to a salon near the foot of the stairs.

Inside, the flames in a gas fireplace crackled. A small group of elders, including Esther, Sadie and two men, were arrayed on brocaded chairs and a maroon sofa, facing Mrs. Michaels, who sat on a gold velvet couch.

He had spent more time than he expected exploring the house, and the only place left to sit was on a love seat next to Cindy. He felt a strange yearning knowing he'd be beside her, a sensation that intensified when he discovered that the aging springs slid the two of them together.

"Excuse me," he murmured when their hips bumped.

At the same time, she mouthed, "I'm sorry." They smiled self-consciously beneath the interested gazes of five pairs of eyes.

Hugh had been trying to put his thoughts in order ever since that punchball game at the pool. He had never suspected a woman's water-beaded skin could feel so velvety, or that their brief contact would arouse such powerful sensations.

Certainly he'd held women during his relationships, but the intensity of his response to Cindy puzzled and disturbed him. Right now, noting the light scent of flowers in her hair, Hugh barely restrained himself from leaning closer to take a sniff.

Too many people were watching. If he weren't careful, these nosy folks might catch on to the marked and rather awkward response in his midsection.

Casting around for a neutral topic of conversation, Hugh wondered if he should mention Thanksgiving. He planned to spend the holiday completing his years-long survey of frozen turkey dinners. Although he'd sampled almost every brand on the market, he'd seen a new one advertised recently. Perhaps he could persuade Cindy to join him.

"I was wondering about Thanksgiving," he said.

Cindy blinked. "Oh."

"Oh, what?" he asked, unable to make sense of her response.

"Nothing. I was just thinking about..." She let the sentence trail off and he realized she'd been daydreaming. "Did you say Thanksgiving? I was planning to ask Roland, but I haven't had a chance."

Before he could reply, Mariah Michaels waved a blue-veined hand for attention. The buzz of conversation fell silent.

"You all know that we've gathered to discuss an emergency," she said. "A threat to our very existence."

Next to Hugh, Cindy's attention riveted on Mrs. Michaels. He thought about taking her hand reassuringly, but Esther Zimpelman was watching from the corner of her eye.

"We have a couple of guests who may be able to help us," Mariah went on. "Does anyone object to their presence?"

"Cindy gave us a ride." Sadie's red hair bobbed in emphasis. "We need her."

"Professor Bemling, being on a campus, could prove to be an asset," said a dapper African-American gentleman, whose name, Cindy whispered, was Hosea O'Donnell.

"Hearing no objections, I'll get right to the issue at hand," said Mariah. "We all know that even though my dear friend Eva St. Clair specified in her will that this house was to be used for our club, the university has had designs on it for years."

"What kind of designs?" Cindy asked.

"They'd like to expand their parking, for one thing," said a jovial man who, by process of elimination, must be Runcie.

"But they can't do that," said Hosea. "According to Mrs. St. Clair's will, the club belongs to our seniors' group for thirty years before it reverts to the university. She's only been dead for seven years."

Mariah made a wry face. "Unfortunately there's an exception in case of dire need."

"Parking hardly qualifies as a dire need," Cindy said.

"That's true," said Hosea.

"The problem is that awful President Martin," Sadie told Cindy. "He's dying for the university to build a medical school."

"For the past six months, he's been cozying up to Bill Sachet," Esther said. "You know, the real estate developer."

"No doubt they're scratching each other's backs," Runcie explained. "If they succeed, President Martin will snag a big donation toward his medical school and Bill Sachet will land the lucrative contract to build the thing."

"Until recently, we assumed that, when they got the money, they'd put the medical center at the back of the campus, near the science complex," Hosea said.

"But…" Mariah paused. The Snoopers exchanged meaningful glances. "This is highly confidential."

"Cross my heart," Cindy said.

Hugh nodded, intrigued. Apparently these outsiders paid a lot more attention than he did to the politics of his university.

"All right." Mrs. Michaels leaned forward with the air of someone imparting a secret. "Earlier this week, Vanessa Sachet dropped by this very house to request a brochure about our activities."

Runcie twiddled with a strand of overlong hair atop his balding pate. "I was reading in the front room. She marched in and asked for a brochure as if we were running a public service! I told her, sorry, we don't put out any publications."

"Maybe she wants to join," Hugh ventured.

"Join?" demanded Mrs. Zimpelman. "She's thirty-one years old!"

"Thirty-two," corrected Mariah. "She had a birthday last month."

"You remember the big party Bill threw her at the Hotel De Lune?" Sadie said. "Runcie had to get his tuxedo cleaned so he could crash."

"They served shrimp, crab *and* lobster," Runcie said. "Delicious salmon pastry puffs, too, and those were just the hors d'oeuvres. I couldn't stick around for the sit-down dinner because there were place cards."

"President Martin sat at the head table," Sadie added. "He got his picture in the paper with his arm around Vanessa Sachet's waist. Pretty chummy, I'd say."

"Why do you think she wanted the brochure?" Cindy asked.

"We believe she's helping her husband plan for the new medical center and apparently they want to build it here," said Mrs. Michaels from her couch. "She might be able to persuade the board of trustees to declare the situation an emergency and dismantle our house if she can show that our members would be just as well served by the public senior center."

"How ridiculous!" Esther sniffed. "We have nothing in common with those boring people."

"Have you heard anything on campus, Professor Bemling?" asked Hosea. "Anything about a medical center, or about tearing down our Senior Center?"

"I'm afraid not," Hugh said. "I'll be glad to keep my ears open, but I'm hardly in President Martin's inner circle."

"Well, we'd appreciate it if you'd keep your ears open at faculty meetings," Mariah said. "Esther can't do anything until her foot heals, but Sadie, you can hang out at the student center. Pretend you're someone's mother."

"I *am* someone's mother," Sadie said. "Unfortunately I never see her since she moved to New York."

"I'll let you know if I hear anything at the Lunar Lunch Box," Cindy volunteered.

"The staff at the Faculty Center never challenges me," Runcie said. "You have to show a card to eat there, but I can hang around the lounge."

"We might not learn much this week," warned Hosea. "Remember, there are no classes Thursday and Friday because of the holiday."

"Times like this, I almost wish we belonged to the kind of Senior Center where they'd have a Thanksgiving dinner." No sooner were the words out than Sadie clapped her hand over her mouth. "I'm sorry! I didn't mean it! It's just that Brad's going skiing over the holiday and I won't have any family in town."

"You can come to my place." The words burst out of Cindy without, Hugh suspected, any forethought. "And, of course, Esther. In fact, everyone's invited. Hugh, Mrs. Michaels, Hosea, Runcie, please come. If everyone brings something, we'll have plenty to eat. I'll invite Dean Pipp, too."

There was no mention of Roland, Hugh noticed. For once, he wouldn't have minded the other man's presence, as long as he didn't have to spend another holiday alone in his loft. "I can pick up some pies."

As it turned out, no one else had plans for the holiday, either. Quickly they each promised to bring a favorite dish and set the time for three o'clock.

When Hugh fell heart-first for his fair ladies, he'd never given a moment's thought to whether they knew how to make people happy. Now he decided that that quality ought to be a priority. If Blair didn't know how, perhaps she could take lessons from Cindy.

He left the meeting cheerfully weighing whether he should bring pumpkin, apple or pecan. He decided on all three.

7

ON SATURDAY, CINDY WENT to the Lunch Box early because both morning-shift waitresses called in sick with colds. Stu Crockenmeyer, who was trying to handle a busy crowd by himself, was snarling at the customers and mixing up the orders.

"Why the devil don't people just stick with what's on the menu?" he grumbled within hearing of the entire room. "This one wants hash browns instead of fries, that one wants apple sauce. What's wrong with these people?"

"Whatever happened to 'the customer is always right'?" asked a balding man with a camera bag hanging from the back of his chair. On weekends, Cindy had learned, the town's quaint shops and picturesque campus attracted tourists, and he appeared to be one of them.

"Who said that?" Daffodil O'Foy stuck her head from behind the kitchen partition. Stu pointed at the offender. "I bet you're the one who ordered a corned beef sandwich with sourdough bread on the bottom and rye on the top."

"I like it that way," the fellow said.

"He's entitled," chimed in the man's companion, a woman wearing tennis whites and a hatless brim secured around her head with a cord. "He's paying the bill."

"You!" roared Stu. "You're the low-fat mayo and

gourmet mustard pastrami with mangos on the side, aren't you?"

"What if I am?" she challenged.

"I'll take care of them," Cindy said to short-circuit a quarrel.

"Good! Because if I have to hear any more of this blather, you might need to call an ambulance." Stu didn't specify whether it was he or the customers who were going to need medical assistance. Turning to another table, he confronted a young couple. "Well? What'll it be?"

Nervously the man said, "Burger and fries?"

"Same for me, if it's convenient," said his companion. They cowered in their seats until Stu marched away.

Cindy hurried to deliver platters before her boss antagonized or intimidated any other customers. She scarcely noticed the time flying by until the crowd thinned out about two o'clock.

When Blair came in by herself and sat at a large table, Cindy would have liked to let Stu wait on her. However, since the place was half empty, he tossed aside his apron and retreated to his office.

Pad in hand, Cindy stopped in front of Blair. The young teaching assistant had propped her sandaled feet on a chair and was painting her toenails purple. "Did you want to order now?"

"I'd like some coffee while I'm waiting for my friends." The young woman glanced up. "Are you busy? There's something I'd like to ask, if you don't mind."

Although she didn't blame Blair for Roland's misbehavior, Cindy had no interest in getting chummy. Still, it went against the grain to turn down a polite request. "Hold on. I'll make the rounds and see that everybody's settled, and then we can talk."

When everyone had been served, Cindy took a seat at Blair's table, positioned so she could keep an eye on the room. At close range, Blair's green eyes had an almost hypnotic effect. With her perfect skin and thick dark hair, it was no wonder she inspired poetry, Cindy thought with an unfamiliar dash of envy.

"I've been wondering…" Blair began. "I mean, you're friends with Hugh, right?"

"Right," Cindy said.

"He's changed a lot since you got here," Blair went on. "If you had anything to do with it, you're a miracle worker."

"He did most of it himself." Although she wished the other woman would get to the point, it felt pleasant to be targeted with such rapt attention. And Cindy was pleased at the compliment, for Hugh's sake.

"Maybe you think I've been cruel to him, but the fact is, I had no idea he was interested in me until I was already involved with Roland." Blair's cheeks colored. "And I didn't know Roland was your fiancé until you showed up. He never said a word."

A tempting idea came to Cindy. Judging by Blair's words and comments, she felt guilty. A mention of how close Cindy and Roland had been since childhood, coupled with a reference to canceled wedding plans and crushed dreams, might be enough to turn her away from the man entirely.

Cindy couldn't do it. For one thing, it wasn't sporting to take advantage of Blair's openness. For another, Roland had to come back of his own choice or she'd never be able to trust him again.

"I know you didn't set out to steal him," she said. "Is that what you wanted to talk about?"

"Mostly I'd like to get to know you," Blair said. "I've

never met anyone like you. You're so calm and confident. Anyone else would have thrown a fit or broken down in tears after what Roland did, but you've just calmly gone about making new friends and getting a job."

"I haven't given up on him," Cindy felt obliged to warn.

"I don't expect you to." Impulsively the teaching assistant patted Cindy's arm. "Don't misunderstand. I'm not trying to influence you in that regard. Actually, I was wondering— I mean, Hugh hasn't read me any poems lately. Do you know if he's found someone new?"

"He's just hit a dry patch. Nothing personal." Glancing past her toward the customers, Cindy noted that her services still weren't needed. Good. She wanted to find out where this discussion was leading.

"Do you know if he's asked a date to the faculty holiday dinner-dance?" Blair asked. "It's the weekend after next."

"I didn't even know there was such an event." Cindy coughed, her throat parched, and realized she'd forgotten to eat or drink anything since breakfast.

Her companion fished a roll of hard candies from her purse and offered it. Cindy took a lemon-flavored piece.

"You know, I'll understand if you want to invite Roland for Thanksgiving Dinner," Blair went on. "I thought I'd mention it in case you were holding back on my account. I'm a dead loss in the kitchen and he's mentioned your cooking several times with that puppy-dog expression on his face. I guess you two mean a lot to each other, huh?"

"We used to." To Cindy's dismay, tears sprang to her eyes. Roland was so much a part of her life, she didn't understand how anything could have separated them.

"I feel awful." Blair obviously hadn't missed the teary moment. "I'm making you both miserable, aren't I?"

"If it weren't for you, I'd never have come to Clair De Lune and met so many interesting people." Cindy truly was glad for the chance to meet Dean Pipp and Esther Zimpelman and the Snoopers. And Hugh, of course. "In fact, I've invited a bunch of friends for Thanksgiving Dinner, and I want to invite you, too. You and Roland."

"Are you sure you want to include me?" Before she could answer, Blair added, "Did you say Hugh's going to be there?"

"Yes, he is."

"I'd love to come," she said. "I'll make sure Roland's there, too. Whatever's between you two, it needs to be sorted out."

"I agree." Food had always been the key to Roland's heart, and what better opportunity to win him back than Thanksgiving?

"How about if we bring some garlic bread? And fresh fruit. There's two of us, so we'll bring two things," said her companion.

"Great! Come at three o'clock. You know where I live?"

"Over Dean Pipp's garage," Blair said. "Everybody knows that."

As she excused herself to wait on some new arrivals, Cindy was glad the other woman had mentioned Thanksgiving. She'd almost resigned herself to not inviting Roland because it would be so awkward, and now Blair would do the asking.

She had a feeling this was going to be a special holiday, one way or another.

"BUY THE TURKEY TODAY," her mother said over the phone on Sunday. "That way it'll have time to defrost in the refrigerator by Thursday."

"Thanks for mentioning it." Cindy had cooked for the first couple of Thanksgivings after her father died, to spare her mother the emotion-filled task, but that had been long ago.

"What kind of stuffing are you planning?" Frances didn't stop prodding until they'd reconstructed an old family sage-and-cranberry recipe from memory.

"How about you?" her daughter asked when the matter was settled. "I hope you're not dining alone that day."

"The minister and his wife invited me," she said. "There'll be lots of us strays at the table. Now tell me, how did that silly rhyme go? The one about the watch?"

"Mom! You always said it was crude," Cindy said. "You aren't planning to tell it on Turkey Day!"

"I'd like to have it handy in case the conversation lags," Frances said. "Besides, our rehearsal pianist has a goofy sense of humor. He's going to be there and I thought he'd enjoy it."

"This rehearsal pianist wouldn't be single, would he?"

"Don't go matchmaking for me!" said her mother. "No one will ever replace your father."

"Is this guy cute?" Cindy asked.

"Just tell me the poem about the watch."

"'Mary had a diamond watch. She swallowed it one day,'" Cindy recited. "'Mary took a laxative, to pass the time away.'"

"I don't think I can say the word *laxative* in public," her mother interrupted. "At least, I'll have to wait till we're done eating. Go on."

"'The laxative didn't work. The time didn't pass,'" Cindy continued. "'So if you want to know what time it is, You'll have to look up Mary's...'" She let her voice trail off, so the listener would fill in the missing word, then finished, "'...sister! She has a watch just like Mary's.'"

"Do you think that's okay to recite at a minister's house?" Frances asked.

"I told it to Dad and he laughed like crazy," Cindy reminded her.

"I don't know if I want to risk offending the pastor. Of course, Albert might find it amusing."

"Albert's the rehearsal pianist?"

"Mind your own business," said her mother, and laughed girlishly.

EVERY DAY THAT WEEK, Cindy added a different item to her "must-make" list. Gravy, of course, and mashed potatoes to go with it. Baked sweet potatoes with orange juice and pineapple. Two kinds of cranberry sauce, because you could never have too much cranberry sauce. Glazed ham slices, in case some of her guests didn't like turkey.

Since she only had one oven, she prevailed on Dean Pipp and Mrs. Zimpelman to lend theirs. Dean Pipp didn't need one, since she was bringing a salad, and Esther's contribution was creamed onions prepared in the microwave.

On Turkey Day, Hugh arrived early with a folding camp table and chairs. Other guests began drifting in, saying they had nothing to do and wanted to inhale the scent of roasting turkey. "It reminds me of the old days when my wife was alive," said Hosea, who'd brought potato salad.

"My daughter used to fix dinner every year, but her husband got transferred to San Francisco," Runcie said.

Although the apartment filled up quickly, Cindy didn't mind. She was glad to have extra hands to set up the serving table and peel potatoes, not to mention caravaning dishes back and forth to her neighbors' ovens. Card tables and chairs, too, made the journey, until the sidewalk outside her apartment began to resemble an ant trail.

When Roland and Blair arrived, Hugh was removing the turkey from the oven while Runcie and Mariah Michaels stood giving advice and encouragement. "Don't tilt it!" "Set it on the burners, not the counter." "That's done just right!"

Cindy, who scarcely had room to move, stood behind them stirring cold water into flour so it wouldn't form lumps when she made gravy. The first indication she had of Roland's presence was when he boomed, "Omigosh! This place smells like home!"

Across the tiny, crowded kitchen, Cindy gazed into the eyes of the man she'd adored since elementary school, even when she was pounding him into a puddle as retribution for his teasing. He looked as familiar as a Winnie-the-Pooh bear and equally cuddly.

Over his shoulder, Blair said, "Where shall I put the bread and fruit?"

"I'll take those," responded Dean Pipp, appearing from the living room. "We've got a buffet set up over here."

Following Mariah's instructions, Hugh positioned the turkey so the juices flowed into one corner of the roasting pan. "You need to scoop the liquid into this pot." Cindy moved closer to assist him.

"I can do that!" Roland tried to join them, but Runcie barred the way. "Excuse me."

"I'm not budging, young man," said the tall Snooper. "You think you can just march in and get first crack at the skin and the bits of turkey that fall in the pan? I was here first, and I've got dibs."

"You don't understand," Roland said. "I always help Cindy."

"You're a little late for that," Hugh replied in an unaccustomed rebuke. "She's been shopping and chopping for days. She was up late last night and early this morning."

Roland's eyes narrowed. "I suppose you were here with her?"

"Not the whole time, but I did what I could," Hugh said. "When I left at ten last night, she was still working. When I got here at eight this morning, she was stuffing the turkey."

It was so unusual to have someone stand up for her that Cindy stared speechlessly at Hugh. Roland had always let her fend for herself and, since she was good at it, she'd never minded.

The surprising thing was how masterful Hugh seemed, despite his spattered apron, steamed-up glasses and rumpled hair. He stood straight, the tan turtleneck sweater emphasizing the tautness of his newfound muscles. Although he was a head shorter than Roland and much less bulky, his air of restrained intensity made him seem more than a match.

Blair noticed, too. As she drew Roland away to check out the hors d'oeuvres, her gaze lingered on Hugh.

Sadie Wilkerson broke the tension by barreling through the door carrying a couple of oversize jars. "I hope everybody likes pig's feet and pickled squid!" she announced. "They're always a big hit with my relatives, so I brought plenty!"

A stunned silence fell over the apartment.

"Now we know why no one in her family invites her to Thanksgiving," Runcie muttered under his breath to Cindy.

"Doesn't anyone want any?" Sadie's mouth trembled as she studied the dismayed expressions. "I was so thrilled when I found them."

Blair tried to reassure her. "Roland likes weird stuff, don't you?"

"Not that weird," he said.

Tears glistened against Sadie's cheeks. "I only wanted to add to the fun. I've made a terrible blunder, haven't I?"

"No, of course not," Cindy said, but couldn't think of anything convincing to add.

"I was hoping someone would bring squid." Hugh set aside his ladle and, easing between Runcie and Mariah, went to take the jars from Sadie. "My grandmother always brought some on holidays. It wouldn't be the same without it."

"What about the pig's feet?" Roland sniped, rather childishly, Cindy thought.

"I've never tried them." Hugh steered Sadie toward the buffet table. "That's the whole point of having people contribute food, isn't it? So we can try new things."

Sadie smiled weakly. "I suppose that's true."

"I'd like some, too," said Dean Pipp. "Who knows, maybe I'll discover a new favorite." Soon the jars were placed on the buffet table and Sadie, mollified, was chatting with Hosea.

Cindy stirred the flour and water mixture into the pan juices and heated them. While the gravy was bubbling, her keen ears—honed from years of monitoring her students while she was writing on the blackboard—heard

Blair say, "Tell me, Hugh, have you written any new poems?"

"Saints preserve us," said Esther Zimpelman. "You're encouraging him?"

"Anyone can write poetry." Roland's belligerant tone made Cindy turn to peek at him. Sure enough, he was displaying the same bulldog determination as he had years ago, when he'd seized the football and plowed through the entire opposition's defense. Even though he'd set some kind of local record, he'd been benched by his coach, who'd been frantically signaling him to pass. "Roses are red, violets are blue..." He stopped, searching for the next line.

"If anyone can write a poem, what's wrong with you?" Runcie finished for him.

"I was working on an intelligent rhyme, in contrast to..."

"Roland!" Cindy bellowed.

He winced. "Yes, ma'am?"

"Get over here and make yourself useful," she said.

"You bet," he said, and came to do her bidding.

Cindy set him to carving the turkey. It took a certain amount of brute strength, and he needed to work off his excess energy.

She tried not to care that Blair and Hugh had their heads together in the living room. There was no reason to object. In fact, it pleased her that Hugh's courtship was going so well.

What disturbed her was that she and Roland couldn't muster their old cameraderie. He had plenty to say about the Minnesota Vikings, but it was like talking to a casual acquaintance.

They didn't finish each other's sentences anymore, either. And when he described the obstacles in setting up the December tournament, she kept having to ask who various people were and what the jousting terms meant. She couldn't even respond with chitchat of her own, because the Snoopers' concerns about President Martin were confidential.

After only a few months apart, their rhythm was off. She hoped it wouldn't take long to restore.

With the turkey carved, the gravy ready and the potatoes mashed, everyone heaped paper plates high with food and took a seat. Roland squeezed between Cindy and Mariah on the couch, while Blair shared a card table with Hugh, Dean Pipp and Sadie.

Half an hour later, the plates had been emptied, refilled and emptied again and glazed expressions replaced the looks of eager anticipation. Before people could begin sliding under their tables, Hosea produced a guitar. "I was hoping we'd be in the mood for folk songs."

"I love folk songs," Sadie said dreamily.

"Thanksgiving wouldn't be complete without a few rounds of 'Home on the Range,'" said Runcie.

"I can't carry a tune to save my life," Blair admitted.

"Don't worry about it," Cindy said. "We're all amateurs here, right?" She considered herself one, although, after years of her mother's choir training, she was sometimes asked to sing at friends' weddings and other special events.

"Start with 'Coming Round the Mountain,'" said Mrs. Michaels. "That ought to bring up the wind."

"Excuse me?" Roland said.

"We need to burp," the matriarch said. "It'll make us all feel better."

"Unless we keel over from the smell," said Runcie. "Now, Mariah, you know I'm just kidding."

So they sang folk songs, one after the other, humming

when they forgot the words. Cindy purposely kept her voice low so as not to stand out, but Hosea shot her a couple of appreciative glances.

Finally he paused and held up one hand. "I'm going to ask you all to be quiet now and listen," he said. "Since my sore fingers need a break, I want our hostess to sing 'Amazing Grace.'"

The hymn, which was usually performed without accompaniment, had been one of her father's favorites. "I'm honored," Cindy said.

She'd never known a touch of stage fright, and she didn't exactly feel any now. Yet the prospect of singing in front of Hugh made her nervous.

Pushing through the emotion, she began to sing.

8

WHEN HE SAT DOWN TO EAT with Blair, Hugh didn't know what to say to her. Not having prepared a poem, he was basically unarmed.

She solved his dilemma by asking questions about his changed appearance. Where had he bought his clothes, how had he bulked up, was he eating differently and who had cut his hair? Sadie listened intently to the answers.

At first, he felt flattered, but after a while the topic palled. Fortunately Dean Pipp took up the matter of transformations with gusto, and for the rest of the meal, held forth on literary werewolves and vampires.

His earlier gallantry forced Hugh to consume several servings of pickled squid and pigs' feet. By imagining himself dining at King Arthur's Court, he was able to down them with an outward show of pleasure that made Sadie beam.

Once the folk songs began, Hugh felt more at home. His parents had matured during the hootenanny era, and he'd grown up with Pete Seeger and Peter, Paul and Mary echoing through the house. With his ear for poetry, he remembered most of the lyrics.

At first, as his tablemates joined in, he didn't pay much attention to the quality of their singing. After a while, however, a painfully discordant sound began to trouble him. Not that he expected perfect harmony when the point was to have a good time, but how could anyone stray so far off-key?

When he began to suspect Blair as the offender, Hugh pushed the notion aside. Surely it must be one of the elderly guests, whose poor hearing might excuse an inability to hit the notes.

The havoc wreaked upon the lovely melody of "Greensleeves" confirmed his suspicions. Beyond question, that horrendous grating noise came from the shapely throat of the woman to his left. How was such a thing possible? In the books of Jane Austen, the heroines always sang exquisitely.

Besides, how could one write a poem to a lark who sang like a crow? Hugh tried in vain to tell himself that it wasn't Blair's fault, but by the end of the song, his mind insisted on thinking of her as Blare instead.

When Hosea designated Cindy to perform, Hugh sat back with a sense of relief and prepared to hear a charming amateur voice. Although he hadn't been paying her much notice, distracted as he was by the squawking on his left, he assumed the guitarist had chosen her for good reason.

"Amazing grace, how sweet it is…"

An angelic voice floated on the wings of heartfelt emotion through a profound silence. Pure, rich melody filled the room, unmarred by wavering pitch or a misplaced breath. Everyone sat enraptured.

Not only did Cindy sound different than usual, but she looked different. When she sang, she took on a radiant air. Her large-boned frame became a sonorous instrument and the wisps of pale blond hair framing her head resembled a halo.

As for Roland, he lounged in his chair, wearing a proprietary smile. All along, he'd known they had this songbird in their midst. Back in Minnesota, she must have sung for him many times, Hugh thought enviously.

The last liquid note fell, leaving them all caught in a spell. It was at least a minute before Mariah said, "That is the most beautiful thing I ever heard."

"I wish I'd brought my tape recorder," sighed Mrs. Zimpelman.

"I don't know why you're waiting tables," added Dean Pipp. "You could sing for your supper."

"Thank you, but no," Cindy said. "Professionals have to put together a band and rehearse a whole list of songs. They also have to put up with hecklers and drunks. I've never been tempted to do it."

She showed no false modesty, Hugh thought appreciatively. Had she tried to downplay her talent, it would only have elicited more compliments to contradict her.

"Is there any more pie?" Roland asked.

"There's plenty," Cindy said.

"Aren't you going to sing something else?" Blair sat hugging her knees. The fact that she'd obviously appreciated Cindy's voice raised her a notch in Hugh's estimation.

"Hey, she's great, but we're missing the football game," Roland said, and reached over to switch on the set.

Although initially annoyed, Hugh was surprised at what a good time he had watching the game and cheering with his friends. He'd never been a fan of team sports, but now he decided he might have been mistaken. There was something to be said for the group experience, after all.

Hugh had never enjoyed such congenial company during high school. He'd grown up in the exclusive community of Beverly Hills, in a rented guest house on the estate of an aging actress. His parents earned decent salaries as college professors, but were nowhere near the same league as the families of Hugh's classmates.

Lacking a designer wardrobe and a sports car, he'd never fit in with the other kids. Maybe if he'd been less sensitive to put-downs, he'd have been able to hang out more, but the sense of being barely tolerated stung Hugh's pride. He'd become a loner, taking refuge in his books and pretending he cared nothing about appearances for so long that he'd come to believe it himself.

Today, he discovered he could feel comfortable in a group of people, and he owed it to Cindy. He was even grateful to Roland for having been foolish enough to leave her, because otherwise she'd never have come to Clair De Lune.

If she hadn't come here, lots of things would never have happened. Hugh wouldn't have changed his appearance, for one thing. He wouldn't be sharing Thanksgiving with these new friends, either. And Blair wouldn't have come to sit by his side to watch the game.

All was right with the world, as long as Blair didn't try to sing.

HUGH'S AIR OF CONTENTMENT pricked at Cindy during the next few days. She was ashamed of herself for being so nosy, but she wished he would at least bring up the subject of Blair. Had he asked her to be his date for the faculty dinner-dance? If not, did he intend to?

It was none of her business, of course. She certainly didn't spend their time at the gym blabbering about how Roland had dropped by on Friday night to watch another game with her. It wasn't really a date, anyway.

Things were working out as she and Hugh had intended. Still, she could see now that, after several months apart, she and Roland needed time to ease into their old groove. There was no sense in rushing matters. In the meantime, she hoped she wasn't going to lose Hugh's companionship.

On Monday when she arrived at the gym, Brad pointed her toward a racquetball court. "Professor Bemling said he'd meet you there."

"Thanks." Cindy started in that direction.

"You'll say yes, of course, right?" asked the attendant.

She swung around. "Yes to what?"

"You mean nobody talked to you?"

"Let me guess. This has to do with the Snoopers." Brad was, after all, Sadie Wilkerson's grandson.

"It's a matter of life and death," the young man said earnestly.

"Then I'd better hurry." Amused by the skullduggery, she hurried to the room he'd indicated.

Inside, she found Hugh thwacking a ball against the far wall, racing around to return his own shots and hitting two of them before the ball went wild.

"Hi," she said.

He pivoted, nearly lost his balance and gave a little hop. "Good, you're here." He patted the racquet against his free hand as he regarded her. "You did buy that dark blue dress with the stars that you were trying on, didn't you?"

Although the question came out of nowhere, Cindy decided not to ask for an explanation. "Yes."

"That should be fine," Hugh said. "Although I'm afraid I'm a little rusty."

"At what?" she said.

"Dancing, of course." He bounced the ball idly atop the racquet. "Too bad they don't give lessons here."

"We're going dancing?" she asked.

Hugh lost his rhythm in midbounce and the ball flew off at an angle. "Nobody called you?"

"I'm out of the loop." Cindy planted her hands on her hips. "Spill it."

Flustered, he uttered a short cough. "It's about the faculty dinner-dance next Friday."

Cindy's heart vaulted at the realization that he was inviting her and not Blair. Then she remembered Brad's comment about life or death. This wasn't a date, it was Snooper business. "Does this concern the university president and his nefarious schemes?"

"Exactly."

"A little more detail, please," she said.

Hugh handed her a second racquet that had been leaning in one corner. "Let's play while we talk."

"You're determined to get in shape for the tournament, aren't you?" she said.

"I wasn't even thinking about it." Tossing the ball into the air, he served it against the wall. "Last night, I got a phone call from Mariah…"

Running to hit the rebound, Cindy missed some of what he said next. Due to the game, it took longer than it should have, and several requests to repeat a statement, before the story came into focus.

On Saturday, Vanessa Sachet had paid a second visit to the Senior Center. This time, she'd pushed for a tour of the premises, and afterward had offered to organize a movie outing, a suggestion that the members had rejected in horror.

After she left the building, Runcie had watched her with binoculars through a third-floor window. From the premises, Vanessa had made a beeline along a footpath, crossed the parking lot and slipped into the college administration building through a side door.

"They're certain now that she's in cahoots with President Martin," Hugh said when they took a break. "As the Snoopers mentioned earlier, she might be gathering ammunition to persuade the college trustees that the seniors would be as well-served elsewhere."

"It seems to me our friends need a lawyer." Cindy set aside her racquet.

"Lawyers don't work cheap. Besides, our friends don't know for sure what they're dealing with." After dropping to the floor, he executed ten push-ups in rapid succession. "They need more facts."

Sweat darkened Hugh's T-shirt, making it cling to his back. Someone ought to massage those muscles to loosen them, and brush the dampened hair off his temples. Someone ought to...

Cindy forced her thoughts back to the subject. "I'll be glad to help the Snoopers, but what does the faculty party have to do with it?"

Hugh swiped a towel across his forehead. "The Sachets are the guests of honor and other local notables have been invited. It's a perfect opportunity for President Martin to do some fund-raising during his welcoming remarks."

"So he might blab about whatever he's planning," Cindy concluded. "The Snoopers want us to report on what he says?"

"Hosea's going to rig a listening device for me to wear," Hugh said. "If we can get President Martin's plans on tape, that'll give the Snoopers ammunition to take to a lawyer or to the university trustees."

"If we're only going to tape his remarks, you don't

need to worry about dancing,'' Cindy pointed out as they resumed playing. "We won't have to stay long.''

Hugh leaped to one side and smacked the ball. "It occurs to me that we could kill two birds with one stone.''

"How's that?''

"The teaching assistants are invited, and Blair mentioned that she's going to be there,'' he said.

An unexpected twinge made Cindy miss her shot. Hugh had asked her instead of Blair to go with him because the Snoopers' business was confidential, but afterward he wanted to dance with the woman he really cared about. *And so he should.*

"If you like, I'll help you with your dance skills,'' she offered. "Since you're getting more coordinated every day, I'm sure you'll impress her.''

Hugh scooped up the ball. "It's not Blair I want to dance with. The thing is, I figure she'll take Roland as her escort. Judging by the way he's been staring at you, he might get jealous if he sees you and me dancing together.''

"Then he'll leave you a clear field with Blair. Good thinking!''

"Cindy!'' Hugh caught her by the shoulders. Even through the glasses, his eyes transfixed her. "Forget about Blair. The point is to win your fiancé back for you. Isn't that what you want?''

"Sure,'' she said, surprised that Hugh wasn't focusing on Blair. He must really be caught up in helping the Snoopers.

"It will only work if he sees me as a genuine threat,'' Hugh said. "Are you working every night this week? With my class schedule, I don't have time to practice during the day, but if we can't rehearse at least once, we can call ourselves the Von Tripp Family dancers.''

"I'll tell Stu I have to leave early one night," Cindy said. "He won't like it, but I've filled in for other waitresses plenty of times. How about Wednesday?"

"I teach Advanced Sonnets on Mondays and Wednesdays, but it's over at eight," he said. "Can you come to my apartment? There's more floor space."

"I'll be there by nine," Cindy said. "And Hugh?"

"Yes?"

"Thanks," she said. "I hope we'll both be happy."

He picked up his racquet where it had slid to the floor. "Don't let the Snoopers know we're trying to make Roland jealous or they'll spread it all over town."

Cindy smiled. "Thank goodness President Martin is keeping them distracted."

"As long as he doesn't get his way."

"Of course," she said, and this time pounded the ball three times in a row until Hugh, blinded by sweat, missed a shot.

NEVER IN HIS THIRTY-SIX years had Hugh gone so long without writing a poem. It had been more than two weeks and still the muse refused to alight on his shoulder.

On Wednesday afternoon, he had office hours from three to five and then a break for dinner. While eating a sandwich at his cluttered desk, Hugh began scribbling on a wrinkled sheet of three-hole paper he'd found in the hallway, probably dropped from a student's notebook.

He tried to picture Blair's bewitching green eyes and black hair. Despite his concentration, the pen made only indistinct scratch marks on the paper, followed by an oily tuna fish blot.

He'd heard that the cure for writer's block was to free-associate, allowing the brain to spew out whatever it wanted, even if it was nonsense. Perhaps this poem didn't have to be about Blair, Hugh decided. Why not start with anything that caught his attention—the faded paint on the wall, say, or the distant blur of students' voices twittering in the quad?

Thanksgiving Day. Hosea's guitar. Cindy's voice soaring over the room. Without allowing himself to worry over the subject, he wrote:

> "On the windy wings of a winter day,
> Cindy sings the chill away."

Although the pen skipped over another oil drop, Hugh felt more words pressing to come out, like water behind a dam. He paused, however, to note that he'd used an interesting internal rhyme between "wings" and "sings."

He used to write more complicated poems as an undergraduate, but since then he'd grown lazy, or perhaps so fixated on his romantic objects that he ignored his muse. That must be why she'd deserted him.

Downing the last of his sandwich, he wrote:

> "When she finishes, not a single breath
> Disturbs the silence. What would I not give
> To hear more? It seems as if death
> Stalks the room. Then she smiles, and I live."

He sat back, thrilled to find himself unblocked. Until now, romance had always been his inspiration, but excessive reverence for his subject matter had made him afraid to take chances. As a result, his poetic skills had atrophied to the point that he couldn't write at all.

It was his love of music that had rescued him. Now Hugh felt as if he could compose poems about anything. Autumn, the planet Venus, the sweet thick lemon filling in a doughnut...

There was time to swing by the student center and grab a doughnut before his evening class began. Happily, Hugh stuck his poem in his briefcase and followed his stomach out the door.

9

STU CROCKENMEYER reluctantly agreed that Cindy could leave early. Despite his admission that she'd earned some time off, he wasn't happy about it. He displayed his ill-temper by ragging on her all evening and by assigning her to wait on Blair and Roland, even though they were sitting in Magda's section.

"Why's he giving you a hard time?" Blair asked as Cindy brought their orders.

"Because I'm leaving early," she said.

"In Oofdah, you never took time off work." Roland frowned, as if the natural order of the universe had been disrupted. To his friends, he said, "She never gets sick, either."

"I'm not sick."

"So where are you going?" he asked.

"That's personal." Cindy grabbed a carafe from a nearby stand and refilled their coffee cups.

"It wouldn't have anything to do with…" Blair's mouth formed an *H* before she stopped herself. "I'm sorry. I have no right to pry."

"It isn't prying. Cindy's an open book," Roland said. "I don't understand why she's being so secretive."

He'd never shown this much curiosity in Oofdah. If Cindy couldn't attend a football game or a movie with him, he'd never asked why. Maybe Hugh was right about Roland's becoming jealous.

She didn't feel flattered, though. Instead she found his possessiveness annoying. "Do you folks need anything else?"

Glowering, Roland shook his head.

"No, thank you," Blair added.

As she went about her waitress duties, Cindy wondered why anyone would want to make another person jealous. She didn't enjoy hearing that aggrieved tone in Roland's voice, and she didn't like being pressured to explain herself.

Yet despite the risk of making Roland even grumpier at the dinner-dance, she wasn't about to give up her chance to dance with Hugh. Around him, she experienced new and tantalizing sensations. The one thing she knew for sure was that she was growing and changing.

Why couldn't Roland see that these experiences would ultimately strengthen their relationship, not harm it? The more Cindy discovered about herself, the better able she was to face life with enthusiasm, and the better she would function as a wife, mother and teacher.

Roland, too, had expanded his horizons since coming to Clair De Lune. He would never have organized a medieval tournament in Oofdah, for example. Painful as his involvement with Blair had been for Cindy, it might prove a blessing in the long run.

She checked her watch. It was past eight o'clock, time to leave for Hugh's dance lesson. Her heart beating furiously, she ignored Stu's scowl and went to take off her apron.

ARRIVING HOME HALF AN HOUR early, Hugh rolled up the grass mat and cleared away some damp towels by throwing them across the fertility goddess. He spent ten minutes digging through the CD collection left by the previous occupants before deciding it was inappropriate to expect Cindy to dance to "Drums of the Tutsi Warriors" or "Pigmy Percussion." He would have to use the radio.

At five minutes before nine, it occurred to Hugh that he ought to serve some type of refreshments. Hopefully, he peered into the tiny refrigerator half-hidden beneath the sink.

It was well-stocked with the essentials: a quart of chocolate milk, half a can of cola, an aging container of cottage cheese, several dead insects in a baggy that he'd collected for his landlady's son's biology project, a pair of socks—he must have stuck those there in a fit of absentmindedness—and a take-out cartoon of Chinese food that couldn't be more than a week old.

At the sound of footsteps outside his door, Hugh slammed the refrigerator shut. He wiped his damp palms on his new slacks and went to let her in.

"Do you think I should take my hair out of the braid on Friday?" she asked when he opened the door. "People around here don't seem to wear this style."

Hugh didn't answer right away due to sensory overload. Cindy smelled like fresh coffee, her skin had a silky smoothness that begged to be touched, and the way her knit top clung to her shapely breasts aroused instincts that no poet since Ovid had captured accurately.

When she waggled her braid at him, he remembered her question. "You might try Solar Snips if you want a new style. Ask for Bernie."

"That's a good idea." She came inside, bringing warmth and vibrancy with her. "You were right, by the way. Roland really is getting jealous. I hope he doesn't make a fool of himself at the dinner-dance."

"Of course he feels jealous. Any man would." Hugh's

voice clogged. Compliments flowed easily when he was
addressing an ethereal object in elegiac terms. It was in-
finitely harder—no, impossible—to tell his good friend
Cindy how likable and attractive she was. "I hope you
don't mind dancing to the radio."

"Have you found a good station?" Spotting the radio
atop a teak chest, she turned it on. At the beat of salsa
music, Cindy began to shimmy. "This is fun, but I don't
know if it's what they'll play at a faculty event."

"I don't know, either. I usually don't attend." If they
played this kind of beat, Hugh was going to have to
leave, because Cindy's seductive movements were de-
molishing his self-control. Moving around her, he spun
the dial past yammering announcers and grating rap
songs until he hit something melodic. After a few bars,
he recognized it as "Strangers in the Night."

"I love that song!" Cindy said. "Take me in your
arms."

His throat tightening and the rest of his anatomy going
on full alert, Hugh looped one arm around her waist and
took her hand in his. He held his body stiffly, the way
he'd learned in fifth grade.

"Don't be so formal." She nestled close. "Let me lean
on your shoulder— Oh, we can dance cheek to cheek!
I've always wanted to do that."

Before he knew it, they were hugging each other while
they swayed. This was dancing? Although Hugh had attended a few mixers during his college years, all he remembered was gyrating somewhere within a few yards
of the girls he'd tapped. Several times his partner had
disappeared into the crowd entirely.

They were pressed together so tight that he could practically measure Cindy's bra size. Every time they moved,
her pelvis brushed his with agonizing sweetness.

"Take the lead," she murmured in his ear. "Sweep me around the floor—not too fast, we might hit somebody, I mean theoretically. I'm melting against you, letting you take over. Can't you feel it?"

He felt it all the way down to the molecular level. What were the long-term effects of this sort of cellular agitation? Could it cause mental breakdown?

Hugh didn't care. For the first time, he understood why the Puritans had disapproved of dancing. Those fools!

When the music stopped, the two of them didn't. They kept on dancing through a commercial for athlete's foot treatment and a weather report. It amazed Hugh how rhythmic the words "partly cloudy with seasonal coolness" could be.

By the time another song began, Hugh was simmering in a cloud of heat and longing. His hands stroked Cindy's back, down along the plentiful curve of her derriere. His mouth grazed the edge of her cheek.

Her chin lifted and her lips touched his, light and daring. Just a taste, really, but it was enough to make him forget about guiding her around the room.

Hugh discovered that by taking a slightly wider stance, he could bring their hips into closer contact. As they rocked gently in place, desire surged through him.

When Cindy's tongue flicked against his mouth, Hugh claimed a deep, thorough kiss. Pure instinct took over. He didn't know where his hand got the boldness, but all at once it was caressing Cindy's ample breasts. Their ripe fullness dominated his brain, removing any last semblance of conscious thought.

O luscious bosom that fills my palm,
Farewell to caution! Goodbye, calm!

Shocked, he drew back. What was happening? **Good heavens, he was composing a poem about Cindy!** She wasn't simply making a guest appearance in an ode to music, as she had earlier, but taking center stage. To target her with verse was unthinkable, a betrayal of their friendship, of her trust, and of his sworn devotion to Blair.

"Hugh, are you upset?" she asked worriedly. "I'm sorry we got carried away."

"It's my fault," he said. "I'm an animal."

"No, you're not!" Her pale blue eyes, slightly enlarged by her lenses, fixed on him reproachfully. "We're both to blame."

"You don't understand," Hugh said miserably. "I was starting to write… Earlier, I thought it was the music… I don't know what's wrong with me."

"There's nothing wrong with you. This is perfectly natural." Cindy caught his upper arms as if to steady him. With her down-to-earth manner and crisp tone, she reminded him of his high-school health instructor. Come to think of it, his health instructor had been a babe. "Men and women are designed to respond to each other. We shouldn't have tempted fate."

Disappointment arrowed through him. "What about the dinner-dance?" he asked. "Does this mean we can't go together?"

"We have to help the Snoopers." Clearing her throat, Cindy took a step backward.

"With a lot of people around, we should be able to keep our instincts in check," Hugh said.

"I hope so," she said. "Although once our instincts get aroused, we apparently have a hard time controlling ourselves."

"Was that true for you and Roland?" he asked, and immediately wished he hadn't. He didn't want to picture her kissing that big lug.

Cindy shook her head. "We never lost control of ourselves. That's because he respected my moral values."

"I respect your moral values!" Hugh said. "I'm sure we can get through the dinner-dance unscathed. After that…"

She averted her gaze. Both of them were surely thinking the same thing: that with any luck they'd soon be back with their real partners, safe and sound.

"We'll be fine," Cindy said, and collected her purse from the wicker settee. With a brisk "See you at the gym tomorrow," she went out the door.

His midsection still suspiciously tight, Hugh unrolled the mat. When he glanced at the fertility goddess, he could have sworn she wore a Mona Lisa smile.

"This is all your fault," he said, and pulled the towels off her.

ON THURSDAY AFTER WORKING out, Cindy went to Solar Snips. The beauty shop was located only a few blocks from her apartment.

Inside, the walls blazed in shades of gold, yellow and orange. Painted sunbursts framed photo blowups of models.

At home, Cindy usually let her mother trim her hair. Each year before the Christmas choral concert, she visited Myrtle Sandfelter's salon to have her locks swept into a formal twist. Frances had suggested going there before the homecoming dance, but Cindy had pointed out that, since she'd be wearing a helmet, it wouldn't make any difference.

As Hugh had suggested, she'd made an appointment with Bernie.

In this relaxed setting, she let her thoughts touch on the subject she'd dreamed about all last night. Hugh. Specifically, dancing with Hugh. In particular, hugging and kissing Hugh and feeling his arousal.

Inside her, something new had blossomed. Like a tightly held bud, her femininity had unfolded at his touch. Her right breast still tingled where he'd caressed it.

Cindy didn't know what to think. How could she be so faithless to Roland? Was it possible to have feelings for two men at the same time? As for Hugh, she didn't understand his behavior, but she knew that he loved Blair.

Cindy had promised to help him. She had to keep her word and her distance, because that was the kind of person she was. As for Roland...

"You!" cried a dramatic voice. Startled, she looked up to see a tall, willowy creature with blond, spiky hair. He or she, as Cindy couldn't tell, scrutinized her through pink-toned glasses. "You are exactly what I needed to brighten my day. That hair! So long and so—" Bernie shuddered. "So in need of my ministrations. Come to the shampoo bowl, my dear, and let us begin working miracles."

"I just want a trim." Cindy got to her feet.

"Of course you do!" With arm gestures worthy of a ballet dancer, Bernie steered her to a row of gleaming basins and reclining seats. "Let me guess. You've worn it long all your life, and your mother cuts it for you. Am I warm?"

She hated to admit it, but the truth was the truth. "Yes."

When she sat back, Bernie whipped a gossamer scarf around Cindy's neck and shoulders. The hairdresser was, she decided, almost certainly male. The tiny row of pearl earrings on each lobe failed to change her mind.

With expert, wiggling fingers, Bernie loosened Cindy's

long braid and fluffed her hair across the sink. "Such a pretty shade of blond, and natural, too! When you were little, I'll bet everyone told your mother it would darken over time, but you proved them wrong, didn't you?"

She didn't dare answer for fear the water would spray into her mouth. Instead Cindy closed her eyes and let herself enjoy the scalp massage.

"So many possibilities," Bernie muttered, as if to himself. "Maylene, what do you think? Short, short, short? Perhaps a touch of purple at the temples?"

"I'm sure you'll find the perfect solution, Bern," came a female voice in passing.

Short? Purple? Cindy barely restrained herself from bolting upright and shaking drops all over the salon like a wet dog. Right now, she reminded herself, Bernie had neither scissors nor a tube of dye in his hands.

The water stopped and, to the accompaniment of a cheerful humming, a towel wound itself around her head. "You must be Swedish," sang out Bernie. "Those cheekbones! You might be related to Greta Garbo."

"Not that I know of."

"I'm sure you are! I never mistake a cheekbone."

When she stood up, Cindy decided it was time to bring this flighty creature down to earth. The fact that she was slightly taller and maybe ten pounds heavier made the job easy. She gripped his shoulders and stared deep into his pink glasses.

"I want a trim," she said. "No dye. No hacking it off. When I emerge from this salon, I want to recognize myself in the mirror." Seeing a trace of fear in his brown eyes, she added, "Do as I ask, and we'll both live long and happy lives."

A sorrowful breath sighed from Bernie, rendering him

almost boneless beneath her grasp. "So sad. Such a waste."

"I am not wasted," Cindy said. "I'm normal." The entire beauty salon was watching, she realized. Well, it couldn't be helped.

"I'll tell you what." Thick eyelashes enhanced his wide-eyed expression. "I'll make a few improvements, but I won't do anything extreme. Do you think you can be that flexible? Because I will absolutely die if I can't bring out your inner beauty."

"Was that *d-i-e* or *d-y-e?*" she asked suspiciously.

Bernie clapped his hands over his heart. "Expire," he said.

"Okay." She hoped she could trust him.

Half an hour later, ensconced in his padded swivel chair, Cindy put her glasses back on and stared at herself in the mirror. He'd kept his word, sort of. Her hair fell to shoulder-length in back, but curved upward on the sides, tapering seamlessly to bangs.

Although she'd approved the style after Bernie waved a magazine picture in front of her, Cindy hadn't expected it to make such a dramatic difference. The sweep of hair made her eyes brighter and her lips fuller. If she'd met herself on the street, she'd have guessed she was Cindy's younger, prettier sister.

"You did a great job," she admitted.

"A little makeup and you'll knock 'em dead," Bernie said. "Do you mind if I take a photo?"

"Go ahead." Cindy didn't see what the big deal was. Okay, she'd improved a bit, but inside she was still the same person.

"Yoo-hoo! Maylene!" Bernie summoned the neighboring hairdresser, a short woman with wild red curls. "Shoot us, will you?"

Looping one arm over Cindy's shoulder, he struck a rakish pose as the flash went off. She blinked. "Are we done?"

"Why aren't you preening yourself, you silly thing?" Bernie reproved. "I hardly ever take pictures of my clients. You're one in a million!"

Maylene handed back the camera. "Make that one in twenty," she said, and returned to her client.

"Tell me what special event you're attending, you fox," Bernie said. "What are you wearing? Oh, dear." An indignant woman, hands on hips, was glaring at him from the waiting area. "I forgot about Vanessa. Well, Cindy, don't be a stranger. *Au revoir!*"

"Thanks again," she said. "I'm glad I trusted you."

As the receptionist took her credit card, Cindy sneaked a glance at the new arrival. The tall woman was in her early thirties, about the right age to be Vanessa Sachet. Dressed in a tailored suit and heels, with pale blond highlights rioting through her light-brown hair, she was every inch the sophisticate the Snoopers had described.

She didn't sound elegant while berating Bernie, however. "I don't expect to be kept waiting while you fuss over a nobody! My time is precious. You may be the best hairdresser in Clair De Lune, but I'll drive to L.A. if you don't treat me right."

At the station next to Bernie's, Maylene's eyes narrowed in disapproval. Bernie himself was fussing with various instruments and jars, clearly distressed. "Oh, Mrs. Sachet, don't do that! I promise, it won't happen again."

If this had been Oofdah, Cindy would have marched over and informed the woman that while no one enjoyed waiting, that wasn't an excuse to humiliate the man. However, this wasn't her town and, besides, she didn't want to draw Vanessa's attention to herself. She and Hugh might need to get close to the Sachets to spy on them at the dinner-dance.

Cindy didn't give any more thought to her hairdo as she walked to the Lunar Lunch Box, until a truck driver whistled at her. Half a block later, a young man turned to stare so hard that the woman beside him cuffed his shoulder.

It was strange and a bit disconcerting. Cindy wondered if she should start wearing a baseball cap when she went out in public.

Well, she couldn't wear a hat at the dance tomorrow night. Fortunately, with peacocks like Vanessa Sachet around, no one would notice Cindy.

10

ON FRIDAY AFTERNOON, Hugh wrote another poem. Even wearing an L.A. Lakers cap, Cindy had managed to look sensual while exercising at the gym earlier, but he didn't write about her. He wrote about the experience of working out and building up his body.

"We thud. We groan. We struggle and we sweat.
Someday we will soar, but we haven't earned it yet.
My muscles ache. Beside me, Cindy's fired
With enough determination to keep even me inspired.
I will make her proud, though I may not do it soon.
I will defy gravity. I will fly to the moon."

It wasn't great art, but it beat his previous efforts, Hugh mused that evening as he dressed in a dark jacket and tan pants for the faculty party. Hosea was meeting him and Cindy at the Senior Center and had promised to bring an appropriate tie, wired for sound.

Although Hugh had offered to pick Cindy up, she'd preferred to take her own car. If things worked out, he might want to give Blair a ride home, she'd said.

Hugh was certainly willing to offer Blair a lift if she needed one. He'd been hoping to take Cindy, though, because she might sing along with the radio.

He didn't focus on his mission for the evening until he stood in the Senior Center's salon watching Hosea demonstrate how to work the tiny microphone in Hugh's tie and activate the miniature tape recorder in his pocket. Then it hit him that he was going to spy on the university's president. What if someone noticed the wire running beneath his clothes?

Hugh lifted his chin and, without thinking, flexed his arm. If matters went wrong, he'd brazen it out. Or he'd freeze like an idiot while Cindy brazened it out. Either way, they were going to make a terrific team.

"There she is!" Hosea nodded toward the door. "My goodness, what a fine female!"

Hugh followed his gaze to a stunning, full-figured woman in a deep blue dress glittering with stars. Blond hair swept from her regal head across the shoulders of her beaded evening shawl.

With a jolt, he recognized his friend and exercise pal. How could she have changed so completely since this afternoon? Her hair...her dress...even her glasses were different.

"Good heavens! Cindy?" Runcie leaped to his feet and tossed aside the men's magazine he'd been reading. "You're lovely tonight."

"Spectacular," Hosea affirmed. He and Runcie were the only Snoopers present.

"Thank you both." Cindy fiddled with the fabric of her gown, acting uncharacteristically nervous. "What do you think, Hugh?"

"I think you're going to sweep Roland off his feet," he said. "He'll be impressed, trust me."

"I thought I'd wear my backup glasses because they're

smaller. I got the larger ones because they seemed more practical, but they're not very dressy,'' she said. ''Oh, and I went to that hairdresser you recommended—Bernie.''

''Isn't she terrific?'' Hugh said. ''A bit odd, but very gifted.''

''She?'' Cindy asked.

He remembered that Jared hadn't been certain of Bernie's gender, but Hugh had assumed at the salon that it must be a female. ''I think it's a she.''

''I thought it was a he,'' she said. ''It doesn't matter. I just hope Myrtle Sandfelter can follow the lines when I get home. This style suits me.''

It certainly did. Hugh could hardly take his eyes off this ravishing woman as they strolled out of the Senior Center and across the parking lot. In the moonlight, the spangles on her dress glimmered and winked.

His body stirred, remembering their passionate kiss two evenings ago. Plenty of bushes lined the campus. If they stepped behind one, they'd have enough privacy...

Hugh gave himself a shake. What was he thinking? Making out had been a mistake, they'd both agreed.

''Are you cold?'' Cindy asked.

''No. Why?'' In fact, since he'd begun exercising more, his body temperature had risen.

''You shivered,'' she said, and drew nearer. ''Would you like to share my shawl?''

''I've got a jacket,'' Hugh pointed out. At such close range, he nearly forgot his resolution to behave himself. But not quite.

They reached the walkway that led past the Administration Building. Ahead, the modernistic Faculty Center shone like a beacon, and through the wraparound glass windows he saw people clinking glasses and exchanging greetings. Soft orchestral music drifted out.

"It's enchanting," Cindy said. "I'm glad you invited me, even if it is only because of the Snoopers."

"You're my friend," Hugh protested. "I like being around you."

In the semidarkness, their eyes met. He got the impression she was asking a question, but he didn't know what it was.

At last she spoke, softly. "I think we're very close."

"You do?" He swallowed hard, pleased but a little taken aback. "I think so, too."

"We may even get there this evening."

Judging by the amount of heat pumping through his arteries, Hugh feared he might start to give off steam. Did she intend to come home with him after the banquet? "You mean tonight?"

"Well, you did say Blair and Roland should be here," Cindy noted.

"Blair and Roland?" What did they have to do with anything?

"As I said, I think we're really close to reaching our goals," she murmured. "When they see us dressed like this, that might do the trick."

Around Hugh, the night got so dark that the glare of the Faculty Center hurt his eyes. "I see what you mean."

Side by side, they strolled into the warmth and clamor of the building. To Hugh, it seemed that they left something precious behind.

CINDY HOPED HUGH HADN'T realized how much she wanted to kiss him. After their embrace on Wednesday, she knew they were on shaky ground. At least, she was, although she had no doubt Hugh's heart remained loyal

to Blair. His kiss had been a natural reaction to the seductive circumstances. Her own response was more
troubling.

Earlier, her heart had leaped at the sigh of Hugh in his
dark jacket, with his hair slightly rebellious and his newly
shaved jawline begging to be stroked. Tonight, she
wished they actually were a couple, that they belonged
together.

It made no sense. What about Roland?

When they entered the Faculty Center, it took a few
seconds for Cindy to adapt to the surge of noise and
brightness. She kept a smile pasted on while Hugh introduced her to various colleagues. One handsome fellow
with lavender-gray eyes made a sweeping bow and kissed
the back of her hand.

"Don't mind him," Hugh said. "Jared's an actor."

"You went to Bernie, I see," the man said.

They both nodded.

"You, too?" Jared asked Cindy. "Of course. You're
every bit as beautiful as Hugh said."

"He must have been talking about Blair." So this was
Hugh's role model, and quite a charmer he was, too.

"You were referring to someone else?" Jared shot
Hugh a questioning glance.

"The two of us are only friends," Cindy added, to
spare Hugh the need to agree. Or perhaps to spare herself
from hearing the truth.

"Then I'm glad he took my advice," Jared said.
"About dating other women to make his true love
jealous."

Cindy felt her face getting hot. Beside her, Hugh
squirmed. Before anyone could speak, two attractive
women caught Jared, one by each arm.

"You haven't forgotten you promised to dance with me, have you?" asked the short brunette.

"And you said you'd sit with me at dinner!" Her blond companion pretended to pout. "Oh, Jared, you're such a flirt!"

"Shameless," agreed her friend as they bore him off, sandwiched between them.

"He isn't usually so tactless," Hugh said to Cindy when they were alone. "I didn't ask you out because of that suggestion he made."

"There's nothing to be embarrassed about." She hoped he hadn't noticed her flush. "We agreed to help each other. What's wrong with that?"

"Nothing." Hugh extended a crooked arm, and she slipped her hand into place. "Let's go act as if we're deliriously happy, and make those certain someones regret they failed to appreciate us."

When they entered the ballroom, the band was playing a fast waltz, and Hugh swung Cindy onto the dance floor. He guided her about so masterfully and gracefully that she thought perhaps they'd fallen into a fairy tale. He was the prince at the ball, and she...must be one of Cinderella's stepsisters, taking center stage before the real heroine arrived.

Cindy refused to feel sorry for herself. With any luck, by the end of the evening she'd have her own prince back. Besides, she was nobody's wicked stepsister.

The strange part was the way people kept smiling at her, especially men. Halfway through the dance, a gray-haired professor cut in on Hugh, only to be replaced by a fellow with a red beard and long ponytail.

"Everybody's wondering how on earth Hugh Bemling managed to find a beauty like you," he said.

"I wasn't so beautiful until I met him," Cindy said.

The fellow puzzled on that one until, a moment later, the music ended and Hugh reclaimed her.

Thank goodness there hadn't been a chance for them to slow dance, she mused as they left the dance floor. Their reputations, and their consciences, were safe.

The two of them got in line for a buffet that was set up along one side of the room. A few minutes later, balancing dinner and salad plates, they found an empty table for four and sat down on uncomfortably hard wooden chairs.

Hugh pointed toward the head table. "The man with the silver hair is President Martin, and the people sitting next to him are the Sachets."

Cindy recognized Vanessa from the salon, although her hair was blonder now. To her left sat a man who must be Bill, the husband who'd dumped his first wife for her. A lean, distinguished figure, he kept trying to get Vanessa's attention, but she was riveted on the man to her right.

Despite his silver hair, President Martin appeared younger than Bill Sachet. In his mid-forties, Cindy guessed. A silver curl dropped like a question mark onto the middle of his forehead, giving his round face the look of a prematurely aged Kewpie doll.

"Who are the other people at the head table?" she asked.

"Mostly university officials," Hugh said. "That couple on the end are patrons. That's James Bonderoff, the computer software magnate, and his wife, Dex."

Cindy decided she liked that couple a lot better than the Sachets. Dex Bonderoff was short and perky, with a mass of brown hair that could use Bernie's ministrations. Her husband, tanned and athletic, gazed at her with open devotion.

The scrape of the chair next to her startled Cindy from her observations. Blair was settling into place, joined by Roland. "Hi!" said the teaching assistant. "I hope you don't mind if we join you."

Hugh's mouth twisted with what she could have sworn was annoyance. Since he must be glad to see Blair, Cindy supposed he was hoping the pair wouldn't interfere with their ability to help the Snoopers.

"We're glad to see you," she said.

Roland rarely dressed up, but when he did, his handsome Scandinavian features and husky build made him a knockout. Cindy found herself admiring him, although without her usual sense of proprietary pleasure. And without that painful lurch of sadness at seeing him with another woman.

What was wrong with her? This was Roland!

"Cindy?" he asked, measuring her with his eyes. "Wow. You did something with your hair, right?"

"It's fantastic." Blair, who made an entrancing picture in an emerald sheath with spaghetti straps, didn't seem to mind her date's enthusiasm for his old girlfriend. "Both of you."

"Me?" said Hugh. "Thanks."

The four of them dug into their food, doing their best to sustain a conversation as they ate. Much of the talk centered on the tournament to be staged the following weekend on the campus athletic field.

"Can you believe it? We had to put down a deposit in case we fail to clean up the pony poop," Roland said as he stuffed a bite of steak into his mouth.

Cindy set down her fork. "Not while we're eating!"

"What did I say?" he asked. "Oh, yeah. Sorry."

"He talks that way a lot," Blair confided. "I never know how to handle him."

"Handle me?" Roland frowned. "Just spit it out."

"He has a thick hide," Cindy explained. "You have to stick a pitchfork in him to make your point."

"Yeah, she understands me." Roland gave her an affectionate grin across the table.

Hugh went into a coughing fit. While Blair fussed in alarm, Cindy marched over and whacked him on the back. Air wheezed out of him with a sound like that of pneumatic brakes.

"I think his eyes just rolled back into his head," Roland said. "You shouldn't hit him so hard, Cinders."

"I can take it," gasped Hugh, and downed a long swallow of water.

"Thank goodness you're all right!" Blair reached across the table and patted his wrist. "I was so worried."

"I'm glad Cindy didn't have to use the Heimlich maneuver," Roland said. "She did that once at summer camp and the guy's whole dinner came up. Oh, did I say something wrong again?"

"It's okay," Cindy told him. "I don't think anybody's eating."

The room quieted, and she saw President Martin standing at the microphone. Under the table, she nudged Hugh's knee to remind him to turn on his tape recorder.

He fumbled with his clothing. "Does choking make you itch or something?" Roland asked. Fortunately Blair shushed him.

Cindy wished the college president would hurry and say something incriminating about his plans to destroy the University Senior Center. Then she and Hugh could escape this awkward situation.

The silver-haired Kewpie doll rambled on about generous donors and the university's goals, but he didn't mention any specifics. Just when all sensation was beginning to leave her buttocks, he signaled the orchestra to resume and asked Mrs. Sachet to dance.

"That's our cue." Hugh stood up.

"I'd be delighted." Blair rose before Cindy had time to push back her chair.

Although Hugh's expression was an unmistakable plea to be rescued, she couldn't think of any graceful way to intervene. "Roland and I will join you," she said instead, figuring that surely one couple or the other could get close enough to overhear their targets' conversation. It was best to get it on tape, but failing that, at least they could eavesdrop.

"I thought you'd never ask," joked her former fiancé, and he came to take her arm.

Cindy had to make a mental adjustment to dance with a man taller than she was. She missed Hugh's cheek-to-cheek contact, but she and Roland soon fell into step.

"I didn't realize how much I like not having to worry about stepping on my partner's feet," he said as they plowed through a crowd of insubstantial faculty members. "Or crushing her dainty bones if I hold her too tight."

"Poor Blair," Cindy murmured. She herself had long ago perfected a sort of Irish dance step that kept her feet out of harm's way.

"She's happy enough now." Roland jerked his head toward where Blair was winding herself around Hugh as they danced. He, Cindy could see, was trying to disentangle his tie and keep it aimed toward President Martin and Mrs. Sachet.

"Your friend seems to have changed her mind about Hugh." Much as Cindy hated to bring up the subject, she couldn't avoid it.

"Yeah, she's got this idea that he's romantic and kind

of dreamy,'' Roland said. ''Makes no sense to me. I mean, he's a nice guy, but you wouldn't want to throw a football with him.''

''I doubt Blair has pigskin-tossing in mind.'' By shifting her balance, Cindy managed to steer closer to President Martin.

''Whatever,'' Roland replied.

Beneath the flow of the music, she heard Vanessa Sachet's brittle laughter. ''Wouldn't that be a lark?'' the woman was saying. ''It's called the Moonlight Motel. Down on Constellation Street near the freeway.''

Surely she wasn't proposing to relocate the seniors from their picturesque mansion into a motel within earshot of the freeway! But what else could she mean?

''Man, I can't wait to see what the people in Oofdah think of your new hairstyle,'' Roland said.

Cindy's attention snapped back to her partner. ''I didn't think you were planning to spend much time in Oofdah from now on.''

''I'm going back for Christmas, of course,'' he said. ''Aren't you?''

''I suppose so.''

''You can't leave your mom by herself!''

''Oh, she moved to Rochester.'' She craned her neck to catch sight of Hugh.

He had his tie draped over Blair's shoulder and was fiddling with it behind her back. From the way she snuggled up to him, Cindy gathered she thought he was caressing her.

He must be frustrated by the need to record the neighboring conversation when he finally had the woman of his dreams in his arms. Cindy wished she'd arranged to wear the tie instead, although it might seem a bit odd with this dress.

"Your mother moved?" Roland asked in dismay. "How could she do that?"

"She got a terrific job offer," she said. "Besides, since we were getting married next summer, she figured she'd be suffering from empty nest syndrome."

"We were getting married next summer?" he asked.

"I'm sure I mentioned it." The crowd had come between them and President Martin, Cindy saw. She hoped Hugh was close enough to hear more of the conversation.

"My e-mail must have come as an even bigger shock than I realized," Roland said, displaying his first trace of guilt.

"Don't worry about it." At the moment, Cindy didn't even want to think about staging a wedding in Oofdah. She was too absorbed with what was happening on this dance floor in Clair De Lune.

"Okay, I won't." Relief shone in his voice. "So…you want to go somewhere after the party tonight?"

"I'm kind of tied up." She didn't want to miss the postevent debriefing with the Snoopers.

"I thought you work every night but Friday," Roland protested. "Hey, I've got an idea. What time do you go to the gym?"

"One o'clock," she said without thinking. Like thunder that strikes seconds after the lightning, understanding roared to life. "You're not planning on joining me!"

"It'll be like old times," Roland said. "Tossing a ball together, breaking a sweat. Don't look so surprised. I'm still your best buddy."

"Well, yes, but Hugh…"

"He won't notice I'm around." At his nod, she saw that Blair was pressed even tighter against her partner. What did that woman think she was doing? Hugh wasn't some toy she could play with, then drop when she tired of the novelty.

"She'd better not play fast and loose with him," Cindy said. "If she breaks his heart, I'll teach her a lesson."

"He's a grown man," Roland told her. "Besides, I don't see him objecting."

Neither did she, Cindy had to admit. And that made her even angrier.

11

THE WAY BLAIR TWINED herself around Hugh was wreaking havoc with his high-tech tie. He had always thought of her as a delicate flower, but he hadn't considered the fact that frail blossoms bloomed on clinging vines.

He doubted he'd gotten anything on tape other than heavy breathing and variations on, "Oh, Hugh, why didn't I see the truth sooner? How could I have been so blind?" Not that he objected to those statements, of course.

The only clear sentence he'd managed to overhear President Martin say to Vanessa Sachet was, "How about Monday afternoon?" That was it. How about *what* on Monday afternoon? Tea with the bursar? Bulldozers at the Senior Center?

The evening was a bust. He hadn't learned a thing that might help his friends.

He'd never even found a second chance to dance with Cindy, although it didn't look like she needed help to make Roland jealous. The way he was sticking to her, she'd have to scrape him off with a spatula, one that Hugh would be glad to provide. That big fellow had no business being so happy after the way he'd treated her.

When President Martin retreated from the dance floor, Hugh suggested to his friends that they depart. Roland lingered briefly outside the Faculty Center, then headed off with a disgustingly cheery "See you!" Since Blair made no move to go along, Hugh escorted the two ladies across the parking lot to the Senior Center.

When they arrived in the salon, he saw that Mariah had joined Hosea and Runcie. She fixed Blair with a disapproving frown. "This is private business."

"I'm sorry," Blair said.

"Would you mind waiting in my car?" Hugh asked, since he was apparently giving her a ride home.

"No problem." She smiled blissfully at everyone. "I'll take a little nap and then we can paint the town red."

At this hour? It was after eleven. Then Hugh recalled that the local art theater had scheduled a midnight screening of the Oscar-winning film *Il Postino,* about the Chilean poet Pablo Neruda. A film about a poet might be worth taking in.

After escorting Blair to his car, he returned and let Hosea disconnect the tie and tape recorder. "I'm afraid we didn't get anything usable."

"President Martin kept a tight lip during his opening address?" asked Mariah, arranging herself on the gold velvet couch.

"He was totally bland." Cindy sat down on the love seat. When Hugh dropped down beside her, she got up and went to stand, arms folded, by the fireplace.

Had he offended her? He wanted to ask what was going on, but the Snoopers were eyeing them both with far too much interest, so he returned to their topic.

"On the dance floor, it was chaos," Hugh said. "There were a few complications...well, maybe you'll pick out more on the tape than I heard. The only thing that sticks in my mind was something about Monday afternoon."

"I heard Vanessa Sachet mention the Moonlight Motel

on Constellation Street near the freeway,'' Cindy added. ''I wonder if the two things are connected?''

Runcie waved them toward the door. ''Time to check the chart.''

For what? Hugh wondered.

''Absolutely,'' said Hosea.

Mariah hoisted herself to her feet. ''The war room was *my* idea and I'll do the tracking, thank you.''

The five of them trooped down the hallway into the room he'd seen on a previous visit. Mariah went to run her finger along a wall map of the town.

On flat paper, Clair De Lune appeared ordinary. You couldn't see the hills to the north or the greenery of the campus, let alone the flowered window boxes and funky architecture in the village-style downtown.

The map depicted the community as a grid of neatly drawn streets crossing each other at right angles. The only break came east of town, where the foothills forced the roads to waver. On this edge lay Constellation Street, which curved its way through rough terrain but fell tidily into place as it neared the freeway on the south side of town.

''This is where the motel is,'' Mariah said.

''Is there a restaurant where they could hold a meeting?'' asked Cindy, who had taken up a position across the room from Hugh.

''I don't believe so,'' Hosea said. ''I'm baffled by this. There's nowhere to hold a business meeting at the motel.''

''Whatever they're up to, we'll nail 'em!'' Runcie said. ''All three of the clerks are on our payroll.''

''You have a payroll?'' Hugh asked.

Mariah waved her hand airily. ''We pool our money. It's a worthwhile cause. Besides, we don't pay them much." She checked a chart next to the map. "Franklin Powers will be on duty Monday afternoon. I'll give him a call."

"Well, I'm kind of tired," Cindy said. "Good luck, you guys."

Everyone said good-night. Hugh did his best to walk Cindy to her car, but she shook her head. "Blair's waiting. Go have a good time."

A thought occurred to him. "Is Roland meeting you somewhere?"

She stiffened. "No."

Now he understood why she'd acted so standoffish. She was disappointed at having had to leave Roland, while he got to enjoy the night with Blair. "I'm sorry."

"Don't be," she said. "Have a good time."

Hugh was on the point of asking Cindy to join them, but she hurried away. The sparkle went out of the evening.

As he approached his car, he saw Blair relaxing in the front seat. Since she hadn't spotted him yet, Hugh took a moment to study the woman he'd adored since he first set eyes on her four months ago.

In profile, she had a pert little nose and a knowing way of holding her head. Her long black hair put him in mind of bewitching Victorian ladies who cast their fate with highwaymen. A man could write any number of poems about her, but the odd part was that he couldn't think of any.

Perhaps it indicated a normal transition in the relationship, from admiration at a distance to growing closeness. The miracle was that he'd ended up with the object of his affections.

A merciful fate had set him on the right course, and Hugh resolved then and there not to blow it.

CINDY DIDN'T UNDERSTAND WHY she'd acted so grumpy toward Hugh last night at the Senior Center. It might have been because he'd practically invited Blair into the debriefing. She was a nice young woman, but she hadn't earned the right to hear the Snoopers' secrets.

That was something he shared with Cindy. Or did he mean to let Blair intrude into every aspect of their friendship?

It was inevitable, she told herself firmly. Now that Hugh and Blair were a couple... Her mind refused to travel any further in that direction.

Cindy decided to call her mother. Frances would be happy to hear that matters with Roland were improving.

"That's wonderful news," her mother said, when informed that they'd danced together last night and that Roland had asked about coming home for Christmas. "I'm not sure whether I'll be going back to Oofdah for the holidays. The house isn't rented yet, so I suppose I might, but..."

"But what?" Cindy pressed. "Is something happening in Rochester?"

"Oh, not much," Frances said. "Albert and I went to a concert, that's all. Two concerts, actually. We both love classical music. He got a kick out of that poem about Mary's watch, by the way. So did the pastor."

"Albert's the rehearsal pianist?" she asked.

"Yes. It's only a sideline. He's a retired carpenter."

"Good with his hands, I see," Cindy observed.

"How on earth did you know—" Her mother broke off in confusion. "I mean..."

The implication struck her. "Mom! Did you make out with him?"

"You're the one who brought up..." Again, her mother halted in midsentence. "Oh. You said he's good with his hands because he's a carpenter and plays the piano.''

"I'm glad to learn he has other talents," Cindy said drily.

"This isn't a proper topic for a conversation," her mother announced, and they spent the rest of the call discussing how well the choir rehearsals were going.

HUGH WASN'T SURE HOW HE got to the gym on Saturday, although he was fairly certain he must have driven, because he was in no condition to walk. After the midnight movie, Blair had still been chipper as a chipmunk, and they'd stopped for ice cream.

He'd fallen into bed at 3 a.m. and been awakened five hours later when she'd phoned to tell him what a wonderful time she'd had. Although he'd rested his head against the pillow, sleep had eluded him.

At the gym, the noise in the exercise room gave him a headache. Since Cindy hadn't arrived yet, he decided to go swimming and trusted her to find him. At least in the pool, if he fell asleep the water would buoy him, or—worst case scenario—he would experience a peaceful death, which was preferable to dozing off and getting caught in the Exercycle machinery.

Although his muscles had developed dramatically from a month of hard work, today Hugh strained to furrow through the water. An impulse to dog paddle nearly overwhelmed him.

He ignored the other swimmers, despite three women faculty members—two from the art department and one from political science—eyeing him and murmuring among themselves. Receiving zero encouragement, they transferred their attention to someone else.

Hugh slowed down and practiced floating on his stomach. Relaxation closed over him, sleepy and soothing.

A huge splash suffused the pool, followed by a tidal wave that flipped him onto his back. Might as well stay in this position, he decided. Maybe he could catch a few winks before the next wave hit.

Hugh's eyes were drifting shut when a hearty—and familiar—male voice boomed, "Seen Cindy?"

"Not lately." He willed the interloper to go away.

"She'll show up sooner or later, right?" continued the pain-in-the-neck. "I hear you're exercise buddies, and Cindy never deserts a partner."

Hugh pried one eyelid open. Darn. He'd hoped he was the victim of a fevered imagination, but no, it *was* Roland. "What are you doing here?"

"Cinders works almost every night," said the blond hunk treading water beside him. "The only way I can figure out to spend time with her is to join the gym."

This lug intended to horn in on their exercise sessions every day? "Was that her idea?" Hugh inquired warily.

"Her idea, my idea, who can tell?" Roland said. "We're so close, we think alike."

Hugh didn't believe it. Still, he could hardly dispute a fiancé's claim on Cindy's time. The wise choice would be for him to bow out of this unholy threesome and exercise alone.

Exercise by himself? What was the point? In high school and college, PE had been a dreary, failure-ridden experience. What made the gym fun was sharing it with Cindy.

His sleepiness vanished. "If you think alike, where is she?" he said. "She's late."

"I didn't say I could read her mind," Roland conceded. "Want to race? I'll give you a head start."

Hugh knew he didn't have a gopher's chance in a concrete parking lot of beating this leviathan. On the other hand, there was much to be said for strategy. "Okay," he said. "And forget the head start."

They started in the shallow end. Hugh pushed off hard from the steps and gained a slight advantage, which Roland erased with a couple of powerful strokes. Because Hugh had chosen his side of the pool with a purpose, however, Roland promptly ran into the school of female professors bobbing and twiddling in the water.

Hugh shot ahead, giving it the old college try. He arrived at the far end inches ahead of his rival.

"Aren't we doubling back?" Roland asked, poised with one hand hooked over the lip of the pool.

Hugh didn't want to admit that he'd blown his entire morning's allotment of energy. He was saved from an awkward situation when he spotted Cindy in the entranceway. Her sleek hairstyle was as entrancing amid the smell of chlorine as in the glow of moonlight, and the modesty of her one-piece swimsuit emphasized the mystery of the ample curves beneath.

"There she is," he said.

Roland issued a wolf whistle. Spotting them, Cindy started forward. "Man, she looks great, doesn't she? And all mine."

Instinctively Hugh's lip curled and a growl started deep in his throat. Whoa, this was not his style! Uncurling his lip and trying to sound nonchalant, he said, "What about Blair?"

"Nice girl," Roland tossed off. "She wears thin after a while, though. Ever tried arm wrestling with her?"

"It never occurred to me," Hugh said.

"That's right, you're more the poetry type," said his muscle-bound companion. "You can write odes to her green eyes till you're blue in the face. Cindy, now, she's poetry in motion."

They both watched as the subject of their conversation swung toward them along the concrete. Long legs, confident stride, troubled expression. "Sorry I'm late," she said. "Esther came over as I was leaving and asked me to drive her to the Senior Center."

"They must be doing more planning for...you know." Hugh barely realized in time that he shouldn't say too much in front of Roland.

"What does she know?" asked her fiancé.

"Just some business involving the senior citizens. They're all atwitter about Monday." Cindy jumped into the water with considerably more grace than Roland had managed and came up dripping next to Hugh. Through the subtle movements of the water, he felt her heat and energy. A yearning that was almost an ache seized him.

"How come he knows stuff that you haven't told me about?" Roland asked.

"Because you haven't been around," Cindy said. "You took yourself out of the picture, remember?"

"Well, I'm back." He stared at her with a trace of belligerence, as if daring her to deny it. Receiving no response, he said, "Want to race?"

She glanced questioningly at Hugh. "I just did it, so you two go ahead," he said. "I won, by the way."

To his credit, Roland didn't mention the fact that he'd encountered an obstacle. "I'm ready to try again."

"Good luck," Hugh said.

He watched the two of them shoulder their way across the pool, making two laps. Cindy didn't bother with strategy. Swimming full out, she touched the finish line a split second ahead of her fiancé.

"Congratulations," said Roland good-naturedly. "It's not my day, I guess."

The three women faculty members started a friendly game of water polo and invited them to join. Roland's well-aimed shots and strong physique clearly impressed them, but Cindy stayed close to Hugh.

"I'm sorry about him tagging along," she said quietly, while Roland was joking with one of the women. "I didn't invite him."

"It's okay," he said. "I'm happy for you. You are happy, aren't you?"

"Sure." She gazed away distractedly.

Hugh struggled against a surge of regret. These last few weeks with Cindy had been a special time, a vacation from the rest of his life. He'd felt free of the usual restrictions, more fully alive than ever before. And, like every kid, he wished vacation could last forever.

But of course, it couldn't.

12

WHEN CINDY ARRIVED FOR work at the Lunar Lunch Box on Monday, Daffodil was pointedly refusing to talk to Stu. After she answered a phone call for him, she said loudly to Magda, "Please tell that man that someone wants to talk to him, although I can't for the life of me think why."

"All I did was suggest we bring in muffins and pastries from Key Lune Pies," Stu grumbled to Cindy after finishing his phone call. "She hit the roof."

"That man seems to think my baking isn't good enough for his establishment," Daffodil announced in a voice that carried to every corner of the restaurant. "Maybe my cooking isn't good enough, either."

"Your cooking's fine," snapped the owner. "It's your attitude I have a problem with."

"Maybe that man would like to fire my attitude and try finding a replacement cook!" roared Daffodil, waving her spatula for emphasis.

Stu knew when he was licked. "I'm sorry I ever brought it up. Your pies are fine with me." He stomped into his office.

"If that man thinks such a mealymouthed response will unruffle my feathers, he's got another think coming," said the cook.

"I'm glad you're here," Magda told Cindy. "It's been one of those days."

"I can tell." Secretly, she was glad for the distraction. The touchiness between cook and owner made her own agitation seem less important.

On Sunday, Roland had dropped by her apartment to say he missed his best friend and wanted to hang around with her on a regular basis. His infatuation with Blair was over, he promised.

Cindy had missed him, too, the lovable oaf. Roland was like a Saint Bernard dog that sleeps on your feet while you're reading in front of the fire. Heavy and awkward, but sweet.

When Roland mentioned Christmas again, Cindy had conceded it wasn't a bad idea for them to go back to Oofdah together to see how they felt in that familiar environment. Yet inside her, a great hollow space had opened, and she didn't know what to do about it.

As Hugh had said, they'd both achieved their goals. Naturally she would miss their close companionship of the last four weeks, but that didn't explain why the colors had bled out of the world.

"That was supposed to be onion rings," said a woman to whom Cindy handed a plate of French fries.

"Oh! I'm sorry. I'll get your order right away." She hurried to the kitchen. Shaking her head, Cindy knew she had to pull herself together and concentrate on her work.

A while later, Roland came in with a group of friends. When Cindy stopped to take their order, he looped his arm around her waist. "We're back together," he told the others.

"Does this mean she's going to be princess at the tournament next Saturday?" asked a young man.

"I have to work that day," Cindy said.

"It wouldn't be very nice to uninvite Blair, anyway," noted a young woman. "She'd get her feelings hurt."

"Cindy's a good sport. She doesn't need to be the princess, but she ought to be there," Roland said. "You're coming as my guest, right?"

"I'm afraid I can't."

Daffodil stuck her head out of the kitchen. Cindy had noticed that the cook possessed keen ears and enjoyed listening to conversations at nearby tables. "Stu will cover your shift on Saturday."

Cindy made a face. "You know perfectly well he won't."

"He will, too, and I'm going to tell him so." Daffodil marched across to Stu's office door and threw it open. "Hey, boss! You're covering for Cindy on Saturday!"

"The heck I am!" came the response.

"If you want to make it up with me, you'll do it, and that's that!"

After a pregnant pause, he said, "No more grousing about Key Lune Pies?"

"Not as long as you never mention that place again," said Daffodil. "And cover for Cindy."

His exasperated breath must have been audible all the way down De Lune Boulevard. "All right."

"There, you see." Daffodil beamed.

"Thank you." Cindy wasn't sure she wanted to attend the tournament, but she couldn't refuse now. Besides, it would be fun to see Roland dressed as a knight, riding around on a pony.

Her heart rate accelerated when the restaurant door opened and Blair and Hugh entered. They paused as if debating whether to join Roland's table, then came over.

Hugh taught his Advanced Sonnets class at six on Mondays, which must be why they were eating early, Cindy thought as she offered them menus. They both requested the corned beef special.

Hugh had appeared tired again at the gym today, but now his eyes sparkled. "Catch a nap this afternoon?" Cindy asked.

"Yes. I had to recover from a late night," he said. She swallowed hard. He must have noticed her reaction, because he added, "They're running Camelot-themed films at midnight on campus this week in honor of the tournament. Sunday's feature was 'First Knight.'"

"It was wonderful." Blair angled her head fetchingly, her black hair falling in a sheer cascade. "But, Hugh, did you really sleep all afternoon? I hoped you were writing poetry."

"Not today," he said.

"You have written some poems recently, though. You told me so last night," she said. "Will you read them to me?"

"I don't have any with me." Hugh sounded ill at ease.

Cindy, on her way to post the new orders for Daffodil, didn't hear the rest of his remarks. It was only natural, she told herself, that Hugh's muse would work overtime now that he'd found true love. Still, she didn't want to listen to the two lovebirds bill and coo.

"Are those tears in your eyes?" Magda asked as Cindy fixed ice-cream sundaes for another table.

"I think I'm getting a cold," she said.

"Congratulations on getting back with Roland," her co-worker said. "He's a hunk! I just heard him tell his friends that you're going home together for Christmas. I'll sure miss you if that means you're leaving us, but I'm happy things are working out."

"Me, too," Cindy said, and tried not to sound miserable.

With the inexplicable ebb and flow of restaurant customers, business slowed down about five-fifteen, just when it usually picked up. Cindy was clearing away dishes when Mariah, Sadie and Esther—who walked with her usual pep again—sailed through the door.

"Champagne all around!" called Mariah as they plopped down at the table next to Roland's.

"We don't have a liquor license," Cindy said. "How about ginger ale?"

"Fine, if you put ice cream in it," said Sadie.

"And butterscotch syrup," added Esther.

After she served them, Cindy decided to take her break. Scooting in beside Esther, she said, "What happened this afternoon?"

Hugh came over and took the chair next to her. "Yes, please fill us in."

Blair half rose from her seat at the other table, but, catching a slight shake of the head from Hugh, sank down again. Roland peered meaningfully in Cindy's direction, but he, too, subsided when she waved him away.

"Here's the straight scoop." Mariah kept her voice low. "The truth about President Martin is…"

"He's having an affair with Vanessa Sachet!" Sadie said. "Isn't that rich?"

"They were never plotting against the Senior Center." Esther sounded almost disappointed.

"We think Vanessa wanted to get involved with us so she'd have an excuse for her whereabouts," Mariah explained. "Then she could slip across the parking lot and have a nooner right in his office."

"They've been doing it like rabbits," Sadie added. "We checked with the clerk at the Wind Song Motel on the other side of town and they've been there, too."

"Insatiable." Esther sniffed.

"Are you going to tell her husband?" Cindy asked.

Mariah regarded her indignantly. "Of course not! What kind of people do you think we are?"

"Congratulations," Hugh said. "I'm glad your center is safe."

"Now, what's this business about you and Blair?" asked Esther, removing a camera from her purse. Her two companions took out notebooks. "Don't tell me Hugh Bemling finally landed one of his fair ladies! How about posing for a picture?"

"And you, Cindy. Rumor has it that you've won Roland back," added Sadie. "How about a shot of the four of you?"

"I liked it better when you were worried about the center," Cindy said. "I don't know how Hugh feels, but leave me out of your gossip." She stood up.

"I'm opting for the sidelines, too." Hugh eased to his feet. "Besides, I've got a class to teach. See you all later." He raised his voice so those at Blair's table could hear, gave Cindy a wave, and walked out.

"That's too bad," Mariah said. "We thought you were our friends."

"If you want us to remain your friends, you'll stay out of our personal business." Pulling the order pad from her apron pocket, Cindy went to assist some new arrivals.

"I guess we've been told off," she heard Sadie say.

"She's right," came Mariah's voice. "We should mind our own business." Her friends squawked in dismay. "At least until this story plays itself out. I have a feeling it's not over yet."

Cindy refused to eavesdrop any further. Besides, she had customers.

HUGH CHEWED OVER ROLAND'S announcement that Cindy was going home with him for Christmas vacation.

Was she coming back afterward, or would she disappear like a dream into the mists of Minnesota?

He had trouble focusing on the lecture he'd planned for his sonnets class. Since the students composed as well as studied poems, he called on them to read their work aloud. He managed to pay enough attention to offer helpful critiques, and everyone seemed satisfied.

Except him.

On the walk home through the quiet streets of Clair De Lune, Hugh barely resisted the temptation to stop by the Lunch Box to see Cindy. Heck, he wanted to go hang around there until closing time, but no doubt he'd run into Blair and have to make conversation with her.

He'd never thought about what it would be like to date her. She'd been an image of beauty, fleeing far ahead of him. Now he felt like a dog that chases a car and doesn't know what to do with it when he catches it.

Of course he liked Blair. He kept hoping that, as time passed and they accumulated mutual experiences, they would slip into the kind of warm friendship he had with Cindy.

The funny thing was that he'd talked easily to Cindy even when he scarcely knew her. From a practical standpoint, he and Blair shared far more in common, since they both taught at the same university and knew many of the same people. Yet he found her boundless enthusiasm wearying and her questions naive.

What was wrong with him? No doubt he'd feel better after a few weeks away from campus. This year, he ought to go somewhere exciting for Christmas break. Like…Oofdah?

Lost in thought, Hugh mounted the steps to his apartment. At the sight of someone sitting on the top landing, his heart skipped a beat, until he remembered that Cindy was still at work.

Blair stood up, chafing her hands together. She wore only a light sweater, although the nighttime temperatures had dropped into the fifties. "Hi! I've never seen your place, and I thought you might enjoy some company after class."

Feeling crowded, he nodded abruptly and unlocked the door. "No midnight movie tonight, though. They're wearing me out."

"That's okay. The next offering is *Camelot* and I've seen it umpteen times." Following him inside, Blair surveyed the room in fascination. "This is amazing. Where'd you get all this stuff?"

"From the previous tenant." He fetched a bottle of wine. "Care for some?"

"Sure."

He poured zinfandel into a pair of plastic cups and handed her one. Sipping, Blair wandered to the fertility goddess. "This is quite a conversation piece."

"The former owners told me she has mystical powers," he said.

"No way!" Blair laughed. "It's a reproduction, made for tourists."

Hugh could have sworn the statue's eyes narrowed and its mouth tightened. Impossible, of course, yet he'd begun to believe he sensed the statue's moods. "Be careful what you say. You don't want to hurt her feelings."

"That's sweet!" Blair turned toward him. "You're so poetic, you invest human characteristics into inanimate objects."

The goddess scowled, startling Hugh. Then he realized that a shopkeeper across the street had turned off a lighted sign and cast a shadow across the statue.

"The real reason I came over was to hear your poems," Blair went on. "Please tell me you brought them home!"

In fact, he had. In his office earlier, Hugh had accidentally stuffed them into his briefcase along with some of his students' sonnets. "I'm afraid they're not about you."

She gazed at him uncertainly. "Is there someone else?"

"I mean, they're not love poems." He didn't want to upset Blair, Hugh realized with a rush of guilt. "They're about impersonal subjects."

"I'd like to hear them." She bounced onto the wicker settee. "Come on." She patted the cushion beside her.

He pulled two scribbled sheets from his briefcase and joined her. The orange spice of her perfume tickled his nose.

"The first one's about music," he said. "You remember, the singing on Thanksgiving."

"Go ahead," Blair urged.

He began. "On the windy wings of a winter day, Cindy sings the chill away..." After he finished, Blair sat with her head tilted thoughtfully and her lips pressed together.

"Do you want to hear the other one?" he asked. "It's about exercising."

"Now there's a novel idea for a poem." She smiled tremulously. What a beautiful mouth she had, Hugh thought, yet he felt no impulse to kiss her. "Sure."

"Here goes," he said. "We thud. We groan..." This one, too, mentioned Cindy, he found. The last lines came out with more forcefulness than he'd intended. "I will make her proud, though I may not do it soon. I will defy gravity. I will fly to the moon."

A long silence stretched between them. Finally Blair said, "Oh, Hugh," in a wistful tone.

"Are they that bad?" He'd believed he was improving. "Maybe I should go back to writing love poems."

"Those *are* love poems, and they're wonderful," Blair said. "They're love poems to Cindy."

"No..." He stopped because he couldn't muster an argument. Now that Blair had mentioned it, he saw that the poems *were* about Cindy. She inspired him in so many ways. "I mean, she's my friend."

"She's more than that," Blair said. "The truth shines in your poetry, and on your face, too."

Was it possible?

Cindy. Images came to him of her laughing as they worked out at the gym, taking charge of the Thanksgiving dinner like a general with her troops, dancing in his arms right here in this apartment. Why hadn't he seen it before?

Yes, he loved her, Hugh acknowledged with a great sigh of relief. It was not only possible, but inescapable. All his life, he'd sought a great love that would sustain him through joy and sorrow. Spurred by the images of King Arthur's court, he'd pursued a holy grail, an ideal maiden, in the mistaken belief that only perfection could bring him happiness.

Instead he'd found the most wonderful woman in the world when he wasn't looking. Before, he'd been in love with the idea of love. Now he knew what love truly was: perspiring together, chopping onions side by side, being inspired not by her beauty but by her soul.

Yet he had to face facts. "She's going to marry Roland. That's what she's always wanted. So I suppose you and I can stay together, if you like."

In Blair's eyes he saw sadness and a glint of appreciation. "I like you, Hugh, but I have to accept that it isn't reciprocal. You wanted me when I was out of reach, but in the meantime, you fell in love with Cindy. I don't blame you. She's a special person."

Impulsively he hugged her, as a brother would a sister. She felt too thin. "You're a good sport."

"Fortunately I'm not in love, just very attracted to you," Blair said. "And you know what? I don't think Cindy's in love with Roland, either. Maybe she used to be, but it's gone now. She found someone who's more of a soul mate, and that's you."

Hugh wanted to believe her. But in the past few days, he hadn't observed anything in Cindy's behavior that would indicate she awaited his return with open arms.

"You'll have to decide for yourself what to do, but don't wait too long." Blair stood up. "I won't be dropping by again, but maybe I'll see you at the tournament." At the door, she added, "It would be fun if you decided to participate. You know what? You'd make a cute troubador."

"I can't sing," Hugh said.

"Whatever." Blair smiled. "See you around, Hugh."

"I'm sorry I can't love you," he said.

She shrugged. "I'll be all right." Out she went, the woman of his dreams brought down to earth.

Hugh genuinely did feel sorry. A little irked, too, though. A troubador! Maybe the role would have fit him a month ago, when he'd been clumsy and physically weak, but not anymore.

He wanted to joust, not for his ego's sake, but to defeat Roland. Sure, he might suffer a few bruises and a squashed ego, but he'd been willing to suffer humiliation for Blair's sake. How much more would he not be willing to risk to prove himself worthy of Cindy?

Of course, muscles had nothing to do with masculine worth, his intellect warned. And defeating Roland might simply send Cindy rushing to her fiancé's side, anguished with worry. Maybe she wouldn't want him to fight the man she loved.

Undecided, Hugh glanced at the fertility goddess. Just then, car lights brushed through the window as a vehicle turned from a side street onto De Lune Boulevard. He could have sworn in that moment that the statue winked at him.

Go for it.

Yes! He loved Cindy, and he was going to make her see that she loved him, too. Even if he ended up getting trampled into the grass of the De Lune University athletic field.

There remained a few obstacles, Hugh conceded. He lacked a suit of armor, a lance and a pony, and the skills to use them.

Hugh's first instinct was to ask Cindy for advice, but she wasn't available. Instead he decided to turn to the next most resourceful person he knew: Jared Benton.

13

"THE BLACK KNIGHT," JARED said. "That's who you'll be."

It was Tuesday, and they were eating lunch at the Faculty Center. Along one side of the large glass-walled room, a cafeteria line dispensed salads, soups, sandwiches and hot entrées. Hugh tried not to think about that night—was it only last Friday?—when he and Cindy had danced here together, blissfully unaware that fate disguised as Roland and Blair was about to separate them.

"You mean I should keep my identity a mystery until the end?" he said.

"Exactly," Jared said. "It makes the whole thing more exciting. Plus there's the added advantage that if you make a fool of yourself, no one will know who you are."

"Cindy will know." Hugh swirled a spoon through his lobster bisque. "She'd recognize me even in a helmet and armor." Thoughtfully he added, "And I'd recognize her even in a space suit."

"You two are amazing." Was that envy on Jared's face? "There's a cosmic connection between you. I hope she wakes up before it's too late."

"So do I," Hugh said.

A female professor from the Medieval Studies department paused on her way past to drop a tan-and-black scarf on their table. "Coming to the tournament on Saturday?'' she asked Jared. ''I'd love for you to wear my colors.''

''I wouldn't miss it, Kerry.'' Giving her his trademark lopsided smile, he wrapped the scarf around his neck. She floated away, her expression blissful.

''You should know about cosmic connections,'' Hugh said.

''Me?'' His friend shook his head. ''I've never experienced that sense of being meant for one another. There was only one woman who came close, but that was long ago, and I lost her. Drove her away, as a matter of fact.''

''You should try to find her again,'' Hugh said.

Jared shrugged. ''What's done is done. Now, getting back to your case, I can scrounge a suit of costume armor from the theater wardrobe. Kerry will know where the other participants are getting their lances, since she's one of the faculty sponsors. As for combat, I can teach you that. It's part of our theater training. What else are we missing?''

''My kingdom for a horse,'' said Hugh.

Jared snapped his fingers. ''A pony! No problem. Kerry owns a stable outside town. She's renting them to the students and she'll rent you one, too, if she's got any left.''

''That would be very gracious of her,'' Hugh said.

''I'm free after lunch,'' Jared said. ''Let's go talk to her. If she doesn't have a class, I'll bet she'll invite us over right now.''

It would mean missing his regular one o'clock gym date with Cindy. Since she probably had Roland joining her, however, he doubted she'd mind. Besides, he had only a few days to get ready for Saturday's event. ''Thanks. I'd like that.''

''Nothing to it,'' said Jared.

CINDY HOPED HUGH WOULD find her and Roland on the volleyball court. At first, she kept checking the door for him, but after missing an easy shot, she forced herself to focus on the game.

The two of them played on opposite sides, by choice. As usually happened when they competed, the session became a challenge just between them. Although the other players operated smoothly, they were no match for Roland's gung-ho vigor and Cindy's fierce opposition.

For a while, she forgot about everything except slamming the ball where Roland couldn't get it. Her teammates, invigorated by the competition, cheered loudly whenever she scored. Unfortunately she stumbled during a crucial volley, and Roland's side noisily trumpeted their victory.

"Good game," she said, coming around to shake hands with him.

"Too bad Hugh didn't make it." He pumped her arm. "Although since we had enough players, I don't know how we'd have fit him in."

They only had enough players because Roland was horning in on her exercise sessions, Cindy thought rebelliously, and then wondered what had gotten into her. She loved playing opposite Roland. Usually when she lost, she couldn't wait for a rematch, but now she hardly cared. Without Hugh, she felt as if she were going through the motions.

Most of the players were women, and they clustered around Roland. He *was* handsome, and affable, too, yet Cindy experienced neither pride nor jealousy. He seemed more like Blair's boyfriend than her own.

Troubled, she excused herself and went to clean up. What was going on? Partly, she supposed, she didn't have the same faith in the bond between them, now that

Roland had broken it. Also, it was hard to relish his company when she kept wondering what had happened to Hugh.

Hugh belonged to someone else, she told herself sternly. End of story.

In the lobby, Cindy declined Roland's offer to come watch him practice for the joust. Although she could have spared an hour or two before work, she suspected the tournament would be more exciting if she didn't see too much of the preparations.

"Did Hugh leave any messages?" she asked Brad at the front desk.

"Let me see." He flipped through some papers. "Oh, yeah. He called to say he's tied up and will be all week."

"That's it?" Cindy asked. "No explanation?"

"Sorry." The young man glanced past her. "Hi, Grandma. I've got my report ready."

"Thanks." Sadie Wilkerson took the envelope he handed her, then gave a guilty start on spotting Cindy. "Oh, hi, there."

"Is that gossip about Roland and me?" she demanded.

Sadie glanced at the envelope, then back to Cindy. "Uh," she said.

Cindy extended her hand, palm up. Sadie put the envelope in it, and Cindy tore it to shreds. "No more of that!"

Brad flushed bright red and retreated to the other side of the desk. "You're right," Sadie said. "We shouldn't spy on our friends. I'm sorry."

"No hard feelings, as long as you behave yourself." The old Snooper was too endearing for Cindy to stay mad at her.

She and Sadie walked out of the gym together. A tow truck whipped by them and pulled into the parking lot of the Venus Motor Inn, across the street. "Don't you love the name of that motel?" Sadie said, getting out of the car.

"I'm sure you have a spy on the staff," Cindy said.

"Naturally." The red-haired woman stiffened to attention like a hunting dog. "We may not need one today. Look!"

Shading her eyes against the afternoon sun, Cindy spotted a well-dressed woman gesturing irritably as the tow truck driver examined an expensive foreign sedan. "That's Vanessa Sachet."

"Ten to one she's not alone." Excitement bubbled in Sadie's voice. "You don't happen to have a camera, do you?"

"Sorry." Cindy was about to get into her car when Sadie grabbed her arm.

"You won't believe what just happened! Nina LaPonz just spotted Vanessa and pulled in. Nina used to be Lynn Sachet's good friend, and I don't think she'd mind getting the dirt on that husband-stealing witch. Don't make me watch this alone!" Sadie said. "I'll burst if I can't share it with someone. Besides, I might need a corroborating witness."

Cindy wasn't keen on turning other people's lives into her personal entertainment. However, she'd never forgive herself if Sadie, who must be around eighty, got overstimulated and suffered a heart attack.

As Cindy returned her attention to the motel, Vanessa was talking rapidly to a skeptical-looking woman of about fifty. The tow truck driver, unconcerned, proceeded to attach hooks to the back of the sedan.

From the hotel office strolled a very satisfied President Wilson Martin. Apparently he hadn't checked himself in the mirror, because even from across the street, Cindy could see that his tie was crooked and he had a lipstick smear near one temple.

Time froze as his gaze met that of Nina LaPonz. Vanessa stopped talking in midgesture and simply stood there with her hands in the air.

"I'm going to die," Sadie announced. "To think that I, Sadie Wilkerson, of all the Snoopers, should be present at this moment.... Well, nothing can ever top this. I might as well die now."

"Please don't," Cindy said.

After turning her back on the adulterous couple, Nina LaPonz got in her car and drove off. As she merged into traffic, Cindy saw her dialing her cell phone.

"She's not wasting any time," Sadie said. "You don't suppose Bill Sachet will forgive Vanessa, do you?"

"He cheated on his first wife, so he ought to sympathize," Cindy said. "Still, I've noticed that people don't generally like getting a taste of their own medicine."

Sadie squeezed her hand. There were tears in the old woman's eyes. "I'm glad you were here to share this moment with me. It's been my dream to outscoop the other Snoopers. I can't tell you how much this means!"

"Congratulations," Cindy said.

Sadie held on to her hand. "Because I like you, let me give you a bit of advice. That fellow Roland is a real hunk, but I like Hugh better."

"So do I," Cindy said without thinking. Corrective phrases popped into her mind—*I didn't mean it, we're just friends, Roland and I suit each other despite our differences*—but none of them survived as far as her tongue.

"Don't worry, I won't tell anyone," Sadie said. "But remember an old piece of advice— Change partners and dance."

"We already did that," Cindy said. "Thanks all the same. Want a ride?"

"You bet!"

She dropped Sadie off at the Senior Center and drove on. There was only one conclusion to be reached, even if it shook her view of the world: If she liked Hugh better, then she shouldn't marry Roland.

Cindy still felt tremendous affection for her old buddy. If she'd never come to Clair De Lune and they'd gone ahead with their plans—her plans—for the wedding, she thought they could have been happy. But events since then had changed her too much.

For the first time in her life, she didn't know what the future held. She didn't even know how she felt about Hugh, except warm and cuddly and passionate. Or whether she should go back to Oofdah, where everything and everyone reminded her of Roland and her old self.

She had a lot to think about.

BY THURSDAY, HUGH COULD stay on his black pony, Ebenezer, while holding the reins in one hand and a lance in the other, as long as his steed didn't go faster than an amble. Wearing a cardboard practice helmet complicated matters, as it muffled his hearing, made his forehead break out in a sweat and gave him the sensation of peering through goggles underwater.

"You're doing great!" said Jared, who'd dropped by to check his progress. "How about a match? I found some cardboard tubes we can use for practice lances."

"I'm game." Breathing deeply, Hugh sniffed one of those unpleasant fragrances frequently met in a paddock. He ignored it. A knight of the Round Table was above such things.

"Be careful," warned Kerry, who had cheerfully

agreed to rent Hugh a pony and supervise his riding. "I don't want to haul anybody off to the hospital."

"We will," Hugh promised. "But I need the practice. I've only got two more days."

"Good luck." She climbed outside the paddock and leaned on the fence, watching.

A short time later, Jared rode in on a shaggy pony about the same size as Ebenezer. The tall man made a goofy figure with his knees tucked up. "I'm sure glad I don't have to ride out in front of the whole school looking like one of the Three Stooges."

"Thanks for the encouragement."

"Don't worry. You won't be as ridiculous as Roland because you're shorter," Jared said. "Remember, hold the lance under your right armpit and aim it over the left side of the saddle."

"Aren't I supposed to have a shield?" Hugh asked.

"You think you're ready to try riding with something in both hands?" asked his friend.

Hugh had his answer ready. "I'm going to be the Black Knight. When I enter the tournament grounds, I want to look powerful and in control, even if I fall on my butt five minutes later. That means no compromises."

"Shields it is. There's a good one with your costume, but for today, we'll use the makeshift variety. Kerry?"

"I'll get them." She returned a moment later and handed them each a cardboard lance and a large cardboard square to use as a shield. Hugh's had Miracle Toilet Tissue printed on the side in large black letters.

He supposed he could use a miracle, even if it came from a packing box.

Following Jared's example, he gripped the square by a plastic handle glued to its center. In his right hand, he wielded the lance, which on closer inspection proved to be several long paper towel tubes taped together.

The two men faced off from opposite sides of the enclosure. Kerry waved a kerchief and let it drop onto her lap.

At the signal, the two men charged forward. Or rather, they kneed their ponies, spurring them to a burrolike saunter.

When they came abreast, Jared thrust his lance around the back of Hugh's wobbling shield and poked him in the shoulder. With a pop, the end of the tube collapsed and dangled uselessly.

At the same time, Hugh found himself a couple of hands short to manipulate reins and armaments. He dropped the shield, pitched forward onto the pony's neck and flailed wildly with his lance, trying to land a glancing blow on his opponent.

Hysterical laughter greeted the two men as their mounts moseyed past each other. Kerry was hanging on to the fence, shaking with merriment.

"The point is not that we were ridiculous," Jared called to her. "The point is, who won?"

"You did." Hugh refused to fool himself. "You landed a blow, however pathetic."

"At least you didn't fall off," his friend said.

"That's a good sign," Hugh agreed.

He'd enjoyed the mock battle, even though he hadn't acquitted himself very well. As he dismounted, he reflected that Saturday might not be so dreadful after all, if he were only participating for the fun of it.

But he wasn't. In two days' time, he was going to risk his pride and possibly his neck to win the woman he loved. None of that mattered.

What did matter was that he might lose Cindy, lose

her forever. Not because he would fail as a knight, but because her heart belonged to Roland. Maybe his mission was doomed before it began.

Yet he had to give it his all. Faint heart ne'er won fair lady, and this was the most important lady in the world.

Hugh drew himself up proudly, ignoring the twinges in his back and legs. Nothing was going to stop him, not fear, not sore muscles, not even common sense. He loved Cindy, and he was going to give her every possible reason to love him back.

ON FRIDAY AFTERNOON as Cindy returned from the supermarket, Mrs. Zimpelman stopped her outside the apartment. "Bill Sachet went to see his lawyer this morning," she announced gleefully.

"I'm afraid to ask how you know that," Cindy said, balancing a sack of groceries on one hip.

"His lawyer is Burt Page at Page, Bittner and Steele," Esther said. "In the lobby of their office building there's a flower stand, and the woman who works there…"

"Also works for the Snoopers," Cindy finished.

Her neighbor beamed.

A loud whistling approached along the sidewalk. Cindy didn't have to check to know who it was. Who else in Clair De Lune would whistle, "Hail! Minnesota"?

"Can I carry that bag for you?" asked Roland, his swinging stride coming to a halt.

"Sure." Cindy handed it to him.

Roland, astonished, barely gripped it in time to avoid a spill. It was probably the first time Cindy had ever taken him up on such an offer, she realized. After a lifetime of dogged independence, she'd become accustomed to Hugh's insistence on being a gentleman.

"Sadie says we're not allowed to snoop on the two of

you,'' Esther said. "So I'm going to go home now. Unless there's anything you want to tell me?" She peered toward them wistfully. "Could there be a little velvet box in your pocket, Roland? Planning any shopping expeditions to, say, a jewelry store?"

"See you later," said Cindy, and led the way upstairs. Disappointed, Esther made her way home.

Roland carried the groceries into the kitchen and began pawing through the bag. "What are we having for supper? Hey, great, pickled herring!" He popped off the lid and rummaged in the silverware drawer.

As Cindy watched him, emotions played tug-of-war in her chest. Affection for her longtime friend battled with irritation at his assumption that she'd bought the groceries for him. Fondness toward this roughly handsome, buoyant soul mingled with disappointment that she had no desire to throw her arms around him.

She had to tell Roland the truth. Otherwise, he might make some public statement about their relationship at the tournament tomorrow.

"We need to talk," Cindy said.

Roland paused with a chunk of herring halfway to his mouth. "Is it my imagination or did the air in here just get chillier?" At her puzzled expression, he said, "Hey, even a ruffian like me knows it isn't good when a woman says we have to talk." He popped the fish into his mouth and put the jar in the refrigerator. "Did I do something wrong?" he mumbled through his mouthful.

"No, of course not." Cindy sat on the couch, the one Hugh had clonked himself on the first night they met. Roland scooted in beside her and stretched out his long legs.

"Well?" he said.

"In that e-mail you sent..."

He groaned. "Don't remind me."

"In that e-mail, you weren't entirely wrong." Cindy discovered it was easier to talk if she didn't meet his eyes. "We're great buddies, but we're not in love."

"I knew I wasn't going to like this," Roland said. "Are you punishing me?"

"What?" Cindy stared at him, aghast. "Do you think I'm that mean? Or that stupid? If I loved a man, I'd never purposely push him away."

Puppy-dog sadness rounded Roland's eyes. "If you keep talking like this, you'll have me believing you mean it."

"I do mean it." A sense of unreality settled over Cindy at the realization that she was rejecting the man she'd always assumed would be her husband. But she had to clarify where they stood. "I don't have the same feelings for you that I used to."

"Because of the way I treated you?" he asked. "I wouldn't blame you."

"How can you be so reasonable?" she burst out.

"Because I understand you." Roland laid one arm along the back of the couch, brushing her shoulders. "Now that the pressure's off, now that I've come back, you're having a delayed reaction. I deserve to be chewed out, so I don't mind. You're still upset about Blair, with good reason. Give it time, Cinders, and we'll be as good as ever."

"No," she said miserably, "we won't."

She didn't mention Hugh, because she had no right to. He loved Blair, and Cindy would never do or say anything that might reach her ears and cause problems. She certainly didn't want to give Roland the impression—which he might mention to his friends—that she and Hugh had anything going on between them.

Yet she missed him terribly. She missed his valiant attempts at writing poetry, and his thoughtfulness, and the tender way he regarded her. She didn't dare allow herself to think too far along those lines or she might start to cry.

"Don't give up, Cindy," Roland said. "We just need to spend more time together."

"I think I'll catch the first flight back to Oofdah," she said. "Maybe when I get home, things will start to make sense."

"You can't leave yet!" Roland gave her shoulders a playful squeeze. "Tomorrow's my big day! You've got to come watch me defend my honor."

"You mean defend the princess's honor," Cindy said. "And no, I'm not jealous of Blair. Okay, I'll stay. One more day won't make any difference."

Roland grinned. "You're going to love seeing me bounce around on that pony fighting challengers. I wouldn't be surprised if you pushed me off and fought a few matches in my stead."

The prospect of pushing Roland off a pony did have a certain appeal. Cindy couldn't resist smiling back. "I'll be there, I promise."

"Great!" Roland said. "Now why don't we see if there's a game on TV?"

"Why not?" agreed Cindy, and handed him the remote control.

She wondered if Hugh planned to attend the tournament. At one point, he'd talked about wanting to compete, but she hadn't seen him at the practices when she'd dropped by and he'd even stopped exercising at the gym.

Still, he would probably come with Blair. Cindy looked forward to seeing him there one last time, even if it broke her heart.

14

HUGH DONNED HIS ERSATZ armor in a dressing room behind the campus stage. Although the theater department was located some distance from the athletic field, he could hear music and crowd noises as people arrived for the big day.

They'd tied the pony earlier inside the theater's scene shop, providing it with food and water and positioning it atop burlap bags in case nature called. A costumer, whom they'd let in on the secret, had stitched up a black-and-scarlet blanket and trimmed Ebenezer's reins to match.

As Hugh dressed, he checked himself in a lighted full-length mirror. Black plastic plates, discreetly sewn to stretch fabric, formed a protective tunic and leggings. Black gauntlets and boots, along with a plumed helmet, completed the realistic but lightweight outfit.

The aluminum sword hanging at his side made walking a bit awkward, but otherwise he could move about easily in the garment, Hugh found. However, there was an unforeseen complication: He couldn't wear his glasses under the helmet, which fit more tightly than its cardboard practice equivalent.

Jared poked his head through the door. "How's it going?"

"I can't see," Hugh said.

"You can lift the visor. It snaps into place," his friend advised.

"I mean, I can't wear my glasses under here," Hugh explained.

Jared started to chuckle, then coughed to cover it. "How nearsighted are you?"

They were standing about five feet apart. "I could identify you by your general shape and the sound of your voice," Hugh said. "Your features are a complete blur."

He stopped, not wanting to sound negative, yet he couldn't help picturing the expanse of the athletic field. He'd been prepared for the embarrassment of getting knocked off his horse, but what if he mistakenly attacked a food booth and made himself a laughingstock?

"I'll put on a costume and guide you out there," Jared said. "Once you're pointed at Roland, you shouldn't have a problem. He's too big to miss."

"Fine." Hugh swallowed his incipient panic. He refused to withdraw. However, as a precaution, he slipped his glasses down the front of the tunic. The stretch fabric held them snugly in place, along with another small item he'd tucked there earlier.

A short time later, Jared returned wearing a red velvet tunic and black tights, with a cocked hat perched atop his thick hair. Despite the black-and-tan scarf around his neck, which he'd promised Kerry to wear, he sported the getup with the panache of a courtier. "This was from last year's production of *Romeo and Juliet,* so I won't break the medieval spell when I escort you."

"I'm impressed," Hugh said.

Jared spoiled the image by producing a cell phone from a hidden pocket. "Kerry's going to call us when the early bouts are over. If you're to be the mystery challenger, we've got to keep you hidden till the last minute."

"Just make sure we don't wait too long." Hugh did

his best to ignore the quivering in his knees. There was no shame in experiencing fear, only in yielding to it, and he wasn't going to.

ALTHOUGH SHE'D BEEN HEARING about the tournament for weeks and had watched a couple of practice sessions, Cindy hadn't grasped what a major production it was until she arrived on campus shortly before the 2:00 p.m. start time. From the parking lot, she could hear recorded music booming from speakers.

In the crisp breeze, banners flew from poles around the athletic field and bunches of balloons swayed wildly, she saw as she approached. Heralds and pages trotted to and fro like medieval cheerleaders, while even the campus security guards sported cavalier-style hats.

The bleachers were jammed. She wished she'd arrived earlier, but she'd been busy packing and making a plane reservation for the following day.

At the head of the field, a temporary stand provided seats for faculty members, tournament organizers and, of course, Princess Blair. Sunrays picked out her lovely face and exquisite golden gown. The circlet of flowers around her black hair added a fairy-tale note.

Although she'd kept an empty seat beside her, presumably for Hugh, Cindy didn't see him. She scanned the field, where half a dozen males in fake armor were cavorting on ponies, but saw no sign of him.

She did spot Roland. If Vikings had fought tournaments, they must have looked like this, although probably better mounted. Wearing a gold scarf to match Blair's dress and carrying a helmet tucked under his arm, he urged his tiny steed up and down the length of the field, reveling in the appreciation of the crowd.

What great fun, Cindy thought. Normally she would

have been out there riding, too, but right now she was more concerned about where Hugh had gone. And, also, where she could find a seat.

"Cindy! Cindy! Over here!" An amplified female voice drew her attention to the princess's stand. Blair, holding a battery-operated megaphone, pointed toward the empty chair.

Cindy hurried to join her. "You saved this for me? How thoughtful!"

"You really should be the princess, because you're the one Roland loves," Blair said. "Anyway, I'd enjoy your company."

Sitting next to the radiant princess, Cindy was glad she'd worn her new rose-colored blouse and skirt. Although jeans were the *mode du jour* among most of the crowd, they didn't suit someone seated beside the princess.

"There's something you should know about Hugh," Blair said, leaning toward her, "although I'm not sure I should be the one to tell you."

Was this "something" the news that they were engaged? A wave of dizziness swept over Cindy. She was grateful when the blare of a trumpet cut off any further attempt at conversation.

On the far end of the field, a trio of costumed heralds blew a salute. The competitors, led by Roland, circled the field, hoisting their lances and grinning as the watchers roared.

Scanning the bleachers, Cindy spotted familiar faces: Esther, Hosea, Runcie, Sadie and Mariah, cheering and snapping pictures. Catching Cindy's eye, Sadie waved, and she waved back.

Directly in front of the princess, the bright-hued pageant halted as the men bowed. There was, Cindy saw, one woman participating, her grin so wide it nearly split her face.

Blair got to her feet and spoke into her megaphone. "My champion, Sir Roland Greenwald, issues a challenge to one and all to joust for my hand. I declare the tournament open!" She sat down. "How did I do?" she asked Cindy.

"Splendid," she said.

One of the knights signaled his intent to challenge, and the battle began. One after another, Roland defeated them all. Key moments stood out: one man split his pants, the woman blew a kiss at Roland after being unhorsed, another contestant's pony refused to charge and bent to chomp the grass, sending its rider into a quick slide to the ground.

The sunlight, the blare of the trumpets, the rich hues and the drama of knight-to-knight clashes thrilled Cindy. Yet she couldn't stop seeking a glimpse of Hugh on the bleachers or among the costumed pages. How could he miss an event like this?

After a month in which they'd spent time together almost every day, they'd been apart most of the week. It seemed unnatural. Could she really go back to Oofdah and never see him again?

Cindy's chest tightened. This was all wrong. She loved Hugh with a depth that astonished her. How could he possibly not love her, too?

She had to see him, had to find him, this very instant. "I'm sorry," she told Blair. "I need to go."

"Wait!" The princess pointed toward the far end of the field. "Who on earth is that?"

The object of her astonishment sat astride an ebony pony, his armor gleaming black and a scarlet plume fluttering bravely atop his helmet. Beside him strode a page in scarlet and black, who spoke through his own hand-held megaphone.

"The Black Knight challenges Sir Roland for the hand of the woman he loves!" the page announced in a deep, dramatic voice.

Cindy would have recognized the knight anywhere. The straight posture, the determined tilt of the head and that lean body belonged unmistakably to Hugh.

She glanced at Blair, but saw by her confused expression that she failed to recognize him. How ironic that Hugh had come to claim the woman he loved, and she didn't know it was him.

Cindy supposed she ought to slip away rather than risk crying and spoiling Hugh and Blair's big moment. Yet she couldn't move.

She didn't want to miss her last chance to watch Hugh's wonderful romanticism, perhaps to hear him read a new poem written for Blair and watch his pleasure at finally being loved back. She wanted to store up the memories, because if Hugh was happy, that was good enough for Cindy.

Her heart went out to him as he squared off against Roland. Even in armor, Hugh was a slender figure compared to his burly opponent.

"I still can't figure out who it is," Blair said. "Can you?"

"It's Hugh," Cindy said.

Blair frowned. "You're kidding." She stared harder. "Yikes, you're right! Won't he get hurt?"

Cindy had the same concern, but she understood why he was doing this. "A true romantic never lets danger stand in his way."

"I hope he wins," said her companion.

"I do, too."

So far, no one had survived more than one round against Roland. His natural strength, coupled with years of athleticism, had dominated easily. With only a month of exercise, Hugh didn't have a chance.

Except for one thing. Even at this distance, Cindy could feel his fierce determination. For him, unlike the others, this was not a game.

The trumpeter sounded the challenge. Blair raised her scarf and dropped it.

Seeing the signal to begin, Roland kicked his pony into a charge. For an alarming split second, Hugh didn't respond. Then his page shouted, "Go!" and he did.

The crowd fell silent. In the stillness, Cindy's heartbeat sounded, to her, like drumbeats.

The men rode toward each other, lances pointed. Although Roland was bigger, Hugh's pony stood slightly taller, leveling their heights. The slender man leaned forward, his entire energy focused as he braced for impact.

At the last minute, a banner tore loose from its mooring and whipped toward Roland. His pony shied, nearly throwing him, and Hugh thudded past.

Roland regained his seat, and the riders circled each other warily. Abruptly, Roland shifted direction and rode back to his original position in front of the stand, preparing for a second charge. His pony sidestepped nervously, apparently still agitated from the flapping banner, but Roland managed to quiet it.

Across the field, Hugh sat in bewilderment, aiming his lance in first one direction and then another. What was wrong with him? As mutters ran through the crowd, the scarlet page attempted to trot toward him, but was stopped by a security guard.

At any minute, Roland would thunder toward the

Black Knight and catch him unprepared. "He can't see!" Cindy said as the truth hit her.

"Why not?" Blair asked.

"He doesn't have his glasses on! He can't see Roland because, where he's positioned, he blends into the background."

"Oh, my gosh." Blair's hands fluttered in agitation. "We can't interfere. Everyone would think we were cheating."

"I've got an idea! Give me the megaphone." Taking it, Cindy tilted back her head and sang out the first line of "The Star-Spangled Banner."

"Oh, say can you see?" The words echoed across the field before halting abruptly. She hoped people would figure she was just fooling around.

Please let Hugh realize I'm cueing him! That I know he can't see, and that he should use my location as a guide.

It took a moment for comprehension to dawn. Then Hugh turned his pony toward the stand and charged, flinging himself with blind trust toward the sound of her voice.

Roland was already underway, and the two men met in midfield. Despite the lightness of their lances, the impact against their shields threw Hugh to the ground and pushed Roland off-center. It also proved the last straw for his pony, which executed a rodeo-worthy buck and dumped its rider to the turf.

"Is anyone injured?" Blair asked, rising.

Since both men were staggering to their feet, evidently there'd been no serious damage. "Don't hurt Hugh's pride by fussing over him in public," Cindy said.

"I wasn't going to." Blair sat down.

Hugh and Roland drew their swords and faced off.

This time, it was Hugh who attacked first, with such suddenness that he caught his opponent off guard. He followed his initial thrust with a series of blows that sent Roland stumbling backward.

The larger man fell to his knees. He tried to get up, but Hugh was battering his helmet with such zeal that Roland apparently couldn't collect his wits. "I yield!" he called, self-disgust evident in his voice. "Hey, cut it out! I said, I yield!"

The Black Knight sheathed his sword and approached the stands where Blair and Cindy sat. "Unmask yourself," Blair commanded.

He tugged at his helmet. When it came off, sunlight bathed the triumphant challenger as if to amplify the glory of his victory.

Gasps of recognition ran through the audience, followed by applause. "Hurray for Professor Bemling!" shouted a female voice. "Way to go, Bemling!" yelled a man.

From beneath his costume, Hugh produced his glasses. After fumbling briefly, he put them on and approached the stand.

Cindy's euphoria vanished. In front of students and faculty, he was going to declare himself to Blair. This must be what the young woman had tried to warn her about.

It was impossible to flee without making a scene. Cindy held herself very still and waited.

"Here." Blair tossed her megaphone down to Hugh, who caught it deftly.

"I'd like to read a poem," he said.

A few giggles in the bleachers were quickly shushed. "You tell 'em, professor!" a young man called.

Hugh peered upward. Cindy could have sworn he was

staring at her, not at Blair, but she knew that must be
wishful thinking on her part.

Squaring his shoulders, Hugh began to read.

"I played at love until I met the one
Destined to bring me from shadows into sun."

Thank goodness he'd found his inspiration again,
Cindy thought, her eyes stinging. She had to give Blair
credit for that.

"Friends and allies, we grew closer day by day
And yet I nearly let her slip away."

Cindy wondered when Hugh had come to see Blair as
his friend and ally. And given his dogged pursuit, how
could he believe he'd nearly let her slip away?

In the hush that had fallen over the field, he dropped
to one knee and removed a jeweler's box from inside his
costume. When he opened it, the sun sparkled off a diamond ring.

Cindy didn't think she could bear to listen to the rest
of the poem. But she'd never broken down in public before and she wasn't going to start now.

"With a heart full of joy, I make my plea." Hugh
caught her gaze. Why was he doing that? Why didn't he
look at Blair? "Cindy McChad, will you marry me?"

A roaring sound filled her ears. She must have imagined that he'd proposed to her. If she responded, she
would embarrass herself and everyone else.

Blair poked her in the side. "Say yes!"

From one section of the bleachers, a reedy voice began
to chant, "Cindy! Cindy!" She recognized the culprit. It
was Runcie.

Soon everyone joined in. "Cindy! Cindy!"

"You'd better answer him before they get rowdy," Blair persisted.

Below, Hugh remained kneeling. His upturned face brimmed with hope and uncertainty.

Cindy signaled for quiet, and the audience desisted. "Yes." She cupped her hands around her mouth and shouted, "Absolutely."

A cheer shook the bleachers. The scarlet page on the far side of the field raised his clasped hands in a gesture of victory. Hugh got to his feet and climbed up to her, holding out the ring.

Scarcely daring to breathe, Cindy extended her left hand and let him slide it onto her finger. It was the most beautiful thing she'd ever seen. "I love you," she said.

"I love you, too," said Hugh. He smelled of fresh exertion, grass and a touch of pony. It was an exhilarating combination.

Then he did something magical. He bent over and kissed her. Inside Cindy, a thousand balloons broke from their ties and soared into the sky.

Their blissful contact broke as lights flashed in her face. "What the—?" Another flash went off. When the spots began to clear from her vision, she recognized Esther behind the camera.

Sadie was snapping pictures, too, while Runcie held out a tape recorder. "Care to comment?" he asked.

"You people are incurable," Cindy said. "And you're all invited to our wedding."

HALF AN HOUR LATER, after the crowd had dispersed and the Snoopers had gone home, Cindy finally got a chance to talk to Roland. She'd forgotten about him during the proposal, but of course, he'd witnessed the whole thing.

"I hope you're not upset," she said while Hugh went to change clothes, after promising to meet her later. "I did tell you last night that I didn't love you."

"You didn't say you were in love with someone else." Roland's dear, familiar face regarded her ruefully.

"That's because I thought he was in love with Blair," Cindy said.

They walked toward the sidelines with Roland's pony trailing behind. "I've learned my lesson," he said. "If I ever find the right woman again, I'm going to buy her a ring before somebody else beats me to it."

"You'll find her," Cindy said. "You're a lovable old chum, you know that?"

"Thanks," he said. "Well, I gotta go. There's a game on TV. After I return the pony, of course." Wistfully, he added, "Oh, yeah, I learned something else, too."

"What's that?" she asked.

"Never say goodbye by e-mail." He gave her a one-armed hug. "Say it in person."

"Goodbye." Cindy smiled at him.

As he strolled away, the female knight approached and shook his hand forcefully. Talking together, the two of them fell into step, her pony ambling next to his until they vanished around a corner.

A matched set, Cindy thought. At least it might be a start.

Her spirits soaring, she went toward the English building to meet Hugh.

15

HUGH HAD SEEN SNOW FALLING before when his parents took him skiing in the mountains of Southern California. But on Christmas morning in Oofdah, the Minnesota snow didn't merely fall, it obliterated the world.

"Awesome," he said to Cindy as they sat in the kitchen, gazing through the curtains and sipping hot chocolate.

"Fortunately, my neighbors have four-wheel drive. They can take us to the airport tomorrow if the roads aren't clear," she said.

"It will be an adventure," he said. "Since I met you, everything's an adventure."

"How could it be otherwise?" Warm and glowing, Cindy leaned toward him across the table. Tendrils of blond hair haloed her face. "You won my hand in a tournament and proposed in front of hundreds of people. I think that set the tone for the rest of our lives."

"Let's hope so."

Hugh's head was still spinning from the events of the past week. Once they were engaged, he and Cindy had found they couldn't bear to wait for a big wedding. She'd given notice on her apartment, and they'd flown to Oofdah for a small private ceremony on Christmas Eve.

Cindy's mother had attended with her new boyfriend before returning to Rochester. Hugh's parents had arrived, as well, then continued on to Canada to visit some old friends for the holidays.

Tomorrow, he and Cindy were flying to a beach resort near San Diego for a week of sheer bliss. They had so many plans for later—she was going to find a teaching post in Clair De Lune, and he intended to buy them a house—but there was plenty of time. All the time in the world.

They'd called Mariah yesterday to apologize for not including the Snoopers in the wedding even though Cindy had issued them a public invitation. She'd waved away Hugh's explanation.

"Don't give it a second thought," she'd said. "We claim the right to throw you a big reception in January, at the University Senior Center."

"We'd love it," he'd said. "How generous!"

"We want all our friends to attend," Mariah had gone on. "In fact, I think I'll invite President Martin. It will be interesting to see if he shows up with Vanessa. Maybe Bill Sachet can come, too. Now that he's divorcing her, he needs to get out and meet new people. Maybe he'll fall in love right under our noses."

"You're hopeless," Cindy had said on the extension. "But wonderful."

After saying goodbye, they'd found themselves alone, with the house to themselves. Their wedding night had been full of laughter and hugs and wonderful, rising passion. For the first time, Hugh understood how physical fulfillment combined with real love bound two people in mystical ways.

"You know what I forgot to do?" he said as, outside, the sifting snow billowed in a gentle breeze. "I never bought you a Christmas present."

"Well, I know what I want, and I'll take it right now."

After setting down her mug, Cindy came around and perched on his lap. Since she was the same size as Hugh, the two of them had to clutch the seat to keep from falling off.

She wound her arms around him, and Hugh forgot about the chair and the snow and everything except the tender, blossoming connection between them. He didn't know how long they sat there, kissing and cuddling, but finally his legs began to fall asleep.

"I hate to mention it…" he said.

Grinning, Cindy stood up. "I don't want to cripple my husband. I've got too many designs on you for later. But first, I want to give you my present."

"You bought one?" he asked, impressed.

"It's not the kind of present you buy." She tugged him to his feet. "We have to go in the living room for this one."

"Sure thing." Despite the pins and needles in his legs, Hugh strode manfully beside his wife. With the confidence gained from becoming the Black Knight, he vowed never again to act the role of an absentminded professor.

At the piano, Cindy took a book, "Beloved Songs of Christmas," from the bench and set it in front of her. "Which are your favorites?"

"You mean I get a concert?" Hugh scooted onto the bench beside her. "Perfect!" He tapped the book. "Every one of these is my favorite carol."

"I'll do my best," said his wife. She opened the book to the first song and began to play.

As her golden voice evoked the melody of "Silent Night," he gazed across the piano and out the window. Snow was piling onto the branches of a pine tree in the yard, angelic against the deep green.

"Silent night, holy night…"

He closed his eyes, carried away by the beauty of the melody. He opened them again as Cindy neared the end, so he could watch her blissful face.

"Sleep in heavenly peace,
Sleep in heavenly peace.''

He'd found his own peace, with the woman he loved. As he listened to Cindy transition smoothly into the next song, Hugh reflected that you couldn't get any closer to heaven than this.

Then he joined her in singing "I'll Be Home for Christmas." That was exactly where he intended to be, every Christmas for the rest of their lives.

The Harlequin Reader Service® — Here's how it works:

Accepting your 2 free books and gift places you under no obligation to buy anything. You may keep the books and gift and return the shipping statement marked "cancel." If you do not cancel, about a month later we'll send you 2 additional novels and bill you just $5.14 each in the U.S., or $6.14 each in Canada, plus 50¢ shipping and handling per book and applicable taxes if any.* That's the complete price and — compared to cover prices of $5.99 each in the U.S. and $6.99 each in Canada — it's quite a bargain! You may cancel at any time, but if you choose to continue, every month we'll send you 2 more books, which you may either purchase at the discount price or return to us and cancel your subscription.

*Terms and prices subject to change without notice. Sales tax applicable in N.Y. Canadian residents will be charged applicable provincial taxes and GST.

GET FREE BOOKS and a FREE GIFT WHEN YOU PLAY THE...

Lucky 7

SLOT MACHINE GAME!

Just scratch off the silver box with a coin. Then check below to see the gifts you get!

YES! I have scratched off the silver box. Please send me the 2 free Harlequin Duets™ books and gift for which I qualify. I understand I am under no obligation to purchase any books, as explained on the back of this card.

311 HDL DRNG

111 HDL DRNW
(H-D-12/02)

FIRST NAME	LAST NAME

ADDRESS

APT.#	CITY

STATE/PROV.	ZIP/POSTAL CODE

7	7	7	**Worth TWO FREE BOOKS plus a BONUS Mystery Gift!**
🍒	🍒	🍒	**Worth TWO FREE BOOKS!**
♣	♣	♣	**Worth ONE FREE BOOK!**
🔔	🔔	🍒	**TRY AGAIN!**

Visit us online at www.eHarlequin.com

Offer limited to one per household and not valid to current Harlequin Duets™ subscribers. All orders subject to approval.

© 2000 HARLEQUIN ENTERPRISES LTD. ® and TM are trademarks owned by Harlequin Enterprises Ltd.

Calling All Glass Slippers

Jacqueline Diamond

HARLEQUIN®

TORONTO • NEW YORK • LONDON
AMSTERDAM • PARIS • SYDNEY • HAMBURG
STOCKHOLM • ATHENS • TOKYO • MILAN • MADRID
PRAGUE • WARSAW • BUDAPEST • AUCKLAND

Dear Reader,

Humor grows from character, and an author never really knows how her characters will develop and interact until they spring to life on the page. Sometimes it's a struggle to help them discover their true natures, but Jared and Laura knew exactly who they were right from the start.

How could Jared, a man so sexy that women throw themselves at him, avoid being egotistical and obnoxious? Simple—he hasn't figured out that women don't behave that way toward all the men in their lives, so he enjoys the fun without getting a swelled head.

As for Laura, she's a sensitive soul, but never a pushover. Jared, who unwittingly broke her heart, brings out every ounce of defiance in her nature. I had fun with her, and loved creating her plays within the story.

I'd be happy to hear from you at P.O. Box 1315, Brea, CA 92822, or by e-mail at Jdiamondfriends@aol.com. Happy reading!

Best,

Jacqueline Diamond

For my friends in the theater,
from the community players of Nashville
to the hardworking publicists in Los Angeles.

1

LAURA PUSHED THE TACK with her thumb. "Get in there, you stupid thing!"

She pressed harder. Ouch! Her thumb throbbed, while the steely tack remained jutting out of the wall.

Laura glared at it. In a few hours, it was going to be New Year's Eve, but she couldn't even think about celebrating until she got the posters up in her new apartment.

Mumbling to herself, she grabbed the sneaker off her left foot and whacked away. The rubber sole produced a series of loud thumps that had no measurable impact on the tack.

She examined the bottom of the shoe. "Great," she said to the empty room. "Now I've put dents in it." What she needed, of course, was a tool kit, but somehow she never remembered to buy one.

A lack of essentials was par for the course. Laura's jeans had patches stitched over the bare knees and her plaid shirt sported a daisy embroidered atop a stain. It wasn't because of poverty, although money was always tight for an aspiring playwright, but because she couldn't spare the mental energy to go shopping.

After wedging the damaged sneaker back on her foot, Laura rummaged through the suitcases piled atop the sofa bed. No hammer, and no feasible substitute, either.

She checked the boxes on the counter between the

main room and the kitchenette. Aha! A loafer with a sturdy heel.

She took aim, squinted, threatened to donate the shoe to the thrift store if it failed, and struck. When she looked again, the tack lay neatly in place.

"Score one for me," Laura said aloud. Her move from Santa Fe to Southern California had been a three-day drag of overpriced motels, flat tires and high gas prices. However, with the superstition common to theater folks, she regarded this small triumph as a good omen.

She set to work unrolling the rest of her posters and whipping her remaining tacks into submission. Soon the walls of the sunny, one-room apartment advertised *Gone With the Wind, Shakespeare in Love* and *Love Story.* Judging by her choices, a casual visitor might assume that Laura had the soul of a romantic, but she knew better.

Every one of those movies ended unhappily for the lovers. That was why she cherished them, because they reminded her of why she'd become a playwright instead of an actress in the first place.

Because of Jared Benton.

Ten years ago, as a starry-eyed freshman drama major, Laura had fallen for Jared while performing opposite him in a De Lune University production of *Romeo and Juliet.* A dashing senior, he'd fallen in love with her just as she had with him. Or so she'd believed.

Then, at the cast party on closing night, Jared had showed up arm in arm with a curvaceous stranger. Her men's-magazine figure and cover-girl hair were a slap in the face to Laura, who had grown up self-conscious about her boyish build and carrot-top thatch. After watching the two of them gaze into each other's eyes, she'd fled in anguish.

That was all behind her, of course. Long ago, out of the picture, practically forgotten. She'd shed her foolish dreams of becoming a glamorous star and honed her wit on the written page, with steady if modest success.

When Laura entered her latest play, *Calling All Glass Slippers,* in her alma mater's prestigious playwriting competition, she hadn't known that the new head of the theater department was going to direct the winning entry personally. She hadn't realized it until last month, when she'd received a congratulatory letter addressed to L. J. Ellison from Jared Benton.

It was obvious from the letter that he didn't remember her. Fair enough, since in all these years, Jared had hardly crossed her mind.

If he'd gone to New York to act and direct, so what? Laura had been busy with a children's theater troupe in Kentucky. If he'd made a name for himself at a university in New Jersey, she hadn't noticed, because she'd been playwright in residence at a Santa Fe theater company. She didn't even recall the color of his eyes. Kind of an odd blend of gray and lavender, maybe, but she wasn't sure.

After standing back to make sure the posters were straight, Laura threw open a window. Even on the afternoon of New Year's Eve, the sunshine heated the room to an uncomfortable degree.

The flat was perched atop the freestanding garage of a house belonging to a retired dean of literature, who lived next door. From her second-story place, Laura surveyed a block of pastel bungalows and pineapple-shaped palm trees.

Glancing toward her landlady's house, she frowned at an unexpected flash of red in a huge eucalyptus tree. Was it a bird? Leaning out, she saw that the red blob appeared to ride atop some whitish fuzz. For the life of her, Laura couldn't figure out what it was.

A series of creaks on the outdoor stairs indicated she had a visitor. Abandoning her examination of the mysterious object, she went to open the door.

"I brought you tea. The mint's homegrown." Into the room bustled her landlady, half glasses perched on her nose and nest of gray hair quivering. Finding the only bare spot on the counter, she set down an antique-style china tray that held a mismatched cup and saucer.

In her fringed shawl, print dress and buckled shoes, the elderly woman—whose name on the lease had read simply Dean Pipp—might have stepped from the pages of an old book. There was nothing otherworldly about her sharp eyes and air of self-possession, however.

'Thanks, but I usually drink coffee,'' Laura said. "Did you notice anything in your tree? I saw something red up there. It might be a bird, but it looked more like some kind of garment."

"It's probably the neighbor across the street, Esther Zimpelman." The dean held out the filled teacup and, seeing no graceful way to refuse, Laura took it. "She and her friends call themselves Snoopers. They spy on people, although I hadn't noticed that she's taken to climbing trees. She's a bit old for that."

Clair De Lune, California, had always been peculiar, Laura recalled. Peculiar places inspired interesting ideas for plays, so she didn't mind. "She spies on people?"

"She's harmless. Drink up," said her landlady. "It's no good cold."

Laura took a sip and tasted mint with a hint of ginger. "This is interesting."

"'Bracing' is more like it," Dean Pipp corrected. "By the way, I'm giving a New Year's Eve party tonight and I expect you to attend, in costume. I had to cancel my Halloween party because of a bad cold and I'm making up for it. I've put together the most marvelous outfit. You'll see it tonight."

"I'm sure I can scrounge something." Laura collected odds and ends discarded by costume shops at the theaters where she'd worked. You never knew when they might come in handy for a future production or, in this case, a New Year's Eve party.

The landlady glanced around the room but, to Laura's relief, made no objection to the thumbtacks. It was a copy of *Calling All Glass Slippers,* bound between stiff yellow covers, that drew her attention. "Is this the play that won the contest?"

"It is," Laura said.

"It's all finished?"

"Yes. Although I'm sure I'll rewrite it several times before opening night." Revisions were part of the process of preparing a new play.

Laura liked the story the way it was, with its ironic tone and a plot that lampooned romantic conventions. Still, you couldn't simply disregard the director's opinions, and Jared would no doubt have plenty of those.

As Dean Pipp lifted the script, her expression softened. Maybe she was reacting to the title, Laura thought. People often smiled at the obvious reference to the Cinderella story.

"Do you know what just popped into my head?" her

landlady said. "No, of course you don't. This February 14th will be my fiftieth wedding anniversary."

"Congratulations." Laura hadn't realized there was a Mr. Pipp in the picture. "Are the two of you planning a big celebration?"

"Hardly," said Mrs. Pipp. "I haven't seen Watley in decades. For all I know, he long ago dried up and tumbled into one of those archeological sites of his. Maybe he's been dug up, mistaken for an artifact and placed in a glass case in a museum. Preferably stuffed."

"You haven't seen him in decades? But you're not divorced?"

"We never got around to it." Wistfully the older woman added, "I suppose I had trouble giving up hope."

"That sounds like a fascinating story." Laura sometimes found other people's experiences useful in her writing, although she tried to be discreet about it.

"I'm not going to tell it. You'd be turned off of romance forever." Her landlady headed for the exit. "Don't forget, the party starts at eight o'clock. I'll expect you to be prompt, although heaven knows no one else will be."

Laura made a mental note not to arrive before nine.

ZORRO WAS READY TO RIDE. He swept the black cape around his broad shoulders, adjusted his hat and strode out of the Spanish-style house into a pool of lighting that temporarily dispelled the darkness.

When he reached his red sports car, the sword hanging from his hip posed a dilemma. That was solved by tossing it into the back seat beside his mask, whose appearance on a driver might draw the attention of the Clair De

Lune police. Zorro might be bold, but he wasn't foolhardy.

Down the roadway that curved past his home sped a small car crammed with young women. University students, he surmised as one of them leaned out the window and shrilled a wolf whistle.

"Hey, Professor Benton!" called the driver, slowing to a crawl. "Need a ride? I'll throw out these losers if you say the word."

"We'll throw you out instead!" cried one of her passengers.

"I'm the one he really wants!" insisted another.

"Thank you, ladies." Zorro swept into a bow. "But I can't possibly choose among you, so have a good evening."

Amid cries of mock dismay, the car zipped off. It was all in fun, Jared mused as he got into the driver's seat. De Lune University teemed with good-natured flirts.

He started the engine and zoomed backward out of the driveway. Even with the seat extended all the way, there was hardly room for his long legs and shiny black boots.

Jared had contemplated riding to Dean Pipp's party on horseback, but he lacked an essential item: the horse. A friend had offered to loan him a pony from her stable, but he couldn't see the masked hero galloping up to his destination with his feet dragging in the dirt.

The little car whipped toward the lowlands. The familiar sight of the town below reminded Jared of the whims of fate. Who would have imagined that, after a cross-country odyssey that had taken him all the way to New York, he would land back here, hired two years ago to rescue the theater department from the doldrums?

By the age of thirty-two, Jared had hoped to be directing on The Great White Way itself. The closest he'd come was directing a revival of *Sweet Bird of Youth* off Broadway, where he'd scored a critical success that had, unfortunately, done less than stellar box office. "Bird Flies Coop," had read the terse headline on the closing notice in Variety.

Not that he was complaining. He enjoyed reigning over his own campus theater and he got a kick out of the high spirits of his colleagues and students. Still, he'd become acutely aware recently that something was missing, which might mean it was time to move on.

Not yet, of course. Not while Jared had a prize-winning play to present, with the near certainty of drawing major critics and producers to the audience. He'd been thrilled to find *Calling All Glass Slippers* among a pile of lesser works. With his help, it could be refined into pure gold.

Something about the play had touched him from the moment he began to read. The playwright's voice resonated inside him like a long-forgotten chord, and the story, despite its surface cynicism, put him in a romantic frame of mind.

All in all, this was a New Year's Eve to celebrate.

Jared slowed as he passed the university. It was after ten o'clock, and by the time he turned from De Lune Boulevard onto Forest Avenue, cars lined the street on both sides. Too bad. He disliked the notion of hoofing it from three blocks away and arriving in less than prime condition.

The sports car prowled along until it came abreast of Dean Pipp's house. The driveway held two vehicles but no one had blocked the entrance. A perfect slot! Swiftly

Jared angled into it and pulled forward until the front half of his car jutted onto the lawn.

He got out to inspect the damage. He was blocking the two cars and half the sidewalk, but he hadn't run over anything except a few spindly herbs. He felt certain his hostess would understand.

From the rear, Jared retrieved his sword and mask and took a moment to complete his costume. Then he stood still, eyes closed, while he blocked extraneous thoughts and transformed himself into Zorro.

A good actor never rushed a performance.

LAURA WONDERED WHY SOMEONE who lived in a tiny house would throw such a huge party. Not only was Dean Pipp's aging interior divided into small rooms and cramped hallways, but every spare inch of space not piled with books was filled by people.

It was so tight that, once she got in, she doubted she could have exited had she wanted to. The entire population of the town must be crammed in here, milling around and all talking at once.

Venturing in search of refreshments, Laura made her way to a shadowy dining room lit by wall sconces. As portraits of Shakespeare, Poe and Twain scowled from the wall, costumed partygoers clustered around the table, helping themselves to salmon log and macadamia nuts and cheese squiggles on crackers.

Laura had made it as far as the punch bowl—only lightly spiked, as far as she could tell—when Count Dracula accosted her. "Is it really you, Morticia?" demanded the mustachioed older man, taking in her black wig, whitened skin and clingy green crushed-velvet gown. "At last I have found my soul mate!"

Although Laura gave the guy points for the spiffy tuxedo and red-lined cape, he had to be in his seventies. "I think you want my grandmother," she said.

"Is she here?" he asked hopefully.

"Runcie, behave yourself!" Dean Pipp appeared in a crumbling wedding gown, à la Miss Havisham from *Great Expectations*. "Laura, this is Herbert Runciland. Runcie, meet my new tenant, Laura Ellison."

"L. J. Ellison, the playwright?" Runcie took her hand and bowed. "This is an honor indeed."

"How do you know I'm a playwright?" Laura raised her voice to be heard over the surrounding buzz.

"Very little escapes my fellow Snoopers and me." Runcie beamed so broadly he dislodged a long strand of hair from atop his balding pate. It hung rakishly over his forehead. "Also, we take a particular interest in anyone occupying your apartment. It seems to inspire romantic developments in the ladies who live there and nothing makes for better gossip than young love."

"It may inspire other people, but not me," she said. A woman whose career required her to relocate frequently couldn't afford—and in her case, didn't want—entanglements.

From the front of the house came girlish shrieks as if to welcome a rock star. "Sounds like someone important just landed," Laura said. "Probably someone male."

"You mean I have competition?" Runcie waggled an eyebrow at their hostess. "Come now, Marie, who have you lured here tonight?"

"I invite interesting people wherever I find them, whether you like the competition or not."

"I like interesting people, too," Laura said, "because I lead such a dull life myself."

Mrs. Pipp gave an audible sniff. "What nonsense! Dull? A woman of the theater who moves from place to place like a gypsy? You pique my curiosity, which is why I'm renting to you even though you'll probably leave me with a vacancy in a few months. I'd rather be out the rent than bored."

"She is interesting, but too young for me. I'm going to investigate the new arrival." Runcie departed and, a short time later, their hostess circulated in another direction.

Left alone, Laura sipped her citrus punch and settled down to observe. Unlike most people, she enjoyed being alone at a party. Other guests' interactions and conversations could be tucked away in memory, to leap forth unbidden when she needed them for a play.

Nearby, a young man with sandy hair and an athletic build was popping nuts into the willing mouth of a sunny California blonde. They were both young and unformed, Laura thought, not yet tested by life. Still, she liked their openness.

A thirtyish woman with an attractive but pinched face caught her eye. Too thin for her big highlighted hairdo and chiffon gown, the woman stalked the room as if seeking someone worthy of her and trailed out, still questing. After engaging in a few casual conversations and keeping her eyes open for useful bits of behavior, Laura was refilling her cup when a stir by the main hallway made her look up. A sigh ran through the female occupants as a larger-than-life Zorro appeared in the doorway, his cape falling back to reveal a broad chest and a lithe, muscular body.

From beneath his mask, intelligent eyes swept the room. Laura felt her throat tighten as the man's gaze settled on her. Her skin prickled as if he'd rubbed a hot pepper across it.

What was making her react this way? The man was well-built, but she'd seen other superhero costumes at the party.

Maybe it was the way he held himself, bristling with energy. And the awareness with which he studied her, as if matching her instinctive arousal with his own.

A connection had formed between them, spontaneous and unmistakable. Laura had no idea why this was happening, but she intended to put a stop to it right now.

THE FEMININE CLAMOR THAT had greeted Jared's arrival buoyed him. Improvising, he'd drawn his sword at the front door and battled an invisible foe to the floor, then taken a bow to applause.

After his mock duel, there were handshakes all around and greetings from friends. Tonight, however, wasn't merely party time but New Year's Eve, and Jared found himself wandering the house in search of adventure. He didn't know exactly what he was looking for, but he had the sense that a new challenge awaited him. He certainly needed one.

As soon as he entered the dining room and spotted Morticia, he felt a rush of anticipation and a sense of daring the unknown. The woman was unfamiliar and complicated, he could see at a glance. There was something else, too, a kind of subconscious link, as if they'd known each other in a previous lifetime.

Jared noticed the pulse throbbing in her throat and the way she shifted backwards. She wanted him, yet she would resist. She wasn't going to flee, though. This one had spirit.

The crowd parted as he sauntered forward. Morticia faced him squarely. In the uneven light, her eyes were wise and wary at the same time.

Jared brought her slim hand to his lips. At the contact, she shivered, as if with a suppressed sexuality struggling to break free. She seemed intensely alive in a way that made everyone else in the room fade into shadows.

"I don't believe we've met," he said.

"I'm Morticia," she replied in a low voice. "You're from a different fantasy, Zorro."

"That makes things more exciting," he said.

"And more dangerous," she murmured.

"All the better." He grinned, and caught an answering glint of eagerness on her face. She had a lovely mouth, full and wide. "Would you grant me the honor of a dance?" he asked.

"Where?" she said with a touch of amusement. "I can hardly move in here."

"On the ceiling," he said with an expansive gesture. "No, among the stars."

When she laughed, the room sparkled. "You're quite an operator, Senor Zorro."

"I aim to please."

"I can tell," said Morticia. "Every woman in the room is pleased."

He caught a couple of hopeful looks from ladies standing near them. Although normally Jared enjoyed spreading around a few casual gallantries, tonight he found their attention intrusive. "We should go out."

"Looking like this?" Morticia asked. "We might be arrested as dangerous lunatics."

"I meant, let's sojourn in the garden," he clarified. "I hear Dean Pipp's bower is enchanting by moonlight."

He wasn't sure what made him so determined to get Morticia alone. Maybe it was her odd mix of vulnerability and tartness, or the nagging sense that he'd met her somewhere before.

"I'd like to refill my cup first," she said.

"Allow me." With a flourish, Jared carried it across the room and dipped punch for them both. A sip told him Dean Pipp had disguised her high-proof vodka with fruit juices and flavorings.

If Morticia was tossing down this stuff, it was lucky he'd come along to protect her from unscrupulous males. Other than himself, of course.

They wove their way through the kitchen and went outside. The night was crisp and starry, with only a hint of illumination from the house. Even in midwinter, Dean Pipp's plantings scented the air, and, although the garden might be modest, the design made it seem larger.

Leaving their empty punch glasses on a stone bench, they followed a winding course between rosebushes and flowering shrubs. Jared wrapped his cape around Morticia's shoulders and, after a brief hesitation, she allowed him to draw her into shared warmth.

"I don't know why I trust you," she said. "Maybe it's because you seem so…heroic."

"I'm not really Zorro," he said, then chuckled at himself for making such a ridiculous remark. "Or who knows? Maybe that's my secret identity."

"I hope so," Morticia said. "I want you to be Zorro tonight. Don't tell me your real name. We'll probably never see each other again, and if I don't know who you are, I won't have any regrets."

"Are you planning to do something you might regret?" Jared was surprised to find that he'd be happy to oblige. Normally he preferred to go slow, to make sure he avoided complications and misunderstandings. Keep it light, that was one of his favorite sayings. Any day now I'll be moving on, that was another.

But it took him aback, the way Morticia made it clear she never expected to see him again. Jared's ego could handle that, but why was she so intent on keeping him at bay?

"I haven't decided what I'm going to do with you," she said and twirled away. "You asked me to dance. Well? Why aren't we?"

"Because you're way ahead of me." In terms of punch consumption and in terms of wildness, he thought. It was a new experience. "Let's fix that right now."

Jared caught the woman in a waltz position, advancing a bit too quickly so they brushed against each other. She had a healthy, lightly sweet scent and a graceful way of moving, and the impact lit a fire deep inside him.

She started humming a song. After a few bars, he recognized Anne Murray's "Shadows in the Moonlight" and joined in. They made a turn around the glade, old-fashioned style with him holding her waist and hand.

What a sprite she was, teasing him with a look and then averting her face, making him want to kiss her. Jared feared this creature of the silver moon might disappear from his arms at any instant.

Maybe, he thought, she wasn't real at all and never had been. But for tonight, he claimed her.

LAURA DIDN'T KNOW WHAT HAD gotten into her. She had a vague suspicion about the punch, but it must be more than that.

Although the mask hid much of Zorro's face, he had

a marvelous strong mouth and a way of sheltering her that banished her usual inhibitions. What she liked best was the puzzled expression that indicated she'd thrown him off balance. There was nothing as appealing as a strong man succumbing to sensations beyond his control.

She'd never acted this seductive, at least not since college. In the normal world, Laura maintained an elusive distance from men, perhaps because none of them were right for her. Love wasn't right for her. She'd realized that ten years ago.

But then, she didn't intend to fall in love with Zorro. She wasn't going to stay in Clair De Lune very long and she already knew he was too much of a ladies' man for her taste.

For now, though, she enjoyed the delicious sensations he stirred. She'd forgotten how pleasant it could be to feel a man's hands on her when she simply let herself go. Who had invented dancing, anyway? She supposed it was too late to write a thank-you note.

As Zorro drew her close, she realized he was going to kiss her. She decided to let him.

His hand slid from her waist to her derriere and drew her against him. At close range, his response became unmistakable. So, Laura realized as her nipples hardened, was her own.

He cupped the back of her head, cradling her gently, and kissed her. The impact smoldered all the way to her toes. Her fingers danced across his shoulders and she tipped her face up, inviting more.

"Let me get rid of this thing." With an impatient gesture, Zorro ripped off his mask and tossed it into the darkness. "That's better."

Laura's heart nearly stopped as she stared into the face

she'd seen a thousand times in her dreams. The slightly crooked nose, the laughing eyes... At some level she must have known that only one man could provoke this response in her, the man who years ago had broken her heart and stoked her resolve never, never to trust anyone again.

Abruptly she felt the alcohol from the punch weakening her knees. Her head spun. She had to get away. Anywhere. Now.

In the distance, a bell clanged. From inside the house sounded the tootle of paper horns amid cries of "Happy New Year!"

"Happy New Year," said Jared Benton.

Laura gave him one last frightened look and took off running.

2

MORTICIA'S REACTION was so unexpected that Jared's usually swift reflexes failed him. A tantalizing woman had drawn him into the moonlight and then disappeared at the stroke of midnight? No way!

It didn't take more than a few seconds to break his daze. He didn't even know Morticia's real name, he realized, let alone what she looked like without her wig. He had to find her fast.

Jared doubted she'd gone into the house, since he hadn't heard the screen door scrape. Instead he raced around to catch her before she got into a car.

In front, it was hard to see through the shifting moonlit shapes cast by the eucalyptus. Some celebrants had spilled out the front door and were toasting each other on the steps, making too much noise for him to listen for an engine starting. He saw no woman, bewigged or otherwise, fleeing along the sidewalk.

Perplexed, Jared stared in both directions, watching for any sudden movement. Drawing a blank, he checked the front yard again, then went inside to make sure she hadn't slipped past the revelers on the porch.

The crowd in the hallway forced him to halt. "Has anybody seen Morticia?" he called in his loudest back-of-the-balcony voice.

"Who?"

"Sorry, no!"

"Happy New Year, Jared!"

"Forget Morticia! Take me!"

Soon he was surrounded by people wishing him well. One lady tucked her arm through his and tried to draw him away. By the time he politely freed himself and eased outside again, Jared was losing hope.

His companion had vanished. He didn't believe she was a figment of his imagination, but considering that she'd been somewhat tipsy, she'd made an amazingly clean getaway.

Well, Clair De Lune was a small town and, wig or no wig, he would recognize that woman the moment he looked her in the eye. He was going to find her again, no question about it.

THIN SUNSHINE FROM THE window bathed Laura as she sat on the rug, cross-legged in her jeans, and studied the script. She was trying to second-guess what comments Jared might make when they had their first scheduled meeting tomorrow.

Their encounter last night had haunted her sleep and left her disquieted this morning. She should have recognized him, even with the mask. Who else moved so sensually while dancing? Who else had such a husky way of speaking?

She wished they didn't have to work together, but it came with accepting the award and agreeing to take part in the production. Laura was stuck here for the next six weeks, so somewhere inside herself, she must find the key to maintaining her composure.

As for Jared, no doubt he'd simply laugh when he discovered that Morticia was his cast-off girlfriend. Okay, to be fair, they hadn't formally dated in college, but they'd spent hours rehearsing *Romeo and Juliet* together. They'd met not only at the theater but at his apartment, where the love scenes had dissolved into heavy petting.

In her naïveté, Laura had believed a bond was forming between them. She'd had the same impression again last night until the removal of his mask stripped away her illusions.

"Darn that Jared Benton!" she told Clark Gable, who was busy inspecting Vivien Leigh's bosom on their poster. "He enjoyed toying with me both times, didn't he? Well, I'm safe now, because I know him for the rat he is."

Determined to prepare herself so his criticisms wouldn't wound too deeply, she flipped through the play, reacquainting herself with the pages she hadn't reviewed for months. Each of the six characters was to be called by the real first name of the actor or actress, so they were listed simply as Male Newlywed, Con Artist and so forth.

In Act One, New Owner, a man in his thirties who'd labored for years as a shoe salesman under his tyrannical father, inherited the family shoe factory. Distressed by the dreariness of his hometown of Sterndale and pining for the beautiful but remote Young Widow, he began manufacturing irresistible glass slippers and shoes infused with a magic potion he'd bought on the Internet.

The potion made anyone who wore the shoes fall in love and win love in return. In Act Two, the result, much to his dismay, wasn't instant happiness for all concerned, but havoc in the town.

A young pair of newlyweds who bought his shoes fell for the first people they saw—total strangers. A Con Artist tumbled for the female Chief of Police, who was so horrified when she learned his true nature, yet so obsessed due to the glass slippers that she turned into a crazed stalker.

As for the dreamy New Owner, he proved no match for the Young Widow, who turned out to be materialistic and grasping. By Act Three, her coarse nature overcame love, and she and the Con Artist conspired to persuade New Owner to take out a fire insurance policy in her name. They then planned to burn down his shoe factory.

By the end, when the spells were finally broken, love had taken a beating and the once-loving couples loathed each other. Even the newlyweds found they'd hurt each other too much to reconcile.

How ironic that the play would open on Valentine's Day! Well, if people expected hearts-and-flowers sentimentality, they were going to be disappointed.

What would Jared want to change? Laura sighed. She'd never been able to read that man's mind. What made her think she could do it now?

Getting to her feet, she went to the bathroom. On the way back, she paused to enjoy the brightness of a Southern California New Year's Day outside her window.

Shrubs blossomed in tidy yards along the block. Despite the season, most of the trees still showed their leaves and some bore flowers, as well. Laura lingered, enjoying the mild climate all the more because she knew her stay here was only temporary.

Across the street, in a shade tree, she spotted a red shape atop a nest of whitish fluff. There it was again! What was it?

Determined not to be put off, Laura stuck her head out the window and whistled. Slowly the thing turned, until she recognized it as a baseball cap perched on a head of white hair.

There was a man sitting in that tree, holding a pair of spyglasses. "Oh, really, this is too much!" she said.

Neighborhood gossips were one thing. Men in trees peering into her window were another.

She ought to call the police, Laura supposed, but the fellow was obviously an old eccentric. In her younger days, she'd shrunk from confrontations. Not anymore.

Pulling on a sweater, she marched out of the apartment. The street lay quiet at this prenoon hour as residents slept off their late night, or maybe they'd all driven over to Pasadena to watch the Parade of Roses. Laura parked herself below the tree. She could see the man clearly now, a gnomelike fellow with a round head and tweedy clothes. He was so absorbed in peering through his glasses that he didn't seem to register her presence.

"Hey, you!" she called.

The man didn't budge.

"Up there in the tree!" Laura said. "Quit spying on me!"

The glasses wavered and a baffled face peered down. Thanks to a round nose touched with red veins, he reminded her of one of Santa's elves with a hangover. "Are you addressing me?"

"You bet I am." She pointed toward her window. "I'm the girl who lives over there. The one you've been watching."

His cheeks colored. "My dear young lady, I assure you, I've been doing nothing of the sort."

She stood her ground. "You're one of the neighborhood Snoopers, aren't you? Well, snoop on somebody else!"

From behind her came a rustling sound, and she turned to see a gray-haired woman descending from the front porch. Around her neck hung both a camera and a pair of binoculars, and in her left hand she clutched a cellular phone.

"He's not the one who's been studying you. It's me," said the woman. "I'm Esther Zimpelman, and if you choose to move in across from me, that's your own fault."

"Excuse me?"

"This block is my beat," Esther persisted. "I've had it for years, and I've snooped on far more interesting people than you, believe me. You've been here two days and not a single male visitor!"

Thank goodness the woman couldn't see Dean Pipp's backyard, Laura thought. "If you're spying on me, why aren't you the one in the tree?"

"I'm too old to climb trees. That man up there is an old friend and he's not even a Snooper. What a waste!" Mrs. Zimpelman waved her hands, nearly dropping the phone in the process. "He's cluttering up my bathroom and my tree, and now he's got you spooked."

"You can't blame me for that," called a voice from above.

"I can so!" cried the woman. "I can't do my job properly since you invited yourself for a visit, Hoagie Gunn! Your family and mine may be best friends, but you're a real pain."

"If he isn't spying on me, why is he sitting in a tree with binoculars?" Laura asked.

"Oh, I see why you're confused," said the man. "I'm a birder. There've been reports of a rare Purple-Breasted Nest-Hopper in the area. Have you seen one?"

"No, but keep away from my window," Laura said. "Both of you." As a matter of courtesy, she added, "Pleased to meet you, Mrs. Zimpelman. Now mind your own business."

"I'll do nothing of the sort," said her neighbor, and went inside.

"It's sad, really," said Hoagie from his perch. "Some people when they get old don't have a life, so they try to steal pieces of everybody else's. Now birds, they're much more interesting than people. Are you sure you haven't seen a Purple-Breasted Nest-Hopper? You can't miss them if they're hanging around. They have striped poop."

"Striped poop?" Laura said. "Spare me."

As she headed home, she heard him say, "I promise not to look toward your window in the slightest. Really."

"Thank you," she called over her shoulder.

When she got inside, she found that one of Hoagie's comments had stuck in her mind. Some people didn't have a life so they borrowed from other people. That sounded like a playwright.

Laura leaned against the door and contemplated this insight. She didn't retreat from life, surely. Everyone who worked in the theater was a bit of a sponge, but although she might absorb borrowed emotions, she then transformed them into something fresh.

Still, his words contained a kernel of truth. She was running away from how Jared made her feel. What she ought to do was to face it boldly, the way she'd faced Esther and Hoagie.

The key to keeping her balance around Jared, Laura decided, was to acknowledge to herself up-front that, first of all, he was a hopeless Don Juan, and, secondly, he still attracted her. Working closely with him, she was going to ache for a relationship she couldn't have.

It might hurt, but it was life, and not secondhand, either. It was an experience to take away so she could use it later.

Laura clapped the script shut. She didn't need to protect herself against Jared. Anything that happened would only strengthen her as a playwright, and that was what mattered.

PERHAPS IT HAD BEEN A MISTAKE asking L. J. Ellison to meet him at the Lunar Lunch Box café rather than at the theater, Jared mused as he sat staring into a nearly empty cup of coffee. He'd figured it would be a relaxing way to get to know his new colleague, but he'd forgotten he didn't even know the playwright's gender, let alone what he or she looked like.

Fortunately there wasn't a big crowd this morning, although the funky restaurant, its walls painted with scenes of fantastical voyages to the moon, was a popular off-campus hangout. You'd think a person could get waited on, wouldn't you? Jared reflected as he looked in vain for a waitress to refill his cup.

"Can I help you?" asked one of the other customers, a pretty young woman who couldn't be more than a sophomore. "I'll get your coffee."

"Please don't bother," Jared said.

She had half risen when Daffodil O'Foy, the chubby cook, emerged from the kitchen with a pot of fresh brew. "I don't know where Stuart's taken himself off to," she muttered, "but if nobody's waiting on Jared Benton, I'll do it myself."

"I was going to help him." The younger girl pouted. "There's a full pot right over there."

"If you want a job, we could use a new waitress." Daffodil filled his cup without spilling a drop. "Stu's real sick of having to fill in himself."

"No, thanks," said the student, and retreated to her seat. After exchanging glances that said, Wow did you see what I did? with her tablemates, she collapsed into a fit of giggles.

"The help doesn't last long around here, I gather," Jared said.

"Stu's hard to put up with, and then our last waitress got married," the cook said.

"I know." The waitress, Cindy, a teacher from Minnesota who'd worked here on a temporary basis, had married Jared's best friend, English professor Hugh Bemling.

"I've thought about quitting myself a few times," the cook went on. "The man's so darn crabby."

"I'm glad you haven't left. Nobody bakes a cheesecake like you," Jared said truthfully.

"Just for that, I'll bring you a slice. It's on the house." The cook departed, returning as promised.

Jared was savoring his cheesecake when a draft of cool air drew his attention to the woman entering the restaurant. Her most prominent feature was a blaze of red hair, echoed in a wild sprinkling of freckles across her cheeks. Slim and intense in a turtleneck and jeans, she carried a briefcase and scanned the room as if seeking someone she wasn't keen on finding.

With a jolt, he recognized her. Laura! He hadn't seen her since...

Ten years evaporated, and it was the night of the cast party. Vibrations had scorched the theater as they performed *Romeo and Juliet* for the last time. They'd scorched him, too. He'd almost regretted asking another date for the party. But he and Laura were getting too close. People had begun making comments, and, although he was a senior and needed to plan ahead, he'd found himself mentally disregarding theater positions on the bulletin board that were located too far from Clair De Lune because Laura still had three years before graduation.

So he'd invited a sex bomb who didn't interest him in the least. Just to calm things down a bit.

He hadn't realized until he saw the dismay on Laura's face that his action would strike her as a betrayal. She'd left the party soon afterward, and for the rest of the semester, avoided him like the plague.

In his immaturity, Jared had decided to play it cool, figuring they'd naturally drift back together. But they never had, and by summer he'd been working on the other side of the continent.

It was wonderful to see her again, but what was she doing here? Why was she regarding him expectantly, unless...

"L. J. Ellison?" he asked, rising. No wonder he'd reacted so strongly on reading the play! Of course, it was well-written and original, but it was also a reflection of the woman he'd once come very close to loving.

"Hello." She walked past a table full of students, whose heads swiveled to watch. "It's good to see you, Jared." She held out her hand.

Normally he would have bestowed a playful kiss on it, but her demeanor warned him off. Instead he shook it with quiet professionalism and gazed straight into her jade-green eyes.

And got a shock.

"Morticia," he said.

"Very good." Laura stowed her briefcase on an empty chair and sat across from him.

No wonder she'd run away. He must have given her a start when he took off his mask, Jared reflected.

"You could have told me who you were the other night instead of vanishing into thin air." Unaccustomed to being one-upped, he arrayed himself sideways in his seat and stretched out his legs. He decided to take things slow and see if his old friend planned to spring any more surprises.

In the clear light, her eyes revealed smoky depths. "When I recognized you, I got an overwhelming urge to make myself scarce."

"I'm sorry to have that effect on you," he said. "You don't hold a grudge from ten years ago, I hope."

"It's all water under the bridge," she said. "I'm glad we'll be working together."

"Are you?" he probed.

"Your reputation as a director is impressive," Laura said without a hint of how she felt about him personally. "I want my play to get the best possible production, especially since I understand some of the Los Angeles critics are expected to attend."

"Not only that, but the *New York Times* is coming." If she didn't want to discuss the past, he decided, neither did he. "Why don't you order breakfast, if we can find anyone to wait on us, and then let's get down to work." Spotting Stuart Crockenmeyer, the owner of the Lunar Lunch Box, Jared waved him over.

The white-aproned man trudged toward them bearing a menu and a truculent expression. "Do you want to hear about the specials or not?'' he said. ''I suppose you'd prefer to make something up to suit yourself like most of the customers. What'll it be? A patty melt with avocados and beets? A bowl of chicken soup with ice cream in it?''

''A cup of coffee, please,'' Laura said without flinching. Either the woman had nerves of steel or she remembered Stu's ill-temper from her student years.

''Decaf, demitasse, espresso, mocha or latte?'' Stu said.

''Espresso, please.''

''We don't have espresso.''

''Just pour something black in a cup,'' Laura said. ''Got that?''

Stuart blinked in surprise at this frontal attack, then retreated, mumbling to himself.

''Good show,'' Jared said.

''So what do you think of the play?'' she asked.

''I love it,'' he said. ''I do want to suggest a few changes.''

''Shoot.'' She held herself very still. The warmth and sensuality of New Year's Eve had disappeared as completely as the black wig, green gown and pasty makeup.

''It needs to be more upbeat,'' he said. ''The play's full of energy and wit, but it leaves a sour taste.''

''I hope you're not looking for a lovey-dovey happy ending.'' Her jaw jutted stubbornly.

''Not at all.'' Jared produced his copy and opened it to a bookmarked page. ''For example, take the Widow. She's too grasping and selfish. What if she had mixed motives for burning down the factory? What if she discovers that the slippers are magic and doesn't like what they're doing to people?''

In a notebook, Laura jotted a few words. "Okay. That might work."

"And the scene in Act Three where the female police chief tortures the con artist with a glass slipper is rather over the top. I think there should be more of a teasing tone…"

She agreed with everything he said in the same remote manner. A man could get frostbite from being in the room with her. If she hadn't admitted to being Morticia, Jared would have thought he was mistaken.

He wanted that other woman back. Heck, he wanted the old Laura back, the sweet, open-faced girl who'd melted in his arms and melted his heart at the same time.

But he had only himself to blame for driving her away. And, of course, you couldn't stop time. People grew up, whether you wanted them to or not.

The play was the thing. In that respect, they were off to a good start.

LAURA WANTED TO ARGUE with every comment he made. She hated to admit she hadn't written a perfect play, although she knew there was no such thing. Grudgingly, though, she conceded that Jared made good suggestions.

Mostly she needed to keep him at bay. He was too likable, that was the problem. In memory, he'd mutated into a monster of egotism, but he wasn't. A hard-hearted jerk wouldn't have such insight into her characters and he wouldn't kindle sparks along her nerve endings.

Instead of showing the arrogance she'd expected, Jared sat there patiently explaining himself, drawing Laura under his spell with each gentle word. She reacted with a mixture of alarm at her own vulnerability and fascination at the discovery that even she, the master puppeteer of her characters' lives, could succumb like any of them to a man she knew was wrong for her.

Laura wasn't really going to succumb, of course. She had too much experience and too much objectivity to be so foolish.

"I'd like to start casting the roles next Tuesday," Jared said after he'd finished giving her his comments. "I want to use actors of the appropriate ages, and it may not be easy finding a couple around age thirty and another pair in their fifties or older."

"That's not the way the theater department used to work," Laura said. "We used to cast students in everything." As an undergraduate, she'd donned a gray wig on more than one occasion.

"Things have changed, partly because of the college president, Wilson Martin. He came on board after you left. He wants us to get more involved with the community," Jared said.

"How do you do that?" she asked.

"At his request, we inaugurated an acting class for nonstudents last semester and we've gotten some interesting participants. Including his girlfriend, who I think is the whole reason he started the class."

"Don't tell me we have to cast her!" Laura groaned.

"She might make a good Widow," Jared said. "Anyway, we'll take a look at her if she tries out, which I'm sure she will. Just a look, that's all."

The owner came back and sloshed coffee in their cups. "We've got a job opening," he told Laura out of the blue. "I like people who aren't scared of me. You interested?"

"Laura isn't a waitress, Stuart, she's a playwright," Jared said.

Laura opened her mouth to agree. And stopped.

She'd waited tables for a short time in high school, but quit after getting teased by classmates. Since then, even during the inevitable gaps in her income, she'd taken pride in performing only white-collar work.

Yet wasn't it her mission to experience life as completely as possible in order to become a better playwright? Besides, the contest stipend barely covered Laura's expenses. She'd borrowed money from friends to make the move from Santa Fe and wanted to pay them back as soon as possible.

"I'll take it." Having a second thought, she added, "As long as it doesn't interfere with the rehearsal and production schedule."

"Oh, all right," Stuart grumbled. With his free hand, he lifted a copy of the script from the table. "Did you write this?"

"She certainly did. It won the University Award," Jared said.

Her new boss flipped it open. "*Calling All Glass Slippers,*" he read. "Hey, guess what? The title reminds me of Cinderella."

"Imagine that," said Laura.

A page turned. As Stuart scanned the words, he began to smile. Laura hadn't realized her opening dialogue was that witty.

"I'll have to come see this when it's produced," he said at last. "My cook might be interested, too."

"Don't tell me you're thinking of asking her on a date!" Jared teased.

Stuart's brow furrowed. "Heck, no. I just meant... So we could discuss it or something." He set the script down. "Come by tomorrow and we'll figure out your work schedule.'' He walked away idly caressing the coffee globe.

Jared leaned forward, focusing on Laura. His attention made her feel protected, even while her brain flashed a warning about his hypnotic effect. ''Are you sure you want to work here? Waitresses have to put up with a lot of guff, and I hear lifting those trays is hard on the back.''

''I need the money,'' she said. ''Besides, what better place than a restaurant to observe human nature?''

Jared covered her hands with his. His palms were roughened, so apparently he still helped make props and scenery himself to get them exactly right. ''Laura, I'm sorry about what happened when we were students. There's no undoing the past, but I hope it won't create problems between us.''

''It helped me become the person I am today,'' she said. ''The person who won the University Award. So I guess I ought to thank you.''

For once, she could see, Jared Benton was at a loss for words.

3

JARED COULDN'T FIGURE OUT why he'd bought the lamp. He kept staring at it on Tuesday morning as he slogged around the house in his green silk bathrobe.

For some reason, after spotting it in a store yesterday, he'd slapped down far too much money, carted the thing home and set it on a table next to the living room couch. His rationale had been that he needed more light for reading, which was true, but the thing didn't belong in this decor.

First of all, it was ugly. Eye-catching, but ugly. Did anybody outside a house of ill repute like lampshades painted with naked cupids? They had a rotund, earthy carnality, as if Rubens had taken up illustrating articles in *Playboy*.

Second, Jared had intentionally decorated the house with the blandness of a hotel suite. It was an investment and a future rental whenever his career heated up. At best, he planned to use the place as a base while running the theater department and flying off every chance he got to direct elsewhere. His collection of scripts and theater books resided in boxes in the spare bedroom. The winter clothes he'd needed in New York and New Jersey were salted away with mothballs inside a trunk in the garage. The point was to keep as little of Jared's personality from showing as possible.

So why had he bought the lamp?

He had no idea. This was troubling, Jared thought as he wandered through the living room again, a Pop-Tart in one hand and a cup of instant coffee in the other. Surely men didn't go through nesting phases the way women did.

He should have stayed home last night to read the revised copy of the play he'd found on his office desk yesterday. According to Laura's note, she'd worked fast over the weekend so he could use the new version at auditions today, and he'd planned to read it last night.

Instead he'd taken his buddy Hugh and his bride, Cindy, on a tour of furniture stores to equip their new home. Jared passed as an expert on shops since he'd bought his own modern Danish gear. Cindy, who'd recently moved to town, and Hugh, perpetually clueless about everything except poetry, had solicited his help.

That was how Jared had come to find the lamp in the center of a Victorian window display. For an instant, he'd imagined he saw the whirr of the cupids' wings and heard the distant plinking of their tiny harps. Without conscious thought, he'd claimed the lamp as his own.

With a shrug at his own inexplicable behavior, he sat at the kitchen table and took out the altered pages. He skimmed them, noting improvements in characterization along with some new, witty lines. As he crinkled the paper, a faint perfume arose, sending Laura's peppery-sweet essence directly into his brain.

He pictured the morning light burnishing her copper-colored mane and the freckles standing out against her fair skin as she raised her eyes to meet his. In their luster bloomed the first love he'd thrown away years ago, when he'd told himself it was more important to pursue his career than to hold Laura close.

Nothing had changed: Jared still couldn't allow himself to get tied down. Mediocrity and despair lay in that direction, as he'd seen in his mother's life.

Resolutely he tucked the pages into his portfolio and went to get ready for work.

LAURA ALWAYS GOT NERVOUS at auditions, even when she wasn't trying out herself. The tautness and twitchiness of the actors seeped by osmosis into her nervous system.

"Would you please stop fidgeting?" Jared asked from beside her.

They were sitting in the middle of the campus theater on Tuesday, feet propped on the seats ahead of them as they put the actors through their paces. Mostly young people were auditioning, and Laura wished now that she'd written more parts for them.

It was a ridiculous idea. *Calling All Glass Slippers* had exactly as many cast members of the right ages as it needed, in her artistic judgment. Still, her heart went out to them.

"It's too bad we can't use more of these kids," she said.

"Don't worry about them." Jared had scooted back in the seat and closed his eyes, so he appeared half-asleep. Nevertheless, she knew he was aware of every nuance from the stage.

When he opened them and glanced her way, she felt herself vibrate like a tuning fork. It was painful how keenly she noticed the warmth in those lavender-gray eyes.

She didn't want to fight her feelings too hard, because if she did, she risked isolating herself from one of life's richest experiences. As a playwright, she needed to ache and to suffer. But as a woman, she needed...oh, heck, right now, she didn't know what she needed.

Since they were between actors, she returned to her previous topic. "It isn't unreasonable for undergraduates to expect you to provide plenty of roles."

"They got their chance with our last production, *Twelfth Night*," he said. "I cast it mostly with students."

"Don't tell me you did a conventional interpretation of Shakespeare!"

"I don't know what you mean by conventional," Jared said, feigning innocence. "I set it in Hawaii, with ukuleles."

"I should have known."

He called some more names, and the two of them settled back to work. The young actors Laura liked best were the blond couple she'd seen feeding each other nuts at Dean Pipp's party. Brad Wilkerson and Suzy Arkhoff clearly had chemistry, onstage and off. Jared made a lot of notes about them, so he seemed to share her opinion.

After all those who'd listed their names for the part of the Young Newlyweds had been heard, Jared moved on to the role of the Con Artist. Laura envisioned him in his fifties, but the hands-down winner was the seventy-something Runcie. Even without his Dracula costume, he projected an engaging rakishness.

"He's one of my adult students," Jared said. "I wonder who we could pair him with?"

A small support group had accompanied Runcie, clapping and cheering when he read his lines. Among them,

Laura spotted Esther, but her nosy neighbor showed no inclination to try out.

After much nudging by her companions, however, another woman rose. She looked even older than Runcie, but held herself with grandeur.

Without haste, she carried a script up the steps to the stage. "Do you want me to read opposite this ruffian?" she said, her imperious voice carrying to the farthest reaches of the theater.

"Yes, please." Jared checked his list. "Are you Mariah Michaels?"

"I am," she said. "I've been on this earth for eighty-nine years. Is that too old?"

"Absolutely not," he said. "But I must warn you that in Act Three, your character tortures this man with a glass slipper."

Mariah's gaze swept over Runcie. "I could do that three times before my morning tea," she said, then blinked as if something had suddenly occurred to her. "Although I do rather like him." She paused. "How odd. I always found him annoying before."

"This should make for some lively interplay," Jared said sotto voce to Laura. To Mariah, he called, "Let's take it from the top of page thirty-three."

There were indeed lots of sparks between Mariah and Runcie. Judging by the amused quirk of Jared's mouth as the woman delivered her lines, Laura had no doubt he was going to cast her.

"Thank you. That was lovely," he said when she finished. "Anyone else reading for the Police Chief? No? Well, let's move on to the New Owner and the Young Widow."

Quite a few hopefuls took the stage, but none of the

men appealed to Laura for her main viewpoint character, and none of the females possessed the necessary haughtiness. Then she noticed a woman seated near the stage, impatiently shaking her mane of hair as she awaited her turn.

Glimpsing her in profile, Laura placed her as the predatory female who'd stalked past the punch table on New Year's Eve. An exclamation of "Well, finally!" issued from her lips when Jared called Vanessa Sachet's name, and she strode up the steps as if en route to claim an Oscar.

"Let me guess," Laura whispered. "She's the university president's girlfriend, right?"

"None other," Jared said affably. "She created quite a scandal last semester when they were caught at a motel and someone informed her husband. In class, she said she's seeking a new career as a Hollywood star now that she's getting divorced."

"Perfect." Talk about casting to type for the self-serving widow!

"I can't read this without someone playing opposite me," Vanessa announced from the stage. A couple of undergraduates in the audience got wide-eyed at her nerve in bossing the director.

Jared didn't appear to notice. Flipping to the last remaining application on his clipboard, he said, "I can't tell from the name whether this individual is male or female. Is Bernie Bernini here?"

A lanky figure with pale spiked hair, hoop earrings, a satiny pink open-collared shirt and tight black pants stood up. "Right here, Mr. Director," he or she said, waggling fingers.

"He can't audition! That's my hairdresser!" Vanessa cried.

"I can, too, audition." Bernie had large doelike brown eyes and a way of shifting backward as if trying to decide whether to flee or do the shimmy. "I mean, if Mr. Benton says so, I certainly can."

"I guess he's a he," Jared murmured to Laura. Aloud, he said, "Go ahead."

With a touch of self-conscious awkwardness, Bernie lifted a script from the edge of the stage and climbed up. He kept space between himself and Vanessa as if afraid she'd bite.

At first, when the two of them read, Laura cringed at their amateurishness. Then, slowly, they caught fire, and before she knew it, the two were bringing her words vividly to life. Vanessa's biting sarcasm appeared to both frighten and thrill the excitable Bernie, whose own interpretation became steadily more seductive.

Was it possible the two were attracted to each other? How odd, Laura thought. If she'd ever met a totally unsuited couple, it was them.

"You know, he's not bad," Vanessa announced after they finished. A student giggled.

"Thank you for your opinion, Mrs. Sachet," Jared said dryly. "Thanks to all of you for coming. The cast list will be posted tomorrow morning on the bulletin board outside my office."

"I don't have a class here tomorrow," Vanessa said. "Please send me an e-mail."

Jared paused for effect before replying, "I'm sure you can find time in your busy schedule to drop by."

"I'll check the board and send you an e-mail," Bernie volunteered.

"Why, thank you." The two of them walked out side by side.

The other auditioners began leaving, as well, some chattering, some subdued. A tall blond woman standing at the side of the stage looked at Jared expectantly. Laura wondered why she hadn't tried out for the role of the widow.

"Who's that?" she asked.

Jared followed her gaze. "Oh, that's Cindy Bemling, a friend of mine."

Laura's spirits dropped. What an idiot she'd been to assume that Jared was unattached. His girlfriend must have been out of town on New Year's Eve. "I see."

"I'd have introduced you, but she got here late," he went on, stretching his long legs as he stood up. "Cindy offered to help, so she's going to be our stage manager."

"Hey, how'd I do?" the woman asked, sauntering toward them. She had a down-to-earth manner that Laura couldn't help liking. "I warned you, I'm used to running the show, but I gritted my teeth and didn't make a single suggestion, helpful or otherwise."

"It's great to have an experienced hand like you," he said. To Laura, Jared explained, "Cindy used to supervise the community theater in Oofdah, Minnesota. And the softball team and the charity bazaar and just about everything else."

"Glad to meet you, Laura." Cindy stuck out her hand, and shook firmly. "I love your play."

"Thank you." Laura's throat constricted. Jared must spend quite a bit of time with this woman if he'd already given her a copy of the script.

"My husband loved it, too," Cindy said. "We got

married last month so we could really relate to all those romantic undercurrents.''

Laura was grateful that no one had guessed how jealous she'd been. But what did Cindy mean by romantic undercurrents? The play was a satire on romance, not an endorsement of it.

''Did it inspire Hugh to write you a poem?'' Jared said as he gathered his papers from the surrounding seats.

''Several of them,'' Cindy said. ''Hey, I hear you got my old job at the Lunar Lunch Box, Laura.''

''I start work tonight,'' she said.

''Well, good luck. I'm applying for teaching jobs, now that I intend to stay in Clair De Lune, but it's the middle of the year so it's not going to happen right away. Anyway, I'll see you at rehearsals!''

''I'm looking forward to it.'' The thought crossed Laura's mind that she could use a girlfriend. Moving from city to city so often made it hard to establish ties, and even during the few months she'd be staying in town, it would be fun to have someone to hang out with.

Someone other than Jared. After that spurt of jealousy, she didn't trust herself around him. No objectivity, no self-protective skepticism—in fact, Laura felt perilously close to jumping into a whirlwind.

She didn't understand why. Jared hadn't flirted with her today. All he'd done was sit there next to her, being himself.

''Want to get a bite to eat?'' he asked.

Laura stared at him in alarm. ''No, thanks!'' she said, and headed for the back of the theater.

''Hey!''

She turned. ''What?''

''Don't you want to review the actors and help me

decide on the cast?'' he asked. There was a note in his voice that pulled at her. A come-hither note, an invitation to spend time together and do things utterly unrelated to casting a play. Or did she just imagine it?

"I'm sure you'll do fine by yourself,'' Laura said, and hurried out into the crisp January sunshine with the sense that she'd barely escaped in time.

JARED STAYED LATE at the theater, making up the cast list. It took longer than expected because he couldn't decide on the understudies.

For the Young Newlyweds, there were plenty of actors to choose from, especially since the understudies would double in walk-on roles as the newlyweds' new love interests. On the other hand, for the older parts, he had no suitable replacements. The play wouldn't work if the chemistry wasn't right.

If one of the men dropped out, he decided, he could fill the role himself. As for the women, Jared would have to hope for the best.

In his experience, theatrical problems had a way of finding their own solutions and, besides, there was no reason to expect to lose an actress during such a short run. They could only hold two performances because the theater was needed by graduate students putting on one-act plays as their theses.

At last the list was complete. Sitting in his office, he rested his chin on one palm and indulged in the image that had dogged him all evening.

It was Laura, wound up as tight as a rubber band, her hair as unruly as ever and her lips moving as she muttered things to herself that he couldn't hear. What had been going through her mind this afternoon?

A strong desire came over him to be near her. There was no harm in it, he supposed. He knew where she was and had a perfect excuse to go there, since he'd skipped dinner.

After throwing on a black bomber jacket, Jared locked his office, posted the list on the bulletin board and retrieved his car from the faculty parking lot. He drove at a leisurely pace along De Lune Boulevard, enjoying the quiet shine of funky boutiques and old-fashioned streetlights.

Much as he loved the fast pace of New York, he relished spending time in this college town. It was fun to greet friends everywhere he went. Also, although he hadn't lost his dreams of stardom, he now appreciated the pleasure of being respected for his position without constantly walking a tightrope, staking his reputation on each new commercial production.

What's the matter, Jared? Getting set in your ways? he asked himself as he eased into a streetside parking slot. You'd better be careful or you'll lose your edge.

Not likely. He wasn't dead yet.

A welcoming glow shimmered through the mullioned windows of the cottage-style restaurant. Atop its shake roof, a cutout of a full moon with a smiling face beamed down. From Jared's angle, the real, three-quarter moon appeared to hang only inches above it.

He pushed open the door. As always in this busy place, the noise and brightness and the smell of sizzling hamburgers enveloped him at once.

"Jared!" "Over here!" "Join us!" called a group of graduate students.

A professor he knew gave him an assessing smile from her crowded table. Although he liked the woman as a friend, something held him back. Or perhaps it was someone, the lady who'd never quite left his heart.

There she stood on the far side of the restaurant, balancing a tray while distributing plates to a group of undergraduates. Laura looked, Jared thought, like a candle, slim and taut all the way up to that flaming hair.

"Can I seat you?" A blond fortysomething waitress popped into his field of view. Her name, he recalled from previous visits, was Magda.

"I'd better sit in Laura's station," he said. "I'm a friend of hers."

"You want to be near Laura?" Magda asked.

The question puzzled him. "Anything wrong with that?"

Magda gave a low whistle.

"Excuse me?" he said.

"In all the time you've been dining here, you've never once joined a woman at a table," she said. "They always come to you."

"You're exaggerating."

She shook her head. "Not only that, but I've never even seen you walk in with a woman. With other professors, yes, and sometimes with the cast of one of your plays, but..."

"I didn't realize you were watching me," Jared said, flattered.

"Everybody watches you. You've got this quality like a movie star that's hard to explain. Maybe it's sex appeal," Magda told him bluntly. "Well, go ahead. Take that table near the kitchen, or you can sit at the counter. Laura's handling that tonight."

"How's she doing?" he asked. "For a newbie?"

"She's a quick learner," Magda said.

Jared decided to sit at the counter, something he hadn't done in ages. The restaurant had comfortable chair-stools perched atop swiveling pedestals, and he had to resist the urge to twirl around like a kid as he settled into one.

He scanned a menu idly, since it was as familiar as the aisles of his local supermarket. Maybe more familiar, considering how little cooking he did.

"Can I help...oh, hi." Laura stopped in front of him and plucked a pencil from behind her ear. "What'll it be?"

"I'll have the bacon, cheese and avocado burger," Jared said.

"That comes with a free course in CPR," Laura said as she scribbled on her pad. "Never mind. Bad joke."

"How do you like waitressing?"

Half a dozen emotions flickered across her face as she mulled his question. The woman never had a simple re-action to anything, Jared thought.

"I feel like I ought to pay them to let me work here," she said. "I can't get over the way people interact! I mean, couples try to control what the other one is order-ing, can you believe that? 'I thought you were on a diet.' 'Remember what the doctor told you.' Then they get into an argument."

"Seen anyone you know?" He wanted to keep her talking, so he could enjoy the rhythm of her voice and the animation on her face.

"Vanessa Sachet and this guy who looks like a Kew-pie doll were in here. I guess that's President Martin, and she fussed at him for ordering onion rings as if there was something low class about them." Laura chuckled.

"It's great to see you so enthusiastic," he said.

"What do you mean?"

"Usually you measure out your words as if they were twenty-dollar bills," he said.

"Do I? I suppose I save them for my writing, but I'm having fun."

Jared was glad to see her so relaxed and talkative. He felt close to her tonight, perhaps due to all the time they'd spent side by side this afternoon.

"After you get off your shift, we can catch a late movie," he said. The campus offered a Midnight Madness screening almost every evening.

"I don't know." She paused with her pencil in midair.

"We can discuss the cast," he offered. "I posted the names before I came over here."

"I'll bet I can guess who— What on earth?" Laura swung around as black smoke issued from the kitchen.

Without stopping to think, Jared leaped around the counter and flung open the swinging doors to the kitchen. "Everybody all right in here? Where's the fire extinguisher?"

Two startled faces popped up between the bank of burners and the ovens. Daffodil had her chef's cap on crooked and Stuart's shirt was unbuttoned.

Atop the grill, smoke poured from flaming black lumps of meat. "I guess somebody ordered those well done, right?" Jared said.

"Oh, my gosh!" Daffodil jumped up from the floor and clapped a metal lid over the burning burgers. "I don't know how that happened. How we...I was walking toward the oven and I slipped."

Stuart turned bright red. "I went to help her and I slipped, too. There must be a, uh, grease spill on the floor."

"It took us a while to get up," Daffodil added. "Guess we're older than we thought."

The howl of a smoke alarm cut off further conversation. Stuart raced to silence it, but not before half a dozen customers poked their faces through the swinging doors behind Jared.

"I called the fire department," said one man, brandishing his cell phone. "Do you need paramedics?"

Stuart found an apron and pulled it over his shirt. "Everything's fine. Just fine."

But it wasn't. Smoke filled the Lunar Lunch Box, and when the firefighters arrived, they sent everyone outside. Since it was nearly eleven o'clock, Stuart announced he was closing for the night, and the waitresses passed out the checks.

"Glad to see you're free now," Jared told Laura when she finished collecting from her customers.

"I guess so." She gazed up at him, oblivious to the evening chill, although she wore only a silver apron over a skirt and blouse. "That was wonderful, the way you rushed into the kitchen without a thought for your own safety."

"It's pure egotism," he told her. "I believe I'm invincible."

"So you really do lead another life as Zorro," Laura joked.

"All I'm missing is the cape," he said.

Overhead, the double moons—one real, one fake—beamed down on them. Jared felt as if they stood in a cylinder of brightness apart from the commotion. He hadn't felt this pleasantly disconnected from reality since a time in college when he accidentally overdosed on cold medicine.

What's going on with you? whispered a still-functioning part of his brain. Usually he was better at staying detached. Tonight, somehow, he couldn't.

Whatever was in the air, it affected Laura, too. She radiated the wonder and joy that had delighted him so many years ago, along with a passion he'd believed he killed that night at the cast party. Fate, it appeared, was giving them a second chance.

Jared took her hand and pulled her through the hubbub until they reached his car. Without a word, Laura hopped inside, and he navigated around the fire trucks and took off, heading for home.

They were going to have quite a night, Jared thought. He hoped it never ended.

4

LAURA SANG ALONG with the radio. Intoxicated, that's what she was. Yet the Lunar Lunch Box didn't even have a liquor license.

She watched Jared's muscular arm as he shifted gears. Zooming into the hills with him felt inevitable, as if fate had been guiding them to this moment for years. Yet only days ago, she'd barely been able to tolerate the thought of him.

What had changed? One kiss on New Year's Eve hadn't made the difference, so what had?

Laura tried to find an answer, but concentration eluded her. Another song came on the radio, and the lyrics commanded her to take a chance on love.

"Magical, isn't it?" Jared said.

"It is," Laura agreed. No, that didn't sound like her, she told herself sternly. "I mean, what's magical?"

"Everything," he said. "The music. The stars. The fire at the café."

"Jared, do things seem a little peculiar to you?" she asked. "As if we're under the influence of something?"

"Don't fight it, Laura," he said.

For a moment, she thought he was going to repeat the line from the song and tell her to take a chance on love, in which case she would know this entire scenario was as fried as those charred hamburgers. But he just hummed slightly off-key and steered up the hill.

"Where are we going?" She hadn't thought twice about accepting a ride, since she'd walked to work, but obviously he didn't intend to drop her at Dean Pipp's. Not that she minded.

"My place."

"Okay."

It was the wrong direction if he meant his old apartment, so he must have moved. Well, of course he had! After years away from Clair De Lune, he would hardly have returned to the same place, she chided herself.

Into Laura's mind popped a vivid memory of his student digs, cluttered with books and clothing and perpetually smelling of aftershave lotion. He and his roommate always had a stack of dirty plates in the sink, and there'd been a dog that wandered through the place, but didn't seem to belong to anybody.

What she remembered best was the lumpy couch on which they'd rehearsed Romeo and Juliet's bedroom scene. One night, in the absence of his roommate, Jared had suggested they try the dialogue lying down, and before she knew it they'd tossed their scripts aside and gone at each other.

It had taken all her strength of will to stop. Jared, to give him credit, had been a perfect gentleman about it, although he wouldn't have stopped if she hadn't asked him to.

"Here we are." The sports car dashed into the curving driveway of a tile-roofed stucco house. He killed the engine.

Below them, all of Clair De Lune sparkled against the darkness. "It's beautiful."

"And all mine in eighteen years, when I pay off the mortgage. If I'm still around." Jared uncoiled from his seat. "Come take a closer look."

Laura joined him on the concrete. It was cold tonight, but she didn't mind. "This would be a great place to dance," she said.

"Inside, outside, all around the town," Jared chanted, and put his arms around her. They didn't need accompaniment. With the stars so bright overhead and the town lights glimmering below, Laura could hear the music of the spheres.

After they circled the driveway twice, Jared steered her inside without missing a beat. They waltzed through the entryway and into the living room, where a flip of the switch produced gentle light.

When Laura noticed the lamp, she stopped dancing to stare in disbelief at the cupids. "I think their little wings are beating," she said.

"You must have eaten too much MSG at the restaurant." Jared kept one arm around her waist.

"Daffodil does put a lot on the French fries," she conceded.

"And so, having resolved that issue, we move on to more important matters." She didn't realize what he intended until he swooped her backward to lie in his arms. Even after ten years, her body responded instinctively with the move they'd perfected in *Romeo and Juliet*. "Now the hero closes in for a kiss."

"Now the heroine comes abruptly to her senses," she said, but instead of twisting away, she touched his cheek and was oddly pleased by the end-of-day roughness.

When he kissed her, Jared tasted of male excitement. Despite her better judgment, Laura responded with pent-up longing, sending the two of them collapsing onto the sofa.

She scarcely registered the impact, as if they were floating. When Jared lifted his head, he wore a dazedly blissful expression that matched her own mood. None of this seemed quite real, and yet it was keenly pleasurable.

Laura heard a faint hum. It must be the cupids' wings, she thought, then forgot everything except Jared.

Leaning over her, he kissed her throat and unbuttoned her blouse. Before she knew it, he had discarded the bra that she sometimes joked wasn't much bigger than a tourniquet, and his hands closed over her breasts. For the first time in her life, they felt lush and full.

Reaching up to caress his vibrant male body, Laura found it as fine-tuned and sleek as a bullet. Deliriously she explored Jared's taut buttocks, hard thighs and well-developed chest. This was as far as they'd gone when they were younger. Now she couldn't imagine stopping.

"I want everything." His voice rang out against the hushed depths of the night. "I want you everywhere."

"Go for it," she said.

Laura hadn't realized he meant not only that he wanted her entire body, but that he wanted her in every room of the house. Wild laughter, most of it her own, accompanied them as Jared transported her into the kitchen and, having shed the rest of his clothes en route, consummated their passion against the refrigerator.

"I've still got my skirt on," Laura said.

"We'll take care of that." How he managed to remove it while they were locked together, she never figured out, but he did.

The next thing she knew, they were in the bathroom, a grand sweep of tile and glass with both a tub and a shower stall. He whisked her into the booth, flipped on the water and drenched them in a warm spray.

"Having fun?" Without waiting for an answer, Jared cupped her buttocks and thrust into her, drawing a cry of surprise and delight.

Their bodies slid against each other, frictionless. Laura clung to him, not that she was afraid. In fact, she'd never felt so worry-free in her life.

Without warning, he picked her up and carted her, dripping wet, straight into the bedroom. "Towel!" she cried.

"Towels are for sissies," said Jared, and plunged both into her and into the bed. It was a low, wide bed that absorbed them so thoroughly that in a moment, Laura didn't even feel damp.

She anchored herself to him as heat coursed through her, intensifying until she was sure she must be glowing. In her arms, Jared morphed into pure white light and they rocketed through dimensions previously unsuspected on the earthly plane.

When at last they came to rest on the tangled sheets, Jared said, "There are two more bedrooms, but they're full of boxes."

"Let's save those for another time." Laura snuggled against him.

She didn't know what had just happened or where it might lead. Right now she didn't care.

JARED AWOKE IN A STATE of happy confusion. What a night! He glanced at the woman curled beside him, her red hair fluffed across the pillow. He wished he'd found Laura again years ago, or that he'd never let her go.

The digital clock blinked to 7:10 a.m. He had to teach a class in less than two hours.

Laura stirred and stretched, dislodging the covers. He loved her unselfconsciousness and the innocence of her slim body.

Her eyes blinked open and she regarded him for several seconds before speaking. "It wasn't a dream."

"You didn't honestly think it was, did you?" He fingered the red fuzz along her nape.

"That bit about the fluttering cupids—what was that?" she asked sleepily.

"Poetic hyperbole," he said.

Laura groaned. "It must have been a spell. Surely it wasn't us doing those things last night."

"If it wasn't us, who was it?" Jared asked.

"Two crazed identities from Dimension X."

"We'll have to get better acquainted with them over breakfast." He threw back the covers. "I have a 9:00 a.m. class."

Laura patted the mattress. "Was it my imagination or did we jump in here soaking wet?"

"We did." He recalled that moment fondly.

"Why isn't the bed damp?"

"I think we were at such a white heat, the moisture evaporated." Jared never worried about the fine points of physics, since the scientists were always changing their minds, anyway. "Also, this mattress is a marvel of the latest Danish technology. It could absorb almost anything."

"I didn't know the Danes were so advanced." Getting to her feet, she helped him pull the colorful, patterned spread into place.

"Think about it," Jared said. "They don't have to

build a huge arsenal like the United States. No laser-guided missiles, no undersea nuclear snooping. No space program, either. So they put all their technical brilliance into furniture. I have it on good authority that whoever sleeps in this bed lives forever.'' He was making that part up, but he liked it.

"That's silly.'' Laura smiled.

The mention of Denmark had whetted Jared's appetite and, after loaning Laura a bathrobe and throwing one on himself, he rummaged in the fridge until he located a package of lemon Danish. Vaguely he recalled that they'd found another use for the refrigerator last night, and started getting lustful all over again.

"Today's Wednesday,'' he said. "I don't have an early class tomorrow, so we can get together again tonight.''

"No,'' Laura said.

"What do you mean, no? You mean no as in 'I can't wait,' right?''

She leaned one elbow on the tale and regarded him with clear green eyes. "I know this sounds peculiar, but what happened last night seemed almost…unreal. As if we'd been showered with pixie dust.''

"What makes you say that?''

"I'm not sure,'' she admitted. "But our impulses didn't come from deep inside.''

"How deep inside do they have to come from?'' Jared asked. "We both enjoyed ourselves.''

"I know.'' She exhaled slowly. "It's not that I want a serious involvement. I don't.''

"Good.'' That was relief, not disappointment, coiling inside his chest, he told himself. "Agreed. We both have our careers to think about. Moving around, taking new assignments.''

''Something like that,'' she said.

''So what's wrong with having fun?'' Last night had merely been an appetizer, as far as Jared was concerned.

''Sooner or later, we'll hit the wall, and that could damage our working relationship,'' Laura said. ''Let's keep it light.''

''Great!'' he said. ''I'll pick you up after work and we'll catch a movie. Then we'll come back here and avoid talking about anything serious while we...''

''No dating,'' she said. ''I'm sorry, I know it's odd, but I think we need to keep our distance.''

Jared finished his second Danish while he mulled his options. Obviously Laura didn't want a boyfriend-girlfriend relationship. He understood, even if he didn't share her apprehension. ''We could do nooners,'' he said hopefully.

''No sex,'' Laura clarified.

''Was it the shower?'' he asked. ''The part about the bed not getting wet? I suppose it could freak a person out. If it makes a difference, I'll be careful not to do that again.''

When she shook her head, the red hair gave a suggestive bounce that turned his midsection hard. ''It's not that simple.''

''Don't tell me you're not tempted,'' Jared said.

Laura swallowed some of the leftover coffee he'd reheated. ''It was great. Perfect, like a single rose. But like any rose, if you let it sit around too long, it will wilt.''

If she was metaphorically referring to his anatomy, she had another think coming. ''It's nowhere near wilting,'' he assured her.

Pink tinged her cheeks. "Please accept my decision. Jared, I'm sure I'm doing the right thing. We both lost control, and, well, wonderful as it was, I don't want to repeat the experience."

Glumly he accepted that she meant it. More importantly, her remark about losing control reminded him of something he should have thought of earlier.

"We forgot the contraception," he said. "Please tell me it's the wrong time of the month."

"You're in luck," she said. "I'm on the Pill."

"Perfect."

The third lemon Danish didn't taste nearly as delicious as the first two. Usually Jared's taste buds were good for indefinite indulgences, but despite his relief at learning that Laura wasn't at risk of getting pregnant, his appetite had vanished.

It wasn't only sex that they were giving up, he admitted to himself. He wanted to spend more time together doing other things—dancing, joking, talking. But he could handle rejection. Badly, maybe, but he could handle it.

Lost in their private thoughts, they dressed quietly and Jared drove Laura home. She darted away before he could kiss her.

It was now clear how she'd disappeared so easily on New Year's Eve, he reflected as she skipped up the stairs of Dean Pipp's rental unit. That time, he hadn't known where to find her. This time, he was voluntarily letting her go.

It was probably for the best, Jared told himself as he headed for campus. So why did he feel as if he'd lost something?

Why was she on the Pill, anyway? There must have

been a boyfriend back in Santa Fe, someone she'd cared enough about to get a prescription for. Someone she'd wanted to spend a lot more than one night with.

Well, whoever it was, she'd left him behind. That knowledge gave Jared a little satisfaction, at least.

AT HOME, LAURA HAD a hard time concentrating. After hearing some of her dialogue at the auditions, she'd been inspired to make additional revisions, but it was hard to focus.

She couldn't believe how freely she'd responded last night with Jared. He'd been magnificent, and she'd been...somebody else.

"Temporarily insane," she told Ryan O'Neal, who continued to gaze sensitively at Ali McGraw on the *Love Story* poster.

Thank goodness she was on the Pill, which a doctor had prescribed to correct irregular periods. Still, last night was going to have consequences, most notably her indelible memories of how irresistible Jared had looked and how wonderful she'd felt as he made love to her all over the house. Apparently Laura's acting skills hadn't entirely rusted, because she'd pulled off an Oscar-quality performance this morning in convincing him of her indifference.

Still, she'd done the right thing. The more time they spent as lovers, the higher the price she would eventually have to pay.

This line of thought was getting Laura nowhere. In a few hours, she had to go to work at the Lunch Box, and tomorrow the first rehearsal was scheduled. She needed to make her latest revisions quickly.

Hoping a change of scenery might help, she hauled an

annotated copy of the script and her laptop computer outside and down the stairs. Although last night had been
chilly, the day was warming rapidly, and a sweater kept
her comfortable as she sat beneath a eucalyptus tree.

Laura didn't fail to notice the red cap bobbing high
above her, but, true to his word, Hoagie was aiming his
binoculars down the block. Since he'd been sitting up
there nearly motionless since Jared dropped her off, she
assumed he didn't want to make conversation any more
than she did.

As soon as she opened her laptop, Laura's mind
clicked into gear. Setting the hard copy script atop some
exposed tree roots, she found the right spot on the screen
and began reworking the dialogue.

Nearly oblivious to the occasional passing car and dog
walker, she worked steadily for the next hour. She barely
registered the man's approach until he turned up the
walkway toward Dean Pipp's porch.

Even then, she deliberately avoided eye contact, but
couldn't help noticing that he was about seventy years
old and in great shape. He wore a safari helmet, camp
shirt and multipocketed shorts that bared knobby knees.

The man rang the bell and waited. After a few minutes,
the door opened and there was a long silence. Then he
went inside.

A suitor? Laura wondered. Perhaps even the long-lost
husband? Well, that was her landlady's business.

She resumed work for another half hour, until a pair
of worn pumps stopped in front of her. One of them
tapped impatiently until Laura looked up.

Esther Zimpelman glared at her. "I need to know
about that man who brought you home this morning. In

the future, don't send him away so quickly. I didn't even get a good look, not to mention a picture.''

''Good.'' Laura returned her gaze to the computer.

Mrs. Zimpelman stuck a sheet of paper over the screen. It was, Laura saw, a form headed Snooper Report. ''Since I couldn't get the information myself, you need to fill this out.''

''Excuse me?'' Laura scanned the questions. ''You expect me to tell you and your nosy buddies who I was with, what we were doing, how long we were doing it and when we plan on doing it again?''

''Here's a pen,'' said Esther, and picked up the script. ''Use this for backing. Go on, fill it out.'' Placing the form atop it, her neighbor started to hand it over.

Amid the rustle of leaves, Hoagie dropped down beside her. ''You should spend your time on something more meaningful than gossip, Esther.'' He took hold of the script.

As he did so, his gaze locked on to Esther's. Whatever he meant to say next, it was lost as the two of them stood with sunlight streaming over them and expressions of wonder on their faces.

''Uh-oh,'' Laura said.

She hoped she was mistaken, but it seemed like a coincidence that these two should react so strongly to each other while holding her play. Other incidents flooded her memory: Vanessa and Bernie's chemistry at the auditions. Stuart's sudden warmth toward Daffodil. Mariah's declaration that she didn't find Runcie annoying anymore.

All had occurred after they handled the script. Then there was Laura's and Jared's own unexpected night of fantasy, complete with fluttering cupids' wings.

It was almost as if the emotions she'd invested in the story had somehow created a real "glass slipper" effect. But that was ridiculous, she told herself. She was taking a bunch of coincidences far too seriously.

Hoagie and Esther were still staring at each other. He swallowed a few times before speaking. "You know, when we were kids, and our families used to get together, I had a crush on you."

"You did?" Esther asked breathlessly. "You never said anything."

Relief swept over Laura. The attraction between this pair was of long duration. Her script had nothing to do with it.

"You were the most beautiful girl I'd ever seen." His face shone. "But I was too shy to say anything."

"You should have." A youthful smile replaced her accustomed frown. "I thought you were cute, too, but you never paid me any attention."

"Oh, yes, I did," Hoagie said. "I was just too shy to let on, and then, before I found the courage, you got married."

"I wish you'd told me." She released the script.

Without taking his eyes off her, he handed it to Laura. "Would it have made a difference?"

"Who can tell, after all this time?" Esther said. "My husband was a good man. I wasn't head over heels in love, but we had a happy marriage."

"I was head over heels," Hoagie said. "I never met anyone like you. I guess that's why I never married."

"You should come to the Snoopers meeting with me this afternoon, so we can get to know each other better," she said. "We're decorating for a party this Sunday. It's a reception for some young friends who got married."

"That sounds like fun," he said.

"Let's go fix lunch." Esther gave him a rare smile. "Tomorrow, I'll help you look for the Purple-Breasted Whatsit."

"Great." They walked away without a word to Laura.

She collected her equipment and went inside. Her play had nothing to do with this, she told herself firmly. All the same, she tucked the script into a drawer where no visitor would accidentally come across it.

5

JARED HAD A GOOD REASON for going to the Lunar Lunch Box for dinner on Wednesday night. He was hungry. Of course, there were other restaurants in town, but Laura didn't work at them.

He returned on Thursday. Since rehearsals started Saturday, he thought it was a good idea to check to make sure his playwright hadn't left town. Or gotten lost. Or fallen through a rabbit hole.

He didn't speak to her beyond a friendly hello because he respected her distance. He didn't sit at her station, either, so he considered himself to be honoring her wishes.

On Friday afternoon at the theater building, she marched into his office and smacked some pages on the desk. Before she could speak, Jared held up his hand.

"I was careful not to impinge on your independence," he said. "Please don't tell me you're mad."

"Mad?" Laura gestured at the papers. "I don't know where you got that idea. I just brought this over."

"It isn't a restraining order, is it?" He glanced through the sheets of paper. Dialogue and stage directions. After a brief disconnect, he realized she'd rewritten part of Act Two. "Oh, sorry."

"Why would I be mad?" About to sit in the one vacant chair, Laura wiped a finger over it.

"There's makeup on here."

"What color?" Jared asked distractedly, reading a snatch of dialogue.

"White."

"That's from Bryan. He dropped in during office hours. He's one of my student mimes."

"He puts makeup on his butt?" After removing a tissue from her purse, she cleaned the seat.

"Students sit on the counters in the dressing room and you never know what sticks to their clothes." As he scanned the revisions, a line startled a laugh from him. "This is clever. You're honing the characters."

"They keep growing inside my subconscious. I don't know how it happens." She sat down. "I wanted you to have the new pages for the rehearsal tomorrow."

"Thanks." Jared tucked them into a folder. "I'll have the secretary make copies."

Laura nodded. Despite her stillness, she glowed like a flame in the center of his office. Watching her, Jared realized that, even after the incredible night they'd shared, she was in many ways a stranger.

If he knew her better, the insights would help him direct her play. The fact that they might bring her closer was immaterial, really. Sort of.

"This small town—Sterndale—is it anything like where you grew up?" he asked. "In fact, where did you grow up? Maybe you told me a long time ago, but I'm afraid I don't remember."

"As far as I recall, we were too busy discussing our futures to talk about the past," she said. "I'm from Denver. My family still lives there."

"Do you like your family?" Jared asked.

"Sure." Laura huddled inside her oversize sweater. "Don't you like yours?"

"That's not the point. I haven't written a play about mine," he said.

"Neither have I." He thought he detected a note of defensiveness.

"I'm only trying to understand you better." Jared leaned back in his chair. "I figure some aspects of your characters have to relate to your background. Your father doesn't run a shoe factory, does he?"

"No. He's a high school teacher," she said. "Shop and PE."

"How about your mother?"

"She teaches math. Dad coaches tennis and baseball, and Mom coaches the math team. Her students win a lot of competitions." Despite the pride in her words, Laura sounded wistful.

Jared had worked with other playwrights over the years and he'd never much cared about their family relationships. This was different, and he didn't need to ask why. This involved Laura. "I seem to remember you had a sister," he said.

"Two sisters." She didn't elaborate.

Drawing information out of her was almost as hard as holding a conversation with a mime, he thought. Bryan, who took his chosen role seriously, communicated through notes scribbled on a pad. Laura, he supposed, communicated through her play, but that was an indirect means at best.

"You don't have to talk about them if you don't want to," he said, hoping to prompt her into doing the exact opposite.

The freckles stood out against Laura's pale skin as she

considered. "It's okay. I want to be the best playwright I can, even if it hurts."

Jared barely restrained an urge to walk around his desk and hold her. It was almost scary how much he liked this woman. He reminded himself that they were only colleagues, and he'd agreed to keep it that way. "Why does it hurt to talk about your family?"

"It shouldn't." In the flat lighting, her eyes took on dark shadows. "I mean, we love each other. It's just..." Before he could question her further, she hurried on, "I'm the middle daughter and I guess I got lost in the shuffle."

"That's hard to imagine." Jared grinned. "You stand out in a crowd."

"I do?" Idly she twisted a strand of hair around one finger. "Oh, you mean this carrottop. We all have red hair, but Leila—she's my big sister—has a gorgeous mane, and Louanne, the baby, has Little Orphan Annie ringlets. Mine's a mop."

"You think your parents ignored you because you're number two out of three?" Jared leaned forward, wishing there weren't a pile of papers and a broad desk between them. "I'm the oldest of four and I used to gripe about having too much responsibility, especially after my parents divorced." He stopped himself. "No, please go on. I want to know about you."

"I thought the point was to get to know my characters." Laura's mouth tightened, a sign that she was pulling into her shell.

"It is," Jared assured her. He meant it, in a way. "You haven't told me about your sisters."

"Leila's a math whiz," Laura said. "She and Mom

were always preparing for contests. She won a full scholarship to MIT, and her husband's a physicist.''

"Impressive," he said. "What about Louanne?"

"When she was three years old, she picked up a swatter and smacked a fly that had been buzzing around the house driving us all crazy," Laura said. "None of us could hit it, but she did, with one try."

"Let me guess. She stars in—is it softball or tennis?" Jared asked.

"Tennis. She won even more trophies than Leila," she said. "Between the two of them, they filled a big glass case in the living room." Her hands clasped in her lap, she added, "I earned a couple of certificates in poetry contests and I had a story published in our school literary magazine. They didn't look very impressive by comparison."

"You did better than me. I used to cut classes in high school to go skateboarding," Jared said. "It wasn't until college that I figured out a person could make a career out of theater, which I'd always loved. I'm glad my parents didn't judge me by my achievements at an early age."

In fact, his father had rarely contacted the family after divorcing Jared's mother. Betsy Benton, on the other hand, was the Number One fan for her four children. Although Jared didn't get to see her often, he kept her informed of his doings by e-mail and phone.

"My parents didn't judge me, exactly. They simply didn't notice me," Laura said. "Maybe that's why I'm so ambitious."

"Trying to prove something."

"Exactly."

"You don't need to prove anything to me." From her

startled expression, Jared gathered he'd become too personal. "Which is neither here nor there. It occurs to me that the character of the Newlywed Woman is an accountant. Good at math, like your sister."

"I didn't register the resemblance, but you're right." Laura took a pad and pen from her purse and made a note. "Now that you mention it, I'm kind of tough on that character."

"She's quick-tempered, but she has some funny lines," Jared said. "I never understood why her husband wouldn't want to try again with her."

"Because they've hurt each other so much." She wrinkled her nose. "Maybe I was taking revenge on Leila without meaning to. She doesn't deserve that. At the end, maybe the couple decides to seek marriage counseling."

"A note of hope," Jared said. "The play could use it."

"I'll do the rewrite tomorrow morning." Laura stood up. "Right now, I'm due at work." In the doorway, she paused. "Are you coming in for dinner again tonight?"

"I thought I might."

"The special is grilled cheese with sauerkraut. It tastes better than it sounds," she said, and went out.

Jared couldn't stand sauerkraut, but he'd be there.

"I TELL YOU, HE'S SMITTEN," Magda said as she and Laura fetched plates of food from the warming station. "Jared Benton, of all people! He comes in here every night and stares at you."

"He comes in every night and gets inundated with friends," Laura corrected. "About two-thirds of whom are female."

"Jared's always been a babe magnet," said her fellow waitress. "I don't think he notices them."

Laura found that hard to believe. Not wanting to sound jealous, however, she refrained from saying so.

A few minutes ago, Jared had strolled in, waved to her, and taken a seat in Magda's section. Already, three women had drifted over and begun vying for his attention.

A couple of male students joined them, then a few more people. Jared presided over his table with jovial carelessness, sometimes absenting himself from the conversation to study his menu as if he'd never seen it before, other times throwing out a comment that inspired uproarious laughter.

He'd always been like that, even in their undergraduate days, Laura recalled. Wherever he went, Jared became the center of attention without trying.

She was clearing away a tableful of dirty dishes when the truth hit her. She was jealous, all right, not of the other women but of Jared himself.

While she'd been ignored not only by her parents but by practically everyone as a youngster, Jared possessed natural charisma. He was born to be popular, while Laura stood on the outside. It was her pathetic place in the order of things, and she...liked it.

She grabbed onto the edges of the tray to keep from dropping it. Why hadn't she seen this before?

Sure, she'd endured some pain as a teenager because of her parents' preoccupation with her sisters, but as an adult she loved being able to watch people. The ability to move among others virtually unnoticed was a gift. She stored up details of behavior that she could never have observed if she were like Jared.

"You look pleased with yourself," said Daffodil when Laura went into the kitchen to deposit the dirty dishes.

"I just discovered I'm glad to be me," she said.

"It's time to move on from there." The cook flipped two burgers, poured a dollop of scrambled eggs onto the griddle and lowered a metal basket of French fries into sizzling hot oil. The heady scents nearly made Laura want to eat a second dinner. "At your age, you should be falling in love."

Laura dumped ice into a pitcher and filled it with water. Although she lacked experience as a waitress, she had plenty as a customer and remembered how uncomfortable it was to run low on water while eating.

"I'm not sure it's safe," she said. "Have you noticed that Cupid's been shooting his darts into the most unlikely couples?"

"You mean like me and Stuart?" asked the cook.

Laura had been careful not to say anything about the two of them rolling around on the floor while the hamburgers burned. She hadn't expected Daffodil to broach the subject herself. "I didn't...I mean, that's none of my business."

"Don't worry about us," said the cook. "We're consenting adults."

"Tell me one thing," Laura said. "If it turned out that what you're feeling wasn't real—wasn't permanent—would you still be glad you and Stuart had gotten closer?"

"Absolutely," said Daffodil. "Honey, I'm forty-two years old. I've been divorced twice and I've got three stepchildren who don't remember I'm alive except when they need money. Playing footsie with Stuart beats

watching reruns of *The Golden Girls*. They'll always b
there. He won't.''

Maybe a little temporary love wasn't such a bad thing
for Daffodil or for her, Laura reflected, and she went ou
to fill her customers' glasses. She was halfway aroun
the room before she noticed that Jared had plopped he
script on the table in front of him.

His former companions had been replaced by Cind
Bemling and a slim, attractive man who must be her hus
band. Apparently Jared had seized this opportunity to dis
cuss a stage manager's duties with her.

Laura got busy taking the orders of a tableful of nev
arrivals. It was half an hour later before she had time t
sneak another glance at Jared. He was chuckling, his hea
thrown back and his lavender-gray eyes sparkling. At thi
angle, his high cheekbones and slightly crooked nos
gave him the look of a classical Greek wrestler.

He could wrestle her to the ground any day, Laur
mused. Her body tingled at the recollection of their ear
lier encounter.

"You've got it bad," Magda said.

Laura jumped. "What do you mean?"

"Honey, I know he's smitten with you, but men aren'
reliable," said her fellow waitress. "I hope you're no
riding for a fall."

"I'll be moving on in a few months," Laura said. "It'
nothing."

Magda clipped a new order onto the metal wheel tha
organized them for Daffodil. "I'd better go see if he an
the Bemlings want more coffee."

For some reason, Laura blurted, "Whatever you do
don't touch that script in front of him."

"What's wrong with it?"

Yes, what was wrong with it? Nothing, most likely. "It's, uh, bad luck," she said. "I mean, to touch a script if you're not involved in the production."

"I never heard that one before." Magda laughed. "Although you theater people are supposed to be superstitious. I heard you won't say the title *Macbeth* because you think it's unlucky."

"We call it 'The Scottish Play,'" Laura agreed. She had no idea where that tradition had originated. "And the way we wish people well on opening night is to say, 'Break a leg.'"

"To each his own." Magda shook her head. "Hey, look who stopped by." She indicated a middle-aged man in an expensive suit. "He's a lawyer downtown, name of Burt Page. He represented my ex-husband in our divorce. What a stuffed shirt! I'm surprised he'd even come into a lowbrow place like this."

The man stopped at Jared's side and leaned on the script while chatting with him. "Why did he have to put his hand on my play?"

"He deserves some bad luck." Magda grabbed a carafe and departed.

Laura went about her duties. A while later, she happened to see Magda move the play aside as she cleared a plate. No big deal, she told herself.

Apparently Burt Page wasn't such a bad guy, after all, she noted as he reached out to help Magda. The couple's eyes locked. Laura could practically hear the violin music.

Her heart hammered inside her chest. You're imagining it. This has nothing to do with your script.

The waitress and the lawyer walked to an empty table

and sat down, talking softly. They kept smiling at each other.

At Jared's table, the Bemlings rose and made their exit. For one unheard-of moment, he was alone.

Hurrying over, Laura slid into a chair. He reached out and cupped her hands inside his. "I've missed you."

"I've been in the same room all evening," she said.

"Too far away." At Jared's lazy grin, her heart turned over.

An uncomfortable notion popped into her mind. If there really was such a thing as a glass slipper effect, it might be responsible for this tenderness. In that case, whatever was between them meant nothing, at least to him.

"Do you think there's something odd going on?" she asked.

One eyebrow lifted. "Care to give an example?"

"The way Magda and that lawyer suddenly clicked, for instance," she said.

"She's an attractive woman, and I think he's lonely," Jared said.

"But she doesn't even like him." That might be because he'd represented her ex-husband, Laura recalled. "Oh, I don't know. It just seems like this whole town is going crazy. Haven't you noticed?"

"I've noticed that I'm going crazy, because you're spending all your time with other people." He regarded her through sexy, half-lowered lids.

"I'm working," Laura said.

"And now it's time to go home."

"No, it isn't." She glanced at her watch, then back at him, startled. "When did it get to be a quarter to midnight? I'd better finish collecting."

"I'll wait," said Jared.

She knew she ought to tell him not to bother. But she didn't.

HE'D BEEN ON A NATURAL HIGH all week, and Jared didn't want to come down. His philosophy was that whenever you stumbled into a euphoric state, you should enjoy it for as long as possible.

A short distance away, he watched Laura make change and pocket her tips. What an appealing bounce she had when she moved. It amazed him that every other man in the restaurant didn't try to pick her up.

He loved being here, although until recently the Lunar Lunch Box's main charm had been its cheesecake. Laura lit up the room, and her grin lit up his heart. Jared couldn't imagine how her parents or anyone else had overlooked her.

A small voice inside, the one he tried to squash whenever it intruded on a good time, reminded him that he'd deliberately broken off with her ten years ago because he hadn't wanted to be held back. Since he still needed the freedom to make his mark in the theater world, why was he dallying with her now?

There was no harm in it, Jared told himself. He wasn't in love and neither was Laura. This infatuation was like a glass of champagne, fizzy and head-whirling and quickly gone. When life pulled them apart, they'd be left with pleasant memories.

He watched as she disappeared through a door marked Employees Only, and returned sans the silver apron. Why was she stopping to talk to Magda? Couldn't she see how impatient he was to get her alone?

At last she turned and walked toward him. As Jared

stood up, his spirits soared like the hot-air balloon passengers rising on the wallpaper toward a painted moon.
He could hardly wait to get Laura home.

There were still two bedrooms, a bathroom and who
knew how many alcoves they hadn't explored yet.

6

"WE'VE GOT TO STOP MEETING this way," Laura murmured as she lay in bed beside Jared on Saturday morning.

"Why?" he asked.

"I should be home rewriting my play."

"You should be here, experiencing lust in all its many forms," he corrected, sliding one hand across her bare breasts.

"We already did that." Laura tried to ignore the heat stirring inside her. "Now that we've run out of rooms, we should quit."

"Give me ten good reasons why."

"Because we both know how this will end."

"That isn't even one good reason," he said, relaxing against the pillow and awaiting her further response.

With the sheets bunched around his midsection, Jared lay exposed above the waist, his muscles tantalizingly male and his lips slightly parted. Laura allowed herself the pleasure of studying him in the morning light.

She wanted more of him, that was for sure. Yet if all she felt was physical desire, she could have enjoyed the affair in the calm knowledge that, postproduction, she would walk away as unattached as he was.

Not that Laura ever sought out purely sexual relationships with men. She'd had only a couple of boyfriends since that painful experience when she was nineteen, enough to reassure herself that she was desirable and had put Jared behind her.

But now that she'd found him again, she liked him too much. Craved him, like those unfortunate women who threw themselves at the man wherever he went.

All week, she'd found herself saving up funny incidents to tell him. She'd imagined conversations in which she proved incredibly witty and he glowed with admiration.

What a fool she was to risk falling in love and getting hurt again! Even to enrich herself as a playwright, it wasn't worth it.

"Because there aren't enough towels in your bathrooms," Laura said, preferring silly reasons to serious ones. "Because your house looks like a hotel, except for that ugly lamp in the living room. Because you don't have any bath mats and there's nothing but beer and cottage cheese in your refrigerator and your pot holders don't match. How many reasons is that?"

"Six," he said. "I think."

"You want more?"

He placed one hand over his heart. "I don't think I can take it. You've wounded me mortally."

"Reason Number Seven. You can't handle constructive criticism." Laura threw off the covers. "I'm going to take a shower. I'll eat breakfast at home, where I have actual food."

They'd be seeing each other that afternoon at the first rehearsal. Until then, she wanted to avoid lingering in Jared's company and falling ever more deeply under his spell.

"Laura!" he called with a note of urgency.

She turned at the bathroom door. "What?"

"You really think my lamp is ugly?" he asked.

She went into the bathroom and locked the door.

When she came out, she discovered that Jared had cleaned up in the other bathroom. Dressed in jeans and a sweater, he was cooking an omelette in the kitchen.

"I did so have something other than cottage cheese and beer in the refrigerator," he said. "You're down to five reasons. They're not good enough."

"You're smug." Laura sat at the breakfast table. "That's a good reason to dump you."

"You need four more." He sprinkled Tabasco sauce over the eggs.

"You ditched me at the cast party ten years ago," she said.

"There's a statute of limitations," Jared said. "You can't use an incident that old."

"There's no statute of limitations on revenge," Laura said. "Also, you leave your socks on the floor."

"That's a universal trait found on the Y chromosome!" he protested. "It doesn't count."

"Here's one that does—the pictures on your walls look like they were purchased from a warehouse." She pointed to a generic seascape.

"I'll have you know that's an original oil painting." Jared cut the omelette in half and slid it onto two plates.

"Then it must be an original copy," Laura said. "Besides, it matches the curtains."

"Art is supposed to match the curtains." Jared poured them each a cup of coffee and brought the food to the table. "The decorator told me so. Also, she had the class to call them draperies."

"Art is supposed to thrill the person who has to look

at it," she said. "And calling them 'draperies' isn't classy, it's pretentious."

"Boring artwork isn't an acceptable reason to leave me." He shook the salt shaker over his plate for so long the crystals began clumping on his eggs.

"The fact that you have a snooty decorator is a good reason," Laura persisted. "Also, you use too much salt. You'll probably have a heart attack before you're forty, although I won't care because I won't be here."

Jared sighed. "I'm not used to this."

"To what?"

"A woman whose tongue is sharper than mine," he said.

"Your lordship was overdue for a dressing-down." Laura dug into her omelette. It needed salt, but after her last crack, she didn't dare touch the shaker. "That must be why fate sent you to me." Jared clearly savored each bite of his breakfast, then leaned back and surveyed his house with a critical eye. Laura followed his gaze.

The living room, kitchen and den formed one large space divided by counters and a couple of partial walls that indicated where one room ended and another began. From where they sat, the blandness of the place was unmistakable.

"Okay, you're right," Jared said. "My decorator was a wuss."

"Define wuss."

"A wimp," he said. "And so was I. That settles it. We're going shopping."

"We?" Laura said.

"We," he replied firmly.

She thought about objecting and decided against it. She

was curious to see what kind of furnishings Jared picked out.

They drove to a large store that specialized in kitchens, bedrooms and bathrooms. "They carry the important stuff," Jared explained as they got out of the car.

Inside, they gazed at floor-to-ceiling shelves and displays in an endless variety of patterns and solids. The aisles were filled with couples of all ages and a few unaccompanied women. Most took their time, examining various objects and, in some cases, holding up swatches of fabric for comparison.

"How exactly would you characterize my current color scheme?" Jared asked.

"You mean you don't know?"

He shook his head. "The carpet is kind of gray, I think."

"It's beige," she said.

"Okay, beige. And the curtains are, uh, greenish with splashes of, mmm, yellow."

"They're blue with accents of beige and pink," she said.

Jared cleared his throat. "Now, the walls, they're white. That much I know."

"They're ivory," Laura said. "The moldings are a slightly darker shade."

"I have moldings?" he said.

"I can't imagine how you got everything to match." She sighed. "Don't tell me—the decorator did it."

"She was great," Jared confirmed. "She furnished the whole place while I was directing a summer production in San Francisco."

"The color scheme no longer matters," Laura said. "The point today is to buy things that don't match."

"Oh, yeah." He brightened. "This should be fun."

He grabbed a cart and headed down an aisle. "How about some of those little china bunnies for the glass coffee table? It needs cluttering, don't you think?"

"China bunnies don't exactly work in a modern decor." Realizing she was getting it backward, Laura decided to go for more kitsch rather than less. "Get the little shepherdesses."

"Wait! Here's something better!" Jared picked up a painted angel. "Don't you think she'd look cute with my cupids?"

"Buy several," said Laura. "Why hold back? We're looking for excess here."

Before long, the cart was brimming with plaid tissue-box holders, marble wastebaskets, a large digital wall clock showing the time in five countries, forest-green towels and far too many purple bath mats, "just in case." Jared didn't specify in case of what.

"Okay, we're done here," he said jauntily, and strolled to the checkout.

After stowing everything in his tiny trunk, he drove through town. Instead of heading for Laura's place, however, he stopped in front of a store called "Male/ Female."

"You're doing more shopping?" she asked.

"You are," he said. "You need a new dress for tomorrow."

Laura took a moment to absorb this comment. "First of all, the only thing I'm doing tomorrow is going to a rehearsal."

"We don't have a rehearsal on Sunday."

"Then I'd better tell Stuart, because he'd like for me to work."

Jared shook his head. "You can't miss the reception." He got out of the car and, puzzled, Laura followed suit.

"What reception?"

"For Cindy and Hugh," he said. "The Snoopers didn't get to attend the wedding, so they're throwing a big blast at their senior center. It's an amazing old house. You've got to see it."

Although Laura suspected she was being manipulated, she knew she would enjoy socializing. "That might be fun. But I can't afford a new dress and, besides, I've already got one."

"One?" Jared quirked an eyebrow. "You're not referring to that green thing you wore as Morticia, I hope?"

It might be a bit over the top, Laura supposed. "I've got a wraparound skirt I can pair with a sweater."

"We are not in high school. Besides, I'm treating." He steered her into the store.

"I can't let you."

"Consider it a thank-you gift for advising me on my redecorating scheme," he said as three salesladies closed in on them.

"Professor Benton!"

"How good to see you!"

"We've got two jackets you'll love, and some pants that will fit you like a glove!" cooed the third woman.

He held up his hands. "Thanks, all of you, but I'm shopping for my friend."

A disappointed hush fell over the group.

"I could use some help here," called a woman customer, who was trying to hang on to a rambunctious two-year-old without dropping an armload of garments.

"I'll be right there." One of the salesladies left, and

the others drifted off glumly after pointing Jared toward a rack of dresses.

It didn't seem proper to let a man buy her clothing, Laura thought, but perhaps that was hopelessly old-fashioned. Besides, although the prices here were moderate, they exceeded her tight budget.

Jared pulled one dress from the rack. "Try this one. It matches your eyes."

Laura couldn't believe he'd noticed that when he didn't know the color of his own curtains. She took the hanger and held it up. Gorgeous fabric, and the shade was perfect, but the style wouldn't work. "It's cut too low."

"What's wrong with it?"

"The neckline's too daring. In case you hadn't noticed, I'm flat-chested." After enduring agonies of embarrassment during her teenage years, she'd come to terms with nature's realities. "I prefer not to emphasize it."

"I like your small breasts," he said.

Laura felt the color rise in her cheeks. "Could you say that a little louder? There might be one or two people in the store who didn't hear you."

"Sorry." Jared didn't sound repentant. "Okay, here's another dress with that color in a print." He continued through the rack, unerringly choosing shades that flattered her, until Laura had more than enough to try on. Thank goodness not all the designers went for cleavage!

In a changing room, she made her way through the selections. The print was perfect, a sheath with ruches across the bust to add fullness. It emphasized her slim hips and legs, and the jade, black and cherry print flattered her skin tone. She had a pair of black heels and a wrap at home that would complete the ensemble.

When she came out to show it to Jared, he directed her to parade in front of him and swivel like a model. "Do you think it's too dressy?" she asked.

His gaze swept her from top to bottom. After a long moment, he said, "What?"

"Do you think it's too dressy?" Laura repeated.

"It's so sexy it should be illegal," he said. "Do they have another one? We should buy two in case you spill something on it."

"Let's not get carried away." Before he could utter any more seductive comments, she ducked back into the dressing room. The slinky fabric made her ache to feel his hands running over her body. Was there time to stop at her apartment?

Laura checked her watch. Their first rehearsal started in half an hour. Saved by the clock, she thought.

She peeled off the gown and took refuge in her ordinary clothes.

THE DESIRE TO SEE A SPECIAL woman in a particular dress and then rip it off her was not compatible with directing a play. Reminding himself of this fact, Jared forced his attention on the initial read-through of the script.

He had a terrific cast, if they could keep their minds on the production. It was understandable that the young couple, Brad and Suzy, held hands under the table and locked eyes, but the older people ought to know better. Mariah Michaels insisted on sitting on Herbert Runciland's lap. Although they kept straight faces, as Mariah explained that it was because the chairs were too hard for her eighty-nine-year-old derriere, Jared knew perfectly well there was hanky-panky going on below the level of the rehearsal-room table.

More troubling was the way Vanessa Sachet kept snuggling closer to Bernie Bernini. For one thing, the smartly styled socialite was an odd match for the flamboyant hairdresser. For another, President Wilson Martin had chosen to attend and glowered at his girlfriend throughout the session.

The room was charged with hormones. This should, at least, make for an interesting onstage atmosphere, Jared reflected. Still, he hoped he wasn't going to have to suffer through the next month with his pants feeling too tight.

It was a struggle not to peek at Laura. He'd meant what he'd said about her small breasts. They tantalized him. There was an elfin quality about her that made him want to...

"Let's read that scene one more time," he said as silence fell over the room. "This time, Mariah, try a little more sarcasm. Bernie, remember that you're supposed to be heartbroken."

"Got it." The young man twiddled one of his earrings flirtatiously at Vanessa. President Martin's teeth gnashed audibly.

Finally it was over. Jared reminded everyone of the next rehearsal on Monday, and locked the theater department behind him.

Then he whisked Laura into his car and drove her home so she could give him a private showing of her new dress.

THE UNIVERSITY SENIOR CENTER, home of the Snoopers and site of the party for Cindy and Hugh, was a three-story house adorned with balconies, a widow's walk, roof peaks and a round tower. Laura loved it on sight.

Inside, the Victorian-style rooms exuded warmth.

Laura drank in the carved wooden moldings and the stately main staircase with its ornate railing.

"Makes you want to slide down, doesn't it?" said Jared, tucking her hand inside his elbow. He wore a tweed jacket over slacks, which was more or less the professorial uniform at De Lune University.

"Not me." With her free hand, Laura smoothed her new dress over her hips. "I'm not dressed for exercising."

"That depends on what kind of exercise you had in mind," Jared said with a low growl that sent tingles down Laura's spine.

"Behave yourself."

"Only if I have to."

They entered the salon, where gas-fed flames leaped on the hearth and old-fashioned maroon-and-gold velvet covered the chairs and sofas. A long table featured an assortment of delicacies.

Cindy and Hugh stood in the center of the room, greeting their well-wishers, who chatted as they drank punch. "I hope it isn't spiked," Laura murmured to Jared.

"I wouldn't put it past the old rogues," he said. Esther and Hoagie twittered at one end of the refreshment table, blind to anyone but each other. At the punch bowl, Mariah was stirring in juice. Runcie tickled her and they both giggled like schoolchildren.

"They're acting more like newlyweds than the guests of honor are," Laura observed.

Jared planted one hand on the small of her back. "There's nothing wrong with a little public snuggling among friends."

"As long as it doesn't go too far." Still, she enjoyed

the physical connection between Jared and her. His touch was a lovely reminder of last night.

Although Laura had worried that he might begin to tire of her, he'd showed no signs of it. At breakfast, he'd been even more cheerful and talkative than usual.

After eating, they'd arranged the ceramic angels around the base of the lamp and she'd helped him position the new clock. As she stepped back to scrutinize it, Laura had had a startling thought: They were making a home together. Despite her desire for independence, she wanted more.

Don't kid yourself. Resolutely she put the whole scene out of her mind.

"Now, there's an unhappy couple." Jared indicated Mrs. Pipp and the man in the safari shirt, who had entered a few minutes earlier. The dean walked two steps ahead of him and glared at anyone who regarded her with even a hint of question.

"You'd never know they were coming up on their fiftieth wedding anniversary, would you?" asked an African-American man standing nearby. "Oh, hello, I'm Hosea O'Donnell."

"I'm Jared Benton." Jared shook hands and introduced Laura. "Are you a member of the Snoopers?"

"Their technical adviser," said Hosea, who looked sharp in a dark suit with a red carnation in the buttonhole. "I'm a retired civil engineer."

"Technical adviser?" Laura asked.

"Hidden microphones, miniature cameras, that sort of thing."

She gave a low whistle. "They take their snooping seriously."

"It keeps them out of trouble," he said. "Or, at least,

it keeps them in the kind of trouble everyone around here is accustomed to. But things aren't what they used to be. The way Mariah and Runcie are acting, not to mention Esther and her old friend, I'll be surprised if they remember to stick their noses into anyone else's business.''

''Have your Snoopers found out much about Dean Pipp's husband?'' Jared asked. ''I've heard rumors about the missing Mr. Pipp for years, but I never believed them. He doesn't look like a Mafia hit man or a deposed Caribbean dictator.''

''His name is Watley and he's an archeologist,'' Hosea said. ''He and Marie met in England and only lived together for about a year after they were married. Most recently he's been working on a Pacific island called Prego Prego that was colonized by Italians. That's all I know.''

''Well, it's more than I knew,'' Jared said. ''Thanks. If you'll excuse us, we'd like to congratulate the happy couple.''

''Pleasure meeting you,'' said Hosea, and moved on.

The next hour passed in a happy hum for Laura. She particularly enjoyed hearing the story of Cindy and Hugh's courtship. It had begun with each trying to help the other win someone else and had climaxed at a campus medieval joust at which Hugh defeated Cindy's old boy-friend and, in front of the whole crowd, recited a poem asking for her hand.

As more and more people drifted into the room, Laura stopped trying to keep them straight and did what she really wanted to do anyway, which was concentrate on Jared. Parties were his natural element. He joked easily, remembered everyone's name, and knew when to listen quietly and when to stir things up with a bit of drama. No wonder women clustered around him.

From a beautiful young graduate student to a sophisticated professor, he showered them with charming bits of nonsense that, she could see, won their hearts. He wasn't being disloyal to Laura; he was just being himself.

In another month, when her job here was finished, Jared wouldn't need to spend a single lonely night, Laura thought. He might miss her, but not for long.

And her? She loved him. Simply, directly, irrevocably.

Her heart twisted as she acknowledged what she'd tried to deny to herself. At some level, she'd loved Jared for ten years, but now that she'd spent passionate nights with him, now that he'd become a part of her life again, she loved him so much she ached.

What, she wondered, was she going to do about it?

7

BEING SURROUNDED BY FRIENDS was the next best thing to acting onstage. Jared got the same adrenaline rush and the same sense of euphoria. It almost made him wish he hadn't given up performing, except that directing gave him an even bigger thrill.

He never lost his awareness of Laura, though. She possessed a beautiful stillness that made her stand out. The most intriguing part was that he knew her mind was always working. While he was showing off, she was registering undercurrents to enrich her next play.

When her attention shifted to another part of the room, Jared lost interest in his friends. Following her gaze, he saw that Runcie had produced a copy of *Calling All Glass Slippers* and was showing it around.

"I wish he wouldn't do that," Laura said when Jared drew closer.

"Why not? It isn't as if anyone's going to steal your ideas," he pointed out.

"I know. I'm just superstitious about having other people handle it." Across the room, Dean Pipp flipped through a few pages and then handed the copy to her husband, who had been introduced to them earlier. "This ought to be interesting."

"In what way?" Jared asked.

"They're the last couple on earth that... Oh, it's prob-

ably nothing. I think I'm about to get my theory dis-
proved, which is fine with me.''

''What theory is that?''

''It's too stupid to mention. Forget I said anything.''
Edging along the table, Laura filled a plate with puffed
pastries and stuffed mushrooms.

Curious, Jared crossed the room as Watley Pipp returned the script to Runcie. He wondered what, if anything, Laura expected to happen.

''That reminds me, I haven't been to the theater in
years,'' the archeologist was saying when Jared came
within earshot. ''I used to love to go. Don't you remember, dear?''

''We went on our first date,'' Dean Pipp said. ''After
we met at the Explorer's Club, you took me to see a stage
version of *Around the World in 80 Days*. It made me
drool to go adventuring.''

''Was that why you married me?'' he asked. ''So you
could come to Africa with me as you'd always wanted?''

'' 'Always' being since I heard your lecture,'' his estranged wife confessed. ''At twenty-six, I thought you
were incredibly romantic. I'd never met such a sophisticated older man.''

''Older? I was only thirty-two, although I'll admit,
sometimes I felt fifty. It got lonely out there, far from
home.'' He took her hand.

''So desperately lonely that you married me for company?'' Marie asked. ''You must have been disappointed.''

''I was heartbroken when you left,'' Watley said. ''I
didn't marry you just for the company, though. I found
you beautiful. I still do.''

''What a sweet thing to say.'' She smiled dreamily.

"This is scary." Laura joined Jared. "It's weird, seeing those two suddenly act like long-lost lovers."

"They are long-lost lovers. What's weird about it?"

Before she could reply, Hugh Bemling held up a hand for silence. "I'd like to read a poem in honor of my bride," he announced.

"We'd be disappointed if you didn't," Jared called, mentally putting aside the subject of the Pipps. Several others shouted their agreement.

Hugh pushed his glasses higher on his nose and, in a moment of boldness, climbed on a chair. Cindy, who was the same height as her husband, grinned as she looked up at him for a change.

From a slip of paper, Hugh recited:

"Home to me was wherever I slept.
Promises were as often forgotten as kept.
My heart wandered, restless and alone
Until you came to bring me home. Now I know
where I belong.
With you, my love is sure and strong.
So, Cindy, my dear one from Minnesota
I give you my love, to the smallest iota."

Everyone applauded. To Laura, Jared said, "Only Hugh would rhyme Minnesota with iota."

"He's cute," she said. "Was that true about him being restless and alone?"

"He fell in love with a different woman every week, but I always knew Hugh would settle down someday, because that's the kind of person he is," Jared said.

"As opposed to what?" she asked.

"As opposed to me," he said.

Into his mind flashed a picture of his house the way it looked now: slightly cluttered, cozy and utterly unlike the spare, impersonal ambience he'd intended. Anyone might think he was being domesticated, but Jared knew better. Not him. Not ever.

He'd grown up in a small, crowded house where his two sisters shared one bedroom and he and his little brother crammed into another. There'd been knickknacks, school papers, books and bills strewn everywhere.

"It's a trap, and worst of all, it's one I made for myself," his mother had said one night after work as she stood struggling to get dinner ready. Once upon a time, she'd aspired to be an actress, but that was before she married, had children and got divorced.

"You don't want to settle down?" Laura asked.

"Being a director requires traveling a lot, and that suits me fine," Jared said. "I'd hate stagnating in one place."

"Or with one person?"

"I can't live the way most people do," he said. "Come on, neither can you. A month from now you're off to—where?"

"I'm not sure," she said. "A theater company in Louisville is interested in producing one of my earlier plays."

"There, you see?" Jared had known she'd understand. "One thing leads to another in this business, and it's usually thousands of miles away. We have to be realistic about who we are and what makes us happy."

"You can't beat realism," Laura said dryly.

In the center of the room, Mariah kicked off her shoes and climbed atop the coffee table. "I will now dance the cancan in honor of the bridal couple," she announced.

"You go, girl!" shouted Esther.

"Shake it!" cried Runcie.

There was no alcohol in the punch as far as Jared could tell, so he didn't understand why he seemed to be the only one aware that an eighty-nine-year-old woman dancing on a coffee table risked serious injury. "Oh, no, you don't." He strode over and swept her off. "You don't have an understudy and as your director, I refuse to let you run unnecessary risks."

Mariah laughed as he set her on the floor. "That was so gallant of you. Jared Benton, you're the best director in the world!" She planted a kiss on his cheek. Everyone looked amused, including Laura. Things were going well, he thought as he partnered Mariah, at her insistence, in an impromptu waltz. Whatever had been troubling Laura earlier, she'd obviously gotten over it.

LAURA SLIPPED AWAY WHILE the party was in full swing, explaining to Cindy that she had a headache. "I don't want to disturb Jared," she said. "He's having such a great time."

The bride walked out to the hallway with Laura. "For an intelligent man, he's kind of dense, isn't he?"

"What do you mean?"

"I don't want to interfere," Cindy said. "But I'm not sure he grasps the fact that you two were meant for each other."

"What makes you say that?" Laura asked with pretended indifference.

"According to Hugh, Jared acts completely different around you than with any other woman," said her friend. "And your love shines through your eyes, even if he's too blind to see it."

It went against the grain for Laura to confide in anyone, particularly when her feelings were so painful, but Cindy's perceptiveness made it easier. "I knew it was dangerous being around him, but I thought I could handle it."

"Give him time," the blond woman advised.

"We don't have time," Laura said glumly. "Besides, it won't help. What he wants most is his freedom."

"Hugh is certain Jared's falling for you."

"It may be temporary chemistry from working so closely together." Laura chose her words carefully. Even after the warming between Marie and Watley, she didn't dare suggest that her play might be exerting some kind of glass slipper effect. "Showbiz romances always fade once the production closes. I have to be prepared to move on."

Cindy strolled outside with her. "I need a little fresh air, if you don't mind."

"Hugh won't miss you?"

"We're not joined at the hip," said her friend. "He'll be fine."

They ambled down the steps and along the curving driveway. Although it was winter, sunshine had warmed the temperature to nearly seventy degrees and, nearby, azaleas were bursting with butterfly blooms.

What was the weather like in Louisville this time of year? Laura wondered. In Santa Fe, it would be frosty.

"I try to keep my distance, but so far I haven't managed it," she admitted. "It isn't easy to push Jared away when he's determined."

"I can see how he would be hard to resist," Cindy said. "He's very charming."

"Yes, when he wants to be," she said. "When he

doesn't want to be, it's like awakening to find that all of a sudden an ice storm has moved in.''

''There's a chilling image.'' Cindy shivered. ''I can't believe he's ever treated you that way!''

''Yes, ten years ago when we were in college,'' Laura said. ''I thought we were crazy about each other. Then one evening at a party, he dumped me without any warning.''

''I knew you two were acquainted before, but I hadn't heard the details.'' Cindy accompanied her across University Avenue as if she were accustomed to walking to Laura's apartment. Which, of course, she was, since Laura had heard she used to live there.

''That night...'' A lump formed in Laura's throat at the memory. ''That night, I didn't know how I was going to go on. He was the only person who mattered to me, and to him, I was nothing.''

''That's awful.''

''The way I got through it was to vow to myself that I'd never let myself get hurt that way again,'' Laura said. ''I may be nothing to him, but I'm somebody to myself.''

''Did you ever ask him why he did it?'' Cindy asked.

''It was obvious. He'd met someone else he preferred.''

''What happened to her?''

''I have no idea.'' In all the comments about Jared over the years from other theater people, his name had never been linked with anyone in particular. Laura had sometimes wondered about it, but concluded the man was simply fickle. Or that he'd finally met a woman as faithless as he was.

''Men don't always know their own hearts,'' Cindy said. ''Neither do women, for that matter.''

"I know mine," Laura said. "It's made out of glass, stuck back together with epoxy."

"That would make it stronger than before," Cindy pointed out. "I got my heart broken once, but I'm much better off now. My reaction was to go after Roland to make him see how wrong he was. It didn't work, or, rather, it did, but by then I'd met Hugh and didn't want Roland anymore."

"You were lucky." Laura couldn't imagine chasing Jared and trying to force him to love her. She certainly couldn't imagine falling for another man, ever. "I'll never meet anyone like him."

"Maybe you'll meet someone different."

Laura didn't want anyone different. Still, she knew her friend was trying to help. "Maybe so."

They parted company at Forest Lane. Cindy, after wishing her luck, turned back with a jaunty stride.

Laura nearly went with her. Jared must be surrounded by women, as usual, and if she weren't there...

He'd find somebody new. That would only prove her point, wouldn't it?

As she mounted the stairs to her unit, Laura got that old feeling of being invisible. She wondered what it would be like if she *were* invisible. If glass slippers could make people fall in love, why couldn't a woman whom everyone ignored gradually slip out of sight?

At the landing, she hurriedly unlocked the door, raced inside and grabbed a notebook. A new play was taking shape, and, in her absorption, she forgot all about Jared and the party.

WHEN IT WAS TIME TO LEAVE, Jared couldn't find Laura. Admittedly he got distracted while prowling through the house when he came across what looked like a war room for the Snoopers, with maps on the walls and shelves full of yearbooks and tapes, not to mention a flowchart where colored lines connected the names of town notables. When it came to gossip, these guys didn't kid around, he thought with reluctant admiration.

After tearing himself away, he finished surveying the downstairs to no avail. Next he enlisted Cindy's help. "Would you mind checking the bathroom? I can't find Laura."

"She left," said the bride.

"When?" As several people called farewells, he responded with a distracted wave.

"About an hour ago."

Jared didn't miss the warning note in her voice. "Did I do something wrong?"

"Not exactly," Cindy said.

"Then what?"

"Come over here." She drew him to a sofa and sat him down. "Tell me something. Why did you dump Laura ten years ago?"

It was none of her business, but Cindy never worried about what was her business or not, which was one of the things Jared liked about her. "I overreacted," he admitted. "We were getting too close and it scared me."

"Are you scared now?" she asked.

He recalled the vivid image of his mother, defeated by life. "When we were talking earlier, I did back off a bit. Some men aren't meant to stay in one place. I don't believe Laura is, either."

Cindy shrugged. "Maybe you're right. But I think she left to protect herself."

"From what? I would never—" Hurt her? Jared

paused, embarrassed. He'd done exactly that, last time. "She left the party because I said I'd never settle down?"

"She didn't specify," Cindy said.

"I'm asking your opinion."

"Something you did upset her," she said.

"I'll go see her." He couldn't wait to smooth it over and spend the evening cuddling Laura.

"And say what?" Cindy pressed.

"I'm sorry?"

"If you try to simply charm your way back into her good graces, you may make matters worse," she said.

"You don't let a guy off the hook," Jared grumbled. What was wrong with charm, anyway? It had served him fine up till now.

"I believe in being prepared," Cindy said. "If you go over there and are mealymouthed, you might make her angry."

That prospect gave Jared pause. If Laura expected a firm offer of some kind, she was bound to be disappointed. "I refuse to make promises I can't keep."

"Nor should you."

"And you think that's what she wants?"

"I think she wants you to be honest," Cindy said. "And to honestly want more than a passing fling."

He thought it over. For Jared, that didn't take long. "I'll hold off and give her time," he said. "We'll be seeing each other at rehearsals all week."

"You think she'll come around?" Cindy asked dubiously.

"I think she'll come to realize that the important thing is to enjoy the moment, not to worry about what may or may not happen tomorrow." He grew expansive, as often happened when he thought out loud. It was a trait that proved helpful in the classroom. "In the cosmological sense, the future doesn't even exist."

"Do I hear intellectual garbage being passed off as profundity?" joked Hugh, joining them. His plate was piled with food.

"And here I thought I was getting away with it," Jared teased back. "Is there any more crab dip?"

"Tons," said his friend.

They chowed down until the senior citizens ordered them to either leave or join the cleanup crew. Jared chose to make his exit.

It was more difficult than he'd expected not to drive to Laura's place. His car kept pulling in that direction, despite his best intentions.

"It's a trap I made for myself," his mother had said.

The first time he'd escorted his mother to a play he directed, she'd burst into tears of joy. At least, Jared thought they were tears of joy.

"Don't make the mistake I did," she'd told him fiercely. "Never give it up." She'd been right. The most important thing was their careers, for him and for Laura, Jared reminded himself, and steered for home.

THE ME NOBODY SEES, which was the tentative title Laura chose for her new play, filled a major gap in her life during the next few weeks.

It was hard on those nights when she didn't have to work, not to tag along when Jared and the cast headed for a restaurant after rehearsal. Reminding herself that she needed to write gave Laura the strength.

Of course, she also had to do more revisions on *Slippers,* but the characters were settling in nicely, at least onstage. Offstage, the cast grew ever more amorous. That wasn't a problem for the youngest couple, and Mariah and Runcie were clearly having fun, but Laura worried a bit about Vanessa and Bernie.

They were such an odd couple, she couldn't imagine them having anything in common after their job here was done. Moreover, President Martin had taken to attending rehearsals and glaring at everyone. As far as Laura could tell, Vanessa hadn't dropped him, but he clearly had his suspicions.

At least the weather continued to be fair. Laura had almost forgotten how lovely Southern California could be in early February while most of the nation shivered.

Poppies bloomed and bare trees cloaked themselves in shimmering yellow-green fuzz. Students strolled hand in hand, and the merry chime of a handlebar bell was heard throughout town as Marie and Watley Pipp raced about on their bicycle built for two.

Since Esther feared heights too much to climb trees, she and Hoagie stood on stepstools, peering into the trees for a glimpse of a Purple-Breasted Nest-Hopper. At the Lunar Lunch Box, Magda sported a beautiful sapphire pin given to her by her lawyer friend, and Stuart Crock-enmeyer covered the main sign with a paper banner that read: Lover's Lune.

As for what Laura was going to do next, some friends in Louisville called and invited her to room with them while her old play was produced. Although appreciative, she put them off. Maybe, she hoped, she'd get a better offer after the critics reviewed *Calling All Glass Slippers*.

That better offer wasn't going to come from Jared, she could see. His manner toward her remained friendly, but he didn't seem to mind that she avoided him outside re-hearsals. Except for a few regretful glances when they were together, he gave no hint that they were anything more than colleagues.

He'd gotten over her fast, Laura thought with a twist of pain. Not that he showed interest in anyone else, but then, with only a week left before opening night, he was too busy.

As always in the theater, things had gone wrong. The set construction crew couldn't possibly finish on time, until Jared devoted a weekend to hammering and painting. Vanessa complained about her costume and had her own dress designer remake it, while Cindy spent the better part of a week scouring Los Angeles for clear plastic shoes that could pass for glass slippers.

It was on the Saturday before the Friday night opening that the bombshell hit. Bernie arrived late for rehearsal and, after stammering and toying with his earrings, announced that he was leaving the cast.

"I'm sorry," he told Jared, "but I received this dream offer from a salon in Hollywood. We're fixing all the hair for a TV special—the cast is absolutely fabulous!—and they've got to have me full-time right away. Evenings, too."

Laura clenched her hands in her lap. If they had to throw in some unsuitable actor, her play's premiere would be a disaster.

The critical fallout would hurt Jared, but it would hurt her more. If Bernie didn't change his mind, she just might strangle him herself.

8

"YOU CAN'T DO THIS!" cried Vanessa. "You can't do this to me!"

Bernie shot a nervous glance at the empty seat usually occupied by Wilson Martin. "He gets on my nerves, you know? I'm having trouble sleeping. I mean, the president of a major university wants me dead. I can feel it. Do you know how sensitive I am to things like that?"

"Don't worry about Wilson," Vanessa shrieked. "Worry about me! I'll tear you limb from limb!"

"You wouldn't," Bernie quavered. He was shivering so hard, Laura felt a twinge of sympathy for the hapless hairdresser.

"I would!" shrieked Vanessa. "How can you leave me? What about our plans?"

"We don't have any plans." Bernie backed toward the wings.

"We were going to have plans!"

His forehead wrinkled. "I feel as if I've been kidding myself. I'm not an actor. All I really want to do is fix people's hair. Make them beautiful." He turned his attention to Laura. "You, for instance. What I could do with that insane red cascade!"

She'd always hated her hair, and from all reports, Bernie was gifted. But this was hardly the time to think about that.

Vanessa ripped off one of her "glass" high heels and waved it menacingly. "You want to see a red cascade? I'll rip your veins open!"

"Make it the arteries and I'm with you," said Mariah, removing her own shoe. When she put the other foot down, she wobbled off balance, in danger of pitching from the stage. Runcie grabbed her.

"I'm sure if we all calm down we can work this out," Jared began, when the president of the college walked into the auditorium. He carried a glittering sword which, on spotting Bernie, he slashed through the air menacingly.

With a strangled cry, the hairdresser fled. Vanessa hopped angrily on the stage, trying to put on her shoe and give chase at the same time.

"Whoa! We don't need for you or Mariah to injure yourselves." Jared regarded the new arrival. "President Martin, can I help you?"

The youthful president, whose silver hair had recently taken on a mottled look, handed over the sword. "Someone left this prop on the playing field during the medieval tournament in December. It's been sitting in Lost and Found and I kept meaning to drop it by."

"Bernie thought you were going to whack him," said Mariah. "None of us would blame you."

"Why?" asked the president.

"He's leaving," Jared said.

"Good." The president gave a low cough. "You mean he's leaving the show, not town, right?"

"What difference does it make?" Vanessa snapped.

"Uh, none." As Wilson Martin brushed back his hair with a nervous gesture, Laura realized that his roots were light brown.

She'd heard that the president dyed his hair to make himself look more distinguished. Now she knew who his hairdresser must be: Bernie. The president had probably been avoiding him out of pique and was badly in need of a touch-up.

"What are we going to do?" Vanessa demanded. "We don't have a leading man. I don't have a leading man."

"Excuse me." Cindy poked her head out of the wings. "Isn't there an understudy?"

"If our director were on the ball, there would be," Vanessa said with typical rudeness. "Unfortunately we all know the only understudies around here are those two teenagers." She indicated the pair who'd been learning Brad and Suzy's lines and had walk-on roles as their new love interests.

Laura felt rather than saw the subtle tension charging through Jared. Of course, she thought. He's going to say... "I'm the understudy," he announced.

She'd assumed he must be. No one else who auditioned could fill the role. He'd do a wonderful job, even better than Bernie.

"You?" said Vanessa. "Who'll direct us?"

"He'll do both," Cindy told her.

"That's great!" President Martin looked as if he might leap into the air and click his heels.

Jared hurried down the aisle, clearly energized by this new challenge. "We're going to have to work extra hard, gang."

"Well, all right." Vanessa made it sound as if the decision had been up to her.

"You and I need to schedule some extra rehearsal time for our scenes together." Vaulting onto the stage, Jared waved his script. "Right now, let's all work on Act Three, Scene Two."

The college president went away whistling. The rest of the cast perked up, delighted to be working with a skilled actor like Jared.

Even on his first time through, he was better than Bernie, Laura thought, watching his presence light up the stage. Not only did he already know half his lines, but the chemistry between him and Vanessa sizzled.

Her brain stuck on that image. Sizzling. Hot. Vanessa, smiling seductively. Jared oozing sexual energy as he reveled in his natural milieu: the center of attention.

Maybe she shouldn't have been so quick to set him free, Laura thought. Sure, she knew she was going to lose him after the play closed, but she didn't want to watch him fall in love—or in lust—with someone else right in front of her eyes.

The trouble was, she didn't know whether he was just acting or whether he really was striking sparks with Vanessa. And if so, what was she going to do about it?

ON SUNDAY MORNING, JARED burst out of bed, his usual morning lethargy dispelled by enthusiasm for the task at hand. Although he'd have preferred to lure Bernie back, he was thrilled to be acting again.

At his request, Laura had printed out and dropped off a fresh copy of the play last night, since Jared's was so filled with notes and revisions that he couldn't be sure of learning the right lines. He'd have urged her to come home with him, but Vanessa had been in his office running lines at the time, and Laura had backed out as if she were intruding on some important ceremony.

For Pete's sake, it was just Vanessa. He'd been glad

when her Kewpie-doll boyfriend collected her. The woman had such a flirtatious nature that she kept giving Jared come-hither looks even when their characters were supposed to be quarreling.

Studying his clean script, he leaned back in a kitchen chair and munched a toasted chocolate-chip freezer waffle. He hadn't realized they'd added so many pages; this copy felt heavy.

When he got to the end, he discovered the reason: Laura had accidentally appended some scenes from another of her plays, *The Me Nobody Sees*. Catchy title. He didn't remember seeing it on her résumé.

The story drew him in immediately. Every line disclosed Laura's offbeat way of viewing the world. The heroine was so much like her, shy and strong at the same time, easily wounded, inventive and subtly sensual. Even while he was reading, Jared felt himself responding.

She'd made a few notes in the margins, he saw, and realized this must be a rough draft of a new play. Laura hadn't included it by mistake; she wanted his input.

He set aside his waffle and began making notes.

How would it feel to be invisible? Laura decided to put herself in the mood with an appropriate costume.

She rummaged through one of the boxes she hadn't bothered to unpack when she arrived in Clair De Lune. There was an outfit in here that should suit her purpose.

At last she found it, an ethereal white gown made of gauze. When she put it on and whirled around, the sleeves floated and, in the mirror, she became a ghostlike blur.

"The lady in white is ready," she told her reflection.

After sitting at the kitchen counter and opening her

laptop, she reached for the pages she'd scribbled on yesterday so she could copy her changes into the computer. Her fingers skittered across the desktop, meeting only bare wood.

Annoyed, Laura scanned the floor and the wastebasket. No pages there, either.

Uneasily, she recalled printing out and hole-punching the script for Jared yesterday. She'd forgotten all about the new pages while she was doing it. "Rats," she said aloud. She must have stuck them on the end of *Slippers*.

It was no problem, Laura told herself. What harm could come from having a director read her script? All the same, the prospect made her jittery.

Letting someone read a new play was like baring her most secret emotions. What had she put in there, anyway?

Scanning the computer version, she realized that the heroine's husband, the man who didn't see her, was a lot like Jared: confident to the point of cockiness, madly popular, stunningly attractive. Would he believe she was writing about the two of them?

Of course, she wasn't. Not in the least.

Outside, the stairs creaked beneath firm, swift-moving footsteps. A man, climbing zestfully.

He knocked three times. Jared, of course.

Laura's first instinct was to grab a bathrobe to cover her revealing gown. Then she remembered she'd spilled her late-night glass of wine on it yesterday. Oh, well. Her white gown might give the impression of translucence, but it had been designed to wear onstage.

She opened the door.

"Great work." Jared held up his script, then stopped

with his mouth open. His gaze traveled over her slim figure. "I like your dress, what there is of it."

She liked his tight-fitting belted jeans and partly unbuttoned blue work shirt, too. She decided not to mention it. "What brings you here at this hour?"

Instead of answering, he tossed his script inside and caught her hand. After pulling her onto the landing, he tugged her down the stairs. "We never finished our dance in the garden. I want to hold you in my arms and whirl you around."

"I'm barefoot," Laura said.

At the bottom, he scooped her in his arms. Although she'd always thought the gesture romantic when she saw it in movies, Laura's first reaction was fear. If he dropped her...but he wouldn't, she realized as Jared carried her easily along the driveway and into the garden.

The trees and bushes glittered with diamond dewdrops. "If I had Hugh's gift, I'd write a poem," Jared said.

"Oh lustrous greenery, oh exquisite scenery?" Laura teased.

"If you're going to be sarcastic, you can do your own walking." Jared deposited her onto a soft tuft of grass.

The texture against her soles made Laura giggle. "It tickles."

From a full head higher, Jared bestowed a crooked grin on her. "Put your feet on top of mine."

He wore soft leather boots. They felt smooth and supple as Laura placed first one bare sole and then the other atop them. For balance, she had to hang on to Jared. "Now I have you at my mercy," he said.

"If I fall and get grass stains on this dress, I'll never forgive you," Laura told him.

He sighed. "Sometimes I don't think you have an ounce of romance in you."

He was wrong. Standing pressed against him, her heart was thrumming wildly. "Shut up and dance," she said.

"As you wish, madame." Jared's grip tightened around her waist, and, careful not to dislodge her, he stepped into a waltz.

It took a few minutes to get their movements synchronized and their humming focused on the same tune—"Shall We Dance?"—but soon they were skimming gracefully through the last tendrils of morning mist. Laura's spirits whirled with them, and she gave herself to pure abandon.

Heat shimmered from Jared's shirt and chest, penetrating her thin dress. Crisp air tingled against her back, making her snuggle closer. She felt safe and buoyant in this place and this time hidden from the world. Alone with Jared.

From the house came the scrape of the back door opening. "What a wonderful idea—dancing in the garden!" cried Dean Pipp, cheerfully unselfconscious in a long flowered nightgown. "Watley, come out here!"

Her husband emerged in a striped nightshirt and a nightcap with a tassel dangling from its pointy end. "Good heavens. There are lovers on our lawn."

"Dance with me!" His wife held out her arms.

He escorted her down from the porch. They danced in an old-fashioned manner, taking large strides and humming a Strauss waltz.

"I like your selection of music," said Jared. "I was getting a little tired of 'Shall We Dance?'"

"I wasn't," Laura said. "I'll never get tired of it."

"And I said you weren't romantic!" Jared nuzzled her ear. "Forgive me."

"We must look ridiculous," Dean Pipp said after her husband dipped her nearly to the ground, then swooped her up again. "You don't suppose Esther and Hoagie are hanging around the trees taking pictures, do you?"

"They wouldn't be interested unless we have striped poop," said Watley.

"I haven't had bizarre health problems like that since we were in Africa." His wife paused to catch her breath. "I haven't danced outdoors since then, either."

"That was so long ago, our camp is now considered an archeological site in its own right," Watley joked to Laura and Jared.

Dean Pipp smiled. "What a honeymoon! I had no idea what I was letting myself in for, going on a dig in Africa for six months."

"You'd have enjoyed it more if that spider hadn't bitten you," said her husband, one arm around her waist. "You swelled up like a balloon and half your hair fell out."

"How awful." Although Jared had stopped circling, Laura remained standing atop his boots. She was in no hurry to end their closeness.

"After that, the heat bothered me more than ever," her landlady said. "It made me so crazy I used to take off my clothes and dance in the moonlight."

"A lovely sight," said Watley. "Everyone assumed we were hippies."

"No, they didn't!" His wife smacked his arm playfully. "That was before the hippies."

"There was life before the hippies?" Watley said. "We're not that old!"

"You've been stuck on your island too long. Time's gotten away from you." Dean Pipp stretched lazily. "You know something, Laura? I feel young again. That's what love does for you. I'm Marie again. I stopped liking my name after I left Watley and his darned expeditions. Every time someone spoke my name, I heard his voice. Marie. I used to love the way you caressed it on your tongue, my dear."

"So did I," Watley said. "I love your name."

The two stood enraptured in each other and their memories. Wordlessly, Jared walked away with Laura still atop his feet, shifting backward as he went forward. They made it to the stairs, where she jumped off and scampered upward on her own.

While she was wiping her feet with a towel, he told her how much he liked the new play. "It has a whimsical quality that's special to your work," Jared said. "The character of the husband seems a little too likable, though. You should make him less sympathetic."

"You're right." Laura was relieved at his positive response and grateful for the feedback. She jotted a note on a nearby pad. "After all, she does leave him in the end, so he can't be too nice."

"Is she going to become visible again?" Jared asked.

"Yes, somehow." Laura hadn't figured out how to accomplish it dramatically. "She's going to have to struggle to get there."

"I'd like to direct it," he said.

She didn't know how to answer. Did she want to come back and work with Jared again months later, when the script was finished? By then, he'd be romancing somebody new.

Yet he was a marvelous director. She'd never find any-one better to help her revise and present a new play.

"It's too soon to decide," Laura said. "I'll have to see where I am and what's going on when I finish it."

"Promise me one thing." Sitting on the couch beside her, Jared plucked a leaf from her hair. "Promise you'll at least let me read it when you're done."

She could hardly refuse. "Of course."

He traced a finger along her temple. Laura's self-control neared meltdown.

"You've been avoiding me, and I've let you," Jared said. "I don't want to push you past your comfort zone."

"Just the sight of you pushes me past my comfort zone," she admitted.

"I wish you'd loosen up," he said. "We make magic together. True, magic never lasts, but maybe we'll be lucky and rediscover it the next time we meet."

"Like Dean Pipp and Watley?" she asked. "Decades later, we'll meet and reminisce?"

"She feels young again," Jared reminded her. "That's what happens when you let love have its way and don't try to pin it down. It blossoms in its own season."

If ever temptation took human form, it was sitting right next to her. Loosen up. Laura wondered if she could.

The problem was, she didn't know how to love half-way. It would tear her apart to see Jared in another woman's arms a year from now or five years from now. And, for Jared, there would always be another woman eventually.

"I can't," she said.

He lifted her hands and kissed them. "Keep writing," he said. "Now I'm afraid I've got to go run lines with the president's lady."

"And I've got to work at the restaurant," Laura said.

It was hard to let him go. But she knew, as she closed the door behind him and went to change her clothes, that it would be a whole lot harder if she didn't.

ON WEDNESDAY, TWO NIGHTS before the scheduled Valentine's Day opening, the technical rehearsal ran late, as tech rehearsals often do. One of the sets showed an unnerving tendency to wobble, necessitating immediate repairs, and the lighting director, a graduate student, encountered a glitch in her computer program.

Matters weren't made easier by the tempers of the cast members. Just as the characters' love affairs began to fall apart toward the end of the play, Mariah and Runcie had begun snipping at each other offstage as well as on, while Brad and Suzy had quarreled openly and were barely speaking.

Although the cast and crew had started at 4:00 p.m., they were still running Act Three at nine o'clock that night, meagerly sustained by sandwiches and coffee. Even Jared felt a bit frayed around the edges, and Vanessa was getting downright peevish. In the back of the house, where she was prompting forgotten lines, Laura dozed in her seat.

He smiled, recalling from years ago how deeply she sometimes napped, like a child. She looked so sweet, sleeping peacefully, that Jared didn't wake her. Since last Sunday, she'd illuminated his dreams and occupied every spare thought. Unlike any other woman he'd known, she refused to stay put in the spare corners of his mind.

He was falling in love with her. He couldn't allow that to happen, he reflected ruefully while waiting offstage for an entrance.

If the critics responded to this premiere as he believed they would, his and Laura's careers were about to rocket into high gear. Although Jared wanted to keep his post at the university, he needed to take on additional, important directing assignments. At thirty-two, he could still be considered a hot young director. And in the entertainment business, youth counted.

For Laura, too. Rising young playwrights were in demand. Neither of them had time for distractions.

When Jared made his entrance, President Martin, who sat on the aisle a few rows behind Laura, was tapping his foot irritably. He'd come and gone several times during the evening, and when the scene ended, he stood up.

"Vanessa," he said, "let's go. They can finish without you and we're late for the Alumni Rummage Sale and Slave Auction."

"Don't be ridiculous." Turning away, she favored Jared with a gleaming display of her dental work. "I would never leave you in the lurch."

Agitated, the college prexy pulled on his De Lune University baseball cap, which didn't quite hide the orange tinge of his hair. It was, Jared gathered, a do-it-yourself dye job gone wrong.

"You're coming with me now," Martin said. "You promised this acting nonsense wouldn't interfere with anything important, and you did volunteer to be auctioned off."

"Nonsense?" She glared at him. "I'll have you know I'm a major talent! And I don't want to be auctioned off, even if you did promise to 'buy' me."

"Everyone's looking forward to it." He forced the words between clenched teeth. "You're embarrassing me."

The cast stood around uncertainly, although an exhausted Laura, who'd worked late the night before, slept right through it. Had anyone other than Wilson Martin interfered with a rehearsal, Jared would have ousted him without a second thought, but he couldn't do that to the head of the university.

"We'll wrap this up pretty soon," he said, hoping to make peace.

"No, you'll wrap it up this minute," snapped the orange-haired man.

"I'm sorry, but if I don't get these lighting cues fixed, we'll be here for hours tomorrow night, too," called the lighting designer from her booth high up at the back of the theater.

Cindy waved her script. "We can't leave now! We've got a charity audience coming in for the dress rehearsal."

"We're leaving now," roared President Martin. "Vanessa, you're out of the cast."

"Not on your life!"

Jared couldn't believe a man in a responsible position was behaving so childishly. He knew better than to say it, however. "I'm afraid we don't have an understudy."

"That's your problem." The man got to his feet. "You'll proceed without Vanessa or I'm closing down the entire production."

Jared struggled to stay calm. "Perhaps you've forgotten that this play won the University Award. A lot of critics have agreed to be here Friday night. It'll look bad if we cancel the show without good reason."

A muscle twitched in Martin's jaw. "Here's a good reason. You don't have a leading actress and you were too negligent to arrange for an understudy. She's out, understand me? And frankly, Vanessa, don't think I don't know what you've been up to.''

"Oh, yeah?'' said the blond actress. "What have I been up to?''

For a moment, Martin's abashed expression indicated he might be considering a retreat. Instead he blundered on. "Running into Los Angeles all week, pestering that bizarre man you've got a crush on.''

"You mean Bernie?'' Vanessa said. "Bernie may be bizarre, but I like him that way.''

Funny, Jared thought. Vanessa had mentioned the other day that she was getting tired of Bernie. If she'd gone to L.A. to see him at all, it probably hadn't been more than once, but obviously she wasn't going to let Wilson Martin boss her around. He had to admire her spirit, even while his brain was madly trying to figure out how to prevent a calamity.

"President Martin, I'll be happy to release Vanessa from the rehearsal now,'' he said. "We can use a stand-in for the lighting.''

"Well…'' The man fiddled with his cap, as if aware that he'd overstepped the line. "I suppose, in that case…''

"I've had it!'' Vanessa jumped down from the stage and scooped her purse off a seat. "Nobody treats me this way. You want an embarrassment in front of the press, Wilson? You got it. I'm out of here. Bernie can introduce me to some of his new contacts in television. I never want to see you or this theater again.''

Speechless, Jared stared at her. He couldn't believe she would jeopardize the production just to get back at her boyfriend.

It was Cindy who spoke. "Don't do this. You're walking out on a bunch of people who trusted you."

"It wouldn't be the first time." Vanessa strode up the aisle and out of sight.

Wilson Martin ran after her. Jared heard them arguing in the lobby. She shouted that she never wanted to see him again, and then the outer door crunched shut, leaving only silence.

"She might come back," Suzy said after a breathless moment.

"She's a witch," announced Mariah. "I never liked her."

"We have to assume she's out of the show." Jared didn't waste time worrying about the fact that he should have arranged for an understudy. Worrying about the situation wasn't an option.

He was going to have to use the only actress available who had a chance of being ready in time. Fortunately she already knew most of the lines and blocking, and she was both more talented and more experienced than Vanessa.

Everyone in the theater appeared to be thinking the same thing he was, because they all looked at the playwright. She yawned, eyes fluttering open as she emerged from her nap.

Puzzled, Laura's green gaze traveled from one face to the next until she stopped at Jared. "Uh-oh," she said. "Did I miss something?"

9

"I'VE BEEN IN LOVE WITH YOU for years," Jared said. "I'm surprised you didn't figure it out before."

"You couldn't possibly be in love with me. It isn't in your nature to feel that kind of emotion." Laura hesitated before plunging on. "Besides, I don't want to take that kind of risk. I can't take that kind of risk, not after how much I've lost."

"Did you?" he asked, coming closer. "Did it hurt you that badly?"

"Line," said Laura.

"'I loved my husband, even though...'" Cindy prompted from her seat in the orchestra section.

"I loved my husband, even though people were always gossiping, saying I was cold." She turned away, making sure the invisible audience could see her smirk. Then she frowned, letting herself feel the pull of the glass slippers as she swung back toward Jared. "Maybe I was cold. But now...now I hardly know myself. I hardly know these lines, either. I left something out, didn't I?"

"It's 'Maybe I was cold on the outside,'" Cindy said.

Wearily Laura leaned against the onstage sofa. "I'm going to have to carry a script tonight."

"That's okay. I'll explain before we start about losing

our leading actress,'' Jared said. ''Everyone knows it's a
dress rehearsal.''

It was 5:00 p.m. on Thursday and they'd been working
since early morning. After last night's near-marathon run-
through, nobody had much energy, although Laura knew
she'd be jolted with adrenaline the moment she assumed
the role for real.

How silly to have feared that rehearsing with Jared
would put her heart in jeopardy! There was no time to
succumb to emotion, not with such a tight schedule.

Her heart was perfectly fine, secure in its armor. Until
Saturday night, at least. Until that moment after the final
curtain fell and she went to the cast party.

It was absurd, ten years later, yet Laura had never fully
recovered from the trauma of seeing Jared with another
woman at what should have been their triumphant moment. Somehow, it seemed inevitable that she was once
again riding for a fall.

''You look asleep on your feet,'' Jared said.

''I do?'' It had been a long day, memorizing lines,
reviewing the blocking and submitting to fittings while
the costume designer adapted a dress from a previous
production.

''You guys need a break,'' Cindy said, ''and I'd better
get home. The last time Hugh cooked dinner, he set the
curtains on fire.''

''That's because he was making bananas flambé.''
Jared had heard about the incident from the guilty party
himself.

''Tonight he's making pizza from scratch. He said he
can't wait to toss the dough like that guy in the window
of the Pizza Palace. I expect to find circles of it draped

all over the furniture like something from a Salvador Dali painting.'' The stage manager collected her script and notebooks.

Laura stifled a yawn. ''I'm glad we only have two performances.''

She went to retrieve her purse from the wings. When she returned, Cindy was gone and Jared stood testing the recalcitrant set to make sure it was stable. ''Looks like we fixed it,'' he said.

''I'm surprised Vanessa didn't have a change of heart and come back.'' Laura found herself lingering to chat, although she knew she ought to go.

''Vanessa doesn't have a heart.'' Jared grinned.

Now that they were alone, Laura's mind flooded with things she wanted to say. That she'd missed him these past weeks, even though they saw each other almost daily at rehearsals. That she didn't want to let go, even though she knew she would soon have to.

Instead she said, ''You want to hear something ridiculous?''

''Anytime.'' He came closer, stopping a few feet away but making no attempt to touch her.

''I had this idea…'' She wasn't sure she wanted to finish the thought, but she'd come too far to chicken out. ''I had this idea that the play was exerting some kind of glass slipper effect. As if reading it or even touching a script could make people fall in love.''

''Like Bernie and Vanessa?'' Jared asked. ''And Mariah and Runcie? Well, if it worked, it wore off.''

''Just like in the story,'' she reminded him.

''In which case, I should be completely over you by now,'' he said.

"Except that you and I just started playing our parts," Laura reminded him. "It might be taking effect all over again."

He brightened. "That explains it."

"Explains what?"

Too quickly for her to protest, he gathered her into his arms. "This ravenous urge I have to carry you back to my house and devour you."

"We don't have time." She felt almost disappointed at finding an excuse.

"We don't have to be back here for two hours," he said. "Okay, make that an hour and a half. If we pick up hamburgers on the way to my place, we can eat while we do it."

"You're kidding!" She didn't know whether to be insulted or amused. "That's the most unromantic thing I've ever heard."

"More unromantic than worrying about grass stains when I'm waltzing you around the garden by moonlight?"

"Definitely," she said.

"I suppose buying food from a vending machine and retiring to my office is out of the question, too?" He looked so hopeful that she could have kissed him. In fact, she did kiss him, because their lips were only inches apart.

As he drew her close, longing coursed through Laura. She'd forgotten how delicious Jared smelled, his maleness heightened by his European cologne. She'd also forgotten that her body needed the hard pressure of him to bring her to life.

"Okay, you guys, break it up!" Down the aisle came

Daffodil O'Foy, carrying a large cardboard box. The scent of freshly grilled cheeseburgers filled the theater and set Laura's stomach to grumbling. "I brought dinner."

Jared hesitated with his arms around Laura. "That was kind of you."

"Kind my foot," said the cook. "Stuart's been a complete jerk. He'd bought tickets for your play tomorrow night and, can you believe, he sold them to a friend? He said he must have been out of his mind to ask me on a date. So I said, take your job and stuff it, and here I am."

"You quit?" Laura asked.

"Temporarily." Daffodil came abreast of them. "I figure that, by tomorrow, he'll be begging me to rescue him, so tonight I'll stay and watch the show. As the price of admission, I brought food."

"There wouldn't happen to be a cheesecake in that box, would there?" Jared asked.

"There would."

Slowly he released Laura. "Well, as long as she's here…"

"I'm hungry, too," she admitted.

A convivial meal à trois revived her spirits for the evening ahead. She supposed she ought to be grateful to Daffodil for saving her from making a big mistake.

But when it came to Jared, Laura wanted to make mistakes. She wanted to keep on making them.

There had to be a glass slipper effect. It was the only possible explanation.

"I'M SORRY, SON. YOU KNOW I'd hoped to fly out to see your play, but we're opening a new store and my company's put me in charge. I can't get away."

Betsy Benton sounded cheerful over the phone despite her obvious regret. Since earning a degree in fashion merchandising and signing on with a large Maryland retail chain, she'd adored her work.

"I figured you weren't coming," Jared said, propping his feet on the kitchen table. It was Saturday morning and he was still coming down from the intensity of the dress rehearsal and the high of last night's opening. "Otherwise, you'd have been here yesterday."

"It opened last night?" his mom said. "I thought it was tonight. Oh, that's right, yesterday was Valentine's Day! Time gets away from me."

"Me, too." A lot of things had gotten away from Jared—most importantly, his plan to carry Laura off for a private tryst following the performance.

Once the curtain came down, several reporters and a producer from the audience had monopolized their attention, and, later, a sea of admiring students had come seeking autographs. By the time the theater cleared out, Laura had been exhausted. Reluctantly, and with a bit of prompting from Cindy, Jared had let her go home alone.

Tonight would be different. The producer, a former actress named Indigo Frampton who'd become a major player at her studio, had invited herself to the cast party, but afterward, Jared had big plans for Laura.

"How did it go?" his mother asked.

"Brilliantly," he said without a shred of embarrassment.

"Of course." She laughed. "I'm proud of you."

"Thanks, Mom," Jared said. "Of course, I didn't do it alone."

"That's right, you've spoken highly of your playwright," she said. "Laura, isn't that her name? In your e-mail, you said she had to step into the leading role. I gather that went well."

"We received a standing ovation and had to take five curtain calls," he said. "I tried to be a good sport about it."

"A good sport?" she asked. "You loved every minute!"

"You know me too well," he teased.

Sure, he'd enjoyed the glory, for both of them. Even stronger, however, had been the sparks that flew between the two of them onstage. They hadn't been acting, they'd been living their roles.

In the latest rewrite, Laura's character discovered almost too late that her cynical soul truly was touched by love. In the bittersweet ending, they'd gazed longingly at each other across a divide, reducing some of the audience members to tears.

"By the way, you have to congratulate me, too. Your sister Ellie's pregnant again," his mother said. "I'm expecting my second grandchild in August."

"Terrific." Jared had only met Ellie's toddler once. He'd found the boy cute but puzzling, as if he were a creature from another planet. "You know, Mom, I'm glad you're having a good time. You worked so hard when we were kids and you gave up your dream for us."

"I gave up my dream?" she said. "Oh, gosh, I used to think that, didn't I? I'd forgotten. You know, looking back, I'm not sure God gave me the talent to become a big star, and obviously I lacked the drive. If I hadn't had you kids, I can't imagine what my life would be like now. Lonely, that's for sure."

"You'd be too busy to be lonely," Jared said.

"It's different for men," Betsy told him. "They can marry at any age and have kids if they want. For women, the years exact a much greater penalty. Anyway, congratulations, and be sure to send me your clippings. Only the good ones, of course."

"I only read the good ones." Jared saw no point in wading through negativity. In his opinion, critics were more interesting in preening themselves than in providing insight. Except for those who praised his work, of course.

After his mother rang off, he called a florist and ordered roses for Laura's dressing room. It was an even bigger bouquet than the one he'd sent last night.

LAURA RESTED HER CHIN on her palm and peered at Cindy. "It's hopeless," she said. "I'm dreading the cast party. Maybe I'll plead a headache and go home after the performance tonight."

She'd accepted the stage manager's invitation to drop by for lunch while Hugh was attending a seminar. After the excitement of the opening had come an inevitable letdown this morning, and Laura was grateful for an excuse to get out of the apartment.

"The party wouldn't be the same without you." The tall blond woman stirred pickle relish into the tuna salad while standing at the counter in her sunny kitchen. She and Hugh had bought a charming bungalow near the heart of Clair De Lune, within walking distance of Dean

Pipp's place. "You're the leading lady and the author. You have to go."

Laura sighed. Yesterday's performance had been an amazing experience. She'd merged with the character of the Young Widow, at first calculating and self-interested, then blindsided by love. By the end of the play, she'd craved Jared so much she could hardly see straight.

It was impossible to distance herself, impossible to defend against the heartache to come. Except by keeping her distance physically.

"What's the worst that can happen?" Cindy asked, putting together a couple of sandwiches.

"He dumps me again," Laura said. "He's probably already got his eye on his next girlfriend."

"He never told you why he invited someone else to the cast party last time, did he?" Cindy sliced the sandwiches, set them on a platter and took a seat at the table opposite Laura.

"Not in so many words, no."

"He got scared," said her hostess. "He liked you too much so he was trying to push you away. Not to drive you away entirely, though. His tactic backfired."

Laura couldn't believe it. "He told you that?"

"He did." Cindy made a face. "Men can be total klutzes when it comes to relationships."

"Unlike women?" Laura joked.

"I guess we screw up, too," she admitted. "You know what? I've got an idea."

It was easy to trust the down-to-earth lady from Minnesota. "I'm game. What is it?"

"You're panicking about the party, so let's plan ahead," Cindy said. "Do you need a dress?"

"I have the one I wore to your reception."

The blond head bobbed appreciatively. "That's right. It's perfect. Okay, now for the rest of you."

Laura didn't know whether to be insulted or amused. "What's wrong with the rest of me?"

"Nothing, except that you don't have confidence in yourself," Cindy said. "What we're going to do is make you the most beautiful woman in the room. If Jared is too stupid to notice, you'll be so surrounded by men you won't care."

"That isn't going to happen." Nevertheless, her spirits gave a little bounce. "How do we accomplish this miracle?"

"We start with Bernie," Cindy said.

THE FIRST THING LAURA noticed when she pushed open the door to the glass edifice in Beverly Hills was the incredible mixture of scents. Perfumes, hair dyes and hair sprays—no doubt called spritzes or something equally tony—marked the transition from the real world to fantasyland.

Potted orchids bloomed and Mozart played as Bernie flitted toward them from an artfully lit cubicle. "Cindy! Laura! Omigosh, I'm so glad I was able to postpone one of my new clients. Of course, I had to promise to come in tomorrow to work on the duchess, never mind what she's duchess of, probably her bathroom, but everyone calls her the duchess, she's zillions of years old and simply reeks of elegance. And this one's on me, completely free, so we're not going to hold back, are we?"

"What do you mean by 'not hold back'?" Laura eyed

a poster of a model who, judging by her hairstyle, had just stuck her finger in a socket.

"He scared the heck out of me the first time he worked on me, too." Cindy had explained on the hour-long drive that her smooth, flattering cut was Bernie's work. "Don't worry, he won't turn you into some rock star, now will you, Bernie?"

The pale spikes atop his head appeared to droop as he surveyed Laura through his tinted glasses. "No? I mean, that red color is so vivid, it fills me with inspiration. I'm positively buzzing. Here, feel my arm." He held it out.

Laura touched him and got a tiny electrical shock. "You're not kidding."

Pleased, Bernie reached out and ruffled her hair. "We're going to weave in some auburn highlights for depth. As for the cut, shorter is absolutely the way to go here. Trust me on this. It will bring out your eyes. Oh gracious me, are they the color of jade? They are, aren't they? Simply fabulous! I don't know why I never noticed before. It must have been that atrocious theater lighting. Well, come along. To the shampoo bowl with you!"

When she learned the process would take several hours, Cindy excused herself to visit the Los Angeles County Museum of Art a few miles away. "Don't worry," she told Laura. "You won't regret coming here."

Laura already regretted it, but after a long drive, it was too late to turn back. "I'll see you later."

The time passed pleasantly. Between the heady scents and the soothing hum of the hair dryer, Laura flipped through magazines and dozed.

When it came time for the final comb-out, Bernie

draped a smock over his mirror. "You can't see a thing till the end," he said. "Say, congratulations on taking over Vanessa's role. I hear you're much better, which doesn't surprise me, because it's one thing to play a hard-hearted Hannah, and another thing to actually be one."

"I thought you liked Vanessa." An image of the two of them grinning foolishly at each other came back to Laura.

"I did, for about five minutes." Bernie's hands moved through her hair, fluffing and arranging. "The minute I drove out of Clair De Lune, and I do mean the very instant my car turned onto the freeway, I remembered all the reasons I can't stand that woman."

"So you're not seeing her?" Laura asked.

"Would you believe, she came here on Thursday and practically ordered me to introduce her to a casting director, as if I'm just lousy with Hollywood contacts. If I did know a casting director or two, which maybe I do, I certainly wouldn't introduce them to her after the way she left Jared's production in the lurch."

He'd apparently forgotten that he himself had left the show at a most inconvenient time. Laura supposed he'd rationalized it.

She forgot all about Vanessa a moment later when Bernie whipped the smock off her mirror. "Voilà."

Laura stared at the unfamiliar image in the glass: chic, radiant short coiffure, huge green eyes, full mouth. Her delicate face had been transformed by the taming of her bushy mane.

On second glance, she noticed that her hair wasn't merely shorter, it was cropped. Glowing, she had to admit, but barely there.

"Wow," she said.

Bernie beamed.

What, Laura wondered as she turned her head from side to side, was Jared going to think? She squared her shoulders. It didn't matter.

Tonight, when the world came crashing down, at least she would know that she looked her best.

10

THE AUDIENCE HELD ITS breath as Laura walked away from Jared the entire width of the stage. She could feel the viewers exerting body English, forcing her to turn back, willing her to say...

"There must be hope for us. We have to at least try to find a way."

Where had that line come from? She was supposed to gaze at him wordlessly as the curtain descended.

"We will try." His voice resonated through the hushed theater.

She stood frozen as the curtain lowered inch by inch. Cindy must be afraid to drop it too quickly in case they intended any further improvisations.

What was going on? She hadn't meant to change the ending. Besides, the other lovers in the cast had become estranged both onstage and off. Why wasn't that happening to her and Jared? The two of them had spoken from their hearts or, at least, she had. At last the curtain brushed the floor. Jared grinned as he hurried across and gave Laura a high-five. Then he caught her hand and pulled her center stage to take their first bow.

Thunderous applause engulfed them. The other actors took their places, and the whole cast reveled in a wave of approval. Clapping, stomping and cheering forced them through another half-dozen curtain calls before they were finished.

At last they were shielded from view. "Next time you decide to get creative, give me a clue, okay?" Cindy said as they drifted into the wings.

"I don't know what happened," Laura admitted.

"We got carried away. And why not?" Raising his voice, Jared called to the cast, "See you all at the Faculty Center!" The party was scheduled at a private room there.

Everyone waved or called back an acceptance. With other faculty and the cast members' friends in attendance, there should be a pleasant mix of people.

Laura hated to separate from Jared even to go change her clothes, but she knew he'd have a crowd of well-wishers in his dressing room. "I'll meet you there," she said. "That way I don't have to hang around while your students drool on you."

"My students don't drool," he said. "They may salivate, but that's as far as it goes. Are you sure you don't want me to walk you over?"

"I'm fine." She could use a bit of quiet to gather her composure.

To her surprise, Laura found people waiting outside her own dressing room. Half a dozen students wanted their programs autographed, while Wilson Martin beamed as he stood with an attractive couple in their thirties. The bright orange of his hair had been replaced by a slightly more pleasing, but still odd, shade of peach.

"Wonderful acting job." He shook Laura's hand. "Much better than someone we won't name could have done, and your play's terrific. I'd like to introduce you to two of our university patrons, Jim and Dex Bonderoff.''

Dex, an attractively chubby woman with a mass of brown hair, greeted her eagerly. "I love your play."

"We're proud that it was first produced at De Lune," added her husband.

"A lot of alumni called to request an additional performance when they learned we were sold-out," the university president said. "Dex and Jim have offered to underwrite the costs if you'll extend it through tomorrow night."

Laura had planned to work at the Lunar Lunch Box, but she knew Stuart would let her off. After begging Daffodil to come back to cook and receiving her provisional consent, he was in a humble mood.

"If everyone else can make it, I'd love to," she said.

"We'll talk to Jared." President Martin clapped her on the shoulder. "Great job!"

After congratulating her again, they departed. An extra performance! Laura felt a twinge of anxiety, wondering if she and Jared would be moved to make even further changes in the script, but decided not to worry about it.

After signing everyone's program, she closed the door to the dressing room and slipped on the jade, black and cherry sheath. It fit with some room to spare, and she realized she'd been working so hard she'd eaten less than usual. Losing weight wasn't a problem, except that some came off the top, where Laura could least afford to spare it.

The woman who regarded her in the mirror was whip-thin, almost fragile, certainly not the stacked men's-magazine ideal. But as long as she suited Jared, who cared?

She pulled on a black coat against the February chill and went out. The campus was quiet and dark. A short distance away, the glass-and-steel Faculty Center, a modern addition that stood out among the ivy-covered brick buildings, glowed like a hurricane lamp.

After slipping inside its warmth, Laura found the window-wrapped second-floor room that bustled with partygoers. Before she knew it, she was exchanging greetings with Mariah and Hosea, the retired engineer she'd met at Cindy's reception. Runcie had another woman on his arm, whom he introduced as Sadie Wilkerson, a fellow Snooper and Brad Wilkerson's grandmother.

Brad himself was accompanied by the female understudy, while Suzy was partnered by a boy Laura hadn't seen before. Cindy and Hugh waved from across the room. Seeing her many new friends made her wish she weren't going to be moving away so soon.

"We want your opinion." Esther Zimpelman, who must have wangled an invitation from Runcie, buttonholed Laura near the bar. "Since you're my neighbor, I expect you to take my side."

"About what?" she asked.

Hoagie Gunn adjusted his red hat nervously atop his white puff of hair. "We were following the striped poop. I mean, I was following it and she was tagging along."

"I wasn't tagging!" Esther protested. "I was taking pictures of it."

"Pictures of striped poop?" Laura said.

"So naturally, when we came across the Purple-Breasted Nest-Hopper, I snapped it," Esther said.

"It's the first picture of a Hopper that's ever been taken west of Gary, Indiana," Hoagie said. "They're very elusive."

"Naturally we intend to send it to *Bird Brain* magazine, and since I'm the photographer, my name will be on the photo credit," Esther said.

"Whereas, being the person who's run this thing to ground, I should get the credit," explained Hoagie.

Both stood with arms folded, eyes averted from each other. So they were estranged, Laura thought sadly. They'd been so happy the past few weeks that she'd forgotten they, too, were feeling the glass slipper effect.

If, of course, it existed.

"I can see both sides," she said. "I'm afraid I can't render judgment."

"Coward!" said Esther.

"I figured that, as a writer, you would understand about giving credit where it's due," said Hoagie.

Now they were casting her as the bad guy? "Stop acting like spoiled children and work out your differences like grown-ups." Laura walked away without waiting for a response.

A cheer from the assembly drew her attention to the door. The cries welcomed Jared, who looked incredibly sexy in a dark suit and open-collared shirt. Laura could hardly wait to unbutton it.

Then she spotted his companion.

Tall and exotic, the woman had raven hair, turquoise eyes and cheekbones to die for. A designer gown swirled about her ripe figure, emphasizing the fullness of her breasts and slimness of her waist.

Inside Laura, disbelief warred with fury. And, deep down, a burning sense of betrayal.

JARED HADN'T EXPECTED Indigo Frampton to show up in a knock-'em-dead dress. Sure, she'd flirted last night, but in his experience, lots of women did that just to keep their skills honed.

As far as he was concerned, he and Indigo shared nothing but a common interest in show business. Still, as vice president of Firepower Productions and the on-good-terms ex-wife of its legendary founder, Hartley Powers, the former actress was too important to brush aside.

Jared hardly noticed her as a woman, because all he could think about was Laura. Every time she came near him onstage, he'd had to fight the urge to pull her behind the sofa. His reaction was exacerbated by the daring new hairstyle that brought out her delicate sensuality.

When he walked into the Faculty Center, he couldn't wait to slip away from Indigo and get Laura alone. There she was, incredibly beautiful in that dress he loved. He started to wave.

Then he saw her staring at Indigo with an expression of dismay. No, worse than that. Utter disgust.

It was ten years ago, all over again. Back then, when Jared had walked in the door with his date, he'd been caught off guard by Laura's shocked reaction. Surely, he'd figured, she knew that he dated around and none of it meant much. Well, he'd been wrong.

Once again, she'd gotten the wrong idea, but this time it wasn't his fault. He intended to set her straight right away.

"I have to go congratulate the playwright," he told Indigo.

"I'll come, too," she announced, snagging a glass of champagne from a waiter. "I'd love to meet her."

Since she was hanging on to his arm, Jared could hardly refuse, so, in his haste, he half dragged her across he room. Fortunately a couple of well-wishers had halted Laura, because she was making tracks for the door.

The first thing that burst out of his mouth was, "We're extending the run through tomorrow night."

"So I heard," Laura said coldly.

"Excellent job." His unwanted sidekick thrust out her hand and shook Laura's. "I'm Indigo Frampton, Firepower Productions."

"Oh, yes, I've heard of you," she said guardedly.

"Who's your agent? You haven't sold the film rights yet, have you?" Indigo asked.

"No." Laura's gaze traveled between Jared and the woman. "I don't have an agent." Jared knew playwrights made so little money that few people wanted to represent them.

"That's going to change now that you're making a name for yourself," Indigo said. "My studio is looking for a prestige film and there's always a need for mature female roles like you've written. I'll write down the names of a couple of agents I can recommend."

Jared was glad Indigo's instinct to find new talent had overridden whatever interest she might have in him. While business cards were being exchanged, he disentangled himself from the producer and shifted closer to Laura.

"I'm glad I was able to introduce you two," he told Indigo when the women came up for air. "Laura and I have a few details to discuss about tomorrow night. You'll excuse us?"

Now that she'd switched modes, the producer appeared to have forgotten all about flirting. "I'll go introduce myself to that handsome young Brad Wilkerson. That scene where he whipped off his shirt, well, I think he's got a future ahead of him. See you later.'' Away she went.

"You thought she was my date,'' Jared teased Laura. As she nodded, he saw moisture brimming in her eyes. If he said anything sentimental, she might overflow, so he added, "When President Martin told me he'd spoken to you first about tomorrow night, I thought I might find you on his arm. I hear he's trolling for a new love, now that Vanessa's vamoosed.''

She started to laugh. "You think I'd date a guy whose hair looks like a fruit bowl?''

"Speaking of which,'' Jared said, "I love your new cut.''

"Bernie did it,'' she admitted.

"You went to see that turncoat?'' he joked. "That's treason.''

"Blame Cindy,'' she said. "Didn't he do a good job, though?''

"I can't wait to take it off you.''

"You're going to take my hair off?'' Her laughter sent delighted prickles up his spine. "You want a bald girlfriend?''

"I'd rather have a naked one.'' Moving closer, he kept his voice low.

She rested her cheek on his shoulder. "That can be arranged.''

If he hadn't felt an obligation to the rest of the cast, Jared would have taken Laura up on the offer that very minute.

SHE'D BEEN FOOLISH TO WORRY about some kind of cast party jinx, Laura thought as she rode home beside Jared afterward. The fact that he preferred her to the stunning

Indigo made her even happier than if she'd never gotten a fright in the first place.

Was it possible that she and Jared belonged together, not just for a few weeks or months, but...well, she couldn't bring herself to think about forever. That was too much to ask. But for a long time, at least?

Maybe he loved her. She certainly loved him. She loved the cocky tilt of his head and his deep chuckle. She loved the way people flocked around him and the way he'd barely concealed his eagerness to whisk her away.

Maybe she wouldn't go to Louisville after all. Why not look for opportunities closer to Clair De Lune? Los Angeles was only an hour's drive away.

When they entered his house, she heard a soft melodic hum. During the dazzling moment after Jared switched on the lights, Laura thought she saw the cupids fluttering wildly on the shade before freezing in place. When she listened again, the hum was gone.

"I think I drank too much champagne," she said.

"There's no such thing as too much champagne," said Jared.

But how else to explain the way their clothes evaporated? Or the almost psychedelic richness of color and texture as they tangled on the carpet, on the sofa, in the bedroom and in the shower?

When they came out soaking wet, they made love again on the fluffy mats, which were lined up on the floor wall-to-wall in the bathroom. Apparently this was what Jared had meant when he'd bought so many "just in case."

"Comfortable?" he asked afterward, propping himself on one elbow and gazing down at her.

"You should line the entire house with these things," Laura said.

"That might be carrying eccentricity too far."

She snuggled against him. "Let's sleep here."

"You got it," he said.

They dozed off. Sometime later, Laura was vaguely aware of being guided into the bedroom, where she curled against Jared under the covers and went back to sleep.

The telephone woke her. She heard Jared pick it up and mutter a sleepy hello. Then he said, "Really?" and "I haven't checked my fax yet. The *New York Times* said that? Terrific. And the *LA Times*?"

She recalled seeing his fax machine in one of the spare bedrooms. With mounting curiosity, Laura pried herself out of bed and went to check.

A stack of papers waited, with more clicking out as she arrived. Jared had mentioned subscribing to a service that faxed him his reviews, she recalled as she flipped through the pile.

The critics waxed ecstatic. For the most part, they loved the play, the acting and the direction. There were a few sour notes, of course, but they came from less important publications.

"We're a hit," she said, reentering.

With the phone pressed to his ear, Jared nodded while scribbling on a bedside pad. "The end of June until mid-July? Yes, I could schedule the rehearsal then."

Producers were calling on a Sunday? That was unusual, Laura thought, and settled onto the bed beside him.

After he hung up, she handed Jared the reviews. "For the most part, they're raves."

"So I hear. That was the High Point Theater Company

in Chicago," he said. "The artistic director was afraid if he waited until tomorrow, I'd already be booked. He wants me to direct *A Streetcar Named Desire* this summer."

"That's one of your favorite plays," she said. So Jared would be gone for a month. Laura supposed it was unreasonable to expect that they'd spend all their time together. She was willing to make sacrifices, as long as they didn't have to be apart for too long.

The phone rang again. This time, she gathered, it was a friend of Jared's in New Jersey asking him to direct a production of a Chekhov classic. "August?" he said. "Who's in the cast? Really...? Terrific! Of course I can do it."

After hanging up, he said, "We might move the show to off Broadway if it does well. I could fly back during the winter break to supervise."

"Sounds like you're completely booked for your vacations." At least he'd be in Clair De Lune most of the year, Laura thought. "You'd better hope nothing else comes along."

"If I get the right offer, I'll take a leave of absence." In a blissful glow, Jared reclined against the pillows.

Laura's chest squeezed as the truth sank in. Jared still meant what he'd said at Cindy and Hugh's reception: He'd never be ready to settle down.

Her rival wasn't another woman, it was Jared's ego. He was in love with his career, not with her.

Hoping she was mistaken, she ventured, "I've been thinking maybe I shouldn't go to Louisville. If we're both willing to compromise, we could spend more time together."

"I'd like that," he said.

"For how long?" Laura asked.

"Excuse me?"

"How long do you want?" she said. "A month? A semester? Because if we want anything more, we're going to have to fight for it."

He didn't answer right away. Laura wondered if she'd pushed too hard. This wasn't like her. She didn't need a man; she didn't even want one.

The heck you don't.

Watching expressions flicker across Jared's lavender-gray eyes, studying the appealing crookedness of his nose and the tumble of his brown hair, she felt her heart expand. It was big enough to hold him forever, if only he felt the same way about her.

"This is what happens when you have a dream." Shifting toward her, Jared caught her hands. "We're building momentum. We can't let it drop. This is it, Laura, the big time. For both of us."

The phone rang. "Let the machine…"

With an apologetic shrug, he answered it. "Hello?" He sat bolt upright. "Good morning, Mr. Powers." That would be Hartley Powers, the head of Firepower Productions. One of the most important players in Hollywood.

"I'm glad Indigo spoke so highly of my work. Yes, I'd be happy to meet with you… Tuesday? Absolutely. Future projects? I'm open to whatever you'd like to discuss."

Laura had lost and she knew it. While Jared was working out the details on the phone, she went to get dressed. There was no point in badgering him after he'd made his position clear.

She left a note in the kitchen saying she'd see him at

the theater tonight, and eased out the door. From the other room, she could still hear him talking.

It wasn't easy negotiating the street in high heels, but Laura found a bus stop about a quarter of a mile downhill. She rode home in a tumult of emotions.

Losing him to another woman would have been painful, but this loss was more final. She had to accept that Jared might not be capable of loving her enough to make compromises. Ever.

By the time she descended from the bus and walked two blocks to her apartment, Laura's feet hurt almost as much as her heart. She replaced her clothes with jeans and a sweatshirt and, barefoot, addressed Gwyneth Paltrow on the *Shakespeare in Love* poster.

"You had to leave him, but at least you made your dream come true for a while," she said. "Were those moments of joy enough to sustain you for the rest of your life?"

Gwyneth didn't tear her gaze from Joseph Fiennes. Oh, well, Laura knew better than to expect sympathy from a photograph.

Still, she had achieved her goal of breaking down her emotional barriers and becoming a better playwright. *Calling All Glass Slippers* was the best script she'd ever written, and *The Me Nobody Sees* would be even better.

She ought to feel grateful, but she didn't.

Laura slumped onto the couch. All great love stories were supposed to end unhappily, or at least generate a memorable poster. If she had a poster of Jared, she'd throw her high heels at him. Darn that man!

When the phone rang, she nearly didn't answer it. He was the last person she wanted to talk to. Still, she couldn't avoid him forever.

She picked it up. "Yes?"

"Miss Ellison? This is George Johnston. I head the theater department at Central Florida University."

"Oh, yes. What can I do for you?" She'd applied for a grant at CFU six months earlier, but since she hadn't heard anything, she'd figured it was a dead issue.

"I just saw your review in the *New York Times*. We already awarded our playwriting grant for the year, but there's another project I want to discuss with you."

An alumnus had offered to sponsor a distinguished playwright-in-residence for the spring semester. Laura could work on *The Me Nobody Knows,* conduct a few seminars and get paid in the process.

Was she interested? You bet she was!

Florida sounded about as far away from Clair De Lune as she could get. Which was exactly what Laura wanted.

11

JARED DIDN'T UNDERSTAND why Laura had sneaked out while he was on the phone. Her note about seeing him tonight sounded ominous.

Why was she making a big deal out of having to spend time apart? They'd both known this was likely to happen.

Irritably he wandered through the house, eating a muffin and letting the crumbs fall where they may. What had he been thinking when he bought plaid tissue-box holders, marble wastebaskets and those ridiculous china angels? Maybe Laura's idea about her play exerting some kind of romantic effect hadn't been as ludicrous as it sounded.

Thank goodness he'd come down to earth in time. In one morning, he'd received more job offers than in the entire previous year. This was what counted, this burst of adrenaline and the knowledge that he was finally on his way to major success.

From one of his boxes, Jared dug out a dog-eared copy of *A Streetcar Named Desire* and began rereading it. New insights jumped at him, along with ideas for the staging. Reviewing a play with an eye to production was, for a director, the creative equivalent of writing a play of his own.

He was lying on his back on the carpet with his feet propped on the coffee table when Jared noticed how quiet the house had become. More than the normal Sunday quiet. Empty. Like his life before he went to that New Year's Eve party and ran into Laura.

Grimly he turned a page and tried to focus on the next scene, but couldn't. The only image in his mind was Laura, the way she'd looked last night with her face shining and vulnerable in that wispy hairstyle.

She ought to be here, even if she were sitting in another room typing on a computer. Why did she have to be so stiff-necked? They could work things out if Laura were just willing to concede that their careers came first.

Determined to bring her to her senses, Jared groped for the phone. Still lying with his feet propped up, he dialed her number.

"Yes?" She sounded distracted, as if she'd been interrupted while writing.

"It's me," Jared said. "We didn't finish our conversation this morning."

"I'm sorry. I was unreasonable," she said.

"No kidding." In his relief, he finally conceded that his feet were going numb, so he sat up. "I'll come pick you up."

"I promised Stuart I'd work for a few hours this afternoon, and again tomorrow," she said. "Then he'll have to find a replacement."

"You're quitting your job?" That might be good. Or not. "Why?"

"I don't know if I mentioned it, but I paid off the last of my debts last week." She sounded too cheerful to be several miles away from him. "Besides, I've landed a developmental fellowship from Central Florida University."

"Wonderful." What the heck was a developmental fellowship? "You mean they'll pay you to write?"

"And conduct a few seminars. I'll be playwright-in-residence," she explained.

"You don't have to move to Florida, though, right?" Jared said.

"That's part of the deal."

She couldn't go that far. Not to Florida or to Louisville, either. "You may get a better offer in this area," he warned. "Remember what Indigo said about scriptwriting."

"That's a long shot, and probably not imminent," Laura pointed out. "This is a terrific opportunity. The university has a cooperative arrangement with a professional theater group…"

He didn't absorb the rest of what she said. The gist was simple: She was leaving.

"No," he said. "You can't go."

"It isn't up to you."

He ought to be able to tease her into staying. Light-hearted charm worked wonders, Jared had learned, but he couldn't summon any, because he cared too much.

"It's a mistake," he said. "Trust me on this one."

"I can't stay unless I receive a better offer," Laura said.

"What does that mean?"

"Think about it," she said. "Gotta go. Bye."

He sat listening to a faint electronic whine, until a snooty voice like that of his least-favorite teacher, the one who gave him a *D* in third grade for not coloring inside the lines, said, "If you want to make a phone call, please hang up and dial again. If you want to make…"

He dropped the handset into the cradle. This was ridiculous. Laura couldn't flee just when things were heating up. The whole point was to share their excitement as they launched the next phase of their careers.

If she finished her new play in Florida, she'd be working with another director to develop it. Someone else would read the first and second drafts. Someone else would challenge her thinking and stimulate her creative leaps.

Someone else would wake up each morning to the flash of those jade eyes. Someone else...

This streetcar wasn't named Desire, Jared realized. This streetcar was named Jealousy.

He could feel himself going a little crazy, as if Laura's play were reexerting its weird spell over him. If only he hadn't agreed to another performance tonight, he might be able to think straight. No doubt normalcy would return by tomorrow, but right now he couldn't stop obsessing about Laura.

Why wasn't she more flexible? Why didn't she want to work exclusively with him?

"I can't stay unless I receive a better offer."

That was what she needed, a better offer than she'd received from the Florida university. Now where, Jared wondered, was he going to find one, and fast?

ON SUNDAY AFTERNOON, WHEN Laura set out for her next-to-last day at the Lunar Lunch Box, she saw Dean Pipp sweeping the front walkway. With a rhythmic *swish-swish*, leaves, pebbles and grass clippings flew toward the gutter.

"You've heard of washing that man out of your hair?" called her landlady. "Well, I'm brushing him off my sidewalk. His shoes probably left some dirt from Prego Prego lying around, and I want it gone!''

Apparently the happy reunion of old lovers hadn't lasted. ''What happened?''

''He gave me a present for Valentine's Day.'' Marie squatted and yanked a weed onto her pile of debris.

That must have been some strange present to tick off his wife. ''What exactly did he give you?''

''A gift certificate for a tetanus shot.''

That was peculiar, even by Clair De Lune standards. ''What for?''

''The whole time he was wining and dining me, he was scheming to drag me out to do grunt work on his dig.'' Dean Pipp scowled. ''With my arthritis, I should go live in a tent and sleep in a bag? I don't think so!''

''You kicked him out?'' Laura asked.

''Lock, stock and carpetbag,'' the older woman proclaimed with satisfaction. ''He still thinks of me as the young sidekick who went gaga over him. Worse, he wanted me to sell my house because his project needs financing. The man's a leech.''

''I'm sorry to hear it.'' Laura was disappointed that Watley had turned out to be so self-centered, not to mention mercenary. ''Are you going to divorce him?''

''If I get around to it,'' said her landlady. ''I should have learned my lesson the first time.''

Although she was due at work, Laura lingered to hear the rest of the story. ''What made you call it quits back then? Was it the spider bite?''

A veined hand waved dismissively. ''I didn't care about losing my hair.'' She shoved the remaining dust over the curb. ''The last straw came when a crazed hyena broke into our tent and ate a rare book I'd been translating from the Urdu. Do you know what Watley said?''

''I have no idea.''

''He said, 'Good, now you'll have more time to spend helping me.'''

What a rat! ''Has he left town yet? I'd like to add a kick in the pants to help him along.''

Watley's remark reminded Laura of Jared's arrogant belief that he had the right to control her actions. So she couldn't leave Clair De Lune without his permission, could she? After tonight, he'd better shade his eyes to watch her disappearing into the distance like the Road Runner.

''I put him on a plane last night,'' Marie said. ''By the way, we saw your play on Friday. I loved it.''

''Thank you,'' Laura said. ''That reminds me, I have to give notice on the apartment. It looks like I'll be leaving this week.''

''Don't worry about it,'' said the dean. ''It's been interesting having you here.''

''It's been interesting for me, too,'' Laura said. ''I'll see you later.''

Her landlady went back to sweeping. Although the windshield of a car parked beneath the eucalyptus tree bore a splotch of striped poop, Laura saw no sign of Esther or Hoagie.

CINDY COULDN'T BELIEVE HER new friend was heading off to Florida so soon. ''What's the rush?'' she asked as she watched Laura apply makeup in her dressing room.

With her new haircut, the delicate redhead looked almost ethereal, although there was no mistaking her underlying strength. Thanks to her own large-boned build,

Cindy had never had a chance of passing for ethereal, but she didn't mind. Possessing physical heft came in handy when you wanted to set straight a gouging repairman or stare down an aggressive softball dad.

"The show's almost over. Time to move on," Laura said.

"I got the impression there was something special between you and Jared." Cindy couldn't help acting like a buttinsky when it came to helping a friend.

"We'd be too busy to see each other anyway." Laura smoothed foundation over her cheeks.

"Jared's reverted to type, eh?" Cindy said.

In the mirror, her friend gave her a wry smile. "Exactly. It's too much to expect him to step out of the limelight, even for...well, even for me."

"Is there anything I can do?"

"You've done so much already." Laura pushed back her chair. "In fact, I brought a little thank-you gift."

Protestations fleeted through Cindy's mind, but never made it to her lips. Why bother saying "you don't have to get me anything" when Laura already had? "How sweet!"

From her oversize purse, Laura produced a fresh copy of the script. "I autographed this for you. In case I ever get famous, it might be worth something."

"It's worth plenty to me now." Cindy handled the script carefully. "I'm thrilled to have it." Hugh took pride in his shelf of autographed poetry volumes. Now she could start her own collection.

"Here's the second part of the gift. It's a more practical souvenir." Laura gave her a shoebox tied with a ribbon.

Curious, Cindy opened it. Inside lay a pair of clear

plastic pumps even nicer than the ones she'd rounded up as glass slippers for the play. "Wow! Where'd you find these?"

"On the Internet," Laura said. "I had to call Hugh to get your shoe size, and then I was afraid they wouldn't arrive in time, but here they are."

If she hadn't been wearing laced jogging shoes, Cindy would have slipped on the shoes, which looked comfortable as well as sparkly. However, she needed to see about her stage managing duties. "How adorable! I'll wear them soon."

"Hugh said he was planning to take you out for a candlelight dinner after the show," Laura said. "You could wear them then."

"I told him I'll be too tired to go out tonight." After closing the box, Cindy gave her friend a hug. "But I'll let my husband take me out later in the week. And I'll always treasure these because of the memories."

"You're lucky. You didn't need the magic," Laura said.

"What magic?"

"The glass slipper effect." She gave an embarrassed laugh. "It's a silly idea I had, that for the run of the show, the magic was real."

"You've got an amazing imagination." Cindy, her arms full, moved toward the door. "Break a leg tonight."

"Thanks."

After stowing her gifts in the wings, Cindy grabbed her checklist and made sure the props were in place. A short while later, as she made a circuit of the dressing rooms giving everyone ten minutes' notice, a nostalgic sadness gripped her.

Cast and crew were like a family, and the end of the

show meant the end of their closeness. Even though they might see each other again or even work together on other shows, it would never be quite the same mix of people.

Still, the future was full of promise. A principal from a nearby elementary school had called Cindy last week about filling in for a second-grade teacher going on maternity leave. Soon she'd be back in a classroom, doing the job she loved.

Rousing herself from her thoughts, she sent a student to give the five-minute warning while she prepared to raise the curtain. Actors took their places, the lights dimmed and the last performance of *Calling All Glass Slippers* began.

The next hour and a half flew by. Cindy grew so absorbed in the onstage action that she had to force herself to remember her cues.

It was during a scene break early in Act Three that, while stowing a prop, she stumbled over a rough spot in the flooring and nearly lost her balance. Recovering, she took a step and nearly kicked off her jogging shoe by accident. When Cindy knelt to retie the lace, she discovered it had broken.

She should have brought a backup pair! Well, she hadn't, so after a moment's debate, she decided to put on the mock-glass slippers Laura had given her.

The shoes fit as comfortably as a pair of bedroom slippers. Even the modest heels didn't bother her, and, when Cindy tried walking in them, they whispered across the floorboards like rubber soles.

As she moved, the shoes gave off a ruby glow in the dimness. It reminded her of the sneakers some of her students used to wear, with heels that flashed red when they tapped the ground.

"That ought to keep me from stumbling," she murmured to herself. "At least I'll always know where my feet are."

She moved to get a better view of the stage as the final scene arrived. Laura and Jared crackled with energy and, even from here, she could feel the pleasurable tension in the audience.

They were so right for each other, she thought. Every time their eyes met, sparks flew. How could Laura leave? How could Jared drive her away?

Warmth bathed Cindy's feet, spreading upwards. That was odd, because usually she found the backstage cold. Come to think of it, she wasn't even wearing socks.

She glanced down. A faint pinkish tinge bathed her jeans in luminescence. Confused, Cindy took a step backward to make sure she wasn't visible to the audience.

But they were too riveted on the stage to notice her, she realized as Laura tore herself away from Jared and crossed the stage. The onlookers let out a collective gasp, as if willing her to stop.

Cindy reached for the lever that operated the curtain. According to the script, Laura was to look back, then turn away forever. Last night, however, she and Jared had made changes, and Cindy didn't intend to lower the boom until she was certain they'd finished.

Laura turned to face him. A rustling noise told Cindy that the viewers were leaning forward in their seats.

"I thought there was hope for us," improvised the actress/playwright. "But..."

From his pocket, Jared produced a jeweler's box.

Cindy frowned. She certainly hadn't provided this prop. What was going on?

"You don't have to hope anymore," Jared said. "Marry me. Live with me. Be my wife."

Cindy had to hand it to the lighting designer. All the way up in her booth at the top of the theater, the woman managed to pick out the brilliance of the diamond ring, although how she managed to do that when the lights were automated, Cindy had no idea. Must be a manual override.

"I...don't know what to say." Laura stood, wavering in her confusion.

Was this for real? It sure felt like it. A wave of heat flooded over Cindy as if she shared their longing for each other. Of course, the one she longed for was Hugh. Too tired? What had she been thinking?

"Say yes!" called a man in the audience.

"Marry him or you'll always regret it!" added a woman. Other people seconded the motion.

"I guess I'm outvoted." Laura broke into a smile. "Yes."

Neither of them moved. Cue! Cindy thought, and pulled the lever. The curtain came down at its measured pace, to thunderous applause.

She wasn't sure where she found the fortitude to stand there raising and lowering it as the cast took bows. She couldn't wait to meet Hugh, who'd promised to come backstage. Where was he? A candlelight dinner, yes! And then they would go home together, and never feel tired again.

"I'm right here," murmured her husband, his arms encircling her from behind. As if he'd read her thoughts!

"Let's go!" Cindy gathered her possessions in record time. "I'm starved!"

"Me, too," he said. "In more ways than one."

"I'll race you to the car!" As they flew outside, laughing like children, her shoes sent ruby flashes into the darkness.

THEY WEREN'T ACTUALLY engaged, of course. At the moment when she said yes, Laura had felt as if she were accepting Jared's proposal, but that had been in the character of the Young Widow. No court of law in the world would hold an actress to a promise she made onstage.

She couldn't have really accepted it, because Jared hadn't really meant it. He hadn't even had a chance to hand her the ring. What a great gimmick, though! They'd certainly made the audience happy.

As she put on street clothes, Laura decided not to change the original ending she'd written for her play. The diamond ring business wouldn't work with any actor less charismatic than Jared.

Suddenly overwhelmed with emotion, she sank into a chair. Who was she kidding? She wished with all her heart that his proposal had been genuine, but she was too old for fairy tales.

A series of sharp knocks made her jump. Before she could get up, Jared scooted inside and closed the door behind him. "What is it with people wanting our autographs?" he asked. "We're not famous yet."

"As long as they don't want it on the bottom of a check, I don't mind." Laura grabbed a tissue and began removing her makeup.

"I forgot to give you something." Her skin tingled as

Jared reached around her and set the black velvet jeweler's box on the counter. He flipped it open.

Inside sparkled the ring. "It looks almost genuine," she said.

In the mirror, he feigned a hurt expression. "Of course it's genuine."

She was embarrassed to ask if he'd been serious about wanting to marry her. Was she supposed to assume that this was all staged for dramatic effect? Or was he too self-conscious to get down on one knee and propose the old-fashioned way?

Jared had never struck Laura as the self-conscious type. But she didn't dare draw any conclusions for fear of looking like a fool.

"What am I supposed to make of all this?" Returning her attention to the mirror, she took a swipe at her mascara.

Jared pulled over a chair, straddled it backward and reached for her hand. "You're supposed to promise to love, honor, and above all obey. That means canceling the trip to Florida."

"I figured that was what you wanted." So he didn't mean it, after all; he just wanted to keep her here a while longer. "Those weren't wedding bells I heard, they were peals of laughter."

"Are you trying to pin me down?" His tone was teasing, but underneath, Laura thought she detected a note of fear. Did he honestly think she wanted to clamp a ball and chain around his leg?

Anger flared inside her. Jared was the one who'd brought up this marriage business, not her. The last thing she wanted was to shackle some man who didn't love her.

"I'm not trying to do anything," she said. "Let's blame the whole thing on the play, all right? You got caught up in your character and went for a happy ending, except it's not suppose to last after the curtain comes down."

"I want this to last," Jared said.

He was sitting so close that, if she turned toward him, her mouth would brush his. Laura fought the temptation by smearing cold cream across her deep-red lipstick.

When she could speak again, she said, "What would it mean to you if I accepted this ring?"

"That we're engaged," Jared said.

"And?" she prompted.

"That we're going to live together."

"Keep going."

"You know what a ring means." He grinned. "That we're a couple. That we do things together. That you don't go off to Florida and leave me."

"But you go off to wherever and leave me," she said.

"Not permanently!"

Was it enough? she wondered. She could use Clair De Lune as her home base, maintain an easygoing relationship with Jared and keep on writing plays.

Yet deep down, something was missing. Laura didn't know what, but she would rather have nothing than pretend this arrangement suited her.

"I can't do it," she said.

The smile vanished from Jared's face. "You're turning me down?"

"I'm turning you down," Laura confirmed. "I'm sorry."

He took her hands and brought them to his cheek. "Come home with me and I'll change your mind."

The man could charm a purple-breasted bird out of a tree. He could inspire painted lampshade cupids to flutter their wings and play their harps. But he couldn't make Laura happy.

If she went home with him, all it would mean was another rude awakening tomorrow morning. That, she thought, would be more than she could bear.

Removing her hands from his grasp, she snapped shut the jeweler's box and handed it back to him. "I appreciate the offer, but I'm afraid I don't believe in long engagements," she said. Without waiting for Jared to try his powers of persuasion on her again, Laura seized her purse, brushed past him and ran out.

12

OF ALL THE THINGS LAURA didn't expect to see on her staircase the next morning, one of them was Esther Zimpelman kneeling down, cleaning it.

"What on earth are you doing?" She eyed her neighbor warily.

Viewed from Laura's position at the top of the stairs, a clump of gray hair sprouted against the dark strands in Esther's scalp. The camera and binoculars around her neck hung down until they bumped the stairs.

"There were some bird droppings," the elder woman said without looking up. "I wouldn't want anyone to slip."

"I'm more likely to slip on wet stairs than on the bird poop." Laura shifted her purse and silver apron to the other arm so she could grip the inside railing. "When did you start taking such an interest in my well-being?"

"Who said anything about you?" Sitting back, Mrs. Zimpelman frowned up at her. "I'm leasing the place from Dean Pipp starting next week."

"You're moving out of your house?" It was hard to imagine that she'd go to such extremes to get away from her longtime friend.

"It's not for me," Esther said. "Hoagie and I put both our names on the photograph and posted it on the Internet. There's a story about our discovery in this morning's paper, too. We've got birders from all over the country who want to come see the Nest-Hopper for themselves and I don't want them moving in with me.''

"That sounds like a lot of people for a one-room apartment," Laura said.

"Birders are used to roughing it. They go on safari, into the woods, all sorts of places." With her cleaning rag, Esther took another swipe at the stairs. "They'll be fine squished in there, as long as the plumbing works and they don't fall on their keisters."

"I'm glad you're so concerned about their comfort." Inching downward, Laura added as a joke, "If I land in the hospital, I'm suing you, by the way."

"It'll be dry in a few minutes." Her neighbor sniffed. "How did I know you were going to show up right now?"

"I do live here," Laura reminded her. "If I break a leg, I'll have to stick around even longer. Ever think of that?"

"Young people are resilient. The worst you'll get are black-and-blue marks." Having held her own when it came to teasing, Esther started to rise and had to grab the railing to keep from tumbling. "My goodness. That is bad. Hoagie! Hoagie!"

The white-haired man materialized in a flash. He must have been hiding in a nearby bush, probably scanning the trees for more specimens. "What is it, honey bunch?"

"She sprayed herself into a corner." Laura edged down the other side of the steps.

"Come to Papa!" Hoagie held out his arms to Esther, who launched herself into them. The couple staggered backward, giggling, and ended up leaning against the garage.

Despite her annoyance at Esther's presumption, Laura was glad the pair had reconciled. She was going to miss these people, she thought as she marched away. By all accounts, Florida had its share of oddballs as well, but they couldn't possibly top Clair De Lune.

BRYAN WAS ONE OF THE MOST talented mime students Jared had ever encountered. During Monday's class, he found himself forgetting the point of the exercise and simply enjoying the young man's performance.

Each mime was required to act out a sketch with a moral that the class had to guess. Most of the students preferred to be part of a pair or small group, but Bryan worked alone. Single-handedly, he created a silent, convincing world.

Bryan had taken his inspiration from an article in this morning's newspaper, the *Clarion,* about Laura's birdwatching neighbors. Around his neck, the mime wore two pairs of binoculars, one white and one black, to indicate different characters. He started on one side of the classroom, wearing a feathery disguise and staring eagerly across the space, then switched sides and became the second birder, wearing a different disguise and staring back at the first.

As the two birders drew closer, each began to wriggle with excitement. Then Bryan pulled a difficult trick: he showed what each personality imagined he was seeing. From the center of the room, a fluttery, gawky, hilarious caricature of a stork faced Birder Number One, then was replaced by a cranky, predatory eagle facing Birder Number Two.

Closer and closer the two characters came, each growing more excited, while the birds became increasingly agitated. At the last moment, the men nearly collided with each other—not an easy moment to depict, since Bryan was playing both of them—and reacted with shock as each realized that his fabulous find was nothing more than another bird fanatic.

Applause erupted around the classroom. "Great job," Jared said. "Okay, everybody. What's the moral?"

"Birds of a feather stick together," someone said.

"A feather in my cap," another student called.

"I don't think so." Jared hadn't figured out the answer himself yet, but he'd know the truth when he heard it. It was hard to concentrate, though, because he was marveling at Bryan's achievement.

"A bird in the hand is worth two in the bush," came from the back of the classroom.

"Don't count your eggs before they hatch," someone suggested.

Bryan shook his head to all of them.

"Try turning it around," he said. It was a piece of advice Jared often gave to actors when they got stuck in preparing a role. "Examine it from a different angle. Forget about bird sayings. Think about people."

A young woman raised her hand instead of shouting like the others. Jared had learned from experience that her reticence hid a shrewd mind. "Amy?"

"I think his point is that people see what they want to see instead of what's really there," she said.

Her answer clicked into place. "I'd agree with that." Jared turned to the mime. "Bryan?"

The young man, who as usual refrained from speaking, scribbled on his slate and held it up. It said, "Bingo!"

The bell rang. Jared had purposely scheduled Bryan for last because it wasn't fair to expect anyone else to follow such a gifted performer. "Wonderful. See you guys on Wednesday. And Bryan, I'm betting we'll see you on Broadway before you're twenty-five."

Beaming, the young man departed in a crowd of admirers. They were unusually quiet, scribbling notes to each other in imitation of their hero.

The image of the two obsessed birders, the ungainly stork and the peevish eagle stuck in Jared's mind as he went to his office. He didn't know why it intrigued him so much. Something was stirring deep within his subconscious, and he supposed he'd have to let it burrow its way to the surface in its own time.

From a folder on his desk, Jared took the cast photos a student photographer had shot at Thursday night's dress rehearsal. They'd been taken in black and white for effect, and some were striking.

Without her vivid coloring, Laura had a pale fragility that made him yearn to protect her. Why on earth wouldn't she let him? Jared couldn't believe he'd finally asked a woman to marry him and she'd said no.

Come on, this isn't about getting married so you can take care of her. Admit the truth, you old curmudgeon, he told himself. You love her.

The acknowledgment sent relief rippling through him. Yes, he loved Laura and craved her and wanted to be with her always. Had he mentioned that he loved her when he proposed?

Jared didn't think so. Maybe he should have.

Her eyes shone from the photograph, vulnerable and wary. How could someone so frail be so tough? Jared wondered as he sank into his swivel chair and plopped his feet on the desk. How could she walk away when he was certain she loved him, too?

She needed to be more flexible. This Florida business, for instance. Why couldn't she postpone it until summer, when it would dovetail with Jared's absence? If she'd try harder, surely they could work things out.

He glanced down at the notes he'd made in class and a line leaped out at him. "People see what they want to see."

In his ears rang the words he himself had spoken, as if someone else were parroting them. "Try turning it around. Examine it from a different angle."

Ruefully Jared conceded that he didn't enjoy the process of self-examination. It was much more comfortable barreling through life expecting other people to leap out of the way.

If he looked through Laura's eyes, what would he see? And once he saw it, would he ever find his own focus again?

STUART TOOK THE NEWS of Laura's imminent departure with a dyspeptic grunt. "I warned you I was only temporary," she said.

"Everybody's temporary. The customers are temporary. The cook comes and goes when she wants to. People keep ordering things that aren't on the menu," he grumbled, standing in front of his office where the entire restaurant could hear him.

"Did it ever occur to you that maybe you're in the wrong business?" Laura said.

Daffodil stuck her head out of the kitchen. "He just likes to complain."

"Then I guess he is in the right business," she said.

"I can work extra hours," Magda offered glumly.

"I've got plenty of free time." The waitress clipped an order to Daffodil's wheel.

"What happened to Burt?" Laura asked.

"We went to your play on Friday night and he said he'd call me again, but he hasn't." The other waitress bit her lip. "I thought we were getting really close. I don't know what happened."

"It's only been a couple of days. Maybe he had some family emergency out of town." Laura glanced at her customers, but they all appeared contented. At two o'clock, the lunch crowd had thinned out, and most of those remaining were lingering over coffee.

"I guess I fooled myself into believing that he loved me." Magda's eyes brimmed with tears. "My friends said it wouldn't last, and I guess they were right. After all, he's a lawyer and I'm a high-school dropout."

"If he's worth anything, he wouldn't care," Laura said stoutly.

"I guess not, but nobody's perfect." Magda hefted a carafe of coffee and went to refill cups.

A short time later, Jared came in alone and sat in Laura's section. He looked cheerful—no, more than cheerful. He looked pleased with himself. She busied herself refilling a water pitcher. Let him enjoy his own company for a while, since he was having such a good time.

"Excuse me!" he called. "Miss! Could I get some service here?"

Magda glanced up with a quizzical expression. Other customers glanced his way and a couple of women looked as if they were considering volunteering to wait on him.

There was no point in acting childish, Laura supposed,

so she walked over in a brisk professional manner. "What can I get you?"

"I'd like some cheesecake," Jared said. "Do you have any with cherry topping?"

"Only sour cream today." She tapped her pencil against her pad. "How about that?"

"No, thanks. When do you think you'll have some with cherry topping?" he asked, and took a personal organizer from his pocket.

"Excuse me?"

"The date," he said.

"How would I know? I'm not the cook." She couldn't believe his nerve, or was this some kind of game?

"Do you think Daffodil could arrange to bake some on June 21?" he asked.

Definitely a game, Laura thought, but one she had no patience for. "I won't be here on June 21."

"You could be," Jared said. "The semester will be over by then at Central Florida U. I checked their Web site."

Against her will, she smiled. "Oh, you did, did you? And why would I want to come back here on June 21?"

"I figure we're both so busy, it was up to me to figure out the soonest we could set our wedding," he said. "You did say you don't believe in long engagements."

The man was unbelievably cheeky. "I never agreed to marry you."

Peripherally Laura became aware that a hush had fallen over the Lunar Lunch Box. Daffodil had emerged from the kitchen and Stuart from his office, and Magda was standing with her mouth open.

"I'll have to cancel attending a theater conference that weekend, but I can see that I need to be flexible," Jared said. "If you don't have anything better to do later in the summer, you could come with me to Chicago and New Jersey."

"What about the honeymoon?" demanded Daffodil.

"How about a weekend in San Francisco?" Jared asked.

"A week in Hawaii," said Magda. "Don't settle for anything less."

Laura folded her arms and regarded Jared. "You can see that I have my agents negotiating for me."

"As long as they don't want ten percent of my time, that's okay," he said. "A week in Hawaii. Done. Daffodil, you'll cater the wedding, right? I'd prefer cheesecake to one of those conventional things in tiers, but that's up to Laura."

"I'll be in Florida. I won't be around to plan a wedding." Her heart was thundering. The man was making a commitment in front of the entire restaurant?

"I'm good at staging things. I can plan a wedding myself," Jared said. "Well?"

"Well, what?" Laura asked.

A couple of dozen faces turned toward him expectantly. "Oh, right," he said. "Hold on."

He got to his feet and, with a flourish, knelt facing Laura. From his pocket, he produced the jeweler's box. "I'm getting a lot of use out of this," he said.

"It's a stage veteran by now," she agreed.

"Laura Ellison, will you marry me?" Jared asked in his powerful actor's voice.

She could feel everyone in the restaurant willing her to say yes. They reminded her of the audience at the end of Act Three. This time, however, she wasn't playing a part, and her future depended on making sure she gave he right answer. "You haven't told me what marriage means to you," she said.

Jared blinked in surprise. Obviously he hadn't prepared an answer for this one. Good. She didn't want him to recite a script, even one he'd composed himself. "What do you mean?"

"As far as I'm concerned, marriage is forever," Laura said. "Are you just planning to stick around for the good times, or what?"

"Certainly not!" he said.

"Then there's the question of your directing assignments," she persisted. "How does marriage fit in with Jared Benton's plans for world conquest?"

"Okay, I get your drift," he said. "Give me a minute. Thirty seconds. Ten seconds. Okay, I got it."

He took a deep breath. Laura's heart was beating so loudly that she was sure everyone else in the restaurant could hear it, too.

"All I ever asked from life was a great career and lots of friends," Jared said. "What I've learned during the past few weeks is that none of that means anything if there's a great gaping hole in my heart."

Magda sighed. Daffodil gave a squeak of approval.

"That's a good start." Laura wasn't giving in this easily.

"I love you so much that I'm willing to meet you halfway," Jared said. "Maybe more than halfway, although don't count on it. I haven't turned into Casper Milquetoast."

"Thank goodness for that!" called one of his female admirers, tears streaming down her face.

"Marriage means that we'll make my house feel like a home even if it requires putting an ugly lamp in every

room," Jared said. "It means that if you have to go awa
part of the time, I'll suffer in silence, except for callin
you every hour on the hour and installing a surveillanc
camera in your hotel room so I can watch you sleep."

"This is the most complicated proposal I ever hear
of," Laura said.

"This isn't the proposal, it's the addendum," Jare
explained.

"Let the man finish," said Daffodil.

"Marriage means that when we argue, sometimes I'l
let you talk more than me even if it kills me," Jare
continued. "I might occasionally admit I'm wrong, al
though I'd rather acquiesce in silence and save face."

Several people applauded his honesty.

Laura should have known Jared would turn his pro
posal into a piece of theater. But what the heck? She wa
enjoying it. "Is that all?"

Judging by the light in his eyes, Jared was barely get
ting started. "To me, marriage means walking throug
life with a friend, having someone I can turn to and wh
always knows she can turn to me."

If she smiled any more broadly, Laura was afraid he
lips would crack. "Okay."

He wasn't finished. "It means that your hopes and
dreams are as vital to me as my own. It means that we're
launching a voyage of discovery together, one that's go
ing to last for the rest of our lives."

Laura could scarcely get a word in edgewise. Tha
word was, "Yes."

"Marriage means…"

"Excuse me." Burt Page stood near the entrance
holding a bunch of daffodils. "As a lawyer, let me sug
gest you get the lady's signature on the dotted line, fig

uratively speaking, before she changes her mind. When it comes to contract negotiations, sometimes the key is to shut up while you're ahead.''

Jared knelt there with his mouth open for a second. Then he said, ''Thank you. If there's anything I know how to do, it's follow stage directions.'' He took Laura's hand and slid the ring onto her finger. ''I'm holding you to that yes.''

''Good, because I meant it.'' She didn't know whether to laugh or cry. The man was outrageous, but she loved him so very, very much.

As if he had springs on his feet, Jared bounded upright and swooped her into his arms. ''My bride,'' he said, and carted her out the door into the crisp sunshine.

Laura dissolved into giggles. ''What on earth are you doing?''

He kissed her. ''Sealing our bargain.''

''Everyone can see us.''

''That's fine with me.'' He carried her inside again, to cheers and clapping. ''I was practicing that threshold business for after the wedding,'' he announced.

Even as she hugged him, Laura noticed Magda standing on the sidelines, holding on to the daffodils and Burt at the same time.

Two happy endings for the price of one, she thought. How could you beat that?

Epilogue

"BURT'S KIND OF BASHFUL, but Jared inspired him," Magda said. "He proposed last month. I hope you'll be in our wedding in September."

"I wouldn't miss it," Laura said.

"If you need anyone to do her hair, I'll make myself available. Any friend of Laura's is a friend of mine," said Bernie, who was putting the finishing touches on the bride's coiffeur in the theater dressing room.

Although it broke with tradition to have a man among the four bridal attendants, Cindy had smuggled him in. She'd explained to Laura that he would sneak out while they whisked her across campus to the chapel.

The last four months had been a whirlwind. Although she'd loved being playwright-in-residence in Florida, and Jared had flown out to see her three times, Laura vowed never again to be separated from him for so long.

She'd also felt more than a few twinges of fear about the preparations he was making for their wedding without her input. Thank goodness Cindy and Daffodil had contributed their expertise.

The cook had declined an invitation to be a bridesmaid, saying she'd be too busy getting the food ready. Magda, however, had accepted, along with Cindy and Laura's two sisters, Leila and Louanne.

Bernie fluttered about, arranging a circlet of daisies

atop Laura's newly trimmed hair. "You know, with all the movie stars I've met and all the productions I've worked on these past few months, nothing means as much as those weeks when I was in your show. I felt like someone else, I truly did. Enchanted, that's what I was."

"I hope my next play is as good," Laura said.

"I'm sure it will be," Cindy said loyally.

"That remains to be seen."

In Florida, Laura had completed the first two acts of *The Me Nobody Sees*. The sticking point was to find a good reason for her heroine to become visible again. With so much going on in her life, Laura had been too distracted.

To her amazement, *Calling All Glass Slippers* was set to open on Broadway the following spring. Firepower Productions had optioned the film rights, with Laura to adapt her own script and Jared to make his film directing debut.

As for her suspicions about a glass slipper effect, after four months they seemed absurd. True, the well-known actor and actress signed to star on Broadway had begun an affair with each other. Also, three years after their divorce, Indigo Frampton and Hartley Powers had decided to reconcile. But things like that didn't require any special magic.

"I love your dress," said Leila. She and her husband had flown in the previous day from Boston. "Did you buy it in Florida?"

"No..."

"It's exquisite," Bernie agreed. "Like something out of a fairy tale. Forget that sleek strapless look! Give me ruffles and tiny roses and puffed sleeves any day."

Laura fingered the French lace on one of the sleeves. "It's an antique. Jared found it in a costume shop."

"The groom?" Her younger sister, Louanne, shook her head. "I can't believe you let a guy pick your gown. But I have to say, he hit a home run."

"In all respects," Laura said. "Remember how stunning the chapel looked at the rehearsal last night? Rose and silver are classic colors."

"I had a little input on that," Bernie murmured. "Just an e-mail or two."

"I thought the color scheme was going to be too subtle, but it turned out beautiful." Cindy tugged at the deep-pink bodice of her bridesmaid's dress.

None of the dresses were alike. Laura's red-headed sisters wore silver, while Magda and Cindy, both blondes, had chosen gowns in rose.

Laura's heart swelled with joy. Until this moment, she'd been so busy rushing from one place to another that she hadn't had time to savor being surrounded by her sisters and friends. "I love all of you," she said.

"What brought that on?" asked Louanne.

"Have you no sense of poetry?" demanded Bernie. "This is a watershed moment. I'll treasure it always, Laura. I've always wanted to hear a bride say she loved me, without actually having to get married."

"I'm honored," Magda said.

"I love you too," said Cindy.

"So do I." Leila gave her sister a hug, light enough to avoid crushing the lace. "I'm sorry we haven't always been close. I hope that's going to change."

"Me, too," said Laura.

"I do so have a sense of poetry," Louanne told Bernie.

"Just because I'm on the tennis circuit doesn't mean I don't have a brain."

"Poetry doesn't happen in your brain. It happens in your soul." The hairdresser stood back to observe his work. "Absolutely splendid. Now I'd better go before anyone sees me."

"We see you," teased Cindy.

"You know what I mean." Bernie gave her a wink. "Before anyone sees me who doesn't love me. I'll treasure your words, Laura."

"Thank you for making me look like a bride," she said.

"You'd better thank Jared for that." With a wave, he was gone, barely in time to miss the photographer, who arrived a couple of minutes later.

The young woman did an efficient job of shooting the bridesmaids clustered around the bride. To Laura's relief, she didn't take long.

"Time to take our show on the road," Cindy said when the woman had gone. "Everybody, let's surround Laura and shield her from view on the way to the chapel. Magda, you're tall, so you should bring up the rear. I'll lead, since I know the way. Leila..."

Once organized, they scooted across the blossoming green campus like a flock of ballerinas, taking little steps to stay in a tight knot. Several people whistled and clapped. A couple of women, no doubt aware that Jared was departing the single state forever, burst into tears.

Through a back door, they swarmed into the chapel. Laura could hear the rustle and chatter of the guests. "Where's Jared? Is he here?"

"He'd better be." Cindy went to check. Returning, she

said, "He's waiting with the minister. Hugh's got the ring."

Laura's heart rate speeded. She couldn't wait to say her vows and become Jared's lifetime partner.

But her brain refused to quit working. It was concerned for her poor invisible heroine, stuck at the end of Act Two with no way to reenter the normal world.

Laura kept mulling Bernie's statement that he wanted to leave before anybody saw him who didn't love him. That phrase seemed like a key, if she could only figure out how to fit it into the lock and turn it.

"The guests are seated," said Leila, who was matron of honor. "Dad's waiting in the foyer. Come on!" In a haze of anticipation, Laura let herself be propelled forward. Her father beamed with pride as he greeted her, and, under Cindy's direction, the bridesmaids lined up, bouquets in hand.

Music swelled. Before she knew it, Laura was beside her father stepping into the small, sunny chapel bursting with silver bows and deep-pink roses. Her heart soared when she saw Jared standing by the altar, a broad smile on his face.

Had any man ever looked so handsome in a tuxedo, or so warm and welcoming? Impossible.

Peripherally Laura saw that the sanctuary was filled with family and friends. Dean Pipp wore a navy shirtwaist dress and a navy straw hat. Esther and Hoagie were holding hands, while Runcie and Mariah sat separated by their group of Snoopers. Suzy had come with one of Jared's students, a mime in full makeup.

Even President Wilson Martin had joined the crowd. Bernie cringed, sitting as far from him as possible.

The closer she came to the altar, the harder Laura had

to fight the impulse to run forward. She wanted to fling her arms around Jared and tell the minister, "Get on with it!"

But this was one of those moments when she needed to slow down, she reminded herself. It was special, never to be repeated, something to savor forever.

"Who gives this woman…?"

Distantly she heard her father respond, and felt his loving kiss on the cheek. To Laura's surprise, her eyes tingled. She wasn't going to cry, was she? She slipped her arm through Jared's. "You look like one hot babe," he whispered in her ear. "You busy after the reception?"

Laura bit back a bubble of laughter. The man was irrepressible.

"Dearly beloved…" After a formal opening, the minister launched into his inspirational comments. Last night at the rehearsal, he'd skipped this part.

He said that, in their earlier lives, they'd learned to walk and now they would learn to fly. Laura hoped Hoagie and Esther enjoyed the bird metaphor. But, try as she might, she couldn't concentrate on his words because she kept hearing Bernie's.

Before anyone sees me who doesn't love me.

There had to be a reason why that phrase kept nagging at her. The heroine of *The Me Nobody Sees!* That was it! She was able to become visible again when people began to love her purely through her voice and her words. And when, as a result, she learned to value herself.

Laura itched to write down her idea. Why didn't they make wedding gowns with pockets? If she had a pen, she could scribble a quick note and…

Suddenly she realized how quiet the chapel had grown.

The minister was frowning at her. Jared regarded her with a puzzled expression. Uh-oh.

"I do!" Laura said.

An audible wave of relief ran through the chapel and the ceremony continued. At last the minister said, "I now pronounce you husband and wife."

Jared kissed her. "What was that all about?" he asked under his breath.

"Do you have a pencil and paper on you? I got an idea for my play."

"I'm afraid not. Hold that thought." Teasingly he added, "I'm glad at least you were using your time productively."

When the minister presented them to their guests, everyone cheered. "Oh, look!" said Mariah. "She's wearing glass slippers!"

Obligingly Laura lifted her skirt a few inches so her guests could see the footgear she'd borrowed from the theater's prop department. As she extended one foot, a ray of sunlight picked out the sparkles embedded in the material. The shoe—both her shoes—appeared to glow.

"It's like magic," said Magda from where she stood clutching her bouquet.

It was magic, Laura thought as, his arm linked with hers, Jared strode beside her up the aisle. There was magic on the faces of her friends and relatives, and magic in the happiness lighting her future.

Real magic, the forever and ever kind.

If you enjoyed what you just read,
then we've got an offer you can't resist!

Take 2 bestselling love stories FREE!

Plus get a FREE surprise gift!

Corruption, power and commitment...

TAKING THE HEAT

brenda novak

A gritty story in which single mom and prison guard Gabrielle Hadley becomes involved with prison inmate Randall Tucker. When Randall escapes, she follows him— and soon the guard becomes the prisoner's captive... and more.

"Talented, versatile Brenda Novak dishes up a new treat with every page!"

—*USA TODAY* bestselling author Merline Lovelace

Available wherever books are sold in February 2003.

HARLEQUIN®
Makes any time special®

Visit us at www.eHarlequin.com

PHTTH